They say it abou~~~~~~~~~~~~~~~~~~~acks, or the Asians. Catho~~~~~~~~~said it about the Protestant planters, Celts about Anglo-Normans; late Neolithics about Bronze-agers; every established group about new immigrants. And laughed. *Ach, they all look the same to me. Can't tell them apart.*

With this final wave of newcomers, it's true. They do all look the same. We see their height, and their thinness, and the skin the colour of new terracotta, and the three fingers on the hands and the oval slits in the eyes and the flat wide nose and the tight buds of ears low and far back on the skull and the strips of dark crimson fur over the top of the scalp tapering into a line down the spine; we see the odd jointings and body postures that make their ease seem discomfort to us; and we think, well, they're not that different, really. Then we look for the sex identifiers, the absolute basis of how we deal with each other: the body shape, the build, the bulges, the breasts or the balls, and they're not there. Is it male, female, man, woman? They look exactly the same.

Jesus, this is weird. Do they have men and women? How do they tell?

They see with more than eyes, that's how.

IAN McDONALD
SACRIFICE OF FOOLS

VISTA

First published in Great Britain 1996
by Victor Gollancz

This Vista edition published 1997
Vista is an imprint of the Cassell Group
Wellington House, 125 Strand, London WC2R 0BB

A catalogue record for this book is
available from the British Library.

ISBN 0 575 60059 4

Printed and bound in Great Britain
by Cox & Wyman Ltd, Reading, Berks

97 98 99   10 9 8 7 6 5 4 3 2 1

Bye baby Bunting,
Daddy's gone a-hunting . . .

(trad.)

March, three years earlier

He knows it'll be bad because they've stolen him a Ford. Nothing good, not ever, about Fords. Cold, hard to start, drive too fast: just like his life. Skidoo's first steal: a '96 Mondeo. Anyone can take a Ford, a five-year-old with half a metre of parcel strapping could, but Skidoo's proud of his achievement. Fleet car: the clothes hook above the driver's side rear window is worn shiny. The night before the job he changes the plates and acids out the licence numbers etched into the quarter-light glass. He checks the engine. Slowly, thoroughly. He always checks the motor before a job. If anything goes wrong, it won't be Andy Gillespie's wheels. But it's a Ford, and that's not good. The bars on the cargo lantern turn the tin garage into a prison of shadows. He mutters mechanic's charms and prayers as he moves around the naked engine.

There are three doing the job: Big Maun, Soupy and Skidoo. They are waiting around the delivery entrance of the Linfield Supporters' Club with their sports bags. Glasgow Rangers. Liverpool. Man U. Skidoo has the sawn-off tucked in safe between rolled sports socks. His job is to keep the place quiet while Big Maun and Skidoo do the work. Gillespie picks them off the street on a wet March lunchtime. Skidoo rides up front. He'll be first in. It's not a long drive, a mile or so from the Castlereagh Road to the Avenue One Bar, but slow. The traffic is heavy.

'Lunchtime rush,' Gillespie says.

'In this town? Where the hell to?' Big Maun says. He is a big man, and he acts hard, but Gillespie knows he's as scared as any of them. Gillespie despises him and all of his kind. All those hard men, all those Big Men. Easy to be big and hard with a gun in your Rangers bag. Gillespie knows Big Maun does not trust him because he suspects Gillespie's loyalties are not true and pure. Gillespie's happy about that.

Skidoo is an easy fool. He'll do anything to please anyone. You talk harder than the hard men, but when the RUC get you in that room up in Strandtown you will tell them everything from the size of your shoe to the length of your cock because it will please them very much. You have it in your face, like a birth mark, and everyone can see it but you. Easy-osy fool. At school, in your family, with your mates, they all knew you'd give them exactly what they wanted: sweets, toy cars, cigarettes, drink, girlfriends, money. Now, a Manchester United bag with a short-barrelled pumper nestled among the jocks and socks.

Teenage mothers push baby buggies over the pedestrian crossing. They form a wide front clearing all before them. Like the war chariot of Cuchulain, Gillespie thinks. They're yakking, and looking to see who's looking at them. Gillespie's looking in his mirror. Job member three. Soup. The inevitable consequence of being born a Campbell. Oh, that rich, rare Ulster humour. Ha fucking ha. But you're the only one who would understand my thought about the war chariots and the ancient warriors of Ulster. The Big One, the fool follower, the pale, quiet, smart one. The usual clichés. With their driver.

The kid Skidoo has his palms pressed to the side window and is licking the glass, showing off to the teenage mothers. They nudge one another and laugh and give him two fingers. Their thin tops, soaked by March rain, cling to their breasts. Skidoo's laughing like a mad man.

'Will you for fuck's sake sit at fucking peace?' Soup says. His voice is thin and penetrating like a blade. Skidoo turns and raises a solitary fuck-you finger to him. Soup grabs it, bends it backwards. Skidoo yelps and fumbles for his sports bag and the piece inside.

'Fuck up, the pair of youse,' Big Maun says. The crossing lights turn flashing amber. Gillespie accelerates smoothly away. Soup releases the finger. Skidoo redirects his testosterone to the radio.

'Woo. Digital FM.' The system scans through fragments from a dozen transmitters.

'Leave it alone,' Gillespie says.

'I only want some fucking music, man.'

The radio drops on to a station.

Dr Coupar: your immediate reaction to the joint statement by the President of the United States and the European leaders. Awe? Fear? Satisfaction?

Well, John, I think mostly it's the sheer relief of incontrovertible proof that we aren't alone in the universe. Certainly, this is the most momentous event in human history.

Yes, but there are eight million of them, and they're as close as Jupiter . . .

Skidoo hits the scan button. The radio hunts for music. It settles on a local FM station of the kind that have it written into their contracts that they must play a Tina Turner song every hour.

'I like the mystery record,' Skidoo says.

'I was listening to that,' Gillespie says.

Skidoo is a gum chewer. He loops the wad around his molars and turns his grin on the back seat. The moment of heat with Soup is forgotten.

'Hey, any of you boys get it last night? Like, you know, night before, special, like? Make it extra good?'

'Jesus, you didn't fucking open your mouth to some bitch?' Soup says. 'Christ, do we have to have this amateur?'

'I didn't say nothing,' Skidoo whines. 'What you think I am? But I picked up this girl at the club, and it was like, because I knew I was going to do it today, I could do anything, and she like knew it too. Wanted it as much as I did. Bet none of youse ever made a bitch cry like a cat. Like a big fucking alley cat, on my bed.'

Soup rolls his eyes in disgust.

'You should keep yourself in,' Big Maun says. 'Keep pure before a job. Like them athletes; they keep away from women before a race. Sucks out your power.'

'Just trying to make conversation, like.'

'Dirty wee shite,' Soup mutters.

The song ends and the DJ announces in his strange Ulster-American twang that they'll be rolling the mystery record over to tomorrow because IRN is doing an extended bulletin at the top of the hour about this thing they've found out at Jupiter.

'Fuck,' Skidoo says and draws his leg up and stamps at the radio with the heel of his boot.

'Hey hey hey,' Gillespie says, checking in his rear-view that the big Montgomery Transport artic really is flashing him into the right-turn lane.

'Sure we're going to torch the fucking thing anyway, afterwards,' Skidoo says petulantly.

'Let him drive,' Big Maun says.

He drives. The rain turns the Victorian red brick of the upper Templemore Avenue the colour of blood. That'd be about right. Dark day: the lights behind the ugly plastic shop signs on the Albertbridge Road are switched on. Across this junction, and it's there at the bottom of Templemore Avenue. He surveyed the run a week ago. Lines, exits, traffic density. The bar is on the corner, the entrance is on Templemore Avenue, but there are lights on to the Newtownards Road. He won't be waiting on the main road either: no, he'll go for the delivery alley down the side that opens on to the entry behind the houses on Tower Street. Across Tower Street another entry leads to Madrid Street. They'll go this way. No one would imagine a Loyalist hit squad escaping into republican Short Strand. Gillespie drives past the bar, turns left at the lights and pulls into a recently vacated bus stop.

'Right, lads.' Sound of sports bags unzipping. Gillespie sees the shake of Skidoo's hand. He can smell fear on his breath. It smells like sick. Gillespie knows then for certain that it's going to be bad. Skidoo sees that Gillespie sees this fear.

'All right, let's do it!' he says, rattling off the safeties on the pumper to show how brave and full of spunk he is.

'Just a wee moment.' Big Maun closes his eyes and clasps his hands. 'Lord,' he whispers, 'we know that you hate all evil-doers and punish the sinner in your sight. We know that drugs, well, they're just about the most evil ever came out of the pit of Satan and we thank you that you appointed us to be your righteousness. Be with us when we're in that bar, Lord. Stand beside us. Remind us that it's your work, we're doing. Don't let us mess it up. Amen.' He pauses for the response. Nothing. 'Right. You know the drill. Keep your bags high, throw them away once you get your piece out. Skidoo, make sure you're out of the way when Soup and me open up. Gillespie'll wait five minutes at the pick up. Miss him and you make your own way on foot. Any questions?'

Shakes of the head.

'Right, lads.'

Gillespie waits until they are around the corner on to Templemore Avenue. Three more blatant hoods it would be hard to imagine. Instead of the names of football teams on their bags, they should read 'Loyalist Hit Squad'.

He parks in Tower Street facing the entry to Madrid Street. Students from the further education college come and go. The girls look denimy. Gillespie rear-views them for something to do. The clock says top of the hour. They should be doing it. He doesn't much want to think about it, so he fiddles with the radio. It works despite Skidoo's boot.

. . . envoys appointed by the United Nations to conduct negotiations with the extra-terrestrial fleet in parking orbit in the shadow of Jupiter's moon Europa. Negotiations are expected to concentrate on granting settling rights in exchange for technology.

Jesus God. They aren't making this up. April Fool's three weeks off. They exist. They're *here* and we're asking Jesus to bless us blow away some kid peddling smack in our parish.

The movement in the rear-view grabs his attention. Running figures. Already? Too early. It's too soon. Something wrong. He starts the car. As he leans across to open the doors, he notices in the wing-mirror there are only two men running down the alley, dodging the grey plastic wheelie bins. Gillespie reverses into the entry. Over his shoulder he sees new figures appear in the rectangle of light at the far end of the alley. Shouts. The rearmost of the two running men turns, lifts his weapon.

Shots.

The figure falls. The other men come running down the alley, guns held high trying to get a shot, but Soup is in the rear seat and Gillespie is burning across Tower Street. Denimy girls scatter. File binders flap and flop like poisoned crows.

'Set-up, it was a fucking set-up,' Soup yells. Gillespie guns down the entry, pushing a wedge of trapped wheelie bins in front of him. If anyone steps out of a back gate now, it's sure death. 'They were waiting inside. Skidoo's down, Big Maun got us out.'

'He's down too,' Gillespie says, wing-mirrors scraping old Belfast brick. Tiny scrolls of plastic swarf flutter from the mirror housings. That close. 'I saw him go down.'

'Jesus Christ, what a fucking mess.'

The woo-woos have started: to the right, to the left, behind. Hunting. Closing down the bolt-holes. Rabbits in a warren. The Ford plunges out of the brick mouth of the alley on to Madrid Street. Gillespie throws a handbrake left. He misses a BT van by millimetres. The vanguard of bins slews across the road. Baby-buggy pushers, old women out on sticks, wee lads with no jobs: every head turns. The woo-woos are closing fast, but not fast enough. Hadn't reckoned on us running right across your own fat laps. The Ford touches sixty-five past the Munster-mansion pile of Mountpottinger police station, bristling with radio masts behind its wire-mesh blast shields. Fort Apache in the alien nation of Short Strand. Long Troubles, slow peace.

Gillespie sees the lights go orange thirty yards from the junction and floors the pedal. The cross traffic starts to move, then stops in a flurry of screeches and horns as the Ford comes through. Something to point out on the teatime news when they get home and say, 'I was there'. Except today I think the schedules will be taken up with something else. The left-turn light is still red but Gillespie goes on to the footway to undertake the stationary traffic and turns on to Woodstock Link in front of a City bus.

'What the fuck are you doing?' Soup shouts.

'They knew we were doing the job, they'll know where we're going. I'm going to dump this thing up off My Lady's Road, burn it, walk away. Catch a bus. They won't look for us on buses.'

Gillespie pulls a ninety degree right across the face of an oncoming Peugeot hatchback down a sudden entry. The Peugeot stops in a smoke of tyres. He knows the secret of getting any other car to stop for you: it's communicating that you are not, ever, going to stop for it. You're not going to think of even

12

slowing down. It's not bin day in Woodstock ward. Gillespie takes a child's bicycle left lying in the entry and smashes it flat. That'll learn you for leaving your toys lying around. The end of the entry leaps towards him. Beyond, the waste ground littered with the charred debris of Twelfth bonfires, where the trouble boys go to smash things. Bonfire coming early this year.

And the red wedge nose of a Ford MPV blocks the square of light. A line of mutual recognition and realization connects Gillespie with the little girl in the back seat. You could be my daughter, my Stacey. Do I look like your dad, is that the expression on your face, or is it that you recognize the inevitability of impact? It is slow, it is perfectly timed. He can shove in the clutch and stand on the brakes, but it won't matter because it's all predestined. He may as well take his hands off the wheel, his feet off the pedals and surrender to it. He does. The glide in to impact is slow and smooth and serene. Front left to back right. Metal, glass, plastic, rubber, detonate. The stolen Ford tail-spins. The MPV slides end first away from the explosion in a shatter of glass. All the back windows have gone. Through the spray of sugar-cube glass comes sailing the little girl.

Gillespie does not see where or how she falls to earth.

The stolen Mondeo has been spun around to face down the entry from which it came. There is nothing left of the front. The windscreen is out. Soup is lying in his seat belt, blinking and gasping. Gillespie steps out of the wreck into the glass-strewn street. The MPV stands in the middle of the road. Its rear end is gone. The woman driver is wailing. People are coming from the houses to help, but the distances seem too great and their movements too slow ever to get here.

How strange your days have turned out, Gillespie finds he's thinking. In your early spring afternoon – weather acceptable – two cars smash without permission or explanation or warning. Wailing woman at the wheel: you pick your daughter up, taking her shopping, maybe to the doctor's, maybe to a relative's; you couldn't foresee that it'll end in smash and the breaking of your life and your daughter in intensive care. Me: Andy Gillespie. You start the day planning the murder of a drugs dealer; you will end it in a police cell. Nation: world: you begin with breakfast shows and cereals and rush to work, you end with new neighbours, other lives from somewhere else, without permission or explanation or warning.

The sirens are closer now, only streets away.

Monday afternoon–Tuesday night

The suit is three years out of fashion, but he wears it. He does
have another one but it's only a year out of date: too soon for
the great wheel of style to have come round to it again. He re-
knots the tie – the first was too small, like a blood-clot on his
throat – but he still looks like a spiv. Outside in Eglantine
Avenue the taxi hoots. It's only a few metres' dash from the
door, but enough to soak his number two suit through. Wet
March. Wet February before it; wet January, wet December, wet
November. Wet April to follow; probably wet May. Used to be
weather in this country. Now all we have is climate. Plenty of
theories, from global warming to atmospheric damage stirred up
by Outsider gravity fields. Can't hoist theories over your head,
like an umbrella.

'Where to?'

'Magistrates' court.'

Court is one destination on which taxi drivers won't quiz you.
He makes one comment, on Great Victoria Street, passing a
humped-back microbus with a cab company number on the
door and roof sign.

'That's what I'm getting, when I get money. Run for ever on
tap water. Amazing.'

'They call it something like zero-point energy, but don't ask
me how it works. Shouldn't work at all, scientists say.'

The taxi bus draws alongside. Steam wisps from its tail piece.

'Oil companies are going to hate it. Surprised they didn't try
to buy it up and bury it, like the everlasting light bulb.'

The traffic barriers are long gone but the security boxes
remain, last legacy of the slow war. They look like a concrete
cruet. They incongruously frame the New Concert Hall, jewel in
the crown of the Laganside Project – if London can do it with
Docklands, Belfast has to do it with Dame Milly Putridia Lagan.

15

The thing looks like a nuclear power station, Gillespie thinks. The signs and symbols have changed in the three years since he last went up the steps to the magistrates' court – two flags clinging damply to their poles, red white and blue, green white and gold; two crests above the porch, lion and unicorn, harp and St Patrick's cross; two names in two languages. The schizophrenia of Joint Sovereignty.

He shivers as he passes through the revolving doors. Inside, cigarette smoke and damp male. Same as it ever was. The usual suspects in this year's sports fashion, laid out along the wooden benches like a team of sent-off footballers. The lawyers sit facing them in plastic chairs. They all have expressions of exasperation on their faces. The floor is cratered with cigarette stub-outs. The walls are graffitied with felt-markered names, fuck-yous and political acronyms.

His case stands head and shoulders above the rest. The humans leave space around it. Even the solicitor looks uncomfortable, chain-smoking, briefcase on her knees.

'Aileen McKimmis?'

Her glasses are too big for her thin face. They slip down her nose and she has to stare at him over them. That's right. A *man*.

'Are you from the Welcome Centre?' she says.

'Yes. Andy Gillespie.'

She doesn't take the offered hand.

'I thought they would be sending ah . . .'

'An Outsider? No. They send their apologies. They've a long-standing appointment with some people from the Joint Authority about political representation, and this did come up kind of unexpected. So they sent me.' You're still looking at me over those glasses, lawyer. You see a squat brick of a man, grey-stubbled, cannon-ball head; three years out-of-date suit splattered dark with rain. But you don't see the inside. There're things you'll never know how to do, in there. 'My Narha is idiomatic; the Centre would not have sent me if they didn't have complete confidence in my ability.'

His hand is taken.

'Could I have a wee word with your client?' he asks.

They say it about the Chinese, or the blacks, or the Asians.

Catholics probably said it about the Protestant planters, Celts about Anglo-Normans; late Neolithics about Bronze-agers; every established group about new immigrants. And laughed. *Ach, they all look the same to me. Can't tell them apart.*

With this final wave of newcomers, it's true. They do all look the same. We see their height, and their thinness, and the skin the colour of new terracotta, and the three fingers on the hands and the oval slits in the eyes and the flat wide nose and the tight buds of ears low and far back on the skull and the strips of dark crimson fur over the top of the scalp tapering into a line down the spine; we see the odd jointings and body postures that make their ease seem discomfort to us; and we think, well, they're not that different, really. Then we look for the sex identifiers, the absolute basis of how we deal with each other: the body shape, the build, the bulges, the breasts or the balls, and they're not there. Is it male, female, man, woman? We look at another one, maybe there'll be some difference, then we can tell. It's important. We have to get these things before we know how to deal with them. They look exactly the same.

Jesus, this is weird. Do they have men and women? How do they tell?

They see with more than eyes, that's how.

The client stands up to greet Andy Gillespie. It's dressed in a men's business suit, way too short in the legs and sleeves, worn over a high-neck green body; a Long Tall Sally label sticks up at the back of the neck. Gillespie takes a long, deep sniff. A female. He shrugs his eyebrows. The client returns the gesture, a flicker of the thin line of dark fur on either side of the central strip. Gillespie offers a hand, palm up. The client bends down and licks it.

The whole room has gone quiet.

She offers Gillespie her hand. He touches the tip of his tongue to the soft centre of her palm. The Outsider tastes of herbs, honey, vagina, rust, hay, incense and pot. Her unique chemical identity. Her name, in perfume.

Aileen McKimmis's eyes are wide behind her too-big glasses.

I bet you smiled, Gillespie thinks, like they taught you in client relations. Put the client at her ease. Except you did the exact

17

opposite. Bared teeth are a threat. You smile to these people by blinking slowly. Like this.

– *I'm Andy Gillespie*, he says in Narha. *The Welcome Centre sent me.*

– *I was expecting a Harridi*, the client says. Her voice is a low contralto, her accent unplaceable; strange yet familiar. The aliens in the movies never have accents, except the ones with boomy Big Brother voices. Echoey. Jehovah speaks. This Outsider talks like music.

– *Like I was saying to—*

– *I heard what you said to my advocate.*

– *I'm here in the capacity of an expert witness. Advocate McKimmis has explained to you that we're here* ... Gillespie breaks off. – *Could we continue this in English? Narha doesn't have the words for the legal processes. Your law is too different.*

'Certainly, Mr Gillespie.'

'I know that by your law you did nothing wrong, but this is a very serious charge and the prosecution – that's the lawyer who represents the state whose laws you've broken – will try to have you sent to prison until the full trial because they think you might attempt to leave the country.'

'Why should I do that? Do you people not respect your own law?'

'In a word, no.'

The Outsider screws up her nose: incomprehension.

'I would have preferred one of our own knight-advocates, a *genro*,' she says.

'Our courts don't recognize them. You've got me, you've got Mizz McKimmis; we'll keep you out of jail.'

You do not want to be there. I've seen what it's like for your people. And I don't ever want to see what happened there happen again. You won't go to jail, none of you will go to jail, while I have strength in me.

The door to court one opens.

'Case twelve,' calls a short usher in a black gown. 'Case twelve.'

Aileen McKimmis stands up, tucks her briefcase under her arm and dusts cigarette ash off her skirt.

'Show time.'

She leaves another butt-end impact crater behind her in the waiting room floor.

Above the magistrates' bench the shiny new harp and cross shoulder in on the chipped lion and unicorn, like a scam merchant with a deal to offer. There's a new name for the prosecution. It's not the Crown versus any more. It's the Joint Justices. Gillespie can't believe that the name made it all the way to statute without anyone getting the joke. Double the civil servants, half the irony.

Defence and Joint Justices confer. Back on their home bench, the prosecution consults palmtops. The defendant comes up into the dock. The court goes very quiet. All rise. The magistrates are in. All persons having business, all that. Then again, in Irish. Case number 451279, Joint Justices versus Fff. Fff . . . Fidiki . . . The magistrates look at the usher. The usher looks at the prosecution. The prosecution looks at the defendant.

'Fidikihana Kusarenjajonk,' she says, very slowly. She takes the usher through it twice.

Andy Gillespie's loving it.

You are Fidikihana Kusarenjajonk, of Occasionally Plentiful Hunting Hold, Tullynagarry Road, Carryduff?

'I am.'

The charge is the attempted murder of Christopher and John Beattie, of Wordsworth Gardens, Carryduff, aged fourteen and sixteen, and of Andrew Coey, of Shelley Rise, Carryduff, age fifteen, on the evening of March the first, 2004. How do you plead?

The Outsider flicks her eyes to her defence brief. Aileen McKimmis nods. No, you don't do that. And Gillespie catches Fidikihana's eye, flicks his head back. *Yes.*

'I am not guilty.'

She doesn't even understand what that means.

The charge of the prosecution: that the accused did confront the above-mentioned Christopher and John Beattie and Andrew Coey while they were playing football in Wordsworth Gardens, pour an inflammable liquid – petrol – over them and set them alight with intent of murder.

And what is the condition of the brothers Beattie and Andrew Coey?

Second and third degree burns to thirty per cent of the body surface. The victims are undergoing treatment at the specialist burns unit at the Royal Victoria Hospital. They are very seriously ill. In view of the extremely violent nature of the assault, on young children, the prosecution recommends custody.

The bench is inclined to agree. This is a most heinous allegation. Ms McKimmis; have you anything to say in defence of your client?

'I'd like to call Mr Andrew Gillespie. Mr Gillespie is employed by the Shian Welcome Centre in University Street, and is qualified to speak on matters of Shian psychology and physiology pertinent to our defence.' The look over the glasses says, *you had better be.*

He does the thing with the book and the hand and the wee note card in the box in case you can't remember the oath.

'Mr Gillespie, could you tell us about the work of the Shian Welcome Centre?'

'Certainly. It's mostly a contact service for *gensoons*; those are young, single Outsiders, who've come into the country looking for Holds – the big Shian extended families – to join. The way their society operates, adolescents leave their birth families and travel widely until they are accepted into another. The Centre has lists of Holds in Ireland, and also assesses the suitability of newcomers for particular Holds.'

'A sort of dating agency?' the magistrate on the left asks.

'In a sense. And a bit like a employment agency as well, in that it sets individuals up with groups. The Centre also provides a liaison service with organizations employing Shian; industry, shops, restaurants, things like that. There's a lot of room for misunderstandings between the two species.'

The prosecution harumph.

'My job is mostly in the field of human–Shian relations and I do quite a bit of translation work as well. I speak idiomatic Narha; that's the lingua franca of the Shian Nations. The Centre also serves as a base for the Shian political organization, such as it is. You've probably been hearing about it on the news lately. I don't have much to do with that.'

'So you're something of a Shian expert, Mr Gillespie?'

'Well, no one can really claim to be an expert on these people. But I think I know them as well as any human can.'

'Could you explain, then, Ms Kusarenjajonk's actions?'

'The primary motivation in Shian society is the preservation of the children. Family lines, bloodlines, are very, very important to them. The Shian law allows any action in defence of a child; including killing. The case notes state that the children of Occasionally Plentiful Hunting Hold had been taunted and bullied by youths from the estate that backs on to their farm. There are at least five complaints from the Hold to the police, none of which were followed up. The police don't want to get involved in Outsider affairs.'

'Police competence is not in question here, Mr Gillespie,' says the magistrate on the right.

'The Welcome Centre had been informed that there was friction between the two communities, and we were attempting some kind of mediation. The boys; John and Chris Beattie and Andrew Coey, had harassed and beaten up Fidikihana Kusarenjajonk's young son Mushedsen on several occasions, and just before the incident, had attacked him on this street, stolen his bicycle and threatened him that if he told anyone they'd come back and kill him. Fidikihana Kusarenjajonk took what she considered appropriate action to end the threat to her child. It may seem extreme to us, but by Shian law, by the customs of her species, she did nothing wrong. By her standards, she showed incredible restraint. In fact, not to have done what she did would have been wrong; it would have been seen as criminal negligence of her child by Shian law.'

The magistrate in the middle twiddles with his pencil.

'Yes, Mr Gillespie, but it is human law, specifically the law of the Joint Authority, that has jurisdiction in this court.'

'In your opinion, is Ms Kusarenjajonk a danger to the community?' Aileen McKimmis asks.

'No more than any Shian is.'

21

'If she is released on bail, is she likely to seek further vengeance on these boys?'

'No. She's removed the threat. They won't be going near her child again. Anything else would be a violation of their individual rights, which is a separate issue in Shian law.'

'Thank you, Mr Gillespie.'

It's the prosecution's turn now.

'Mr Gillespie, are you a qualified xenologist? Degrees? Diplomas? Certification with our fine new Department of Xenology in Queen's University?'

'Well, not qualified.'

'So you don't have any accreditation for your expertise on Outsider affairs?'

'No.'

'I see. You speak Narha idiomatically. Where did you learn the language?'

You fucking fuck of a smug bastard.

'Mr Gillespie?'

'The Maze Prison.'

'Where you were serving a term for conspiracy to murder. I'm glad to see you spent your time constructively.'

Aileen's on her feet.

'I must object to the relevance of this line of questioning. This is not a trial.'

'But Mr Gillespie's qualification as an expert witness is surely highly relevant here.'

Middle magistrate does the pencil thing again.

'It really is a bit cheeky bringing up Mr Gillespie's prison record, Mr Magrory,' he says. His colleagues nod. 'Where Mr Gillespie learned his -- Narha? Is that is? – is hardly relevant.'

'No further questions. Thank you, Mr Gillespie.' Smug fucking fuck bastard Magrory sums up. Then Aileen's on her feet.

'What we have here is a clash of cultures. I don't deny that a very serious act took place, that severe injuries were inflicted on these three boys. What is in question is my client's state of mind, which the bench must recognize is very, very different from our mind-set. In my client's view, she has committed no crime. Had she killed those boys, she would still have committed no crime.

22

She has no sense of having done wrong; in fact, she has done right. Like very young children are assumed to have no conception of right and wrong and can't be held morally accountable for their actions, Shian morality, and their concepts of right and wrong, are equally alien to us, and must be taken into account. These are the early days of contact between our species; there must be a certain amount of leeway in dealings between us, a period of mutual adjustment. I sympathize with the sufferings of the victims, and the anguish of their families, but I do not think the law, justice, or relations between humans and Outsiders would be served by custody.'

The magistrates look at each other. They mutter. They nod. Then the middle magistrate says, 'This is a nasty, vicious attack on three vulnerable members of society. The victims will in all likelihood bear the scars of this attack for the rest of their lives. Such an offence, if proven, would normally warrant custody. However, there are unique features to this case that demand special consideration. We find ourselves in a delicate state of rapprochement between two markedly different cultures, and while the Outsiders must recognize that their law has no remit in our society, deeply ingrained cultural and social beliefs can only be changed over time. Ms Kusarenjajonk, I believe you are convinced that you have done nothing wrong and that you acted in the best interests of your child, but you must reflect that in defending him you have caused suffering to the parents of other children. I am also inclined to believe Mr Gillespie's testimony that you are unlikely to pose a threat in future, and I am persuaded by counsel's argument that community relations would not be improved by sending you to prison. Therefore I am remanding you on bail of three thousand pounds to appear for trial on the fifteenth of May in the Crown Court.'

Yes! Result!

'Central Court of Justice, your Honour,' smug bastard Magrory interjects.

'Yes. Exactly. The Central Court of Justice. It takes me a while to get used to these new names. Who is tendering bail?'

'The Welcome Centre's putting it up,' Gillespie whispers to McKimmis. He slips the plastic out of his wallet.

'The Shian Welcome Centre, your Honour,' Aileen says.

Back in the waiting room Aileen McKimmis thanks Gillespie.

'Sorry about the prosecution. That was underhand.'

'It's not where you've been, it's where you're going to. That's what I tell myself. Most of the time I believe it.'

– *Thank you, Gillespie, though I am not quite sure what it is you prevented me experiencing*, Fidikihana says in Narha. *My Hold will recompense the Welcome Centre as soon as possible.*

Gillespie tilts his head from left to right, an Outsider gesture of dismissal. – *Don't worry about it. The Harridis have more money than they know what to do with. But I wouldn't count on that defence working in the real trial.*

The usher's out again, moving through the hard lads and their briefs, frantic in his little black gown. 'Case sixteen,' he's crying. 'Case sixteen.'

It's only a stud-wall box he shares with the photocopier and sixteen boxes of old gold A4 (they like old gold, they do everything on old gold), but it's more home than his flat over on Eglantine Avenue. He still despises suits and shirts who'll tell you their real home is the office; they say it because it's where their families aren't. For him this office is home because it's where his family is.

Seyamang and Vrenanka are chasing each other around the desk legs on their tricycles. When they get bored with that they'll come and stick their faces in the photocopier or climb up the stacked old gold. Seyoura is on the phone – hers is the next stud-wall box to Gillespie's – trying to get some kid who's had his money lifted in the bus station a place for the night in their Transients' House on Palestine Street. Senkajou is in deep communion with the computer – Gillespie'll never understand how that direct chemical interface works, looks too much like snorting cocaine to him – and Muskravhat is making an appointment to see someone from one of the big Holds in London's Docklands.

Senkajou's out of the machine and pops his head into the Gillespie box.

'Excellent result, Andy.'

'Cost you three grand.'

Senkajou does the Shian shrug, which is a flexing of the shoulders back and a slight opening of the mouth. It's money, that's all. It won't bother them if the Kusarenjajonks don't give it to them. These people have no idea of the value of money. They've built starships, colonized ten planets across one hundred light years without a functioning economy.

'I am most impressed, Andy,' says Muskravhat, stopping on his way to the downstairs kitchen to make something for the kids to eat. He's not their father; neither is Senkajou. It's the Shian way.

Gillespie blinks slowly. It's taken him three months to unlearn the automatic human greeting smile.

'How was the meeting?'

'Most satisfactory. The British and Irish Joint Authority Directorate is prepared to recognize us as a distinct political entity and negotiate on an equal status as the main Unionist and Nationalist parties.'

'The Chinese and the Indians'll be wanting their own parties next.'

'Of course. They should have had them long before we arrived, but the Unionists and Nationalists insist that there is no such thing as ethnic identities outside their own. There is no Chinese political identity. There is no Shian political identity. If we wish political representation it should be within the framework of the existing parties.'

'You're either a Nationalist Chinese or a Unionist Chinese. Nationalist Shian or Unionist Shian. Can't just be Shian or Chinese, or Indian. Bastards have to divide everything between them. You're either one or the other. Can't be neither. Can't be just for yourselves. That's sitting on the fucking fence. You know why I haven't voted in ten years? Because these wankers aren't worth my vote. If you're not one, then you must be the other.'

'Neither side trusts us. The Nationalists suspect us of being planted by the British government to dilute the Catholic population; the Unionists suspect we have been settled by the Irish government to minoritize the Protestant population. The truth is that we have been settled here by both governments to

25

introduce a third element into this country's political dynamics. But we have land. We have space. And soon we shall have a say in how we live in this land. The real problem is not with the Unionists or the Nationalists, however, but with our own people. There is a strong tide of opinion that we should not involve ourselves in human affairs, or at least not yet. Persuading the Nations to participate as one species will be the great challenge. But that will have to wait until after the season is ended.'

Everything bows to *kesh*, the spring and autumn seasons. It's less than a week now to the first moon; the Welcome Centre has been working at a soft scream, like an ant-hill doing speed. Traditionally, all affairs must be set in order before Shian culture effectively shuts down for five weeks. But there's a more intimate urgency, an inner compulsion. Gillespie's caught momentary electric tingles of otherness in the air; the chemicals, the pheromones, are stirring. The heat is coming. Gillespie tries to think of it like a big holiday, like Orangemen's Day and Christmas and New Year and birthdays put end to end, and then end to end again, like summer holidays were when he was a kid. But it's not. It's nothing like that. It's sex. It's the mating season. It's the rut. It's the time that the Shian become alien even to themselves.

There's an old joke. There's some psychologist doing a sex survey. First of all he asks, how many do it three times a week? About half stick their hands up. All right, twice a week? About a third. Once a week? All the rest, except one wee old man sitting in the corner, grinning away like an eejit to himself. Once a month? the shrink asks. The wee old man just sits there, but he's looking ever happier. Once every two months? No. The old boy's looking ecstatic. Once every six months? Once a *year*? The wee man sticks his hand up. He can hardly keep himself still. 'Why are you looking so happy?' the shrink asks. 'You only have sex once a year.' 'Yes,' the wee man says, 'but tonight's the night!'

The Shian have built an entire civilization around that joke. Only it's twice a year, and for five weeks at a time. Other times, nothing. Sexless as a nun. Sexlesser. There're lots of old jokes about nuns and candles. Sexless as a baby. But when it's on, it's on.

How can they live that way?

They probably think the same about us. Neither hot nor cold, just this lukewarm half-passion, how can they live that way?

At least someone will be getting sex. For Andy Gillespie it'll be five weeks of sitting staring out at the rain and the red brick cliff-face of the Holiday Inn with its hundred black-plumaged businessmen nesting in its eighty-pound-per-night ledges, answering the phones and saying, hello, you're through to Andy Gillespie at the Shian Welcome Centre. Normal service has been suspended during the spring season, but if there's any way I can help you . . .

'Incidentally,' Muskravhat adds, 'I have had a call from a Mr Sinnot, who is the manager of McDonald's drive-thru at Spruce-field shopping centre. Could you talk to him?'

Gillespie phones him back. Mr Sinnot's relieved to be talking to someone with a Belfast accent, with a Belfast vocabulary to match. The Outsiders learned their English by chemical interface with the brain; they have the words but the idiom you learn from experience. It's this Outsider employee he's been sent. She's refusing to follow company policy of smiling at the customers. Gillespie makes an appointment to visit and sort it out, then Seyoura puts her head around the door.

'I have just had a call from Occasionally Plentiful Hunting; they wish to pass their thanks and congratulations to you for helping Fidikihana. You have the makings of a *genro* in you, Andy.'

'Wrong species, I think.'

'Rights are rights whatever your native species, Andy. Other-wise they are not rights at all. There is no bar to us practising your law, if we can understand this idea of law; so why should you not study ours?'

'This is not a great country for upholding individual rights.'

'You are making excuses, Andy. Yes. A thing. By way of thanking you for your contribution, we have arranged a small celebration later this evening, upstairs, in our apartment. We would be much honoured if you accepted this invitation.'

'A party? For me?'

'That's correct. Your facial expression indicates a possible negative reaction. Have I given offence?'

'No, I'm just surprised. I hadn't expected this.' Upstairs. Home. Into the fold of the Hold. Accepted. Family. 'Thank you, I'd love to.'

'Very good. If you wish alcohol, you should bring your own.'

Andy Gillespie catches a movement in the corner of his eye. He moves too slow: Seyamang brings down the big stack of old gold A4. Thud, wail. Seyoura consoles and licks bruises. Vrenanka's out the back, stalking the cat from the other side of the entry.

Then it is quitting time and the kids are rounded upstairs and as he's putting on his coat Gillespie decides that he won't go back to the flat, he'll grab something to eat down Botanic Avenue. On the way out the door, as he arms the alarm and waits for the confirmation message, he imagines he feels something brush past him, a touch, nothing more. Imagination. Nothing. The roofs and church spires stir the wind up to all sorts of weird things down this street.

The staff in the diner are all dressed in denim and try to move him to a smaller table in case a group comes in but Gillespie folds his arms and looks them his three-years-in-the-Maze-terrorist-related-offence look and they go and pick on someone safer. The service is fucking awful. He wasn't going to leave a tip anyway. He plays strip-mines and slag-heaps with the sugar in the sugar bowl and decides that the music is too loud and the food is average and the serving staff are getting their own back on him, but it's better than going back to that flat. Too many nights he sits with tinnies and Chinese and the remote control in the dark, smelly living room, looking at his pictures of Stacey and Talya on the mantelpiece. But he's thinking about Seyoura and Muskravhat and Senkajou and Seyamang and Vrenanka Harridi, folded and curled together in their little suite of rooms upstairs.

In the bright loud eatery, Andy Gillespie thinks about families, human and Shian. There's something great and sane to Andy Gillespie about the Hold, the amorphous social unit of the Shian species. Two or two hundred, great roofs or small, lives packed close together under them. Lives come, lives go, lives pass through, the Hold endures. Less than a marriage, more than a friendship or a club. Communal. Dirty word. Nasty word. Discredited word. We've forgotten how to be communal. We've exalted the individual over the corporate. We're afraid of others. We are ourselves, we are independent, individual, we live our own lives and we are free. And we end up in our separate rooms with our tinnies and our takeaways and our remote controls individual and independent and apart.

A family, Andy Gillespie has concluded, is what works. A functioning arrangement. Blood is not enough.

He's brought copies of the photographs of his daughters into his office. They sit on a shelf above the photocopier. They should get to know this new family. Maybe someday they'll all be part of it.

The staff are cleaning his table around him now, and taking the salt and pepper away to be refilled. OK, OK, I'm going. He turns his collar up against the dark and the rain. Girl students huddle past under umbrellas; the boys in their wee bum-freezer jackets just get wet. It's a machismo thing. The cafés and diners are bright and loud and busy.

You'd almost think you weren't in Belfast.

Sirens. Woo-woos. Always something to bring you back. They sound close. He hates the sound of sirens. There is nothing good in them, ever.

In the offie he buys two six packs of Guinness. He's missed the chemist by five minutes, but the all-night Spar by the station does a wide range of aspirins. It always makes him smile, the aspirin thing. What a great cheap way to get out of your head. You have to have a Shian physiology, though. They're as knowledgeable about different brands as wine connoisseurs about clarets. There's a new soluble aspirin-codeine out that's the thing at the moment. Chemists can't keep it in stock. The Spar doesn't do it, but it's got Junior Disprin, which is almost as sought after. Some day the pharmaceutical companies are going to wise up to this and start putting out their own designer brands. Shortly after that governments'll be slapping tax on them.

He'll stick to the black stuff. Each to their own poison.

He's early so he goes the long way through student land. The old East Belfast Woodstock Road thing was that you couldn't live over here, it was uninhabitable, it wasn't proper Belfast. Students and Chinkies and fags and republicans lived over there. Weird Outsiders. Not real people. Now he wouldn't live in any other part of town. He likes living among students and Chinkies and fags and republicans and weird Outsiders. They're real. It's the Woodstock Road, East Belfast Wee Ulster mentality that's uninhabitable. Fake people living by fakes rules and fake principles. Fake lives. Everything sacrificed to playing the role, being the man, doing the things. Do the friends, do the family, do the wife and kids and house bit. What if it isn't right? What if it isn't what you want? Doesn't matter. It's the way. You follow it, or you don't exist.

So, Gillespie, is being what you want to be worth the price of family, friends, wife, kids?

The question makes him falter as he comes round the corner of Wellesley Street on to University Street.

And he stops dead.

There are five police cars, one police motorbike and three ambulances outside the Shian Welcome Centre.

Those woo-woos . . .

There are police in yellow jackets and paramedics in green coveralls. There are people in suits and coats. Blue lights pulse; uniforms are pushing back bystanders and stringing up *Police Incident: Do Not Cross* tape.

Andy Gillespie starts to run. It all goes very slow. It all goes very smooth, very soft, very pure and distant. As he crosses University Street he notices how a policewoman has the traffic stopped, and that every bedroom window in the Holiday Inn is open and a salaryman is leaning out into the rain. He's under the tape and past the uniforms. The coat and suit cops turn – they're shouting something – but they're too slow. They'll never catch him. There's a Shian leaning against the side of an ambulance, a blanket around his shoulders. A woman in a beige raincoat is offering him a foam styrene cup of something. The Shian is shivering.

Up the steps. Into the hall. Into the office. He's still got the bag of Guinness cans in his left hand, the aspirins in his right. The room is full of suits in coats and baggy white bodies with rubber gloves. They turn with a communal squeak.

'Get him out of here!' a voice shouts.

'I fucking work here!' he shouts. 'These are my friends!'

Uniforms lunge like monsters in a cheap Hammer Horror, tackle him, wrestle him back to the door. A camera flashes. By its brief light, he sees it all.

There's one body in the middle of the room. It's lying on its back, its hands are balled into fists, folded on its chest. He can't tell whose body it is. It has no face. It has no head. Blood fans out from the severed neck across the carpet. Shian blood is dark as venison; it smells very strongly. There is more blood around the groin, a mess of it. The second body is against the far wall, by the fireplace, underneath the year planner. It lies in the same position as the first, it has no head. Its groin has been mutilated. The third is to the left, in the short corridor beside Gillespie's office, lying on its back, fists on its chest, cut open below. Beyond, in the back room, are two smaller headless bodies, curled around each other.

All this he sees with absolute clarity and precision in the white lightning of the camera flash.

Detective Sergeant Roisin and Mr Michael Dunbar of Cotswold Close, Dunmurry, are celebrating the arrival of a new dining room suite. It was delivered at seventeen thirty-five by Gribben Weir Reproductions of Dunmurry Lane. It is reproduction Victorian, six fiddle-back chairs and a circular pedestal table in real, but sustainably forested, mahogany veneer, seating four, extendable to six. While manoeuvring it into the cramped dining recess of the Dunbars' Frazer Homes C5 'Sittingbourne', the delivery men contrived to put a six-inch scratch on the table top. Detective Sergeant and Mr Michael Dunbar are considerably fucked off about this. Gribben Weir have admitted liability and will send a French polisher, but the problem is whether the job will be done by the weekend when the Dunbars plan to host a dinner to baptize their new table. At present, they are sitting on their fiddle-back chairs around the scratch, which is shaped like a tick on Nike sportswear, playing Fantasy Dinner Guest League.

'Thing is, if it's one police, it has to be all police,' Michael is saying.

'No it doesn't,' Roisin Dunbar says. 'You just think that my friends aren't compatible with your friends.'

'I thought we were talking police, not friends.'

'There's Darren Healey.'

'You can't stand him.'

'He's all right. He's good crack, when he loosens up a bit. His wife's nice.'

'His wife's about to give birth. Anyway, I remember you saying that he cooled off towards you when you made sergeant over him.'

'Well then, who do you think we should have?'

'There're a couple of clients I'd like to invite. Potential clients.'

'I thought we were talking friends, not clients.'

'My clients are my friends.'

'Who then?'

'John and Kylie, for a start.'

'Jesus, not them, they'll sit around and talk about that bloody twenty-four-hour golfing range all night.'

'That bloody twenty-four-hour golfing range's worth five grand a year if I can steal John away from his current accountants.'

'The idea is to have a decent dinner, couple of bottles of wine – each – general conviviality and crack; not discuss how home working and the information revolution can cut so many hundred a month off accountancy fees. I don't want to talk shop the whole evening.'

'Same goes, Rosh, for the Northern Ireland Police Service.'

'All right, no police, no clients. Who then?'

'Conrad and Pat.'

'They're gay.'

'Things have moved on a little in this country since they chained the playground swings up on Sundays. We're supposed to be tolerant, a multi-cultural, rainbow nation. There are aliens living down the road, for God's sake.'

'We'll have Louise here.'

'It's not an infection, it's not like whooping cough or meningitis. She's not going to be scandalized or have her emergent sexuality warped. And they're good crack.'

'OK. Conrad and Pat. Who would go with them? What about Sean and Donna?'

'Sean and Donna. This is going to be an alternative lifestyles evening, I can see. We'll be the boring bourgeois farts.'

'Next problem,' Roisin Dunbar says. 'What will you cook?'

At the moment Louise, aged six months and eight days, decides she's bored with *Coronation Street* and starts to grizzle in her plastic baby carrier. Roisin Dunbar and Michael dive simultaneously to attend to her. Within seconds they're disagreeing over which end of Louise is causing the distress and who's to do the picking up and cooing and rocking thing. And that, Roisin Dunbar thinks, watching Michael jiggling his daughter and singing songs and snatches from Gilbert and Sullivan, is the ur-problem underlying the trivialities of who to invite and who not to invite and what to feed them.

Babies change things. They'd warned her, she didn't believe them. She'd thought she could be police and mother. She'd opted for the shortest maternity leave because there was promotion dangled at the other end of it, and this affirmation of her abilities would slop over into the rest of her life, turn her into wonder-mother, -wife, -supporter while Mikey got his consultancy airborne, -social Rosh, -everything. But you can't be police and mother; you can't be police and anything; wife, lover, supporter, friend. It won't let you. You're police, and you're police.

Louise had been more than a baby. She'd been a career opportunity for both of them. Somebody had to stay at home and do the parent thing, and Mikey had wanted to get out of Renswick Bart and do it on his own, one man, one accountancy package, one Internet connection, freeing Roisin to go back to three stripes on the sleeve of her detective's beige trench coat. Except she knows that the parent thing is more time-consuming and boring and schedule-disrupting than Mikey's saying. Louise is sitting in her trug and waving her fists and smiling and bringing it down around him. She knows he's lost one client because of a missed deadline. He's never said. He never will. Like he never will say that he's jealous she's moving on and he's running to stand still. Maybe not even standing still any more. Watching her pull away from him.

Jesus, Mikey. You should tell me this. Communicate with me. You spend three hundred quid a month on connecting with the infosphere through that white box on the study floor, but you won't connect with me, for free. Or is that what you want, contact without communion? The great lie of the network age, that connection is communication.

The Communication Age is great and dandy while it's just ourselves to talk to. Suddenly there's another voice to answer back, and we realize we've never really had very much to say. What we have on show doesn't impress them, our scrap-books and fetishes and football stickers and Star Trek collections. What we want to sell them, the trinkets and tack of our racial Home Shopping Channel, they don't need.

It's hard, sitting on your fiddle-backed chair at your scratched repro Victorian pedestal table in your Sittingbourne in Cotswold Close, to believe in eight million settlers from a world sixty light years away, one hundred thousand of whom are in these six wee counties of North East Ireland.

Mikey has got Louise settled. She's going off.

And Roisin Dunbar's mobile rings.

Mikey looks thunder at her as Louise screws up her face for the inevitable explosion.

It's Willich. Her boss. At this time of night, this has to be big shit. It is. There's been an incident down on University Street. A major incident. He needs everyone in CID there, now. Seems someone walked into the Shian Welcome Centre and blew five Outsiders clean away.

DCI Willich whispered the secret key of all police work to Roisin Dunbar the day she was promoted to DS. Everything is either a fucking mess, or a bloody fucking mess.

34

Holds good for life in general, DS Dunbar's found.

Three ambulances, five patrol cars and a bike: this is a bloody fucking mess. Plus most of CID: she recognizes, in addition to the SOCOs' evil little black van, Richard Crawford's Nissan, Darren Healey's bashed Ford, Tracey Agnew's scarlet lady VW – the ultimate girlie-mobile – Ian Cochrane's white Toyota. New alloys. Flash git.

'Police. Let me through, please. Police.'

The crowd of gawkers parts guiltily. Bad consciences about being here at all. She notices the salarymen leaning out the windows of the Holiday Inn. One of them has a camcorder. She points him out to a uniform. The officer goes over to shout up at him to turn that bloody thing off. Old paranoias cling. In the old days, the camera could steal much more than your soul.

There's an Outsider leaning against the side of an ambulance, shaking violently. Tracey Agnew is offering it a cup of tea and trying to coax forth information. She's wearing aerobics gear under her raincoat.

Detective Chief Inspector Bob Willich is in the hall. He looks like cinders.

'Bloody fucking mess, boss?'

'Bloody fucking mess, Rosh.'

She goes into the room. Walls, ceiling, floor, things on the floor swim for a moment. She grasps the door frame, one, two, three slow, deep breaths. Steady. You're all right.

Barbara Hendron the pathologist is crouching by the side of the first body in her scrubs and rubber. She looks up from her work, nods to Roisin. Dunbar's never been able to see her without her imagination dressing her up in Middle European evening dress, cloak and plastic fangs. She must have seen Christopher Lee look up from a drained corpse in exactly that way, once upon a Saturday night Horror double bill. There's a man with her, vaguely familiar; tall, tweedy, Gerry Adams beard. His hair could have been painted on with black vinyl silk.

'Who's this?'

'Dr Robert Littlejohn, Department of Xenology in Queen's,' Barbara Hendron says, poking at something with sharp steel. 'I called him in. I'm out of my depth here. I need someone who knows what should be where, and what shouldn't. And he only lives around the corner.'

Dunbar knows where she knows him from. All those Outsider Specials they did on BBC Northern Ireland when we discovered we'd been volunteered to billet an entire shipload of aliens: that calm, reasonable, slightly smug voice telling us everything was going to be all right, they were just like us, really, no more different than Chinese or Indians or anything else.

Ah hah.

Dr Robert Littlejohn stands up, wipes his fingers on his green plastic pinafore, offers a hand to Roisin Dunbar.

'You ever hear those urban legends about old Californian spinsters who shampooed their poodles and then put them in the microwave to dry?' he says.

Ian Cochrane of the new alloy wheels looks up from what he's doing with the computer, grins, mimes an explosion.

'The word "maser" mean anything to anyone?' Littlejohn asks.

Ian Cochrane frowns.

'Maser. Microwave laser. Poodle in the microwave effect, with a vengeance. Our killer comes in, one shot.' Littlejohn stands over the body on the floor, both hands gripping the imaginary weapon. 'About half a megawatt in an invisible beam no wider than a thread. Totally silent, totally effective, totally untraceable. No cartridges, no powder burns, no rifling, no shell to retrieve. Water flashes to steam. Steam pressure detonates the skull. Boom! Head goes off like a hand grenade. On to the second.' He steps to the body by the fireplace. 'Click. Boom! Turns, takes out the third, then goes into the back to kill the kids. Two shots. Boom, boom!'

'What about the hands?' Dunbar asks. 'The posture of the victims?'

'Haven't a clue, my dear.'

Roisin Dunbar remembers that she'd never been able to watch more than thirty seconds of Dr Robert Littlejohn. Too full of himself by half.

'You certain it was a maser?' Ian Cochrane asks.

'The necks are cauterized. The intense heat seals the wound.

36

Also, you may have noticed a damp pink haze sticking to everything. Vaporized brain.'

'I've been hearing something about these Outsider weapons,' Cochrane says. Murder isn't his area of expertise. He's a terrorist boy, from way back, clearing up those other leftovers from way back who have yet to learn that Joint Sovereignty is supposed to safeguard their freedoms and cultures. Old paranoias cling exceedingly tight. Old political dogmas cover petty war-lordism. This is our pissing ground. Ours. Ours. 'There's word that the gang bosses are looking for them. They're paying top dollar for any Outsider gadgetry they can get their hands on, if it doesn't blow their hands right off them first.'

'You think there could be terrorist involvement?' Willich asks.

'It's a theory,' Ian Cochrane says. He pokes at the computer. 'Jesus, how is this thing supposed to work?'

'You stick it up your nose,' Littlejohn says. 'Shian technology is largely based around information-carrying chemicals. With humans, sight is the pre-eminent sense; with the Shian, it's smell. So, if you have to interview any Shian, don't wear aftershave or strong perfume. It's the equivalent of wearing a mask. Disguising your identity. Better still, get me to do it. I know these people's languages, verbal and physical. There are gestures and expressions in human non-verbal communication that are at best insulting in Shian body language, at worst an outright challenge. You'll be needing help with these people.'

He has just pitched for a retainer, Roisin Dunbar marvels. Five dead Outsiders at his feet, two of them kids, for God's sake, and Dr Robert Littlejohn is pushing for a consultancy.

'A simpler theory is that it's some Outsider feud, one clan blowing away another,' Roisin Dunbar says.

Littlejohn is wearing a look of superiority.

'For a start, they aren't clans. They're Nations: semi-geographical social units. There are a thousand of them, most older than the pyramids. They have ancient and complex cultures; they build starships, colonize other worlds. They are not the Mafiosi. And for second, it's physiologically impossible for a Shian to have committed these murders.'

He waits for a leading question, a *How so?* an *Oh really?* He doesn't get one.

'What's the first thing you notice about the Shian? They all look the same. Boys look like girls, girls look like boys, no external gender identifiers, all the naughty bits neatly tucked away behind decorous little flaps of skin and they only pop out once the season comes. The guys can even suckle young. But this is just whitewalls and chrome fins, just trimming; where it really matters is in here.' He waves a finger at his forehead. 'They don't have the strong-man, weak-woman set-up that is the absolute foundation of human society. There's no possibility of physical strength being equated with sexual domination. They have no concept of dominance or submission, no concept of sexual violence. A male Shian hits a female, she hits him back every bit as hard. Even better, it's all chemicals with these people. Sex is entirely moderated by chemicals; changes in daylight trigger the hormones that kick the Shian into *kesh*, but also, when they actually do get down to having sex with each other, it's governed by a series of pheromones exchanged between males and females. She can't lubricate without a male pheromone, he can't have an erection without a female pheromone. It's all some evolutionary adaptation to make sure that if you only have sex twice a year you're blooming well going to conceive, but from the human point of view it makes rape impossible. They don't even have the concept. The idea of it horrifies them. No sexual violence, no rape. Tell me, what do you see here? An entire family, murdered. Look at the way they were killed; look at the way the adults' hands are folded; tidy. Obsessive. Ritual. Look at the way the killer mutilated the bodies.'

Barbara Hendron stands up, wipes her fingers on her plastic suit. Ten red wounds on the white vinyl.

'The male and female sexual organs were excised immediately after death. I'd say some jagged-edged weapon. The usual hunting knife, commando knife sort of thing. You can get them in the Scout Shop. We found three piles of charred biological material underneath the window in the back room.'

'The, ah, organs?' Willich asks.

'Maser set on grill for thirty seconds,' Littlejohn says.

I really don't like your bloodthirsty humour, Roisin Dunbar thinks. Pathologists, SOCOs, even we are allowed to make bloody jokes, because we make our livings out of this stuff and it's how we stop it crawling into the back seats of our cars and riding home with us and creeping up the stairs to sit on our pillows at night, staring at us. But you make your living out of knowing things about people, things you've got out of books and off screens and from libraries, and our jokes turn sick in your mouth. In fact, Roisin Dunbar thinks, I really don't like you at all.

'Mutilation, ritual killing, and the clincher: the kids. Protecting the children is the primal law of Shian society. The third one there was probably on her way to the kids when the killer got her.'

'Her?' Dunbar asks.

'You get to recognize the details. The point is that no Shian could have done this. Their physiology makes the kind of psychosis evident in this crime impossible. No, a human did this. A human male. A single, unattached, human male, under-socialized, bit of a loner, on the edge of society. Classic serial killer profile.'

There's an altercation at the door. Uniforms are politely but firmly holding back a short, bulky man with a near-bald head. He is dressed in a French *Nouvelle Vague* leather jacket, and is wet through. He's shouting about working here, his friends.

'Get him out of here,' Willich orders. The uniforms struggle him down the hall into the street. 'Who the hell was that?'

'Andy Gillespie,' Littlejohn says. 'He does work here; the Harridis took him on last November. I've seen him on a couple of occasions, but not socially. I don't know exactly what it is he's supposed to do, but he does, unfortunately, speak even more perfect Narha than I. I think he must have had access to a *souljok* at some time.'

'A what?' Willich asks.

'An instant language chemical. I told you everything about these people is chemical; that's how they all learned English overnight. Turn the language into tailored chemicals and snort

39

them up your nose. I suppose if you were of a picturesque turn of mind you could think of it as a kind of super-snot.'

Ian Cochrane laughs out loud at that.

'Cochrane, find out about this Gillespie,' Willich says. 'Rosh, go and talk to him. Get his story. And give him back his tinnies. What's in the other bag?'

'Aspirins, boss.'

Willich frowns.

'They do it for them,' Littlejohn says.

'Would you mind continuing this little conversation in the hall?' Barbara Hendron says, waving in a bag team. 'We're about to take them out and I wouldn't want anything to leak or rub off on to your good coats. And you know what forensics are like if you muss up their lovely scene of crime. Pack of anal retentives, the lot of them.'

A team is on its way upstairs to break open the private quarters and pick and sniff through the furnishings of lives.

'You recognized Gillespie,' Willich says to Littlejohn. 'So you knew the victims?'

'I'd met them several times, professionally. These are not, let's say, your average Outsiders.'

'How not average?'

'The Harridis are the largest and most powerful of the Shian Nations in Ireland; and the Welcome Centre Hold held the most powerful Harridis. They'd been in negotiation with the British Northern Ireland Office and the Irish Joint Sovereignty Ministry about setting up a political organization to represent all Shian. Their policy was for much closer integration between Shian and human societies, economies, political and legal systems.'

'So the killer has knocked over the Shian equivalent of Peter Robinson, or John Hume, or McIvor Kyle? Jesus fucking Christ. This is a bloody fucking mess. The Northern Ireland Office, Dublin and the bloody Outsiders are going to be sitting on me for a quick result.'

'Serial killers never yield a quick result.'

'I know this, Littlejohn. What worries me is the backlash when the news gets out. And it will. I saw that wanker Fitzhugh from the *Newsletter* out there sniffing around like a squaddie in a

40

brothel, and I'm sure his mates from the *Telegraph* and the *Irish News* and the *Irish Times* are out there keeping him company. They put it out that it's Outsiders killed with an Outsider weapon, and it'll be bloody *Independence Day* and *War of the Worlds* combined by morning. Look, I'm taking a risk here, but I'm putting you on the pay-roll as Outsider adviser, whatever the fuck you call it.'

'Try "Xenological Consultant".'

'If I could pronounce it. I need you to run interference for us, give interviews, go on the news, tell what you told us, that it's biologically impossible for the killer to be an Outsider. Keep the peace while we look for the real boy. Right?'

'How much?'

Willich rolls his eyes in the way that says, *there are five bodies being zipped into black butyl rubber bags in there, and a gentle dew of vaporized brain all over a late Victorian living room, and you are talking money?* But before these thoughts can make it to his throat Tracey Agnew comes in to tell him what she's got from the Outsider outside. She wraps her coat close around her very bright exercise gear.

'His name's Ongserrang something or other. I can't pronounce these Outsider names. He's in from Iceland, on his *wanderjahr*, you know, travelling around. He's eleven, could you believe it? He had an appointment here this evening; the Harridis were going to fix him up with a new Hold or something, find him a place to stay the night. He's kind of worried that he doesn't have anywhere to stay. He turns up at the allotted time, finds the outside door open, thinks nothing of it, goes in, finds the inner door open too, thinks, what a nice trusting welcoming place that they can leave their doors unlocked with humans around, and walks into that.'

'Do you want me to talk to him?' Littlejohn asks. 'He might say more in his own language.'

Willich sighs. It's a very dry, tired sigh, like a man makes who has seen far too much of what no one should have to see, and doesn't want to have to see any more but the world isn't kind that way.

'We'll get a statement off the poor bastard in the morning.

Great welcome to Ulster this is. Find him a hotel, book him in, tell him we'll pick him up in the morning. Eleven years old. Would you send your kids off on their travels at eleven? These people.'

Now it's Ian Cochrane. He's looking pleased. He's looking like a man who's cracked it.

'Our boy Gillespie,' he says. 'I managed to open the computer and get his address. I checked with our database and surprise, surprise, Mr Andy Gillespie has form. Three years in the Maze for conspiracy to murder. Interesting case; he was the driver in a botched assassination on a drugs dealer over on the Newtownards Road. Mountpottinger had been tipped off, our lads were waiting for them. You might remember it, it was the one wee Skidoo McGann got knocked over; we put Big Maun Patterson in a wheelchair.'

'This rings a bell. It was the day the Outsiders came, wasn't it?'

'Didn't even rate a line in the news. But Big Maun Patterson was Divisional Commander, Third East Belfast Battalion UVF. Our Mr Gillespie has immaculate paramilitary connections.'

'Gun-running?'

'And they found out, and he silenced them and made it look like some Outsider feud. Except he doesn't know enough about them to know that they can't do a thing like that, according to our friend Mr Littlejohn here. You have to admit his timing's, shall we say, intriguing? If not him, some UVF buddy of his. Contract killing.'

'Down to the last kid,' Willich says. 'Jesus.'

'It fits,' Cochrane says. 'Gillespie lives alone in a flat over on Eglantine Avenue, divorced from his wife shortly after he got out, two kids – wee girls; no evidence of any significant others. This is his first job since getting out. What was it you were saying, Dr Littlejohn? Single, unattached, human male, under-socialized, bit of a loner, on the edge of society? He's got prime suspect written through like a stick of Portrush rock.'

Willich leans against the wall. He looks out at the rain. He does the sigh again.

'Here's what we do. Get the lads out door to door, find if

anyone saw anything; there's a bloody hotel across the street, someone must have noticed something. We go for the gun-running approach, it's the best we've got so far; Andy Gillespie is our prime suspect. Littlejohn, you come with me up to the morgue; Barbara might need your expertise, I don't think she's ever done a post mortem on an Outsider. We'll haul Gillespie up there with us, officially to make an identification, if he can make anything out of what's left. Unofficially, he might let something slip. I'll prepare a press statement; we do not, repeat, not mention the mutilation of the bodies. I want everyone to know that like they know their kids' birthdays, all right? They don't even whisper it in their partner's ear in the throes of passion. Complete silence on the mutilations. Every fucking nut case from here to Timbuktu is going to come out of the woodwork claiming responsibility once the news goes out. Are we right? Cochrane, send Rosh, Agnew, Crawford, any CID you can lay your hands on, in. This is a bloody fucking mess.'

It's not because he's cold and wet and shocked numb that Andy Gillespie's shivering. It's this place, this morgue. This porcelain, these tiles; these cold cold reflections of himself, an infinite regress of pale ghosts. Everything clangs. Everything bangs. Everything echoes. And he doesn't think he'll ever get the stink of preservatives and cleaning fluids out of his sinuses.

The seats are bloody narrow and hard. Everything aspires to the condition of the slab here.

He knows they have suspicions about them. They'll have checked him out. They'll have opened up all his sins and failings and handed them round like a bad school report card amongst virgin aunts. Andy Gillespie; fucked up by thirty-five, well, that's it. You get one shot and one shot only. Redemption? Change of life? New start? We don't subscribe to those notions. Leopards, spots; mud, sticking; smoke, fire; those are the maxims we heed.

In his teenage years, when too many of his friends had become Christians for the same reason that other friends started smoking – peer pressure – he had been hauled along by some recent converts to a wee meeting. Teenage Christianity seemed to be about little else than hauling yourself from one wee meeting to

43

another, presumably so you wouldn't have any idle time for sinful things, like smoking. There had been a talk – he'd learned there always was a talk, and a lot of singing, and not much else – on the Will of God. The speaker had impressed Andy Gillespie, for he was that rarity in Christian meeting society: a man of genuine spiritual insight. Most people think of God's will as a mountain, the speaker said; a big sharp ridge, like the side of the Matterhorn, and if you wander you will fall off and be lost, and it's a constant struggle to stay on that sharp ridge against the gales and buffetings of the world. But God's will is not like that at all. God's will is a valley with many ways through it, and if you wander too wide the steepness of the way will take you back on to easier paths.

The valley and the mountain. Yeah. Andy Gillespie's trying to live his life like a valley, following the flow down to the sea. Too many others are pushing up the side of the mountain, clinging to the sheer rocks, waiting for the slip and the big fall when the rope won't hold them.

They think I did it. They think I blew their heads apart like a dropped egg, Muskravhat and Seyoura and Senkajou and little Seyamang and Vrenanka. They think I did that thing with the knife on their bodies. That bitch in the beige coat who didn't say one word to me as she drove me up here; that thin bastard with the look that says *I know who you are, I know what you are,* that wee girl with the gym gear under her coat; that big DCI bastard who looks like a Russian president with a vodka problem; even Littlejohn, they're waiting for that one little slip, and they'll cut the rope.

They send the bitch in the beige coat for him.

'Whenever you're ready, Mr Gillespie.'

Someone has opened the big meat larders and slid them out; he's glad of that, he doesn't want to have to hear five sets of chromium runners squeak and clack to a halt.

'All right?' the pathologist woman asks. Gillespie nods. She pulls back the first sheet. Gillespie closes his eyes. It's too close; there's nowhere he can look away from what has been done. The dead Shian is thrusting its wounds in his face, like Jesus on a crucifix: *look at me, look at what they've done to me.*

'Can you identify it?' the woman asks.

The DCI and his DS and Little Miss Reebok Shorts and Littlejohn are smiling to themselves. Gillespie fixes Littlejohn's eye. He bends to the corpse's hand, licks the palm.

'Senkajou Harridi.'

You're not looking so fucking pleased with yourselves now, are you?

The Work-out Queen's expression says she might suddenly boke.

He goes to the second trolley, licks the second corpse's palm.

'Seyoura Harridi.'

He doesn't need to identify the third, but he does it anyway.

'Muskravhat Harridi.'

To the end, then. He goes to the first of the smaller mounds of white sheeting, pulls a spider-thin arm free, presses tongue to palm.

'Vrenanka Harridi.'

And the last.

'Seyamang Harridi.'

Little Miss Cycle Shorts is losing her weightwatcher's dinner in the wash-hand basin by the door.

'Take him down to the Pass,' the big boozy DCI says, shaking with fury and outrage. 'There's things we want to know from you, chummy.'

There's a leaking sprinkler in the corridor outside Interview Room number two. Andy Gillespie can clearly hear it through the heavy wooden door. If it doesn't keep the sound of a drip out, what hope when they start in with the riot batons? 'Romper Room', they used to call it. That was the good old bad old days, though. They have Amnesty International breathing garlic and macrobiotic yoghurt down their collars now; they need subtler methods. Psychological methods. Like the drip drip drip drip drip of a leaking sprinkler on the floor. Chinese water torture. And in the chair across the table from you is Dr Robert Fucking Littlejohn, xenologist. Wanker.

At least the Romper Room was quick.

'Interview with Andrew Gillespie commenced 00:15 Tuesday

March the third, 2004. DS Roisin Dunbar in attendance, also Dr Robert Littlejohn in a consultancy role.'

Down go the buttons. On goes the red record light. Same as it ever was, Andy.

'I haven't had my cup of tea yet. I'm gagging.'

DS Roisin Dunbar sighs. She doesn't do it very well. Gillespie thinks about telling her this, decides against it because she does genuinely look tired, greasy, creased. Her make-up is flaking.

'Look, Mr Gillespie, I've got a kiddie, a wee six-month baby. I'd kind of like to get back home to see her some time tonight.'

'I've two girls myself, Stacey and Talya. I'd show you their photographs except you've taken my wallet. I always fancied a boy, but you get what you get, what else can you do but be happy with them?'

'Mr Gillespie, let's go over this one more time. You state that you left the Welcome Centre at twenty past six.'

'I remember the time was on the alarm system. There've been a lot of break-ins in the offices of University Street recently; I think it was a Crime Prevention Officer from here told us we should put the alarm on even if we're leaving the place unattached for just a wee while.'

'But the Harridis were upstairs.'

'Yes. I was going back there later. They'd arranged a wee hooley because I'd helped a client of theirs in the magistrate's court. It'll be in the court records.'

'That's not in question. It's what you said you did between leaving the centre and returning there at eight thirty.'

'I've told you, I went to eat at the Denim Diner on Botanic Avenue. They'll remember me, I made a fuss about the table. I had lasagne and chips, two pints of Harp, a wodge of banoffee and a coffee. Banoffee, coffee, heh? Then I bought two six-packs of Guinness from the offie at Botanic Station – the time is on the receipt – then I bought soluble aspirins from the Spar on the other side of the station, the all-nighter. I don't have the receipt for that, should I have kept it? Then, because I was early, I took a longer way back and found you guys at the Welcome Centre. You know this. This is the fourth time I've told you it without any self-contradictions or holes in the story.'

'But no alibi.'

'Do I need one?'

'Ongserrang Huskravidi, who arrived at the Centre for a seven-thirty appointment, found both the front door and the office door open. The alarm was switched off. How do you explain that?'

'The bodies were in the office. Maybe they'd switched it off when they came downstairs.'

'But the outside door, Mr Gillespie?'

'But if I did it, which you think I did, Ms Dunbar, then why the fuck did I come back with twelve cans of Guinness and a bag of aspirins?'

'Why indeed, Mr Gillespie?'

'Oh, for fuck's sake! Can we have a proper police officer in here? Look, instead of trying to pin a multiple murder on me just because I've a bit of form and some dodgy friends in my last life, you should be using me to help you. Jesus God, there is some seriously sick fuck out there who has blown five Shian to pieces and cut them up, and you need all the help you can get because you don't have the first clue about how to deal with Outsiders. Littlejohn here's as much use as tits on a boar; you need someone who knows the language, who knows the people, who can work at street level. What you're forgetting is, these weren't just any old bunch of weird Sheenies; they gave me a chance, they trusted me, they were my friends, and I want whoever did it caught and fucked right up the ass.'

'You use the word "fuck" very easily, very comfortably, Andy,' Littlejohn says. 'Fuck this, fuck that, fuck it up the ass. But there are other words you have difficulty saying. The word "mutilated". The word "genitals". The words "sex organs", or "penis", or "vagina". Do you not feel as comfortable with those words as you do with fuck?'

'Hey hey hey hey, what's going on here?'

'I'm curious about how you come to be working for the Welcome Centre. I think I can safely say that you must be the only member of your generation on the Woodstock Road that's given up fixing cars for Shian–human mediation and translation services.'

'Like they said about Elvis, good career move. Aren't we supposed to be an opportunity culture, finding out wee gaps in the market, squeezing ourselves in, making money?'

'Yes, but why this opportunity?'

– *I learned the language, I wanted to do something with it,* Gillespie says in Narha.

– *In jail,* Littlejohn replied.

– *In jail,* Gillespie answers.

'Could we keep this to English, please?' Roisin Dunbar says. The verbal warriors eyeball each other across the table.

– *If Dr Littlejohn's Narha isn't up to it,* Gillespie says in a very difficult sexual innuendo mode with phallic connotations. He repeats it for Dunbar's benefit in cold English.

'Your Narha is beyond reproach,' Littlejohn says. 'It's your English lets you down with the odd significant slip. When you were talking about your children to Sergeant Dunbar, you said, "I always fancied a boy". Do you?'

'Jesus God, you think I'm one of these pervs gets off on Shian because they remind them of men, or women, or kids, or something?'

'You'd be amazed, Mr Gillespie, the lengths paedophiles go to to get to work with children.'

'You are trying to make me out to be something I'm not, some kind of perverted psycho killer. I work – I worked – with the Shian because I wanted to.'

'Well, that's not good enough. Why did you want to?'

'It's something I had to do. Something I had to put right. Something I owed them.'

'What?'

Gillespie looks at the table top.

'What?'

Gillespie looks at the turning spindles on the tape machine.

'What did you owe them?'

Gillespie listens to the flat drip of water in the corridor. He won't tell them. They can keep him here all night, as long as the law lets them hold him without charge, but he won't tell them about the thing in the Maze. It's his, all his. They don't deserve to know it. This is one piece of his life he won't let them unfold and pass around and snigger over. He sits. The tape winds. The sprinkler drips.

At last Littlejohn speaks.

'One last thing, Andy.'

'Don't you ever fucking call me that. Ever.'

Littlejohn manages a sick smile. 'If that's what you want. Let's go back to the trouble you had talking about the mutilation of the sex organs. Look, you're squirming in your seat at the mention of it. Why do you find it difficult to talk about?'

'It makes me sick, what that bastard did to them.'

'I noticed an odd thing, did you notice it too? The children, they'd been left intact.'

'Yes,' Gillespie hisses. 'I know.'

'Don't you think that's strange?'

'Yes. It's strange.'

'Why is it strange?'

'You tell me.'

'Someone comes in, blows their heads up like grenades with five maser shots, then gets out a hunting knife, goes to the bodies of the adults, cuts out the men's penises and testicles, cuts out the female's vagina, womb and ovaries, puts them against the wall and incinerates them with the maser, but leaves the kids. Why leave the kids? Why not cut them up, make a perfect job?'

'Will you shut the fuck up about—'

'About what?'

'About fucking mutilations.'

'Why? Why, Andy? Tell me, what is it you find so hard about this?'

'Because they were my fucking family!' he shouts. And he's calm. He's cool. He's all right. He's all right. 'And I told you never, ever to call me Andy. You know why the kids weren't cut up as well as I do. Because they weren't adult. They weren't mature. Hell, they didn't even have a sex; Shian kids don't become male or female until puberty. They're just kids. You know that, Littlejohn.'

'And you know it. And so, it seems, does the killer.'

The soft hum of the tape machine changes pitch as leader-tape runs over the heads and the cassette comes to an end. Drip,

49

says the sprinkler. Dunbar turns the tape over, carefully noting times and durations. They check these things rigorously in this age of Joint Authority.

'Your work with the Welcome Centre must have brought you into contact with all aspects of Shian society in Ireland,' Roisin Dunbar ventures.

'What are you trying now?' Gillespie can hear the weariness in his voice and hates it.

'I'm sure you'd have encountered all kinds of strange Shian technology.'

'Oh, I get it. You really should leave this to Littlejohn; he throws you a curved ball. You, straight down the middle. I can see where you're coming from. Shian technology, meaning weapons? Like masers? Look, I do translation work, I offer a mediation service, like if some employer wants to know why his Shian staff want five weeks' holiday, or why all the men turn funny and aggressive twice a year when they come into contact with a Shian male employee, or if some poor bastard Outsider is up in court without a fucking clue what's going on, like I was doing this afternoon. I do know a lot of people, human and otherwise, I do have a lot of contacts; none of them are UVF, UFF, Red Hand Commando, UDA, Ulster Young Militants, Free Men of Ulster, Protestant Action Force, Militant Orange Order, which is MOO and just about the most fucking stupid name for a bunch of loyalist wankers I have ever heard. I don't know, I don't care. I'm done with all that. I am certainly not running Shian weapon systems to Loyalist paramilitaries. Jesus Christ, these guys are psychopaths. You want to find the killer, try them. Fucking wired to the moon on this insane Holy Ulster bullshit and Nazi Master Race stuff. They think they're the Lost Tribe of Israel. Outsiders, Shian? They'd be queueing up to drop the gas pellets on the lot of them.'

A knock, the door opens a crack. Willich puts his head in, beckons Dunbar into the corridor with a twitch of his eyebrows.

'Result?'

'It would be a hell of a lot easier without Littlejohn there. He keeps changing my tack; he goes off into all this psycho-killer profile stuff, trying to trick Gillespie into slipping up and confessing that he did it.'

'Gillespie?'

'He has a chip on his shoulder about everything. He protesteth much.'

'His kind always do. Protesteth too much?'

'Hard to tell. He's as dodgy as a nine bob note, boss. But he's not going to give us anything, even with Littlejohn rattling his cage.'

'He give you anything on this weapon-smuggling line?'

'He protesteth mightily much about that too. You still think it's the way to go?'

'It's the best we've got. This is Ulster, we only have two tricks, the orange one and the green one. Even our crime has to be Unionist or Nationalist. Everywhere else has proper, ordinary murders for good, old-fashioned, classical reasons. Not this place. So why should killing a bunch of Outsiders be any different? No, we'll go with the gun-running angle. But a wee word: don't push Gillespie too hard. There's a whole operation out there; if we charge him, they'll vanish. Give him about another ten minutes, then let him go. We'll stick twenty-four-hour surveillance on him, see where he goes, what he does, who he talks to.'

'Who're you getting?'

'We're stretched, Rosh. This kind of thing is not what the accountants want to hear about at this stage in the fiscal year.'

'You mean me.'

'I mean you. And Darren Healey, and Paul Connor. And I want to know everything; when he takes a shit, how many sugars he has in coffee.'

Roisin Dunbar sighs the police-mother, scratched dining table, husband's - professional - jealousy - eight - hours - day - behind - a - wheel-watching sigh.

'It's a bitch,' Willich says. 'Remember, ten minutes, then you let him go.'

He walks off down the corridor, deftly side-stepping the puddle of water on the floor beneath the leaking sprinkler.

*

Andy Gillespie is watching the local television news and learning about anger. The two are related. It's a dark, wet March night; the rain is overflowing the sagging gutter and splattering on to the coal bunker roof. Like that leaking sprinkler in the Pass. Took him all last night to get the hammer beat out of his head. The local television news is talking about the Harridi killings. It's the lead story. It's about the only story, now that people have stopped killing each other politically. They're spinning it out in every direction; they've got half an hour to fill. They've got local politicians on, giving the response from their parties. The usual political suspects. There's Peter Robinson, looking like a serial killer himself, stating that the Democratic Unionist Party has always maintained that something like this was bound to happen when an alien and hostile population is foisted upon the Unionist people of Ulster without their consent. There's David Trimble, with that lemon-up-his-ass look on his face that seems to come with the job of Official Unionist leader, saying that this is an inevitable consequence of the politics of Joint Authority, and that no decent, law-abiding citizen can feel safe in his bed while the killer is out on the streets. There's John Hume, looking more and more like a boozed-out poet, saying that the SDLP fully supports the efforts of the NIPS to bring the killer to justice and that he hopes that this incident has not done irreparable damage to the on-going political dialogue between the Shian Nations and the constitutional parties. There's Wur Gerry Adams, in his Barbour waxie and cords looking like the lord of the manor, giving the Sinn Fein opinion, which is that this is a ploy by the Outsider planters on behalf of their British masters to further detract from the real issues of the six counties and destabilize Sinn Fein's presence in the Joint Authority process. There's M'Lord Alderdice, going love, man; peace, man; let's all sit down together and think about this rationally and ascertain what the real problem is, not rush off at the mouth in hysterical over-reaction; as if rationality, love and peace, man, ever had anything to do with Ulster politics. And there's Pastor McIvor Kyle, that evil little man, giving the Ulster Democratic Front position, which is that they're all maniac pervo killers, the lot of them, and Ulster would be better off without them, and if the

UDF held power, they would shove the lot of them back into their rocket ship and send them back into the sky.

What are these fucking jokers doing on my television? Talking about something they know nothing about? Something they don't want to know about? What has this got to do with them? Anywhere else this would just be a murder. In this country, a new Sainsbury's opens, a cat has kittens, a cow farts, and they wheel the politicians on for the Reaction of the Parties.

'Jesus God!' he shouts, but it's not the politicians using five deaths to score party political coup that he's angry at. It's not even because the police need a name in the frame and his sounds better than anyone else's. That's their nature, like it's the nature of Shian to hunt, and dogs to piss on gates, and Andy Gillespies to be suspects. He doesn't like it, but it can't hurt him. They'll see that he didn't do it, that he couldn't have done it.

He's angry because he's helpless. Because five people – people, not Outsiders, not planters, not aliens – that were the closest thing he has to a family died while his back was turned. A moment's inattention, a brief look away, and they died. He's crucified himself for the wasted moments: if he'd eaten some-where else, if he hadn't had that fight over the table, if he hadn't had that coffee refill. If he'd gone straight to the Spar instead of checking the pharmacy first. If he hadn't dithered over whether to get the Guinness or the Caffrey's. If he hadn't decided to take the scenic route back, and been there those few minutes earlier. But he did what he did and none of it can be undone. The universe won't give you any moments back.

He's angry because when he got out he swore that no Outsider would ever suffer again because of anything he did or did not do. He took what he swore to the Harridis, and told them why he had come, and they accepted him and the thing he'd been given and they gave him family. And now they're dead. Like that, too quick for his slow feelings to understand what has happened and move him into positions of shock and grief and loss. Anger, that's all he has. Angry that they have been taken away in a moment. Angry that the police suspect him because they haven't tried to understand what he felt for Muskravhat and Seyoura and Senkajou. Littlejohn just wanted to make it cheap and dirty, the well-thumbed page that the text book on sexual deviations falls open at. Angry because he couldn't do anything then, angry that the police have assumed all rights to do anything now.

You have the makings of a genro *in you, Andy,* Seyoura had said just before the invitation to the party that never was.

Genro. No real word for it in English. Knight-advocate is the usual translation; good on the sense of valour and questing for truth and right, but it can't catch the spirit of the Shian law it embodies; of personal right and the absolute commitment of the lawyer to defend those violated rights. A kind of loving. A marriage of client and advocate.

Rights are rights whatever your native species, she had said. They are inviolable for everyone, or they aren't rights. You don't have to be a Shian to practise the Shian law.

But he's only Andy Gillespie of Hatton Drive, Woodstock Road, Belfast, ex-con, car mechanic, with a gift of tongues. He wouldn't even know how to start.

You are making excuses, Andy, she had said, almost last of all.

Andy Hero. Knight-advocate.

At least he'll be looking in the right directions. At least he won't be following big smelly presumptions up his own ass. At least it'll show the police that he wants to find out as much as they who killed them.

Where to start?

The one who found the body. Ongserrang Huskravidi.

And after that?

Make it up as you go along. It's done you all right so far.

Then his emotions see the three bodies in the crowded front office, and the two smaller ones curled in an innocent parody of soixante-neuf in the back room, and he falls into his chair and shudders and heaves and cries out aloud in his small, smelly flat.

He's noticed this thing about the weather. Every time he goes out of the city it stops raining. This isn't to say that it rains all the time in the city – it just seems that way – but he's never seen it rain in the country. Sort of a miniature arse-up of the dumb Loyalist slogan you'd see painted on gable ends: *We Will Not Surrender the Blue Skies of Freedom for the Grey Clouds of an Irish Republic.* Usually spelled wrong somewhere. *Surender. Blue Skys.* Grey Clouds of Belfast. Blue Skies of Everybloodywhere Else.

It's not court, so the taxi driver can talk this time, and he talks. Gillespie doesn't want to talk, but taxi drivers are skilled at circumventing the silence of fares.

'Not a bad day.'

'Not bad at all.'

'Wettest winter I can remember.'

'Wettest I can remember too.'

'I reckon it's those big ships of theirs, coming and going all the time. I reckon it's putting holes in the ozone, all that coming and going. Can't be doing any good, and all that messing around with weight and things. Not natural.'

'Gravity.' He's not going to explain Mach's Principle to a city cab driver, especially because he doesn't understand it himself.

'Yuh. That.'

They go another couple of miles and the driver tries again.

'What's this place you're going to?'

'It's called South Side of the Stone. On Sketrick Island. You go down to Whiterock, and it's just before you get there.'

'Oh, I know where it is all right. Used to be a good pub on Sketrick, before.' Gillespie makes no response. 'So is it the Outsider place you're going to?'

'It is.'

They're into the country now. Green fields, cows, bare trees, tractors ploughing. Black crows pick over the fresh furrows, like fragments of broken storm.

'Bad do back in the city, that Outsider murder. The whole family, Jesus.'

'Bad do.'

'Said on the news that they'd used some kind of gun makes heads blow up. The bodies had no heads, can you imagine that? Even the kids. What kind of person would do a thing like that?'

'Lot of sick people about.'

'Had this man on, some kind of expert, Jesus, they have experts on everything these days; anyway, he says that it's impossible for these Outsiders to kill each other. Says it's like impossible for their chemistry or something for them to do something like that. I don't know, I mean, what do we know about them? What do we really know about them? Not exactly like they've gone out of their way to be friendly, you know, living out there in their weird hippy communes. Not that I'm saying they don't have the right to believe what they want to believe, have their own religion or whatever, but they've not exactly gone out of their way to adopt our customs and ways and all, you know; live like us, be like us.'

'I don't think it's that they don't want to, but that they can't.'

'I'm telling you, they had that McIvor Kyle, the one gets on like he's the new Paisley; I'm telling you, that man made a lot of sense to me. A lot of sense. I mean, what do experts know? You can't believe them, I mean, what if they're wrong? What if these Outsiders all of a sudden come out with guns and they start shooting everyone and everything? They don't know, so I think it would be better to take them and put them all on some wee island where they can keep an eye on them until they're sure they're safe to be let loose on society. Better safe than sorry.'

'This is that wee island.'

The next mile is passed in silence. Gillespie notices the driver glancing repeatedly in his mirror.

'Something the matter?'

'You upset someone?'

'Why?'

'There's a blue Ford Escort been behind us since the city centre. Woman driver.'

Gillespie looks out of the rear window. Blue Ford Escort. No danglies from the mirror. No trims, no direction finders stuck to the dash, no whip aerials. Mrs Beige Coat Lady Detective from last night at the wheel. Serious expression.

'Slow down,' he says to the driver. 'About twenty.'

The taxi slows to a crawl. The blue Ford drops gears to match.

'She's not going past,' the taxi driver says.

'Didn't think she would,' Gillespie says. 'Looks like I've picked up a police tail.'

'No shit?' The taxi driver can't keep the note of interest out of his voice. A real hood. In my cab. 'What are they after you for?'

'Those murders you were talking about.'

'The Outsiders?'

'With no heads. They think I did it.'

A real multiple murderer. In your cab.

The driver's not quite so voluble after that, but he does dare to ask, 'Did you do it?'

'Think I'd tell you if I did?'

The driver thinks about that for half a mile or so, then offers, 'Want me to lose her?'

The cab driver's Number Two Dream. After *follow that car; lose that tail.*

'I do not. I want her to see where I'm going, and what I do when I get there, who I talk to, what I find out, and then I want her to follow me all the way back to my front door. I want her to see that I have absolutely nothing to hide from her.'

She clings close as a condom over the twisting switchback drumlin roads along Strangford Lough, across the bridges and causeways linking the drowned hillocks to the shore. The long tide is out, flocks of over-wintering geese are moving over the chilly mud flats, dark speckles in the glare of the low sun from the wet silt. Yachts stand keel-down in the shallows; burgees and sheets rattle against the aluminium masts in the northerly wind. In the huge car park opposite the beached Ballyhornan lightship two cars and only two cars are parked, nose to nose outside the public toilets.

Jesus, it must be grim to be queer out here, Andy Gillespie thinks.

'Left. Here.' He almost missed the turning. The driver turns on to the single-track causeway to Sketrick Island. At the end of the causeway is the tumbledown stone tower of Sketrick Castle. Used to climb all over it when I was a wee kid, Gillespie thinks. Always loved it down here, those rare days out when the car was actually working and we'd stuff in a picnic and Coke and just go off. Never liked the beaches, got bored on beaches; just sun, sea and sand. A good castle to climb up; forests, hills, somewhere you could push with your imagination into something like those sword 'n' sorcery books I used to love when I was wee: that was my kind of day out. Changed a bit since then; in a direction outside my imagination. Or anyone's imagination.

There's a gateway and cattle grid. The gateposts are old country style: whitewashed round pillars of stone capped with angled slates. Fourfold yin-yangs have been set in coloured pebbles on each post; the most ancient and powerful of Shian symbols. Every Shian is two selves, the everyday, and the burning self of *kesh*. Male, female, cold, hot. Gillespie directs the taxi driver between the gateposts, down a rutted track that runs at the edge of the water. Bladder wrack is heaped on the seaward side of the lane; it crackles and pops beneath the taxi's tyres.

South Side of the Stone has grown around a farmhouse, yard and outbuildings overlooking the open water. 'Grown' is the best word for it, Gillespie thinks. The constructions that surround the old limewashed farmhouse look as if they have sprung from the ground in a single night, or been spun in the darkness by something best not seen by daylight. Nothing is straight, nothing is level. The Shian abhor the straight line: roofs dip and wing like birds in flight; walls slope and curve, annexes bubble out of each other, windows blister. Surfaces are as smooth and perfect as the skin of a chestnut racehorse or the shell of a porcelain vase. To the left of the farmyard entrance a number of tall, slender objects shoot from the roof of a tent-like building. Smooth boles rise twenty feet, then unfold into a green-yellow tiger-striped parasol. They look like kiddy-book giant mushrooms in the enchanted forest. It would take a motherfucker of a leprechaun to sit on top of one, Gillespie thinks. But they contain magic more mighty than faery gold. Real alchemy: the transmutation of the elements. They're machines; nanofacturers, processing atoms, taking things apart and knitting them into something new. They can make you anything. You want a car engine that'll never wear out, an artificial heart valve, a jet engine, half a kilo of Colombian? In goes the shit, out comes the gold. And they'll customize it, shape it to fit, personalize it for you and none other. It's just putting the atoms together in the right order.

Might as well be magic for what Andy Gillespie understands of it. But it scares the hell out of the big chemical and manufacturing companies. Who's going to buy their goods when anyone can get whatever they want built just down the street, in their own back gardens? We were so desperate to get what you had; your starships, your zero-point energy, your nanofacthingies; come to us, stay with us, have some land, have some money, have whatever you want but don't forget to bring your technology with you; and now we've got it and the people who wanted it have realized that it's a gun down their throats. Wam! and they're blown to fucking pieces.

All be better with a hell of a lot less people controlling things, Andy Gillespie thinks.

'You can drop me here,' he tells the taxi driver and gets out in front of the farmhouse. 'I don't know how long I'm going to be. If you get bored you can always have a chat with the copper. She might even buy you a cup of coffee. Where is she, by the way?'

'She pulled in back down the lane.'

Probably got the high-powered glasses in the glove box, or is she going to risk getting her good shoes muddy and follow me on foot?

The driver settles down with today's *Sun*. Not a soul else in the farmyard. Must be off doing whatever rural Shian do. Andy Gillespie goes over to the big mushroom farm. There's a white BMW parked outside – a customer, no Shian would drive a white BMW. The skin of the big tent-like construction is translucent; a golden glow fills the interior of the factory. The air smells rich, soily, musky, as if it's been put through the molecule-weaving machine and come out with added value. The stems of the processors hold up the roof like the poles of a big top, the bases flare out like whiskey stills. They can probably make you that too. There are two figures at the end processor. One is tall, the other is wearing a Pringle sweater. No difficulty spotting the BMW driver.

'Looking for Ongserrang Huskravidi,' Gillespie calls.

'Who's looking?' the Shian says.

'Andy Gillespie.'

'Are you from the police?'

'No, I'm from the Welcome Centre.'

'I will see.' The Shian goes out a back door.

Pringle sweater has had a golf club made. Looks like some kind of driver to Gillespie, who's more a football man. He practises his swing in the golden light of the nanofactory.

'Look at that,' he says, shoving the grip end in Gillespie's face. His eyes are shining with delight. 'Custom made. Built to fit my grip. Do you know what it's made out of? Diamond. They take carbon fibres and they weave them into diamond. If this was a jewel, it would be about fifty thousand carats, but it's only cost me a hundred quid. Incredible.'

'Incredible,' Gillespie agrees.

The Shian returns with two others, both males, one older than the other. They sniff, lick, do the greeting thing with Gillespie.

'This is Ongserrang Huskravidi,' the older one says. He is carrying a staff taller than even his tall self. Gillespie recognizes the insignia of a *genro*. 'I am Saipanang Harridi, of this Hold. I have been appointed to protect the rights and interests of Ongserrang Huskravidi. Shall we go somewhere we may talk in more privacy?'

They walk down to the shore. The tide has turned and is advancing around the keels of the stranded yachts and orange anchor buoys in little fondlings of foam.

'I thought you people were suspicious of water,' Gillespie says.

'The Harridis are a coastal Nation,' the *genro* Saipanang says. 'Many do not trust us for that reason. Too much water in our blood.'

Gillespie finds a rock and sits down. He pulls his jacket tight. The wind is finding every crack and gap in it. It's always cold or wet. Or both. The Shian look comfortable in T-shirts and skirts. Higher body temperature. He used to be able to warm himself by the University Street Harridis. Those high-output metabolic furnaces need stoking with big food every couple of hours.

'I don't see why we need your lawyer here,' Gillespie says to the younger Outsider. 'I'm just going to ask you a couple of wee questions.'

'With respect, Mr Gillespie, that is what the police said,' Saipanang says. 'Whatever your judicial system, your investigative process makes a presumption of guilt in those it turns its attention on.'

Don't I know it, lawyer.

'There are a few things I want to find out for myself,' Gillespie says. 'You could say I'm a sort of *genro*, for them. The victims. My friends.'

'My client has given a comprehensive statement to the police,' Saipanang says. 'You could have saved yourself a journey by consulting it. My client will not be telling you anything that is not already contained in it.'

'I'd like to hear Ongserrang's version of it.'

'My client had arrived in Belfast on the airport bus after travelling from the Occasional Aurora Hold in Reykjavik in Iceland. He is on his *gensoon*. I believe your expression is *wanderjahr*.'

This thing in a T-shirt, a foot taller than you, Gillespie, is eleven years old. He's come all the way from Iceland, and before that a planet sixty light years away. Where's the furthest you've been? Glasgow. What were you doing when you were eleven? Wondering what an erection meant, and if Liverpool were going to do the League-Cup Double. That white blur was childhood, that sonic boom was puberty.

'I really would rather Ongserrang told me this himself.'

Ongserrang looks at Saipanang. There are eye movements, facial gestures that even Gillespie can't translate.

'As my knight-advocate says, I have come from Iceland,' Ongserrang says. Does Gillespie detect a slight accent, physical hints of a different ethnic background? He realizes that all the aliens he's ever known are Harridis. There are a thousand Nations beyond this one. 'I had had an appointment made for me by the transients' office in Reykjavik with the Belfast Centre to introduce me to a number of Holds with which I might be compatible.'

'This you should know, Mr Gillespie,' the *genro* says. 'My client arrived at your premises at the arranged time . . .'

'Please, could Ongserrang tell it his way?'

Must be a universal law, like gravity, or that weird quantum shit; that briefs put words in their clients' mouths.

'I found the outer door was open, so I went in. The inner door, the one to the office, was also open. I went in, I found them—'

'Yes. I know. I saw it too.' And you still see it, like a distraction in the corner of your vision that you turn to look at, and there they are: one in the middle of the floor, one against the chimney breast, one behind the desk, and in the back room the kids, curled around each other like aborted twins. 'How long before you called the police?'

'My client was in a state of considerable shock,' Saipanang says.

'I'm not trying to suggest that you held off calling the police, I'm just wondering if you called anyone else as well as them.'

'Who would I have called?'

'Other Shian.'

'Why would I do this?'

'Mr Gillespie, you are still employed by the Welcome Centre,' Saipanang interrupts. 'You have the authority to find out where calls were made to. If you do I think you will find that only one was made that night, and that was to the police at Donegal Pass.'

'Only a thought,' Gillespie says. He is stabbing in the dark. That smug *genro* bastard is right, he could get all this from the statement. There's no reason for him to be here. Except that he wants to. He needs to ask these questions, to get his own, personal answers, addressed to him, Mr Andrew Gillespie of the Shian Welcome Centre, University Street, father to Stacey and Talya, ex-husband to Karen. He needs to show the woman in the beige coat in the blue Ford that he is doing something that an innocent man would do. Put on the coat and the hat and smoke the cigarettes of the great old television detectives; play Andy Hero.

Oyster-catchers sweep in across the tideline, swift deltas of black, white and orange, trilling to each other. Gillespie's ass is numb on this rock. Probably getting piles.

'When did you come here?' he asks Ongserrang.

'Yesterday evening.'

'And before that you'd been, where?'

'The police found me a place in a hotel in Belfast.'

'Why did you come to this Hold?'

'This Hold asked me to.'

'Why? You see, like your lawyer says, I should know about you. And I do. I saw your contact list, and this Hold wasn't on it. It's kind of out of the way, isn't it? Easily overlooked. Quiet, out of things.'

'Is this a suggestion of some irregularity on our part?' Saipanang asks. 'Are our actions in any way suspicious?'

'Well, all I know is what I see, and what I see is suddenly your client, the person who found the bodies, is taken in by a Hold who don't know him, and given a lawyer to help him with kind of basic, innocent-enough questions.'

Saipanang flares his nostrils. At the same moment Andy Gillespie becomes aware of a smell. It's nothing he can give a name or a label to, but something's itching at the base of his brain.

'Mr Gillespie, I believe you have been interviewed by the police. Why is this?'

Bastard.

'You know fine well.'

'The police and their consultant Dr Robert Littlejohn are working on the basis that this is a purely human affair. Ongserrang tells me they have a theory about smuggling unlicensed Shian technology.'

'It's bullshit.' The smell, it's getting stronger. Where's it coming from? Is it the sea? The mud?

'I am quite sure of this, Mr Gillespie. I am also quite as sure that it was no Shian did this thing. I have done some research into this, I know the act of human murder has a predominantly sexual motive, and that all serial and spree killers have been *men*, or acted under the influence of human male sexuality. With you, sex and violence are inseparable. I understand the physical inequality of your sexes makes this so; we Shian still have great difficulty, Mr Gillespie, in treating men and women as the same species. Your strength alarms us, your aggression dismays us. Sexual aggression, physical dominance, the need to express power through sex; these are hard lessons for us to learn of the species with whom we must share this world. Even your word for intercourse is a term of verbal aggression: fuck you, fuck off, you're fucked. It is all competition with you, competition to best each other, to a sexual partner. With us it is display. We dress, we dance, we make ourselves attractive, not aggressive. We certainly do not kill each other out of perverted sexual desire.'

'You don't need to lecture me about what human males are like.' I was in the Maze. I know what their lust did. I saw it, I heard it, I smelled it. I hated it, it made me ashamed, but I won't have you telling me I'm an animal, looking at me from your extra foot of height like you're looking down on some kind of alien slug with disgusting reproductive habits. 'We're not all like that.'

'Are you not? I sense that you are becoming quite angry, Mr Gillespie. Is this aggression because your sex has been maligned?'

Too fucking right he's angry. He wants answers, he gets insults. He get sniped at by some tall poncey fairy of an alien in women's clothes. Well, look then, at this decent, hot, *man* anger. This male aggression. This testosterone power. Because I'm going to tell you now what it's really about, what it's running on.

'Fuck my sex, Mr Harridi. Fuck all this playing with words. Five Outsiders – Shian, your own species – have had their heads blown off, and you are standing on this freezing cold beach lecturing me about sex and violence. And that makes me angry, because they aren't even my species, but I feel something for them. I want to do something. You, you just stand there, and it's like you feel nothing. Jesus Christ, you don't need me to tell you what it was like, your client there can give every bloody detail, but it doesn't seem to worry you in the slightest. You, youse. None of youse seem to give a fuck. If this was a Shian taking out humans, Jesus, there'd be panic on the streets. There'd be – I don't know, people mouthing off, making demands for more security. There'd be fucking McIvor Kyle and all those DUP Nazis and Sinn Fein and all talking about protecting their communities from the Outsiders and vigilante groups forming and it would be fucking mental. You, you hire a lawyer, you sit on a rock, and it's no more to you than, than' – Gillespie quests around in the high-tide flotsam for a' simile – 'this crab.' He flings the dry husk away from him. A gull swoops, but it's only an empty shell and it sweeps up into the cold north wind again.

'What should we be, Mr Gillespie?'

'I don't know. Show some emotion. Be shocked. Be angry. Be human.'

'Be human, this is what you mean. We may look human, but we are not human. We are nothing like you at all, Mr Gillespie.'

Groups of South Siders are moving along the tideline, scavenging plastic bottles, crumbling cubes of styrene foam, condoms, scraps of nylon line and net from the flood. They are barelegged and barefoot; they leave long, four-toed prints in the tidal ooze, like the spoor of birds.

'Mr Gillespie, what is it you want to know?'

He looks at the beach-combers, and the birds running along the edge of the waves, and says, 'I want to know why someone would want to kill a whole family of Shian who never did anyone any harm in the world.'

'We all want that, Mr Gillespie. But you will not find the answer here. If you do find it, I should be grateful to hear it. Now, I think you are getting cold. Shall we return to the Hold?'

Thirty quid taxi fare down the toilet. He's not going to learn anything here. That might be because they don't have anything to teach. But it might be that they have something they're not saying. Not saying to humans. You're not going to get one past that *genro*. Bastard played you like a harp. You Shian know enough about human male aggression to know what buttons get what response. That smell, it was of your making. You were weaving pheromones, speaking in your chemical language, saying, *Gillespie, get tetchy, Gillespie, get mad.* But maybe you were just a little too fucking clever, Knight-Advocate Saipanang Harridi. Maybe you pushed the buttons too hard. Maybe the buttons are wondering why you pushed them at all. Of course, maybe I'm just making words out of worm tracks on the sand; you aren't like us, your differences challenge everything we know about ourselves, but ex-cons get a sense for lawyers like daft old men get a leg for weather.

There are other Holds. There are different Nations. There is a whole island full of Shian, and a bigger one than this heap of shit at the end of its causeway. There are new answers to old questions. I'll find out if you're lying to me.

And what'll you do then, Andy Hero?

'You done?' the taxi driver asks.

'Yeah, I'm done. You can take me back.'

'My pleasure. Gives me the creeps, this place.'

Pringle sweater and his white BMW have gone; there is now a big red Citroën estate with a bike carrier on the roof parked in the farmyard. As the taxi drives off Gillespie can see a man standing beside a racing bike talking with a Shian at the door to the magic mushroom farm.

Signs and omens greet Roisin Dunbar when she comes down to her fitted pine breakfast table in her fitted pine kitchen. Louise in her fitted pine high chair has managed to hit the mug cupboard door with a gout of yummy apricot breakfast, simultaneously setting new distance and altitude records for boking. There is no caff coffee. Michael's wearing the '98 Lark in the Park T-shirt over his jogging bottoms and ludicrous slippers. Nothing good has ever happened while he is wearing that T-shirt. There's a bank statement in, and a credit card statement, and a net provider bill. Outside in the garden, which the estate developers have promised will be a grassy paradise come summer but in early March resembles the Ypres salient, a lone magpie is stamping around in the mud, defiantly remaining one, singular, all alone, and ever more shall be, oh. And the headlines in the morning newspapers and free sheets read 'Paramilitary Arms Link in Outsider Killing' and 'Terror Weapon Murder Link' and 'Ulster in Alien Fear'.

The signs and omens say *shit day, Detective Sergeant Roisin Dunbar*. Maybe she's retrofitting them. It's going to be a shit day – any day you spend driving around following someone who knows you're there, and all the time your knickers are sticking to the upholstery and your neck's killing you because in these days of interstellar travel and zero-point energy from water they still haven't invented a comfortable car seat, is a shit day – and she's finding signs and omens to prove it.

'So, what are you going to do today?' she asks Michael, who's spooning even more yummy chocolate and banana pudding into Louise. *Here comes the helicopter, wheeeeee . . .*

'I'm going to see if I can get the Donaldson-Lyle account to run. Bastard needs it yesterday, of course, but if I submit it as it is the thing's just going to come back to me again and it'll end up costing double. It's going to be another morning of that fat schmuck attempting telephone sarcasm.'

'At least you don't have to deal with them face to face.'

'You can stick a fist into a face. Try that on a screen and you get severed arteries.'

The signs and omens must be bad to Mikey too, this morning.

Louise screws up her face, waves her fists and specially for Mummy hits the window with a gob of choccy-banana goo, surpassing all records. It looks like a condor shit on the glass.

And, *and*, Michael's wheeked all the decent CDs upstairs and left her Chris Rea and Tina Turner and fucking Chris de Burgh to stack in the multi-changer in the back of the car.

And, *and*, *and*, it's down to three miles per hour on the motorway and when she gets to the delay it turns out to be a French artic that's shed its load of Golden Delicious. Traffic branch are chasing rolling apples across the carriageway and the driver is standing on the hard shoulder with a look that says, *that's for Jeanne d'Arc, rosbifs*.

'You're late,' Paul Connor the graveyard shift says at the hand-over.

'Anything?'

'Came home, went over to ex-wife's, spent night with kids at McDonald's, came home again, slept. Is still sleeping. Milk's still out. Post came at seven-thirty, two bills, one electricity, one phone. At least you get to drive around a bit, I just sit here all night and freeze. Have you any idea how bad the radio is at four o'clock in the morning?'

As bad as the CDs in my boot, I'm sure.

Connor hands over the camera and the radio and drives away to an Ulster fry and falling asleep in front of *Richard and Judy*.

Dunbar's contemplating phoning in the answer to Spot the Star competition on the radio (Tina Turner) when the taxi draws up outside 28 Eglantine Avenue. The driver honks the horn. Andy Gillespie comes out and gets in. The taxi does a careful U-turn. Roisin Dunbar repeats the manoeuvre and follows.

Heading west. Into enemy territory. Police thinking: you are one of the enemy, Roisin Magdala Dunbar. This is your home country, these shitty streets are the capital of your state of mind. Except it isn't. This is no more my nation than Karachi. My spiritual home is Marks and Spencer's; Habitat; B & Q; our mortgage company; the Internet service provider; the health club we joined but never go to; the wee Italian restaurant in Dunmurry where we and the staff call each other by name. Sold out my heritage. Fuck my heritage. The nations aren't Protestant, Catholic, Unionist, Nationalist any more. The nations are have and don't have. Punters and petty bourgeoisie. And the Outsiders. Good name. Outside. Not part of. Looking in, looking on. An alien nation. The police; that's another nation. We're the ultimate outsiders; we look like humans, we walk like humans and smell like humans and you think we are humans but we are very, very alien indeed. Strange nations under those nice new blue Northern Ireland Police Service uniforms they've given us to wear.

And how does a wee girl with a saint's middle name come to be driving up the Whiterock Road with a NIPS warrant card and a piece in her handbag?

By being useful. Useful Roisin Dunbar. Serve your fellow humans, help your community, have babies, do the things by the numbers, live the right life. Don't be selfish. Think of others.

God first, others second, self last. The worst thing is to live a selfish, useless life. Like her older brother. What did he do? Wanted to be in a band, be a DJ, cut dance tracks. Useless, selfish. Don't be like him, Roisin. We brought you up better than that. And what did you do, oh mother, apart from have babies and bring them up the way you wanted? What did you do, oh father, in McClatchey Concrete Products that was of such value and service to humanity?

Nothing. And you could not stand the guilt, that you were just ordinary wee people with ordinary wee lives and the world was never going to resound to your names and achievements. So you try and live it through your children. You commissioned and sent them forth to do what you couldn't.

OK, Rosh, but you're still Detective Sergeant Dunbar driving up the Whiterock Road on a Thursday morning, because if you turned in the warrant and piece in your bag you couldn't live with the guilt either.

And how do you, Mr Andrew Gillespie, three years for conspiracy to murder, come to be driving up this self-same Whiterock Road where they paint the gable ends with murals of the saints of the new Ireland: St Gerry the Peacemaker and St Brendan the Escapee and St Bobby the Anorexic and SS Donna and Sean and Nessun of Gibraltar (Martyred)? I suppose you grew up with your own Dulux pantheon watching over you; I mean, it's not as if anyone believes in these beings any more.

The taxi turns left into a reclaimed industrial site. The Outsiders have settled among the ruins of the old plant. Shawls of plastic skin stuff are thrown over old red brick and steel cladding. Dunbar parks at the limit of the zoom lens, but two Outsider kids on BMXs spy her and cut across the scabby concrete to check out the stranger.

'Are you taking pictures?' the larger one on the bigger bike asks. They're both long, lithe, impossible to age or sex. Their deep voices are disturbing, like men dressed up as schoolboys.

'I'm at the Art College,' Dunbar lies – rather well, she thinks. 'Doing a photography project.'

'Can we be in your pictures?'

'Certainly.' Provided I can get that cold-looking man in the leather jacket who is talking with one of your relatives into shot as well. She makes notes in her NIPS notebook. 'What is this place?' she asks the kids.

'Interesting Weather Hold,' they answer together.

Andy Gillespie, arrived Interesting Weather Hold, Whiterock Industrial Park, 10.25, departed 10.45. Talked with two Outsiders.

'Are you not going to take any more photographs?' the Outsider kids ask.

'I'm done. Thanks for your help. By the way, shouldn't you be in school?' Always the cop, Rosh.

'What's school?' the smaller one asks the taller one.

North now, along the Ballygomartin Road, between the foot of Divis mountain and the grey estates of the 1970s. Left up Glencairn, winding up into the hills, climbing away from the estates past tinker caravans and scavenged car wrecks orange and black with rust and smoke; then a sudden right into a farm gate. She overshoots, stops, reverses back. There's a lay-by twenty yards down from the turn. Good camera angle on the front of the farmhouse. More Outsiders. More kids. Don't they believe in school, or do they home educate, like those spooky Christian fellowship churches?

Arrived 11:05, unnamed Outsider residence at 228 Glencairn Road. Spoke with three Outsiders. Departed, 11:15.

What are you at, Gillespie?

East by north, to the scablands by the lough where the Outsiders have grown a haven out of the landfill and yellow-bag shit of Belfast. I'm a bird-watcher, Roisin Dunbar will tell anyone who asks her her business. Photographing ducks and geese and gulls. Mostly gulls. No one asks. Gillespie's here twenty minutes, meeting, talking; then the taxi takes him on again.

You aren't making it easy for me to believe that you're not involved, Gillespie.

Dunbar follows him down a complex inward spiral through the Holds of Belfast City. South, then east across the river to the big settlement in the shipyards, except there haven't been any shipyards since the turn of the century, when the Koreans bought them up to asset-strip away any possible competition with their home peninsula. The two huge construction cranes stand over the new Nation. Symbol of the city, once. You could see them from everywhere. Two fuck-yous from the Protestant work ethic. But it was already dying then. Like the pyramids; monumental epics of engineering are symptoms of the end game. Engines rust, winding gears seize tight. You can still see them from all over the city. Cost too much to pull them down. Now lander 769 fills the dry dock between them, where one hundred years ago the *Oceanic* and *Titanic* were built side by side. And tall, lithe, androgynous creatures that the hard-man welders and caulkers couldn't begin to imagine slip through their cutting sheds and plating yards.

She remembers the day when the lander came down, Number 769. She and everyone else had watched it on television, the escort helicopters hovering at a respectful distance as the big dark red thing came in over the lough. She remembers its shadow sliding across the sheds and yards and the runways of the Harbour Airport; she had shivered with delicious awe. Like a Spielberg movie on your doorstep. The thing had hovered over the empty dry dock and for a moment she'd known, known absolutely, that this was not FX; this was everything it said it was, this was an alien spaceship, this had crossed sixty light years clinging to the stalk of a Shian Interstellar Craft, this was carrying eighty thousand beings that were not human, that were real, genuine aliens, not actors in silly make-up with American accents. Then it had done the thing with gravity that the physicists still don't understand, and touched concrete. There had been two-mile-tail-backs for a week as sight-seers came for a look at a genuine alien spaceship. They'd laid on buses from as far away as Cork. She hadn't gone. A couple of miles across the river, but this is the closest she's ever been to it. Like Parisians never go up the Eiffel Tower.

In the few years since the doors of 769 opened and the Shian came out, they've made Queen's Island the capital of Outsider Ireland. A city within a city. You're not in Belfast any more, Rosh. The place gives her bad vibes. Shivers. It might not be so bad if they had levelled the lot and built from the ground up, but the way they've recycled the old sheds and hangars and fused them with their own sinuous architecture feels like a corpse dressed and polished for a wake, or one of those sci-fi films Mikey likes where they take dead cops and patch them together with technology and send them with big guns out to bust crime. She follows Gillespie's taxi through the warren of buildings and alleys and walkways. She shoots him talking to twelve different Outsiders. Could as well be the same one twelve times, for all she can tell them apart. He's here an hour, enough time for her to call in lunch on the mobile. It comes on the back of a mountain bike ridden by an impossibly tall, impossibly thin, impossibly young and impossibly beautiful girl sandwich courier.

'There's mayonnaise in this, I didn't order mayonnaise,' Dunbar says meanly.

'Take it or leave it,' the impossible lunch girl says with a wave of a gloved hand.

Dunbar takes it.

He's on the move again. South to an Outsider outpost on The Mount; then along by Laganside to Annadale Flats. Onwards, inwards, spiralling back across the river into her own parish, to the Holy Land, those few streets of tiny, red-brick terraces with Biblical place names. Jerusalem Street, Damascus Street. I used to live here, when I was at Queen's. *There*, that one. The landlord still hasn't cut the hedge. I'm sure you can still harvest mushrooms in the bathroom. Five of us in there; how did we survive? I wonder what the others are doing now? Something trivial, probably. Something glorious and useless and *fun*. The Catholic guilt ethic is every bit as good at shafting your life as the Protestant work ethic.

Palestine Street. He's talking to an Outsider at the front door of Number 37. They seem to know each other. Must be one of those transient houses the Welcome Centre set up for newcomers. Clickety-click. Got you. Again. Gillespie doesn't look happy. They mustn't be giving him what he wants: information, alibis, weapons? Back in the taxi, off to a cash point – note place and time, the bank'll give transaction details if we tell them it's the Outsider inquiry. The taxi takes him right past the scene of the crime. You're a cool one, Mr Gillespie. The SOCO vans are still there. Tape and no parking cones all over the place. Then home again home again jiggety-jig. Where he stays until Roisin Dunbar's replacement on the evening shift draws up. Just in time. If she has to listen to one note more of Phil Collins she'll take a tyre jack to the disc player. Do you take this man to be your lawful wedded husband, with his Phil Collins albums, and his Tina Turner discs, and his Chris Rea records? I did.

Darren Healey on the evening session is in no smooth humour. Andrea's imminent, and so he reckons he deserves special treatment from everyone. It's the first, he has to be there for the whole thing, when the waters break, when the first contraction comes. He wants it all on video. They'll break with or without you. Andrea'll just call a taxi and give you a buzz on your mobile.

'Anything?' he asks.

'He's been all over town, calling on Outsider Holds. I'll take the disc back to the station. You got a new one?'

Darren Healey checks his inside pocket.

'Yes. They really should have two of us on surveillance.'

And you could slope off home to Bump of the Year. 'Cutbacks, Darren. We're not a police state any more.' She hands him the camera and the rest of the stuff. It's new uniforms for everyone, but they can't afford more than one SLR. The accountants probably have this entire inquiry budgeted. We overspend, and the bastard gets away on financial grounds. 'Anything from the office? Any breaks yet?'

'Politicians are pissing and moaning about crazed aliens murdering good decent law-abiding citizens in their beds. The papers have got hold of it; the *Telegraph*'s gone apeshit about the "alien menace". Littledick's—'

'What?'

'You haven't heard that one?'

'I like it.'

'Anyway, he's going on the local news to try and sell his theory that it's biologically impossible for Outsiders to kill in this way.'

'Good luck to him. I can think of half a dozen good decent law-abiding citizens I wouldn't mind seeing murdered in their beds.'

'Where do you start?'

'Where do you stop? See you, Darren.'

She finds she's laughing in her car as she drives back to the Pass to print out her photographs and make her report. Littledick. Heh.

Gillespie hates being suspected, but he hates being followed more. It'll be back there, that cop car. He can't see it, but it's there, and it can see him, perched up in this tinny bus with the big glass windows, like a bird in a cage. Here I am! Look at me! Off I go on a wee bus ride. Can you guess where I'm going today? Follow me and find out.

The following isn't the worst of it. The watching; he loathes that. It makes him feel like his life is one big bus window, and faces are pressed to it, hands shading eyes so they have a better peer at the things inside.

It's like the Maze again. Everything public and open and noted and commented on, somewhere that he can't hear what they are saying. He wants to press that red button up there and stop this bus and go to that bitch in the blue Ford, or maybe it's the fat guy with the stupid hair-cut and the attempted moustache, and get into the car and say *all right, we're going back to your place now, and I'm going to walk around outside your house and peek in at your windows and listen at your door and see who comes and goes and who they are and what they do.*

If you want to know what I know and think what I think, talk to the people I talked to. Go back to those Holds I visited yesterday. Ask them what Andy Gillespie was asking. What reason could there be for killing the University Street Hold down to the last child? And they'll tell you what they told Andy Gillespie. No reason. The Harridi Nation is loved and respected by all Shian. Their Welcome Centre has helped hundreds of *gensoon* to find new homes and relationships in this island. And their political aspirations? A Shian party, a third force in Northern Ireland's playgroup politics? If that smug bastard Littlejohn is as good as he makes out on television, then he'll pick up what Andy Gillespie picked up in response to that question: that the Shian Nations are divided, the Holds are divided on this question. There are factions that welcome Muskravhat's movement to integrate the Shian into the Joint

Authority's political structure. And there are factions that think it is way too soon. We're only three years on this world; that's not time enough to get to know our new neighbours. Human ways aren't our ways; everything they do is split down the middle by this man/woman divide and they can't accept us as either. Time, and only time, will teach us to appreciate each other's genders. Until then we are close, but separate. And Littlejohn'll pick up that talking about this to a human makes them uncomfortable. They don't want us to see that they're as petty and disunited and opinionated as we are. There are only eight million of them. They have a toe-hold on this world, and nothing more. And if he's really good, Littlejohn'll pick up what Andy Gillespie surmised from a word here, a look there, an unguarded gesture somewhere else: that something is scaring them. Something beyond playing politics, beyond divisions in the species over integration or segregation, beyond the sex politics of man/woman/Shian. And he'll understand, as Gillespie understands, that they will never say what this is to a human.

And so he'll understand why Andy Gillespie needs to talk to someone who talks like a Shian, walks like a Shian, looks like and lives like and lives with the Shian, but is not a Shian.

Not last time he saw him.

The country bus dawdles by B-roads, through townlands with names longer than their main streets, past endless hacienda-style bungalows raised on plinths of barely grassed soil so that all may appreciate the wealth and taste of farmers. Cathedrals couldn't be more incongruous. God's own country, the devil's own architecture, with satellite dishes. At every stop old people and mitching schoolkids get on. The schoolkids sit at the back. It's mandatory. They're headed for Larne to hang around shopping centres. Urban boredom beats rural boredom. The bus fills up in Larne, passengers for the Antrim coast villages. The bus service has been cut to ribbons, two up, two down. Gillespie reassures himself that if he misses the last one Eamon'll find him a bed for the night. The bus winds in and out of the bays and headlands of the Antrim coast road. As it swings out on to one headland, he can see the blue Ford in the bay behind. Following. Nice day for it. She'll be getting a big mileage cheque

75

at the end of the month for this. Scotland is clear across the water. If you can see Scotland, it's about to rain. If you can't see Scotland, then it is raining.

The bus drops him in the centre of Glenarm village. It's mile walk up the valley; the day is bright, there's warmth in the sun. After half a mile Gillespie takes his jacket off. The land smells green; maybe there will be a spring this year. Eamon's invitations, which Gillespie had ignored, until now, said a mile up the Ballintubber Road and you're at Peace in the Valley. The Surreptajongseng Nation originates from the central south of the Great Continent; their customs are different from the northerly, coastal, Harridis; their Holds are diffuse, houses and lodges spread over the whole of the demesne. There are five hacienda-style bungalows, three farmhouses and two converted barns to choose from. Start with the closest. Which is another bloody hacienda-style bungalow, thoroughly Shianized.

Two kids from it take Gillespie on the back of a tractor to a late nineties mock-Georgian farmhouse with a big stable block further up the valley to see Genjajok Surreptajongseng, the closest thing to a head of household in Peace in the Valley. His Narha title translates as *Facilitator of Guest's Questions*. Always a problem for humans dealing with Shians: who's in charge here? It never bothers the Shian.

For some reason there are two Group Four security vans in the stableyard.

'Mr Gillespie, it is good to meet you at last,' Genjajok the Facilitator says. He shakes hands the human way. He smiles, the human way. It doesn't look right to Gillespie. 'Eamon Donnan speaks of you with great affection. You were most close in jail.'

'Everyone's close in jail,' Gillespie says.

'But you were closer than most,' Genjajok says, leading Gillespie into a large awning-cum-room the Peace in the Valleyers have tacked on to the ugly house. There are human wicker chairs, and Shian stools. 'Eamon has told us about the Maze.'

'All about the Maze?'

'All. Might I offer you some tea?' Genjajok whistles, a piercing shrill. A Shian appears and Genjajok asks for Earl Grey tea for two in Narha.

76

'I'm glad he's found a place here,' Gillespie says, listening to the rising thunder of a kettle boiling in the kitchen. It's the mundane humanities, like kettles and tractors and God-awful hacienda bungalows that lull us into the seduction that they're really just people in silly costumes. They're not. Don't fool yourself. 'When he got out, you know, after what happened, well, he was a little crazy. I suppose we both were. He wanted nothing more to do with human society. Anything could have happened to him; he could have ended up anywhere. I'm glad he found you, and that you took him in.'

'We loved him very much. But you also have found a place.'

'And lost it.'

'Had it taken away, do you mean? It is a severe business.' The tea arrives. He knows it's barbarous, but Gillespie takes his with milk. Genjajok piles in six sugars.

'You've heard.'

'I think it was before even the newspapers got the story. Word travels quickly in our community. Bad news has big wings and a strong wind.'

Gillespie blows on his Earl Grey and watches the Group Four people. There's a lot of coming and going from the stable block.

'What does Eamon make of it?'

'I would not know,' Genjajok Surreptajongseng says. 'He is not a member of our Hold any more.'

For a second, one second, a hideous, hideous suspicion thrashes in Andy Gillespie's mind like a gutshot dog.

'What's happened to Eamon?'

'I recognize a tone of concern in your voice, Mr Gillespie. He left Peace in the Valley happy and healthy in mind and body. His life-hunt is taking him on; in a sense it is his *gensoon*. His childhood is over, and now he has embarked on the journeys of adolescence.'

What kind of seduction has gone on here, Eamon? What have you let them do to you?

'Do you know where he's gone?'

'I do. Before he left on his *gensoon*, he had been expressing an interest in the *hahndahvi*. He had been experimenting, unsuccessfully, with psychotropic substances to try to simulate the

77

effect of the dreaming. He felt he could not properly be a member of our community without being able to dream; therefore we advised him to go to a sacred space and place himself under the tuition of the warden. We have heard that the human nervous system is susceptible to sacred space architecture; this might have the effect of stimulating Eamon into the dreaming state.'

The Shian religion makes eminent sense to Andy Gillespie. If something with no gods, no theology, no ritual, can be called a religion. Belief system. Except you don't need belief for this. No faith, either. It comes to you out of the unexplored regions of your head every night when you click over into dream state. Every culture that understands the importance of dreaming has made up systems of interpretation, but the Shian have purified it into a language. The Narha of the unconscious. Learned in the womb, like Narha: foetuses curled up among the words and spirits. Freud, Jung, all those interpretation of dreams, collective-unconscious people, they would have loved it. The Shian dream the same dreams. They see the same things. They speak a common tongue of archetypes and dream landscapes and symbols. Signs and signifiers. While they are still folded in the womb, they have ten thousand of these archetypes folded into their skulls: the *hahndahvi*, the Guiding Ones. Like casting the bones, or reading the leaves, or that Chinese thing that means whatever you want it to mean. Something Ching. You have a problem, you sleep on it, the right *hahndahvi* comes out of your collective unconscious and gives you the answer. No pissing around with coins or yarrow stalks or genuine plastic runes, no rituals, no smells or bells or making yourself pure and good and holy. Clear, unequivocal, the right answer. Every time.

What's most sensible to Andy Gillespie about the Shian dreaming as a religion is that no one is ever going to kill anyone else because they have a different dream.

'So you sent him to a sacred space?'

'Yes. I can tell you exactly where he is gone. There is only one in this part of Ireland. It is in the Queen's Island Hold, in Belfast, where you have just come from. He is under the tutelage of Thetherrin Harridi, the current warden of the sacred space. I

78

regret you have had a fruitless journey, Mr Gillespie. A simple phone call would have saved you time and wealth.'

Gillespie recognizes the root of the expression, it's a Narha idiom; the fruitless journey, the unlucky hunt. No prey. All covert, tucked down in the undergrowth. Gone to earth.

Yeah, that's about it.

'What I need to say to him, I need to say face to face.'

'Then you will have to go to Queen's Island to say it. Do you wish to stay and take an evening meal with us? An intimate friend of Eamon Donnan's is a most welcome guest at Peace in the Valley.'

Gillespie recognizes another Narha thought underneath the words 'intimate friend'. He means 'lover'. But not in the human sense. In the Shian sense, of love without sex.

'Thanks, but I've got a bus to catch.'

'I will have one of the tractors take you down into the village, Mr Gillespie.'

In the stableyard the Group Four people are getting ready to go. They're wearing a lot of heavy armour for a Shian Hold way out in the glens of Antrim.

'What are they at?'

'Oh, that is one of our profit-making operations,' Genjajok says. 'It seems that self-sufficiency is not enough to be a member of human society, we must subscribe to the profit economy. Thus we are manufacturing stasis coffins, which we keep in the stable block. There must be over a hundred now.'

Gillespie finds the image of eight million Shian sleeping away sixty years objective/six subjective (and relativistic time contraction is just another thing about the World Ten Migration he takes as read) in stasis coffins chilly and sinister. As if they really were dead and have come back to life like vampires, an invasion of the undead floating down upon the earth. Step off the space elevator, find your coffin, in you get. Feeling like a little doze, and you wake up thinking, that was the best sleep I've had in years and all the people you left behind are sixty years older. Or dead.

'What do you do with them?'

'We lease them to Group Four Securities to keep prisoners in.'

'You what?'

'It is a most efficient system. It is vastly cheaper to keep a criminal in stasis than in prison, it ameliorates overcrowding, as your Joint Secretariat seems intent that every human male under the age of thirty spend some time in prison, and there is no possibility of escape, nor are there any problems of discipline, or of drug trafficking or prisoners being corrupted by others. Or rape, Mr Gillespie. Would you like me to show you?'

'Um, no. Thanks.'

Jesus. That's protecting society with a vengeance. But they couldn't do it to long-sentence offenders. They'd go under and come out to find they hadn't aged but the world was ten, fifteen, twenty years older. Their wives, their girlfriends, their parents. Their children. Childhood wiped out in a single sleep. Jesus, that's cruel and unusual. But they wouldn't be a day older. Everyone else would be old, but they'd be young, strong. Is that a punishment or a blessing? It's a shit world where the crims needing protecting from society. And how would it have been for you, if instead of taking you in the big blue van through the gate of HMP (Cellular) Maze, some private security clowns in paramilitary uniforms had brought you up to this farm and stuffed you into a box and sent you to sleep for two years? No Eamon. No Narha, no great gift of language. But the bad thing wouldn't have happened either. You'd all have slept in your cold boxes and woken up no different from when you went in. Eamon Donnan wouldn't be trying to turn himself into a Shian; you'd just be another unemployable ex-con, orbiting in towards the gravity of the old boys, the old ways, the old places. But someone that no one saw, some invisible killer, would still have gone into the Shian Welcome Centre on University Street and killed five people with five maser shots and then cut up their bodies with a knife.

'Whole new meaning to "suspended sentence",' Gillespie comments.

The Peace in the Valleyers turn out to wave Andy Gillespie off in the tractor. They all smile the human smile. They have it very good, but he's not convinced. Truth is in the chemicals. I can smell it in the wind. I can smell it off you like sex. You're as scared as the rest of them.

The taxi drops him under the third light on Queen's Quay Road. It's as close as the driver will go to the sacred space. He gives Gillespie a look, like he's a transvestite, or a terrorist of the wrong colour, or a celebrity he personally doesn't find particularly entertaining. *I don't like you. I don't like what you've paid me to bring you to.*

He doesn't like Gillespie's money.

'Don't take animal money.'

'They haven't had animals on since it went decimal. That's Dun Scotus. Ancient Irish scholar.'

'Don't take punts.' He exaggerates the Irish word into a small mockery. *Phunts.*

'We got joint authority, haven't you heard?'

'Not in this taxi we don't.'

Gillespie opens his wallet like a mouth.

'Dun Scotus or fuck all.'

The driver takes the Irish twenty. Tips of fingers, like it's printed in liquid shit. Gillespie asks for *all* the change. Thank you. Fucker. The taxi throws a U-ie inside the cone of light from the third street lamp. Gillespie turns up his collar against the cold drizzle. His jacket is silvered with fine droplets. They float and eddy in the sodium light like spirits. Dreaming is all around. You move through two worlds as you walk along this wide, wet, empty road towards those white arc lights. Every step sends clouds of *hahndahvi* twisting away, like the veils of mist that swirl in behind you as you pass. As real, as touchable and touching to them as this physical world. Ordered dreams; places and faces that you can visit night after night because you can trust that they will remain the same. Not like human dreams, where people you love wear bodies that are strange but familiar. Trustworthy dreams. Faithful dreams. How would that be? Dreams that don't lie when they whisper you the way to success and the path of fulfilment, and when you wake up you find that the golden key to the universe is *pancakes should not be pissed on by robins and wolverines.*

And this place, under the white arc lights, where waking and sleeping meet. Unseen is seen. A building for meeting God. A holy place that works, every time, without fail, or faith. A divinity machine.

Gillespie breathes in the cold, damp air through his nostrils. It's beginning. He can smell it. A faint, salty tang. A little jizz in the atmosphere, a little jolt of pheromonal electricity. Like a change in climate, the season is coming.

The sacred space is on the edge of the Shipyard Hold, a disused Harland and Wolff loading dock with its front open to the water, like an old man taking a slow piss in the river. It doesn't look very holy on the outside. True holy places never do. Holiness is always within. Outside holiness is no holiness at all.

An orange Volkswagen campervan is parked on the Hold side of the road. The interior lights are on; figures move behind steamed-up glass and in the darkness underneath an awning erected against the open tailgate. Bass blast: dunh dunh dunh dunh dunh dunh dunh duhduh dunh. Divine architecture junkies. God is the best addiction of all. But the dynamics of the sacred space work unpredictably on the human nervous system. It's not always the face of God you see. They find them in the river sometimes, churned up with the plastic beer glasses in the jet-wash from the car ferries, or down on the mud flats with the shore birds mincing around them. Heart failure. The eyes. You can't describe the look in them, the last thing they saw. But the kids keep coming in their campers and caravans and tents and little wet encampments smelling of piss, wood smoke and wet wool. Hungry for the face of God.

Maybe that's the look in the eyes of the next-morning wash-ups.

The loading dock is a shell. The sacred space is constructed inside, a building within a building. Gillespie's senses slip off the web of wooden beams and live-polymer sheeting. Its geometry eludes him. As soon as he sees it as *this* it changes shape to *that*. Dimensions shift with every step he takes towards it: the sacred space grows bigger than perspective allows, the loading dock dwindles until it seems smaller than the object it contains. The emotional resonances extend outside the space. He can feel his balls tighten, his belly tense, his breath grow short, the quarter-inch of stubble on his head prickle as he approaches the chamber. Something wonderful. Like Christmas to a child. With snow, like when Stacey was three and it was pure wonder.

Andy Gillespie's never known the subtle movement of spirit dwelling in a temple or a shrine. He's never stood awed and silent beneath the ancient lights of Christianity's cathedrals. But he knows that whatever you might feel there is only a shadow cast by what is contained here. A place for experiencing God. There are angels in the architecture. There are sick buildings and healthy buildings and buildings that make you feel at peace and buildings where you feel agitated the moment you step into them but do not know why. Buildings that make you feel vulnerable and vertiginous, buildings that enfold and nurture you like a placenta. The first stone tombs of the Shian are thirty thousand years old. Enough time to learn to build so skilfully that every nuance of architecture and decoration and geometry and lighting and the subtle movements of air stimulate your senses into a perception of the divine.

A Shian arrives around a corner of the sacred space. Smell of a female. A second sniff: an *old* female. She is dressed in a long skirt split to the thigh and a silk blouse. It is cold in the loading dock but the blouse is open. Her nostrils are circled with white make-up.

'You are Andy Gillespie.' The nostrils flare, identifying him. 'I know you from the Welcome Centre.'

'Thetherrin Harridi?' he asks. The old Outsider tilts her head back in confirmation. 'I'm afraid I don't remember you.'

'We all look alike. Eamon Donnan is at the focus. I will take you to him.'

'I'm sorry. I didn't mean to disturb anything.'

'It is nothing. He is at the stage of searching for a *hahndahvi*. This requires that he spends much time in the focus. Your presence will not trouble him. He will be glad to see you. You loved each other once.'

The enforced intimacy of prison is a kind of loving.

'I will take you by the north door. The effect is less there, but you would be advised to close your eyes to minimize the disorientation.'

'I had a couple of big vodkas just before I came.'

Without speaking, the Outsider leads Gillespie round to the north door. She opens it. They pass through into the sacred space.

Two big hits of vodka blur the edges of Gillespie's senses, but the lift into God-consciousness makes him want to fall on his hands and knees. It's here. Every good thing. Every moment of awe and wonder and beauty and mystery. He is floundering in *numen*. He breathes it in; it is everywhere and nowhere, like all good gods should be. Infinite and intimate. Terrible and wonderful. All those paired contradictions that divinities maintain so effortlessly.

It's only because of the alcohol that he is able to look around him to try to see how the trick is done. It is very good. When he looks at the walls straight on they seem to stretch away for ever, but on the edges of the fields of vision they curve intimately around the space so that it is both very much larger and very much smaller than it looks from outside. The light is at once directional and unfocused; shadows shift, clouds of tiny flames appear, swirl, vanish. Tongues of fire. In the centre of the space is what he can only describe as a globe of woven light. A stained glass window made of fire. There is a shadow in the light, a seated figure.

As Gillespie walks towards the figure, the walls move across his peripheral vision, stealthily opening up planes and dimensions. Invitations to strange rooms and niches. He pauses, shakes his head. There is something in it.

'Above the range of your hearing,' Thetherrin says. 'The space modulates the passage of air through it into sound.'

But he felt it. It was a sharp, sudden sense of loss and freedom. A great divorce. In one of the chambers in the corner of his eye he glimpses a kneeling figure – human, Outsider, he can't tell. It's wrapped in a shit-coloured coat. It beats the floor with a fist. He hears weeping. He turns, but the walls have closed.

He knows instinctively that it would have been very different entering through one of the other doors.

The illusion is seamless. That is because it is not illusion. A real magician can do all the same tricks as a conjuror. It would have been an illusion if Gillespie had seen the face of God, but the Shian do not believe in gods. Their *hahndahvi* come out of themselves. The sensations of the sacred space come out of themselves, from that fold of the mind that holds the faculty for spiritual experience. God is within. God is in the chemicals. Twelve vodkas, a tab of LSD, eight hours' dancing on MDMA: thou also art God. Like those people who have near-death experiences where they fly towards a great white light and see the faces of their loved ones and angels. Oxygen starvation of the visual centres of the brain. Chemical heaven. God doesn't make us. We make God. The answers aren't out there, waiting for the right question to be asked in the right way with the right degree of faith and self-deprecation, then *maybe* they might get an answer, provided you accept that *No* is a valid answer from an omnipotent deity. The truth is in there, among the heroes and the villains, the lovers and the rogues, the thieves, fools and pretenders of the *hahndahvi*. This light is my own.

Jesus.

'I will leave you here,' Thetherrin says at the edge of the central globe of lights. He turns to thank her but she is gone. Swallowed by the numinous. Gillespie steps through the curtain of light, into stillness. At the centre, all influences come together and cancel each other out.

'Andy.'

'Eamon?'

He doesn't recognize the voice. It's high, accented. It doesn't sound right. It doesn't sound like he remembers. He doesn't recognize the figure kneeling on the meditation stool. It's dressed Shian fashion, wrap-over jacket, leggings and boots: the formal hunting garb that the Outsiders on earth wear only on ceremonial occasions. Its hair is cut Shian fashion: shaved into a central crest, dyed red. A hand is offered, palm up. The Shian way. It has five digits.

Gillespie licks it. Eamon Donnan doesn't taste human any more.

'Yeah.' But Donnan tilts his head back, the Shian way.

85

'Jesus, you look like Robert de Niro in *Taxi Driver*.'

He laughs, but doesn't return Gillespie's smile. He blinks slowly.

Suddenly, Gillespie finds he wants to seize Eamon Donnan and shake him. In the still centre of this spiritual space, he wants to shake all this stupidity and play-acting out of his prison friend. What do you look like? he wants to shout into his face from a distance of very few centimetres. Do you think you are one of them? Do you think that because you shave your head and wear the clothes and speak the body-talk and smell of their food that you are one of them? You can't even sit on their stool because your legs are too short and your hips are the wrong shape and your joints are in different planes, and you think that you can dream their dreams and give a home in your head to their archetypes? You look stupid. You look as stupid and undignified as those thin white boys who shave their heads and put on saffron robes and dance about in Cornmarket on Saturday afternoons singing *Krishna Krishna* and everyone laughs at them and wonders what kind of a god makes you dress like a dick. You look like a dressed-up chimpanzee. You look like a monkey at a tea party.

He wants to say all this and shake this thing in front of him back into the Eamon Donnan he knew. But he does nothing. He doesn't know why this angers him so much. He doesn't like to think that he is jealous that Eamon Donnan has found the courage to do and be what he desires most.

'Good of you to see me,' Gillespie says lamely. He declines the offer of an empty stool and squats down to sit uncomfortably cross-legged.

'Hey, you know . . . Any time.'

'How long do you have to stay in here?'

'I don't have to stay anywhere. I want to stay here.'

'How long have you been here?'

'Five days. I think the *hahndahvi* will be coming soon. I've seen things, on the edges of my dreams.'

'How does that work? I thought you had to have the dream language passed on in the womb.'

'Yes, normally. But Thetherrin reckons that because I have –

we have – the structure of Narha imprinted, the dream language could be grown around that grammar. They're both language-like structures, they both share the universal grammar. The sacred space stimulates archetype formation in the subconscious, and they crystallize around the language structure. This is the first English I've spoken in six months, Andy.'

'We can talk Narha if you like.'

'It's all right. But watch your dreams, Andy. You got given it too. What are you here for, Andy? Not pretty talk about linguistics.'

'You know.'

Donnan shrugs. Human shrug. 'Everyone knows. No one's talking about anything else. What have you been told?'

'They aren't talking to me. They won't say anything to me. But they're split; right down the middle. Even the Nations are split. Goes all the way down to the Holds. Even this one, I think. Most of all this one, maybe. If the Harridis are divided, everyone is divided.'

'I didn't think they would tell you anything,' Donnan says. 'You're a threat.' He sits back on his contemplation stool. The illumination from the veils of coloured lights shifts. He looks very alien. His eyes are the most alien.

'Me? The Welcome Centre? Humans?'

Donnan, by saying nothing, implies all three. And more.

'Can you think of anywhere more typically human than this country?' he says. 'They know they're an experiment. Some think your Harridis and their movement for integration into human society is premature.'

'You're telling me Shian could have done this to their own kind?'

'If they won't tell you, I can't tell you. What do the police think?'

'They think I did it.'

Donnan looks at Gillespie. A long look, that Gillespie can't read because it means two things in two languages of looking.

'They think I'm the link man in a weapons-running operation to the paramilitaries. They think the Welcome Centre found out, and I kept them quiet. They've someone following me. This bitch. She'll be out there now, in the rain.'

The silence at the heart of the sacred space is palpable. Gillespie hears his voice speaking in it: flat and dull and lifeless.

'The police are fools,' Eamon Donnan says.

'They've got a man in from the university. Some Shian expert. Littlejohn.'

Donnan blinks his eyes slowly. A smile. Gillespie leaves him space but he does not speak.

'He thinks it's some kind of psycho,' he goes on. 'Serial killer. The police don't want to hear that. They want a quick result. A serial killer has to strike again before they can begin to get a pattern.'

'What do you think?'

'I agree with Littlejohn.'

'Littlejohn knows nothing,' Donnan says. Then, in Narha: – *Littlejohn is a fool.*

– Am I a fool then, too? Gillespie asks.

– You don't know what you're saying. Donnan snaps back into English. 'The police, Doctor Robert Littlejohn, you: you don't know anything. The rules are different, Andy. You don't even know what pitch you're playing on, let alone where the goals are. Leave it, Andy.'

'I can't.'

'Playing fucking Andy Hero again, isn't that it? Just like in the Maze. You couldn't stop it happening then, you can't stop it happening now. And you cannot live with that. Hand the man his staff and stones and give him a pair of tights and a big black cape to dress up in and watch him leap from rooftop to rooftop. Play-acting Andy. You aren't the Masked Avenger. You see all this stuff about defending rights and personal commitment to pursue justice, but the Shian Law isn't the Lone Ranger. There's a price to it. Maybe you won't pay it this case, maybe not for ten years, twenty years, but every Shian lawyer knows that in the end it will cost them everything. Justice isn't free.'

'You think I don't understand this?'

'I think you don't understand that there is no word in Narha for *guilt*. Shian lawyers don't take cases because they can't bear feeling guilty.'

His friends say there are many unexpected things about Andy Gillespie. One is that you never know what he is going to do until he does it. Another is that, for a broad man, he moves very fast. Almost as fast as a Shian. His left hand is clutching a fistful of soft jacket, his right drawn back to strike, before Eamon Donnan can throw himself off the contemplation stool to safety.

Donnan looks at the hands.

Gillespie looks at the hands.

Gillespie looks at Eamon Donnan. Striking distance is as close and intimate as loving distance. Gillespie feels the body under his fingers. He sees its muscles move. He smells its sweats and its perfumes. He breathes them in. Chemistry is identity to the Shian. The thing in his grip does not smell human. This is not an ape in a costume, pretending to be a man. This is not a man. To hit this would be like hitting a woman. A totally different violence. It would be as incomprehensible as hitting a Shian.

A third thing Andy Gillespie's friends know about him is that his anger burns hot and fast and soon goes to ash.

He rubs the back of his hand across his forehead.

'Jesus, I'm sorry.'

Donnan rearranges his clothing, adjusts his position on the contemplation stool. Beyond the curtains of coloured lights, God waits.

'Do you remember what you said the day you got out, Andy?'

'I remember saying I was going to do something with what I'd been given. Use it to make sure the same thing never happened to another Outsider.'

'Not that, Andy. What I remember is you saying that you were going to hold on to your kids. Whatever. They were the most important thing you had. The most important thing any man could have. You were going to go out and try to be a proper family. I remember that because I wanted it. You had what I wanted, but I couldn't have it. I'd have killed you if I could've had that.'

'It didn't work. Outside, it'd changed too much.'

'We're all looking for something to belong to in this country.

Protestant, Catholic, Irish, British, Unionist, Nationalist; human, Shian, we have to be a part of something. We're not allowed to exist outside. Independent. We're not allowed to be ourselves, alone. I've found where I belong, Andy. I've got my family. My proper family. What you had, I've got now. In the Maze I saw men at their most typical. Men at their most *man*. I hated them. They were fucking animals. I didn't want to be like them. I didn't want to be a man any more. It sickened me. Male, but not a *man*. Can you understand that, Andy?'

'What are you trying to tell me?'

'I won't tell you what you want to know. What the Shian are scared of. They're my family. Even if they're wrong. I won't go against them. No more than you would do something against your children, Andy.'

'Is that all you can tell me? I came all the way here for this?'

Donnan nods his head. The human nod. Gillespie stands. The sides of his knees ache from sitting cross-legged. Old bones. A tall shadow waits in the divine light beyond the protecting veil around the sanctuary: Thetherrin Harridi, to guide him back to the mundane world.

'I can tell you one thing, but you already know it.'

'Tell me anyway.'

'The Shian do not die for love, but they will kill without thinking to protect their children.'

Andy Gillespie shivers, though it is not cold in the quiet place in the eye of God.

The dripping sprinkler in the corridor is one of those annoyances that you never think about when you are not around them, but when you are you wonder how anyone could forget something so intensely aggravating. Of course they haven't fixed it. And some clown has put a metal waste-bin under it to catch the drips, when anyone with a functioning cerebellum would know that a resonant *plop* is much more infuriating than a flat splat on cigarette-cratered vinyl floor tile.

Not enough money to fix it. But enough to reprint every form in two languages and bilingually sign everything down to the bogs and stick up pictures of the Blessed Saint Mary Robinson on the wall next to not-so-Bonnie King Charlie. Always enough money for window dressing. Always enough money for politics.

A single desk light in the room of shadowy geometrical furniture. The red eye of the coffee machine is open. Dunbar recognizes Littlejohn's hairy hands on the lit desk-top.

'What are you doing here?'

'Awaiting the fruit of your unrivalled professional insight.'

He's got it from serial killer books and TV cop shows; this Wayward But Brilliant Police Consultant repartee. Do you know what they're calling you? Littledick. But if you get me a coffee, I won't call you it to your face.

He pours two coffees.

'Non-dairy creamer?'

'Yah.' She fishes in her overcoat pocket for the sweeteners. Police-plan Diet. Sell a million copies: pig out on takeaway food in your car, then salve your conscience with Diet Coke and sweeteners.

'Still wearing that ghastly Arpège.' Littlejohn sniffs as he sets down the mug. It has a faded print of ex-Princess Diana on the side.

'I forgot.'

'It's important. It's like you doing door to door wearing a Mickey Mouse mask.'

She can still hear that bloody drip. Plop. Plop.

'I did remember not to smile.'

'Shouldn't be too hard for the NIPS.' He lingers over the components of the acronym. 'So, what did the shifty Mr Gillespie do this day?'

Her palmtop is unfolded, the stylus in her hand, the empty report document open on the grey screen.

'I really do have to make this report.'

'Come on. We're on the same side. No "I" in team.' She looks at him. He smiles through his black beard. 'Heard it on an American sit-com. I know you don't buy the gun-running theory any more than I do. Where did he go, who did he see, what did he say?'

Littledick, she thinks. OK, I'll talk. If it will stop him being chummy. Save me from intimacy. It's better when he's a supercilious bastard.

'Down to Queen's Island.'

'Ah. Our friends the Harridis.'

'He went to an old Harland and Wolff dock they've turned into some kind of church.'

'Sacred space. Police literary style has sadly declined since the days of "I was proceeding along Victoria Street in a westerly direction when at nine-thirty-three precisely I perceived a certain gentleman . . ."'

'Do you want to hear this? I don't have to tell you any of this.'

He holds up his hands.

Plip goes the leaky sprinkler.

'Does the name Eamon Donnan mean anything to you?'

Littlejohn purses his lips, twirls a strand of beard between thumb and forefinger, shakes his head.

'He's living with the Outsiders. Wears the clothes, got the Mohican, talks the language. He's gone native.'

'It happens. There must be a couple of dozen sub-cultures have grown up around the Shian. Most of them are kids; the kind would've ended up as New Age Travellers ten years ago. They set up these parodies of Shian Holds, try to live like them in mutual harmony and understanding. Of course, they don't understand that the Shian aren't just tall thin people with nice colour skins and funny haircuts. They are not human. Nothing like human. Sexual jealousy usually kills these communities in six months dead. We can't live their way.'

'This Eamon Donnan seems to be trying.'

'It's the difference between a transvestite and a transsexual. One wants to be *like* the opposite sex. The others wants to *be* the opposite sex. Same with your friend. For some it's not enough to be like them, like those kids you see going around town with their heads shaved Shian-style. It's not even enough to want to fuck them, like the frooks. Some want to be them. There're a lot of folk out there know they're aliens trapped in human bodies. There're operations they can do to bring the alien out. Of course, their surgery is centuries ahead of anything we're capable of. Bone grafts for the extra height, eye-jobs – whole new irises.

92

Various cosmetic rearrangements of the facial features; they can even implant smell receptors in the nasal passages. They can reprogramme the melanin in the dermal cells. Like sun-tan, only it stays. That's all surface stuff. For the more radical transformations, they implant nanotech hormone pumps in the pituitary gland. Twice a year, when the season changes, so do you. They'll also redesign your personal plumbing so you can actually do it with them. Oh, it's mighty impressive stuff. Then there's all the psychological business as well; language implants – like your friend Gillespie got from his buddy in the Maze.'

'Donnan has one too. He and Gillespie were inside together. He got out three months after Gillespie and went straight to the Peace in the Valley Hold in Glenarm.'

'And now Gillespie's checking up on his old cell-mate. What was Donnan in for?'

'Possession with intent to supply.'

'They still bust people for that? I can see your mind working, Detective Sergeant Roisin Dunbar.' The liquid metronome in the hall ticks off moments of significance. Little. Dick. Little. Dick. Little. Dick. 'The old paramilitary and the insider ex-pusher? Setting up the deal? Checking his supply?'

Dunbar twiddles the palmtop stylus. The screen wakes from its saver of Next Generation Starship *Enterprise*s. Go away. Don't want you. It's cold in the office, despite her street coat. The heat went off hours ago. Beyond the plip, plop she can hear robot polishing machines waltzing each other up and down the corridors. She shrugs.

'I thought you were on my side, Rosh.'

Christ, he's trying to come on to me.

Littlejohn holds his left hand up in the desk light, wiggles his fingers.

'How many fingers does he have, this Eamon Donnan? It's the first step, amputation of the minor metacarpal.'

'I didn't get to see him. Some Outsider told me he was in meditation in the sacred space and could not be disturbed.'

'Allowed Gillespie to see him, though. Did the Shian tell you what Gillespie and this Eamon Donnan talked about?'

'Didn't. Wouldn't.'

'I'm not surprised, you smelling like that. At least you didn't smile. You want my opinion?'

'Do I have a choice?'

'Pull Donnan in.'

'What grounds?'

'He's your boy.'

'I thought Gillespie was your boy.'

'Eamon Donnan is more my boy than Gillespie.'

'What's your evidence?'

'With humans, everything comes down to what you want to fuck or be fucked by. My dear, you take a kid. A boy. Ordinary enough. Well brought up. Brighter than average. Good at school. Friends. Popular. You take his father away one day. Just like that. Gone. Maybe it's a car smash somewhere, or his heart, or the big C. Most likely a divorce, a separation. One day, Dad's just not there any more and the kid's asking, where my father, what's happened to him? When's he coming back? He's never coming back, his mother tells him, and that's where it starts. He begins to feel responsible. They broke up because of him. He's bad. He's strange. He carries this terrible secret around with him: *I'm the little boy who made his father disappear.* He's different inside. He's horrible. Then one day the horrible inside begins to come out. It comes out as one single, thick, black pube. Jesus help me! he thinks. I'm turning into a monster. I'm weird. But he can't tell anyone. And to make matters worse, he's in love with the pretty boy in his class – we all were, at that age – and all of a sudden there's the pet lizard he keeps down his pants that won't stay still when he's sitting on the bus, or sharing crisps with his pretty boyfriend, and in the school changing room he's got half the Matto Grosso in his groin while the others are as smooth and pure as Dresden china and he wants this pretty boy more than anything but he knows the pretty boy is going to be repelled by him. He's a monster. He's an ogre. He repels himself. He wants, but can't have. And later, when it comes to women, it's worse. You have to talk to them. But he can't talk. He's a hairy monster. And anyway, they've got these lumpy bits, and that sucking-in, biting-off bit – that's really scary. They don't have the smoothness he wants. Not the flatness, the Dresden china perfection. He fantasizes about racing cyclists. He buys albums by androgynous bands. He shaves off his body hair and panics when it won't flush down the toilet and has to scoop it all out and hide it where his mum won't find it. But it doesn't make the women want him, because the monster is inside, always growing outwards. And now the men he once fancied like mad are all hair and balls and testosterone and team games. They disgust him. He disgusts himself. There's nothing, no one, like him. He's absolutely alone.

'Then the Outsiders come. They're tall. They're thin. They're smooth. They've got no nasty pulpy or dangly bits and you can't tell the boys from the girls. People like me, our man says. Schwing! Instant stiffy. But there's one big problem. He wants them, but they don't want him. Intellectually, he knows it's the chemicals – he knows everything there is to know about these folk, he keeps scrap-books on them, for God's sake – but emotionally, it's another rejection. The perfect lust object, and it doesn't want him. He's still a monster. So he tries to make himself like them, so they won't be afraid of him and reject him. Gets the look. Buys the clothes – a real turn-on, clothing fetishism's one of the best, maybe some day he'll have the courage to go out on the street dressed. It's not enough. He learns the accent, maybe even the language. Goes to clubs, tries to get close to them. Still not enough. Maybe if I lived among them, that would be close enough. No. Doesn't do it. Because it's not enough now to be with them, or even like them. He wants to *be* them. And he can never be that. He doesn't want to fuck them any more. He wants them to fuck him. He wants them to get inside him. He wants to take, not give. And of course, they can't fuck him. It's absolutely impossible. They don't even possess the *idea*. He's come this far, he's done all this, and still they don't want him.

'He's a monster again. He's a monster like no one ever was a monster before. No one wants him. Nothing. He's hated. Despised. Laughed at. Monster. Freak.

'Well, then, if they won't fuck him, he'll fuck them. Fuck them good. So, he gets hold of a maser, blows five heads to red smears. Hah, now you're really fucked. Then to make sure they can't

95

fuck him about any more he gets his knife out and cuts off their dangly bits and slitty bitey bits so they can't fuck anything ever again, and fries them with the maser on defrost cycle.

'He's destroyed the thing he loved. Shian don't do that. Shian can't do that. He's not a Shian. But he's not human either. He's the monster he always knew he was. It's grown out from inside, taken him over. Strangled by his own wiry pubes. And the monster will keep doing it again and again and again, until someone stops it.'

Littlejohn swills down the cooling dregs of his coffee.

'Was that a bit horrid for you? You don't like the idea that inside us men there's something that only needs to be bent the tiniest bit out of true and we start killing things and can't stop?'

The polishers have danced off down the corridor. Slow foxtrot. The solitary metronome drip is unchallenged.

'You don't join the police if you can't hack "horrid",' Roisin Dunbar says. 'You're a psychologist, somewhere? Make something of this. When I was a wee girl, I was the one in our family buried the dead, cleaned up the shit, wiped away the boke. Dead sparrow in the garden, pet had to be taken to be put down: wee Rosh's job. Cat shat in the bath, dog boked his dinner on the hearth rug; everyone would run away and hide behind the door because it would make them sick if they went near it. I'd be the one who would go and get the kitchen roll and the plastic bag and the carpet cleaner and the cloth, and take it all away.'

'Now they pay you to do it,' Littlejohn says. 'That big gun under your jacket blow much sick away?'

'The thing is, I'm used to it. It's my job. Someone had to do it. Someone still does.'

'Don't you deserve more than sick and shit?'

'Everyone does. No one gets it, though. It just keeps coming. But what no one ever stopped to think was, maybe all this stuff I had to clean up made me feel as sick as it made them. Maybe I wanted to throw, maybe I was as disgusted as they were by this shit. Maybe the only difference was that I understood someone had to face the stuff to clean it away.'

Littlejohn sits back in his chair. His face is deep in office darkness. Roisin Dunbar can see his eyes looking at her. She does not like the way they look. They are over-educated eyes. They study.

'Do you have to finish that report tonight?' he says. It is not what she is expecting him to say.

'No. Why?'

He puffs a sigh-ette through his lips.

'Just that, well—' he makes a throwaway gesture with his left hand. 'You finish your report. You go home. Marks and Spencer's boxed dinner. *News at Ten*. Half a bottle of Chilean Chardonnay, which you can't enjoy because your darling infant's screaming in one ear and your husband's bitching and moaning in the other about what a hell of a day he's had up to the elbows in spew and baby shit and you can't even have a bath all to yourself because the baby'll start crying or the phone will ring or hubby will come slinking in with the bottom half of the bottle of Chilean Chardonnay and two glasses and ask you if he can rub you up with his extra special soaping device.

'And this bearded, corduroyish congeries of academic clichés will go back to his leaking Victorian terrace furnished in books he's never going to read again, with the piano he can't play and there's no one there who can play it any more, and he'll pour himself a wee gin because contrary to expectations he doesn't like whiskey, and he'll see what's on Sky Sport, because again, contrary to the script, he doesn't like either Dizzy Gillespie or Wagner. And then he'll sleep. And you'll sleep and we'll both wake another day older.

'And maybe two people with nothing to go home for might just enjoy a drink – or two – nothing more, honest, and a few brief moments of intelligent conversation.'

'A drink?'

'Or two.'

'That's all?'

'Aha.'

Dunbar clicks off the palmtop. Starship *Enterprise* dematerializes into plastic screen, flat and grey as February.

'Maybe it is baby spew and bitching and the local TV news telling me and the whole street I'm doing a bad job, and maybe it will be Marks' microwave linguine and half a bottle of white

97

wine; but it's my baby spew, my bitching, my television and dinner and wine, in my house, sitting on my sofa with my central heating on, and maybe it's stupid, and maybe it's fake security or just plain head-in-the-sand, but for a while I won't have to think about the monsters out there, the horrid things, the shit. They can huff and they can puff, but they can't blow my walls down. So, thank you for your invitation, Dr Littlejohn, and no offence, but I won't be accepting it because, despite your efforts to convince me otherwise, with you it's all script. Nothing but script.'

As she gets up and picks up her bag to leave, she sees his smile out of the corner of her eye.

'Next time, Rosh.'

'Please don't call me that.' *Littledick.*

He speaks to her as she goes through the door into the lighted corridor.

'Pull Donnan in. He's your boy!'

A quick flick of her foot shifts the waste-paper bin from under the leaking sprinkler. The water falls flatly on the polished vinyl floor. Flat. Flat. Fhlat.

Andy Gillespie is watching football but thinking about language. It is not hard to think about language when the football you are watching is local teams playing a Coca Cola Cup second-round qualifier and the score is nil all after eighty minutes with the prospect of an equally scoreless half hour of extra time to follow. An insight surfaces through his thoughts on language, like a barnacled U-Boat flying a swastika. What the hell kind of a name for a football trophy is the Coca Cola Cup? Do the twenty-two men in shorts running around in the dark on a freezing wet March night think it is worth it all for something named after American carbonated water? Then he goes back to thinking about language. The language he is thinking about is Narha. He is not thinking about Narha in Narha, though he could if he wished – the molecular structure of its grammar is imprinted into his frontal lobes. Thoughts about a language are most clearly worked through in another language.

He's thinking about something Eamon Donnan said in Narha.

Shortly after the start of the second half Andy Gillespie had been thinking about Eamon Donnan, but his thoughts slide off that man. It's something like shock, Gillespie thinks. Like a death, or a divorce, a terrible change that happens to someone you know and you can't keep his face in your mind, you can't think about him afterwards, because you don't want those emotions that what has happened to him makes you feel. He can't think about Eamon Donnan because Eamon Donnan is dead. Better – easier – to think about Distillery nil all with Glenavon than to have to try to understand what Eamon's done to himself.

– *Littlejohn is a fool*, were Eamon Donnan's words.

But it's not what Donnan said in Narha Gillespie's thinking about. It's how he said it. His *tone*. Gillespie's no linguist, but he understands that every language has unsayable things. Ideas, objects, emotions that its vocabulary cannot properly describe. He's read somewhere that the Eskimos have fifty names for snow. Maybe more. An Inuit-speaker looking at a snow-covered land will see a more detailed and descriptive landscape than an English-speaker, who sees only snow. The French officially despise Anglic borrowings like *le weekend* or *le sandwich*, but their language has no other way of describing these concepts. Narha recognizes its unsayability with a special tone of voice. It says, *the word I am speaking cannot fully convey the concept I am trying to express.* It's the oral equivalent of crossing out a word you have written, because it will not work, but leaving it legible, because no other word will work better.

What Eamon Donnan said, was – *Littlejohn is a ~~fool~~.*

Hrachar is the Narha word. *Hrachar*, spoken with a rising inflection, guttural in the back of the throat. Taught speakers can't learn that tone. Only chemicals give you the right way to speak it.

What is Dr Robert Littlejohn, consultant xenologist, that is more foolish than *hrachar*?

Ding da-da-da-da-da-da-da dang.

Jesus.

That doorbell'll kill him yet.

Eleven-thirty-five. Karen? Wouldn't be the first time she's dumped the kids on him at this time of night because her current won't shag her with an eight- and eleven-year-old in the next bedroom. You want to be a father? Then be a father. While the guy's out there in his car, drumming his fingers on the wheel. *Come on come on come on before I lose this hard on.* She's supposed to phone, but there are a lot of things she's supposed to do. Always when the place is like a bomb-site. She does it deliberately. Call yourself father with a week's dirty dishes in the sink and three bin-bags of unlaundered underwear and T-shirts humming gently?

Call yourself a mother, when you drag your daughters out of their beds at eleven o'clock at night, drive them across town in a complete stranger's car and dump them here with school the next day because your boyfriend can't get it up if he's afraid an eight-year-old might wander in and catch a glimpse of his spotty bum.

Upstairs' mountain bike is all over the hall again. Gillespie catches a trace of vodka off himself. Shit. He opens the street door.

It's not Karen with Stacey and Talya.

It's an alien babe. She's dressed in skinny black leather. She has a red motorbike helmet in one three-fingered hand. In the other, a large red, white and green-striped pizza box. She is holding this box out to him.

'Mr Gillespie.'

Her accent is unfamiliar. *I ♥ Pizza* is printed in diagonals across the flat square box.

'Your pizza.'

There's a little Yamaha motorbike propped up against the balding hedge. A big box on the back says, 'Pizza Di Action, 385 Lisburn Road'. He can't read the phone number.

'I didn't order a pizza.'

He's heard about these revenge trips. It'll be taxis at three in the morning, alarm calls, deliveries from record and book clubs. Half tons of coal.

'I know. But I have brought you one anyway. Do you like pepperoni? I do not. Therefore I have left it off my half of the pizza. Would you have liked artichoke hearts? I have some.'

'Are you sure you've got the right house?'

'Yes. This is twenty-eight Eglantine Avenue. Flat one. May I come in? I am quite hungry now. As you know, we must eat more frequently than you.'

She steps past him in a creak of leather. Her long legs take her over the tangle of mountain bike in one stride. She fills the hall like some terminating robot from a sci-fi movie.

'Your flat is this on the right?'

She goes in through the open door. She is greeted by a television roar. Goal!

Gillespie finds her on her knees on the carpet in front of the electric heater. The pizza box is open in front of her. She unzips the top foot of her leather jacket and pulls out a shining silver pizza cutter. She lifts it high. It glitters in the light. With two slashes, swift and vicious as a sacrifice, she quarters the pizza. She lifts a dripping wedge for Andy Gillespie.

'Please forgive this unorthodox introduction, but it is imperative that I speak with you, Mr Andy Gillespie. Accept this pizza as a gift. It is my last delivery of the night. Eat, and I will explain why I am here. My name is Ounserrat Soulereya, of the Not Afraid of the River Hold in Docklands in London. I have come to Ireland to defend right and pursue justice.' She feels inside her jacket again. She brings out a small cloth bag and tips its contents on to the floor. Stones. Black stones, white stones. 'I am a knight-advocate of the Shian law.'

'*Genro*.'

'Yes.'

She holds out her naked left hand to him. Most slowly, most luxuriously, Andy Gillespie licks the palm. He's never tasted a female like her before. Scent of a different Nation. And something beside, a frizz, a jizz, like you catch a wisp of perfume in the street and it pulls your head round and you want more than anything to find the woman it belongs to but she's gone. Way gone.

He returns the greeting. How do we taste to Shian? He imagine it's like just-off pork. He vanishes the Coca Cola Cup into the screen. Won't be going to extra time after all.

'A drink? Aspirin?'

'Water, please. Sparkling.'

She gets tap. His isn't the kind of flat does sparkling. He hauls himself a Guinness from the fridge, drinks it from the tin. Head forms in your mouth. Mildly narcotic experience.

The Shian folds her legs up under her and sits on the floor. They aren't comfortable on human furniture. She unzips the rest of her biker jacket. Gillespie notices the swelling of a breast under her black rib top. She's feeding a kid, then. Probably her own – they're born to breed, these people, though in their big Holds they pass children between them like joints.

'So, what's this imperative?' The pizza's not bad. Could use anchovies.

'You may have heard of the arrival in your country of Sounsurresh Soulereya. The model?'

The *Telegraph* had made something of it. SPACE QUEEN DESCENDS ON PROVINCE. The photographer had shot her in front of the landing craft in the shipyard, as if she'd arrived on it from out of orbit and not by British Airways. A Division Two model is Premier League in a city as starved of genuine celebrity as Belfast.

'She brought her kids. She said she was going to visit her birth Hold.'

'That is correct. However, she did not return to Not Afraid of the River when she said she would.'

'Is this unusual?'

'It is not uncommon for individuals to move to new Holds. We assumed she had done this, and felt loss, of course, but wished her well in her new family.'

'So?'

'Her modelling agency contacted us and told us that she had failed to turn up at a shoot for a client. We grew concerned. Emotions are one thing. Profession is another. The consequences of breach of contract are quite severe. Her agency had contacted the Hold she was visiting in Ireland. She was not there. She and her children had left on the day they were scheduled to return to London. It was at this point that Not Afraid of the River asked me to be *genro* to Sounsurresh to defend her rights against the advertising agency.'

'And you're here to look for her. You've checked she got on the plane?'

'Yes. She did not redeem the return section of her ticket. I have contacted all the airlines flying out of this city. They have no records of issuing one-way fares for an adult with two children.'

'She could have left by boat. Or gone down south on the train or bus.'

'This is a possibility. Or she could still be here.'

'When was she due to go back to London?'

'Ten days ago. I have been in this city for five days.'

Delivering pizza. Gillespie thinks it's a pretty good system where lawyers practise their art for the love of it rather than the remuneration.

'Who's minding the kid?'

Ounserrat Soulereya blinks slowly.

'My partner Ananturievo. We have a *planha* in the transients' wing of the Annadale Embankment Hold.'

Annadale's a FreeHold of Outsiders from many Nations. *Planha*: a Hold of two. Cosy. Like a marriage.

'Who is minding yours?'

She's looking at the photograph of Stacey and Talya on the mantelpiece between the clock and the bills he hasn't got round to paying yet.

'Their mother.' He doesn't want to talk about his fuck-up of a family in front of a lactating pizza-deliverer alien mother lawyer babe, so instead he takes a long cool pull from his tinnie and asks, 'What do you want from me?'

'If Sounsurresh was still in this country, she and her children might have joined another Hold. I had heard that the Welcome Centre in this city operates a contact service for those searching for new relationships. I thought that it might have a record of Sounsurresh Soulereya.'

'I don't remember her. Believe me, I would.'

Ounserrat blinks again. Gillespie doesn't have the vocabulary to interpret this one.

'I made an appointment to visit the Centre and consult the files.'

'When was this?'

'The afternoon of the second.' While he was at the magistrates' court. 'Mr Gillespie, I am now exceedingly concerned for my client.'

'You think what happened at the Centre and your client's disappearance are connected?'

'There are disturbing features in the University Street killings that incline me to think so.'

'Such as?'

'It would not be in my client's interests to mention them at this point.'

Andy Gillespie picks up a black stone from the carpet. He likes to feel things in his hands. Small, exact things, like engine parts or jury stones.

'Your client may be dead.'

'Her rights have still been offended against, Mr Gillespie. You could assist me greatly by giving me access to the Welcome Centre records. Have some more pizza.' Andy Gillespie declines. He feel Guinness foam up in his mouth and watches Ounserrat Soulereya tear apart artichoke and mozzarella pizza with her long fingers and bite it down. Everything is hunting with them. But we are traders. Deal-makers.

'I'll do it if you let me work with you.'

Is that eating, or the hint of a *smile*? A *genro* may be refused no reasonable request. To do so is to compound the violation of right. Sheathe your teeth, huntress. He's not refusing her request. Just capitalizing on it.

'Why do you wish this, Mr Gillespie?'

No word in Narha for guilt, Eamon Donnan had said, and Andy Gillespie had wanted to smash his eyeballs open for it, because he can still hear the cries in the corridor of the H-block. In the dark. Through doors. Through walls. Through time. Such strange cries.

You should tell her this. You should tell someone this, and stop carrying it around like some precious, lovely jewel. It's not. It was bad. It was evil. It was not your fault, but feeling guilty is all you have now. But he's never told anyone, and he fears he never will, so he gives her another reason, a lesser reason.

'The police got me as a suspect. Their prime suspect. They've people on me, they take shifts. There'll be someone out there; dark blue Ford, probably. Eating chips, noting that a Shian turns up with a pizza at eleven thirty-five, leaves however long it is later. And I don't like being a suspect. I don't like being mistrusted. I don't like the idea that the cops think I blew the heads off three adults and two children. Folk I worked with. Folk who gave me time when no one else would. Gave me respect. And I want the cops to know I didn't do that to them.'

She's flaring her nostrils, taking scent. Finding the true trail. The *genro* is a lonely hunter. He remembers that, from the Maze. He remembers everything from the Maze.

'The police are working for the law, but who's working for the victims? Who's defending their rights? Who's hunting down justice for them, not for the law? Who's their *genro*?'

'You do not know what you are saying,' Ounserrat says.

'There's a price. I know that.'

'You are not prepared to pay it.'

Pictures of the kids above the fire because that's the most you can keep of them. Thirty-eight, still in a rented flat in student land. No car. No job. Money running out by the second. Prison record.

'Oh, I think I am.'

Ounserrat Soulereya blinks again the smile that is not a smile.

'Very good. Then I shall meet you at the Welcome Centre tomorrow morning. Eleven o'clock. Is this satisfactory?' She scoops up her black and white stones of justice, uncoils from the floor and zips up her leather jacket. Fingers hook up the red helmet, like it's the skull of some Hearthworld thing she's run down and killed and skinned and carries for its totemic power.

'Hey.'

The door's open. She's half out it. She turns.

'We're supposed to be partners.'

'This we agreed to. Yes.'

'Partners trust each other. Give me something back.'

'What?'

'This Sounsurresh Soulereya. What Hold did she come to visit?'

'It is one in the country, not the city. It is called South Side of the Stone.'

He doesn't tell Ounserrat Soulereya what he knows about South Side of the Stone. Could be coincidence. There are not many Outsiders, and they like to stick together. Common adversity. Enemy of my enemy. It's always been an inhospitable planet for settlers, Ireland of the hundred thousand welcomes. But then again, it could be something more than just coincidence. Poker could only have been invented by a species of traders and deal-makers. He won't show his cards yet, and if the punter gets burned in the game she'll have learned something.

He sees the *genro* on to the street. She straddles the little motorbike like some devouring black insect. Imagine being sucked up into that thing. He watches her red tail lights weave down the street.

'She's gone now,' he shouts to the unseen watcher in the dark blue Ford. 'We didn't fuck.'

But when he goes back into his flat and closes the door, he kicks his half-full Guinness can into the far end of the kitchen in a comet-tail of white foam, suddenly angry because the fucking place is so small and so shabby and so empty and at the same time so full of the personal perfume of the tall, elegant alien. The ghost of her clings. He can't even contemplate sleeping, but the only things on any channel are topless volleyball and ads for Internet sex pages and the radio doesn't speak his language any more.

He used to have mates who smelled of blood this way. Well, not mates really. Acquaintances. The ones who would come into the club and everyone would pause for a moment in whatever they'd been doing. Hard lads. They'd sit in the corner with their pint and you'd nod to them and say, 'Right, big man', because it was their due, and you'd catch it off them, the smell of someone else's blood. A kicking, maybe a Black and Decker job on kneecaps and elbows. Community policing, they'd call it. They sloshed on Brut for Men or Aramis their girlfriends had got them for Christmas but it couldn't disguise it. Nothing disguises the smell of blood on a body.

Nothing disguises the smell of blood in a building.

The cleaners are at the back of the Welcome Centre – he can hear their radio. They've got the stains off the walls and carpets – hell of a job – but he can smell blood through the pine-mountain lemon-fresh spring-meadow multi-surface cleaners. It'll never go away. It'll be a marked house. People will buy it years from now but they won't stay in it. Something bad about it. Vibes. Shivers. Old blood in the walls and floors.

It's like a physical assault on Ounserrat's Outsider sense of smell. She stops dead in the hall, eyes wide open, teeth bared in a smile.

'You should have smelled it on Monday night,' Andy Gillespie says.

The files are in the front room. The cleaners have made an attempt on the mess the SOCOs have left behind. The police never tidy up after themselves. They burst into your home, throw everything into a heap on the floor and then go away without an apology. You made the mess, you fucking tidy it up. Holds for everyone except the NIPS. They still have that warrior-elite mentality from the Troubles. We're the fucking samurai, we can do what the hell we like. Cut your balls off and you can't do a thing about it, because the rules that apply to you don't apply to us.

Where is she this morning, faithful hound-dog?

The people walking past in the street are glancing in. That's the place, isn't it? They look away when they see people in the front room – *the room*. They never looked before. Embarrassed by the Outsider embassy. Like folk down town who walk past sex-shop windows full of leather and lycra and pink plastic with their eyes firmly fixed on their feet. But now the weird Outsiders are gone. They've been murdered. So you can look up.

Monday night, there was a body *here*, and one here against the chimney breast.

'Are you all right, Mr Gillespie?'

He tried to rub the memory out of his eyes.

'Yeah. It's just hard. I keep seeing things, remembering.'

'I am sorry. Perhaps you should have given me the key so I could come alone.'

'No. Needs doing some time.'

He's always been thankful that he can't use the direct interface. Information inside him, in his head, horrifies him. Ounserrat sits down and lets the thing creep up her nose while Gillespie turns on the monitor the Centre keeps for its human visitors. The police'll have been all through the hard drive and the disks but unless they had Littlejohn with them they won't have been able to use the liposome memory. Ounserrat's eyes are moving beneath her closed lids. Watching the chemicals. That's all we are, so the scientists say. Dancing chemicals. She's done in the time it takes Gillespie to make wee icons appear on the screen.

'Nothing?'

'Nothing.'

The wonderful-woman-in-the-crowd smell from last night is stronger today. It's in-the-room-with-you. Sitting-next-to-you. Know it.

'My clients have not approached the Centre.'

'What now?'

'I will have to ask around the Holds.'

'I've done that. I went round asking about the murders here.

108

They wouldn't talk to me. They're scared of something. They won't tell me what.'

Ounserrat Soulereya expands her pupils. Slits to circles. Cats in the moonlight.

'What does that mean, what you just did?'

'It is an expression of interest.'

Andy Gillespie looks at the images on the monitor. After a time listening to the cleaners' radio, he says, 'There's something we could try.'

'What is that?'

He's already opening the icons, making the connections.

'Someone like Sounsurresh coming to Belfast'll have been noticed in, ahm, certain circles.'

'Do you mean frooks?'

'I mean frooks. They've got bulletin boards, web sites, contact points. They might have something about her.'

As he speaks he's flicking and clicking. Menus, sub-menus, addresses of page after page. Rubber Boys in Bondage. Crucifix-ion Babes. Lttp.comco@shit-eat.ftp. Pony Girls. How many teenage girls call that one up by mistake? Mr S. M. Frooks. We want frooks. We don't want this old-shit human-on-human stuff. Or even pony-on-human. We want twenty-first-century devo. Give us frooks. Shit. There're fifty pages of the bastards. Alien Invaders. Outsider/Insider. Alien Babes. Come on, can't you do better than Alien Babes? Alien Gay Boys. They're making that one up. Human body-double run through image processing software.

He smells Ounserrat at his shoulder. He doesn't like it. It's not invasion of body space. He doesn't like the way this thing that isn't human is seeing all the tricks and treats and turns of human sexuality spread in front of it. Boys do it for us. Rubber does it for us. Rope and leather do it for us. Dogs and donkeys do it for us. Nails through the palms of the hands get us hot. We eat our lover's shit and cream ourselves. We fuck our children. We fuck dead humans. We'll fuck any fucking thing. Including you.

A filter would help here, if he can remember how to do one. Belfast. Northern Ireland. Sounsurresh Soulereya. Models.

The screen gives a choice of fifteen pages. That much. That quick. Devos don't hang around. Always whispering to each other, sharing furtive wee things.

He really doesn't want Ounserrat on his shoulder when he's looking at this stuff. Softer options first. *She's Here!!!* is a file of long-lens pics taken at the City airport. See!: Sounsurresh Soulereya coming down the steps from the plane. See!: Sounsurresh Soulereya glancing behind her to make sure her kids haven't been sucked into a jet engine. See!: Sounsurresh Soulereya asking the ground staff where's the baggage reclaim. They get off on this, they beat the meat to a Shian bending over to ask a taxi driver how much to take her to South Side of the Stone.

He hits target on the next file. It's a city-web bulletin: Club Ochre. 16 North Street. Cum 2 R $1000 Opening. *See* London hyper-space-bay-bee *Sounsurresh!!!* 4 1 Nite Onlee. First drink free. Beer and aspirin promotion. There's a little animation of a Shian in knee boots and hot pants pulling a Star Trek phaser and firing it two-fisted. Fab Feb 20. 10 'til late. DWSAA. Dress With Style And Attitude.

Just a themed night club. The real frook joints do only aspirin. The serious ones, the kind who buy the gear and the contact lenses and get the fingers lopped, they can actually get high on it, he's heard.

He'd got Junior Disprin from the Spar by the station, that night.

'Was she still at South Side then?'

'Yes,' Ounserrat says.

'Did they say anything about her opening a night club?'

'I did not ask.'

'They didn't offer.'

'Should we go there?'

'Someone might know something.'

'I shall try to change shifts at the pizza shop. It will not be easy.'

'If you call round at the flat, I'll book a taxi.'

Ounserrat wrinkled her nose. *Affirmation.*

'Have you thought what you want to ask?'

'I have not.'

'Me neither.'

There's a tap and small cough at the door: the bravest of the cleaners, come to ask for money.

In her beige plain-clothes police person's coat, Roisin Dunbar is as inconspicuous in the club as a papal litter on the Shankill Road. She's going to hang Darren Healey by his balls: of all shifts to switch. It'll be another false alarm. Funny how Andrea's contractions start when there's a job he doesn't fancy. Michael was furious. What does he have to be furious about; in the warm, and the dry, with the kid? He hasn't been twelve hours behind Andy Gillespie, with hours more to come by the look of it.

Upstairs clubs conform to a universal condition. Too small, too hot, too loud. They'll have turned off the taps in the bogs to sell club-brand water, which is relabelled Ballygowan at six times Ballygowan prices. The floor is so crowded there is not even room for one handbag to dance around. High density funk: little jiggings and fingers and feet.

You spent some of the greatest nights of your life in places like this. But you could dance to the music then. This is just noise.

It's not even real Outsider music. A lot of that is beyond human hearing. This is two white boys with Mohawks in a bedroom with a MIDI system and more drum samples than they can shake a pair of sticks at. Fake alien. Everything about this place is fake. Fake computer animé of deep space and starships and *manga* characters video-jiggered into fake *hahndahvi*. Two fake Outsiders dancing in the shadows behind the decks, faking being DJs from another planet, man. That skin colour comes off in the shower. That height is platform soles. Baby-blue round-eyes behind those cool, cool shades. Fake punters heaving on the floor. The ones with money have bought fake Shian costumes from specialist catalogues. The rest make do with cross-dressing and mondo leather. A small group in front of the decks are wearing three-fingered white gloves. Beats amputation. They thrust their hands up into the black light. They look like fluorescent Mickey Mouses.

Fake *kesh* musks. Smells a lot like girlie sweat, Chanel and dry ice to Roisin Dunbar.

She's amazed to see a couple of real Outsiders head and shoulders above the shove. You can tell them by the way they dance. The humans look like ironmongery next to them.

Gillespie and the Outsider are at the bar. The barboy is pointing to a door. Jesus, they're turning round. Hide. Hide. She takes her coat off, slips behind a group of Mohican boys passing around a bottle of club water. Their faces are ecstatic as Orthodox saints.

One generation down, they are as alien to us as the Outsiders. When Louise hits these years, will I even recognize her? It's 2004, citizens, do you know what your children are?

The door opens, Gillespie and the Outsider go in. Dunbar excuse-mes her way through the bodies to the bar. The boy is checking twenties under a UV scanner. INLA have been waging economic warfare against the Imperialist Monolith of Joint Authority with fake Bank of Ireland notes. For once they're not waging warfare against themselves. Dunbar surreptitiously slips him the warrant card. He's already worked it out from the cut of her cloth.

'I haven't had any and I've no idea where they're coming from,' he says, fists full of notes.

'Those people who were talking to you just now, what did they ask you?'

'They wanted to know about the opening night.'

'What about the opening night?' She's having to yell. Her throat's going to punish her in the morning. If there ever is a morning after this.

'I don't know, I've only been here three days. I said they'd have to talk to the manager.'

'Can I talk to the manager?'

'Manager's busy now.'

'Later.'

'I suppose.'

God, it's hot. She can feel sweat balling up in her armpits and rolling luxuriously down her sides.

'A bottle of that water, please.'

'That's five fifty.'

'How much?'

The other secret key of detective work, Boss Willich said on the day of her promotion, is that you pay for information, one way or the other.

No glass. No furniture to put glasses on. She finds a place by the corner of the bar, sips her relabelled Ballygowan and watches the dancing. There's some kind of boys-only competition going on. Boys and Outsiders. The girlies are standing in a circle, pretending they aren't looking, but the music's moving them. No contest, really. The Shian are moving around the wee lads like smoke. She finds her feet are twitching to the rhythm. That old dance-hall magic never dies.

'Excuse me!' A dim yell in her ear. She almost drops her water. They've made a covert approach through Roisin Dunbar's wild years, Gillespie and the Outsider.

'Detective Sergeant Dunbar, fancy seeing you here,' Gillespie says. He's smiling, and sweating heavily. 'Really, you don't need to do all this sneaking around. We're on the same side, you know, like I told you when you had me in the other day.' Dunbar notices that the Outsider's nostrils are flared. Scenting. 'Here, a wee proposition. Would it help convince you that I'm not the villain you think I am if I was to tell you what I'm doing here? I presume that's why you're here. Or maybe you like a dance on a Saturday night?

'This is Ounserrat Soulereya of Not Afraid of the River Hold in Docklands.' The Outsider blinks slowly. Dunbar remembers not to smile. 'She delivers pizza, but she's really a knight-advocate. A *genro*. You know what that is?'

'A Shian lawyer.' She's not stupid. Except she is, getting jumped by the suspect she's supposed to be following.

'I am representing Sounsurresh Soulereya,' the Outsider says. 'Mr Gillespie is helping me discern why she has not returned to my Hold in fulfilment of a professional contract. We have identified that she attended the opening of this dancing club.'

'We're going to another club now,' Gillespie says. 'The manager here told us that Sounsurresh had an appointment with a man at this club. The man was a Mr Gerry Conlon. He seems to be big in business; some kind of biotech company called GreenGene, though I'm told it's all ripped-off Shian technology. Incidentally, this club? It's a frook joint. I thought you should know before you decide to follow us. If you do, you could offer us a lift, and try and look a little less police.'

'You didn't have such a smart mouth when Littlejohn was talking to you, Gillespie.'

'Well, real police talk. Think about this: would a guilty man tell you all this?'

'He might if he wanted to look innocent.'

Gillespie shakes his head.

'Too devious for me. I'll never make detective. Well, we're going. I'm getting hoarse shouting. You can come with us or not. The club is on Little Howard Street, above a Chinese supermarket. See you.'

Clubland parts before the Outsider. Gillespie follows in her wake.

The dance competition is down to three survivors. They're all Shian.

Roisin Dunbar hits the ladies' toilet like a dam burst.

'Shit! Shit! Shit! Shit!' She kicks the pedal bin full of water bottles and panty liners the length of the room.

One girl is bent over the basin while another is giving her a Shian with a Ladyshave. The Ladyshaver looks up.

'Quit pissing around or they'll call the fucking polis,' she says.

'I am the fucking polis!' Roisin Dunbar shouts. When the toilet is empty, she pulls out her mobile and tells the Pass to find anything and everything on the Soulereyas of Not Afraid of the River, Docklands. Especially their legal division.

He used to love the night. Deep night, empty night. He loved the fellowship of the people of the after hours, who are unseen and which is unspoken except in the slur of taxi tyres on wet concrete, or the figures in the third window of the night bus, or the drone of robot street cleaners vacuuming the gutters, or the soft, conspiratorial voice of the pre-dawn radio disc jockey saying, *it's just thee and me, comrade.*

He loved to walk in the deep night, to feel it press down on his city like living flesh. He loved to walk beneath the yellow lights, seduced by a stray rhythm from a club door, dazzled by neons, following the shining damp snail tracks of the street cleaning trucks. Every soul was a fellow pilgrim: the gorillas in tuxes, the sallow-faced women behind the BBC, cold in all seasons; the greasy youths manning the burger vans, the midnight kids behind the glass of the all-night petrol stations; the drivers of the big artics, high above it all riding through. He saw the night people and they saw him and their looks said, *we live more intensely, we see and hear and feel and taste and smell more richly than the bleached-out people of the day*.

He loved the night, he trusted the night, he was one of the people of the dark night, until the dark of the night turned on him, and with five swift lunges tore apart everything that gave his life meaning.

It scares him now. He doesn't know it any more.

The frook club is very discreet, but there are signs to the wise: a single red Chinese duck hung in the grocer's window, the outline of a three-fingered hand sprayed in red car lacquer on a steel security door.

'Red, swinging meat,' Gillespie says. 'The ultimate frook fantasy is having sex with a Shian in free fall.'

Ounserrat Soulereya flares her nostrils.

'You know a lot about this perversion, Mr Gillespie. Are you a frook?'

'You get a lot of this stuff on the fringes of the Welcome Centre. Chancers would come in pretending they wanted advice on Shian employees. I got to know the signs, threw the bastards out.'

'Human sexuality mystifies me, Mr Gillespie. And you did not answer my question.'

He's already rung the door bell. Footsteps descending, a spy-hole goes dark. Hey, look! Real red swinging meat, on the hoof!

The door is opened by the Chinese grocer. He's dressed in Shian formal hunting costume. He's wearing nostril make-up and the bridge of his nose is patterned with black. Ounserrat stares at him as he lets them up the stairs.

She really stares when they go into the club. What must have been an upstairs store has been transformed. There is a small bar with a sullen teenage girl sporting a stubbly Mohawk crewing it. Her stock seems to consist of bottled water and aspirins. There's a small dance floor. Eight people are dancing on it without causing each other injury. There's a small sound system, a domestic hi-fi unit rammed through a guitar combo, and a lighting rig consisting of Christmas tree lights stuck over the ceiling pretending to be constellations. Music is techno-kitsch, arrangements of old pre-Advent sci-fi shows. *Doctor Who. The X Files.* The tables wobble, the seats have cigarette burns through to the foam. A drinking club is a drinking club is a drinking club, Andy Gillespie thinks, beer or water. Except for the clientele. Now that is different from the clubs he knows. He must be the only basic human here. Judging by the heads that turn, Ounserrat must be the only pure Shian.

For some, it's just cross-dressing. These are the ones who take any opportunity to dress up in the clothes of the opposite sex, but they can't do it like the Shian do, mixing and matching, wearing what's comfortable without consciousness or shame, not because it gets you wet. For others it's gear. Alien gear: the traditional Shian hunting dress and the elaborately exotic *kesh* dance costumes shuddering with sequins, ponderously embroidered, swathed in miles of veil and topped off with mirror-ball-scraping headdresses. For others it's skin. Ochre skin. Red-earth skin. Gillespie doesn't doubt that among the rub-on fake tans there are some who have had their melanin altered.

Even Eamon Donnan hadn't done that to himself.

With the skin goes the hair and the eyes. Contact lenses; ophthalmic surgery jobs? For a few even that is not enough. They need it to be perfect. They've had bits of themselves taken away, other bits expanded and augmented and adapted.

How do they live? Gillespie wonders. Where do they hide themselves by day? Do they change their names? Do they drive buses, sell you things in shops, sit behind desks? Do they smirk at you when they serve you, because you don't know what they really are, which is fake fake fake? Do they go down to the wee shop to buy the paper or stand at the bus stop or put petrol in their cars and think to themselves, you think I'm an Outsider, don't you? Well, I am, I am, I am now.

Gillespie shudders.

'Does Roisin Dunbar know this is going on within spitting distance of her office?'

'That is that police woman who followed us to the other club?' Ounserrat asks. Most of the heads are turning away, but the hardliners continue to stare.

'And's following us to this club too. Place has probably got half a dozen cops done up like carnival queens anyway. That's how it's survived so long.'

'Should this place not be here?'

'If it's not actually illegal, it's certainly not lawful. And it's definitely immoral.'

'These distinctions confuse me. But these people are enjoying themselves. Why should the law infringe their right to do that?'

'Because the law still gets on like there's a big God up on a chair in the sky telling everyone sex is a bad thing.'

'I know good sex and sex that has not been good. Is that what the law means by sex being bad?'

'Wicked, I mean. Sinful. Sin.'

'I know this word, but its meaning eludes me.'

'Sin is what people are doing here, because they aren't a married heterosexual couple having straight missionary position sex in bed with no clothes on. Normal. Good.'

Ounserrat flares her nostrils again. Gillespie bangs his head on an Airfix model starship dangling from the ceiling as he steers between the tables to the bar. The barkid's staring at Ounserrat like she's never had a real Shian in smelling range.

'Could we get a drink?' Gillespie asks. They get water, and soluble aspirins. 'In my life, these are for after the drinking,' Gillespie says, ruefully watching the plink-plink fizz and the slow sashay of tablets to the bottom of the glass. 'Any beer?'

No beer. Just water and aspirins. Ounserrat has a water. No aspirins. Gillespie leans against the bar and studies clubland faces. Ounserrat sips her water very elegantly.

'And the law tells you what normal and good is?' she asks.

'The law. And the politicians, though one lot would say eating children is normal and good because the other side say it's a sin. "We maintain that this condemnation of eating children is just another typically cynical stance by the British government in an attempt to further hinder the peace process by placing obstructive preconditions regarding the legitimate and democratically mandated rights of Republicans to All-Ireland consumption of offspring." And then there's the churches. They've still got this idea that they're important and have something to say because when you guys arrived everyone thought it was the end of the world and packed the pews out. They're the real experts on sin. They wrote the book on it. Tell you this, if Reverend Doctor McIvor Kyle and his Dee Pee head-the-balls ever get in, they'll have you lot classified as animals and anyone who wanted to could shoot you on sight. Make the big BSE cull look like a Brownie Guide picnic. Ethnic cleansing. And they'd take all the Catholics and queers and gyppos and Pakis and Chinks and southerners out with you too. Put a wall of Lambeg drums up along the border. Fuck off out of here. To them, what these guys do is like doing it with a sheep or a pig or something. Bestiality.'

'I cannot understand why they should be troubled by something for which they have no desire.'

Gillespie turns around to study the other half of the upstairs club. A tall woman in a *kesh* dancing costume hitches up her skirts and sits on a stool beside Gillespie. She lights up a cigarette. The mirrors in her headdress catch the reflections from the glitter and throw them over Gillespie and Ounserrat like an infection of light.

'You people.' Gillespie shakes his head. 'You need looking after, you know? This your first case, *genro*, that you don't know what humans are like yet?'

'Yes, Mr Gillespie.'

'Oh, for fuck's sake.' To the bargirlie: 'You sure you haven't anything stronger than water?' She hunts under the bar, rattling the bottles a lot so Gillespie will know just what this is costing her cool. She comes back with alcoholic lemonade. Gillespie's had days when his piss looked and smelled like that. 'Has Gerry Conlon been in yet?'

Shave-head goes from sullen to sullen+suspicious.

'Gerry Conlon. You know. Guy owns GreenGene, that genetic engineering company? He comes in here.' The Chinese club owner is edging nearer to the bar. Sullen/suspicious is edging nearer to him. Full metal headdress is edging as far away as a ten-inch bar stool will allow. Glitter fragments dazzle him. Inspiration. 'I've got his babe. The one he wanted? Thought maybe he'd like to see the goods before he buys. Take it for a test drive. She's genuine. Real thing.' He lifts a paper coaster from the bar, wipes it across Ounserrat's forehead, holds it out to the club owner. 'Have a sniff. Pure undiluted Shian. Can't fake that.'

It's sullen+suspicious+disgusted now.

'What did you do there?' Ounserrat asks.

'Pimped,' Gillespie answers. Ounserrat wants an answer, but Gillespie doesn't feel like giving her one. At the moment. 'This could take a while. Fancy a dance?'

'Will it help our investigation?'

They go to the minute dance floor. Full metal headdress has picked up the scented bar coaster and is decorously sniffing it.

'Mr Gillespie,' Ounserrat whispers, bending down to Gillespie's five and a bit feet. 'That woman asked if she could have sex with me.'

'At least she asked.'

He doesn't know any of the tunes – Andy Gillespie has reached the age where a continued striving to be up to date in popular music is pathetic – but it's intercourse music, for couples dancing together, not the wank-music of Club Ochre, where you dance by yourself for yourself.

'Mr Gillespie, I am beginning to understand what it is to be troubled by something for which you have no desire.'

She is like liquid. She is like smoke. I've got lead boots next to her. Like an old deep-sea diver. Clump clump. Lump of lead. But then all the girls said I couldn't dance to save myself.

'You mean sex between species?'

'No. I mean sex with another female.'

'You mean lesbianism.'

'What a pretty word. It would make a fine name for a child.'

Gillespie catches a little laugh at the back of his throat. He's

119

never met an Outsider who understood laughter. A threatening braying and snapping of teeth. Ha!

The woman is watching every play of Ounserrat's muscles. Gillespie finds he doesn't like that.

'To her it's not sex with another female, it's sex with a different species. That's her kink. It doesn't matter if you're a boy or a girl, as long as you're Shian.'

'She would not have sex with a human female?'

'Probably not.'

Ounserrat flares her nostrils briefly.

'But how would she have sex with me?'

It's hot on the tiny dance floor. Gillespie tells himself that's why his face is flushed.

'You can get dildos. Fake penises.'

'Really? Do they tumesce and detumesce?'

'They're made of plastic. Or rubber.' Like the old-style rubber bullets the RUC used on petrol bombers and wee lads throwing stones. Girl's best friend, after they'd locked the men folk up in Crumlin Road. The new plastic baton rounds weren't as good. Right colour, that sort of sex-toy pasty fleshtone, but they didn't have that nice pointy end for deep penetration.

Ounserrat blinks. 'And she would fuck me with this?'

'Yes.'

'But what would it do for her?'

That, my alien pizzagirl lawyer babe, is the question.

The tempo's dropped. Slow-dance time. Couples are getting up all over the club and coming on to the floor and flopping over each other. Stick tongue in ear and mutter drunkenly *I love you, I really love you* time. Outsiders don't dance that way, do they? He hopes not. He's not sure he wants to clinch with this elegant Outsider. There's something about the way she smells tonight, the way it clings to the folds of her denim jacket, that frightens him. Ounserrat carefully dusts dandruff off his shoulder, adjusts the collar of his shirt. Grooming. Like monkeys, they're always fiddling with each other.

'Mr Gillespie,' she says. 'You are really a very bad dancer.'

Then he spots the face by the bar, the face that shouldn't be there at all, that shouldn't be anywhere Andy Gillespie is likely to be because the last time he saw that face it had seen Jesus, big time, and after that wouldn't look at anything else. That face saves him.

From what, Andy lad?

'Got to go. Just seen someone.'

'Is it our Mr Gerry Conlon?'

'Ah, no. Someone I know from, ah, way back.' From the Maze. But you don't want her to know that, yet.

'May I come with you?'

'I'd rather you didn't.'

'I shall sit at a table, then. I will endeavour not to be seduced into sex with anyone.'

Gillespie comes through the swaying couples on the blind side. He's on a stool, a big straight water in front of him. Black suit. Black shoes. Shiny. Cuff-links wink at the glitterball. Still that same fucking hideous haircut. Comb straight up, cut off across the top, shave the back and sides. Looks like a gun-loving, nigger-hating, born-again fundamentalist. He is.

'Peterson. Gavin Peterson?'

The shoulder muscles clinch beneath the tight-pulled jacket. Jesus, he's jumpy. Suppose he has reason to be. Caught out in Satan's lair. He relaxes. He knows this voice.

'Gillespie. Andy Gillespie.' He swings round on his stool. He's got a handshake to match the haircut, but he's as pleased as Gillespie's ever seen him be at anything. Both go to say *what are you doing here?* at the same time. At the same time, both realize it's better left unasked.

'Last time I saw you, you were into Jesus in a big way,' Gillespie says.

'Still am.'

'Last time I heard you were with the Dee Pees.'

'I'm working for the church now. On Reverend Kyle's staff. Security.'

When you get so big, so holy, you can't trust God alone to mind your ass. Gillespie tries to read the line of the black jacket for a weapon bulge, but it's either too well cut or the piece is too cunningly made.

'Kyle's always made good use out of the repentant sinner.'

'I know where I'd be going if I died tonight, Gillespie. Do you have the same assurance?'

Did he stand you up at the front? Did the tears fall, did you go down on your knees in front of all those terrible suits and Sunday hats and beg Jesus to forgive you for that Catholic father of four you blew away in his own front room, and the kid whose head you blasted off outside his girlfriend's front door, and the pensioner you took out because you couldn't tell 121a from 121b? Did he lead you weeping to the water and push you under and wash your sins away and cleanse you of the hate in your heart for anything that isn't your own? Or did he just sanctify it, did he just say *you can hate now because it's hating for Jesus*, and dress it up in a suit and a job description and now you're sitting at the bar of a frook club at twenty to three in the morning in your black suit with a gun over your washed-in-the-blood heart? Just because a thing is born again doesn't mean it comes back different.

'Forgive me if I'm cynical about prison converntions.'

Peterson's lips are like a knife wound across his face. A twitch at the corners, his smile: stitches pulling.

'I seem to remember you had something of a religious experience yourself. Born again frook?'

'I'm working.'

'So am I.'

'I thought Shian were sperm of the devil to you people.'

'You always were a mouth, Gillespie, but I believe the Word of God.'

'Great thing about the Bible, you get to pick and choose what bits apply to you. You can justify anything with it. Frook club. Twenty to three. Where is that written?' Peterson smiles his stitches-tearing smile but Gillespie's scored a hit.

'God's work, Gillespie.'

'Me too.'

'You're in that place those Outsiders got blown away.' His face says *five less*.

'I'm technically unemployed now.'

'I hear they pulled you in for that. Real mess, I hear. Blew their heads clean off.'

'Your spiritual leader was economic with his condemnation.'

'Well, I mean, you wouldn't shed any tears if it was five dogs got killed.'

'Except they aren't animals.'

'You should read your Bible more, Gillespie. In the end times, people will bow down to the creatures of Satan. Satan's apes, a mockery of God's handiwork. First comes the anti-Adam, the perversion of man. Then comes the anti-Christ. Last days, Gillespie.'

'You didn't think that in the Maze. You were one of the ones went that night. Did you hold him down, or were you one of the ones stuck it into him? He never told. He never said who did it to him. The shame was too great. He had too much dignity even to speak your names, but we had our suspects. He died because you just had to show what big, hard men you were. What I can't work out is, was it lust, or was it hate?'

Gillespie finds he's looking past Peterson to Ounserrat sitting at a table with a real-or-maybe Shian, because if he were to see the sanctimonious smirk on Peterson's face he would shove the broken end of a bottle into it.

'Jesus washed my sins away, Gillespie.'

'Is this what Kyle's got on you? The blood not take the stain out completely? Left behind at the lower temperature wash? You going to introduce another one to the new cultural experience of rape tonight?'

'I'd be careful with that mouth, Gillespie. I don't know what you're doing here, but you don't know anything about what's going on. Stay ignorant, Gillespie. It's safer that way.'

'The Dissenting Presbyterian Church is threatening me?'

'Not the church.'

'The UDF?'

'The Ulster Democratic Front is a legitimate political party promoting the abolition of Joint Authority, the affirmation of Northern Ireland as part of the United Kingdom under the Crown, the re-establishment of a devolved government in Northern Ireland, and the upholding of the traditional rights and culture of the Protestant people.' Straight off the manifesto.

'The hard men are in on this, aren't they? What is it they call themselves now? Aye, the Free Men of Ulster.'

'There is no connection, and there never has been any connection, between the Dissenting Presbyterian Church, the UDF and the Free Men of Ulster, or any other terrorist group. The Dissenting Presbyterian Church and the UDF condemn all acts of terrorist violence.'

Except when they're done to Outsiders. Jesus, you fucker. You fucking fuck.

'They did it. Them or some other wee splinter group with a stupid name thinking they're hard men. They're all headcases in those wee Loyalist gangs; all think they're the chosen people. Their own wee Holocaust. And hey, great joke, we'll do it to them with their own weapon, because, well, they're animals – worse than Taigs – but they make neat guns. Was it the Free Men? Those fucking Outsiders getting too big for themselves, thinking they can be treated like real people, well, we're going to show them who's boss here? No wonder the Shian are shit scared.'

'There's a power play going on, Gillespie. Don't get involved in it. Even asking questions might make one side think you're on the other. You're out of the paramilitaries, stay out. Things have changed since your day.'

'I don't give a fuck about your power plays. You've been playing pretend politics for most of my life and it's just one gang of hoods taking over from another. No one cares. The world doesn't care. Why should it care? We've done it to ourselves. Self-inflicted wounds. They patch us up, put us back on our feet, give us some money in our pockets and set us off on our way, and we go and do it all over again. Well, now we've got aliens from outer space living down the road, and some of us are looking at the sky.'

'It's your country, Gillespie. Your people. Your kind.'

'I don't give a fuck about my country. What did wee Ulster ever do for me except give me thirty-five years of bad politics and pointless violence? I don't owe it a fucking thing. It owes me. My kind, my people? Jesus, fifty glipes in stupid uniforms and wee tam-o'-shanters banging a big drum and playing the

124

flute badly? That's it? The sum total of what it means to an East Belfast Protestant? Maybe some of us don't have a culture. Maybe some of us don't have a community. Maybe some of us are just people. Individuals. Getting on with it.'

'You'll have to decide where you stand, some day. It all comes down to it in the end. What you are. Who you are is what you are.'

He sees Ounserrat in Peterson's face before he smells her. Contraction of the pupils. Involuntary twist of mouth. Twitch of muscles. Christ, he hates them. Or is it he's scared of them?

'Mr Gillespie, I have been engaged in a most interesting conversation.' Peterson doesn't know that when a Shian smiles you reach for your piece. He attempts a smile back at Ounserrat. 'It is with a young *gensoon* at that table.' She leads him away. Looking back, like the hard lads do who won't be first to break eye contact, Gillespie sees the bargirlie get a small package from a just-open door and slip it over the counter to Peterson. He's peeking into the padded envelope, smiling properly. God's work, eh? Then God should be able to tell you about the cop car that'll be waiting somewhere, watching, noting, dates and times and faces. I'll leave it to God.

'Who was that man?' Ounserrat asks, steering Gillespie to a table where a to-all-appearance Shian is sitting alone. 'I did not like him at all.'

'Someone I once knew.'

He's gone. The stir is settling. The night Andy Gillespie comes, it's the most hassle they've seen in months. The club owner and the bargirlie will be ordering him out for upsetting the regulars. Let them try.

It is an Outsider at the table. A kid. Smells no more than twelve, thirteen. Got the hormone rush, got the airline ticket, and he's footloose in the big world. Whole alien planet under his feet. And he has to end up in this country. This city, this street, this room. Does your ma know you're out? What're you at?

Understand pimping now, *genro*?

– Gillespie, this is Serrasouhendai. He is from the Safe In Winter Hold, near Norkoping, in Sweden. Gillespie and the kid

125

meet, greet. The boy's dressed in a mohair top and long satin skirt.

– You're looking for Gerry Conlon. You want to know what he wants with Sounsurresh Soulereya. His accent is different again. There are odd inflections and shifts in his Narha, as if he's speaking dialect. But Narha is the common tongue. Its grammar is inviolable.

– You know Gerry Conlon? Gillespie asks.

– I have done work for him.

– What kind of work?

– Video work. No word in Narha for the moving pictures in the little box. In eight thousand years of technological civilization, they never invented it. Lucky them.

– Porn? They have a word for that, but it's more family fun than solitary vice.

'Work-out videos,' Ounserrat says quietly in English.

'You mean, like Jane Fonda, Cindy Crawford, all that up-down two-three feel the burn?'

– Please, speak in Narha, Ounserrat says. *We are attracting enough attention already, without being eavesdropped.*

– It is a kind of porn, Serrasouhendai says. *Underground . . .*

– I didn't catch that word.

– Erotica, Ounserrat says. But the kid hadn't said that. What Gillespie heard was a string of sounds that made no echoes in his head. Could it be wearing off? Could he be losing it, word by word? The chemicals unravelling like knitting?

– It is sold in the shops as ordinary entertainment, Serrasouhendai says. *Many people buy it as such. But for frooks it is secret erotica.*

Long lean bodies in skimpy lycra pressed together in some industrial funk gym. Can't tell the boys from the girls. Step to the rhythm, alien effort, alien sweat. Shot smoky and dark, lots of red light. Who's pumping what, here?

'Jesus.' Then: *– Our friend, Gerry Conlon, he's something to do with this?*

– He is a member of a production company. It is based in Dublin. I cannot remember the address. Upstairs, on the south side of the river.

– Can you remember the name of the company?

'Hot Sweat Video.' Gillespie scrawls it on the back of a match book. Ball pen ink slides off glossy card.

– He'd be keen to get a famous name like Sounsurresh Soulereya.

– Yes.

– And that's all Conlon does?

– It is all he asked me to do. A few hours of work. He paid for the train ticket. The costume was supplied. I had to buy my own food.

– Thank you.

The kid's staring at him. He flares his nostrils.

– The genro *gave me to understand that you would remunerate me for my services.*

'Ach, Christ, Ounserrat.'

'Serrasouhendai is attempting to make a living from this style of life. I would give him money, but unfortunately I do not have any with me. I will pay you back, Mr Gillespie.'

Gillespie looks into the open mouth of his wallet. Too few paper things in there. He tries the smallest. It does it.

'Can't teach you folk anything about prostitution.'

As they leave the table, the desperate woman at the bar in the dance-floor costume cuts in and sits down. Who'll be using Steely Dan on whom, tonight?

'Dublin then, Mr Gillespie?'

'Looks like it.'

'This may be difficult. I shall have to come to another arrangement with the pizza company. But yes, this has been most productive.'

'Are we done in here? This place is giving me the creeps. Listen, you getting hungry again? Fancy something to eat?'

Serrasouhendai and the dildo queen are on the floor now, dancing slow. They've got it all to themselves. For some reason, the bargirlie is on top of the bar, walking up and down. She's wearing a pair of black spike-heel shoes and the punters are playing a game where they put their hands flat on the counter and pull them away quickly before she stands on them. They're laughing a lot. The club owner is smiling, but he's looking around him all the time.

Out on the street it's drizzle, same as it always is. Gillespie looks for the ever-faithful dark blue Ford. Dark green one tonight, gleaming with rain drops. More than one Ford in the police car pool. He whistles: *wheet!* 'Hey. Detective Dunbar! Dublin, Hot Sweat Video, director, Mr Gerry Conlon. You can go home now!' He turns up his collar, shoves his hands deep in his pockets and heads for the all-night kebab van he knows will be open on the corner beside the Empire Bar.

At his side, Ounserrat Soulereya is almost black in the sodium light. Like the Ford, she's gleaming with rain drops.

'Does it not bother you?' Gillespie says.

'Does what not bother me?'

'What they do back there. What that kid – what you call him? Serrasouhendai – does for his living. Selling his ass to humans.'

'It is only sex. Human sex, which is not true sex. If they wish to give him money for their pleasure, that is excellent. You give money to people who stimulate your laughter reaction, or make very fine meals. I do not see any difference.'

'It's what you were saying; it's only sex. No feeling, nothing. No love.'

'This is why I think you were more disturbed by that club than I. What disturbed me was that that woman would have had sex with me, another female. That is beyond our experience. But I was not disturbed that they would have sex with another species, nor that it was sex without emotional attachment. They were like us, in that way. And surely your own prostitutes do not make this equation of sex with love, so why should it trouble you that Serrasouhendai does not?'

'I don't know. It's kind of, ah, dirty. Nasty.' But wasn't that how it was with Karen? Sex without emotional attachment. You moved around that tiny house like weather systems, edging around each other, carrying your own independent climates, occasionally passing through without significant precipitation. And you paid her. Hooking for white goods. So many for a washing machine. Blow job for a three-piece suite. Big fake screamer that gets the Orrs next door looking at each other in that way, *oh aye, ah-hah, wink-wink* for a Dolby pro-logic Nicam stereo widescreen television with satellite. Wipe yourselves down, shake on the deal and go back to your separate sides of the bed.

'It is what men are supposed to want.'

Until they get it.

There's a gang of early-morning people gathered in the fluorescent light from the hatch of the kebab trailer. Kids in nightclub fashions, shivering and wet. They never dress for this country. Fashion's always worn by those it least flatters. One's talking on a mobile. Gillespie can't imagine who the hell to. The drizzle has steepened into rain.

'Never had anything from one of these vans when it wasn't chucking it down,' he says. Chip fat and rain. He's got a theory: kebab and burger vans make it rain. Wheel one out into the middle of the Sahara desert, wait for a passing camel train to buy one, and it'll be pissing down within thirty seconds. Ounserrat wrinkles her nose and shows a tiny glint of teeth at the smell of hot grease. She watches with distaste the proprietor carving grey kebab meat from the rotating, fat-dripping cone. Meat's poisonous to them, Gillespie remembers. This stuff's probably poisonous to humans too.

'Sun bed for salmonella,' he says.

'I will have just the vegetables,' Ounserrat says. 'Could you put the chips in it too? And please use a different knife.'

The boys look like they want to say something smart about an Outsider at a kebab van. Impress their girls. Ounserrat's a head taller than the biggest of them, and Gillespie's glance dares them, just dares them. As they walk away, he hears the high whicker of girlie laughter over bass boy muttering.

They hit them on the third street along. In a dark entry there's a rustle and click of feet on wet concrete and two men are behind them. At the same instant the green Ford shoots past and two more big lads jump out. One's got a baseball bat, the other a crow-bar. He doesn't know what the ones behind him have got, but he can hear them scraping them along the gutters and walls as their footsteps break into a run.

'Jesus!' he yells as he realizes that however fast he runs it won't be enough to make it past the two in front. Then something hits him in the back of the knees and down he goes and they're on him and he's rolling up with his arms folded over his head as the hurley stick comes down. His arms. They've broken both his fucking *arms*, but he holds himself tight, tight as the edge of the stick whaps at the backs of his hands. Not my face, my face, my fucking face. No! Jesus! He uncoils: his kidneys have exploded. He tries to roll away, scrabble away, scramble crawl run away. There's a guy with a twenty-pound sledge hammer up over his head. No pissing around. They want Gillespie dead. He rolls out from under the warhead. Kerbstone cracks and shatters. He makes it to his knees. He's not sure his feet will hold him. He sees Ounserrat moving like a blur of red between the swings of the baseball bat. The boy can't get a fix on her at all; staring like a hypnotized rabbit. Too fast.

'Go!' he croaks at her. She turns, stares. The bat catches her in the belly. In an instant she's halfway across the street, still on her feet, but crouching, staring. The howl stops the hard lads dead for the instant it takes. Gillespie sees her reach inside her denim jacket, pull out a short, fat cylinder and in a shake of the wrist it's a *genro* staff tall as a Shian hunter.

Gillespie doesn't see what happens next because Hurley Stick knocks his legs out from under him and he rolls over on to his back to see the Hammer, the sledge high and looking for the space between his eyes. It looks. It waits. It never comes, because there's the tip of a *genro* staff rammed hard into the guy's breast bone. A shove, he goes over backwards, toppled by his hammer.

And the hurley stick is spinning across the street and a high-pitched voice is moaning, 'My wrist, it broke my fucking wrist, my fucking wrist.' From ground zero Gillespie hears a new car crunch to a wet halt in the middle of the street. He recognizes Ford hub caps. He recognizes a pair of sensible flat heels and the hem of a beige coat. He hears a woman shout, 'Police! Stop!', and sees four pairs of black shoes running towards open car doors. Exhaust fumes cling to the street. Doors slam, tyres shriek. The green Ford reverses, swings round. And it's gone.

'GZA 1880,' he hears the woman say. It's getting very difficult to make things out. The road feels very very soft and comfortable compared to his body. Nice to sleep. Roll over. Pull the tarmac around you. Lights have gone on in windows, though half-closed eyes you can make kind-of faces out of them. Holy faces: Jesus and Blessed Mary Ever Virgin, looking down at him. Face of Jesus. Face of Mary. Oh Jesus. Oh Mary.

'Jesus, he's a mess,' the Blessed Lady says.

'He must be got to a hospital,' Jesus says gravely.

And something's lifting him. Something's carrying him, something's putting him in the back of a dark blue Ford. It hurts. It hurts. It hurts, but he knows he's safe in the arms of Jesus.

Sunday

Roisin Dunbar notes as she comes down the corridor that someone's shifted the litter bin back under the leaking sprinkler. In the office Darren Healey is standing on his desk with a pair of Snuggies over his pants and a bib round his neck and Tommy Tippee beanie hat perched on the back of his head like a papal skull-cap while the CID Outsider squad applauds him on the birth of a son, a Darren-ette, at two thirty-eight this morning, weight seven pounds. No phantom labour, this time.

'Congratulations, Darren. Remember, a child is for life, not just for Christmas.'

He's obviously had as little sleep as her, he's dishevelled, unshaven, creased and smelling of hospital, but nothing can bring him down. Not that he's done any of the hard work. He made his contribution nine months ago. You deserved your big clap then. He holds up a palmcorder.

'Anyone want to watch the birth?'

'Almost got to see it live, Darren,' she says.

'Aye, I heard you were up in casualty,' Healey says. 'How is your man Gillespie?'

'He'll not be running any marathons for a while. That Outsider lawyer he's hanging around with is looking after him back at the Annadale Hold.'

Darren Healey gives her the look that suggests all manner of sexual deviations. It also says that she should thank the police-person's god that her client is in the Annadale Hold and not the morgue.

I know, I know, Darren. I take my eyes off the ball for one second to call the office about Gavin Peterson, and they hit the boy you're supposed to be minding with your life. But for that Outsider, he would be on the slab.

Oh God. Willich is going to fry me.

And then when you creep in with the dawn's early light, Michael's doing his Zen Bang Breakfast Routine where he pretends to move things slowly and carefully because wee Rosh has been up all night, but which somehow contrives to make the maximum amount of impact noise. I'm the one's been out all night cruising clubs and saving suspects and somehow I've done something that makes you annoyed with me? She learned long before Michael that you can't argue with a man in Zen Bang. When it starts to blur into Good Father/Bad Mother, Good Father putting his time/job/life on hold for lickkle Louise because Bad Mother's got so many things that are more important than lickkle Louise and Daddy, it's time to go to work, however shitty you feel. Jesus, do you think I like this? Do you think anybody would choose to spend all night alone and cold and scared deep in the weird? No. No. Leave it. You came here to get away from him. Don't bring him in. Leave him out there under that cold drip in the corridor, all day, maybe it'll wear him away like a stone.

Darren Healey's off in his disposables and bib and hat and smug grin to see if they will persuade his boss to give him his European Union Statutory Paternity Leave early. Lots of luck, Darren. Hope you never end up hiding from partner and heir behind other people's crimes and misdemeanours.

Word of her fuck-up has spread. On the way to hot strong black coffee Richard Crawford shouts out, 'Hey, Rosh! Good thing that Outsider lawyer bit Gillespie's hanging around with pulled some kind of Wonder Woman stunt, or we'd be down one prime suspect and Willich wouldn't like that.'

'Fuck off, Richard,' Dunbar growls.

'*Kethba*,' Littlejohn says, sitting on Dunbar's desk, which she wishes he wouldn't. 'Superhuman strength. Controlled hysteria. Like those stories you've heard about grannies single-handedly lifting cars that have fallen on their sons. The Shian can switch it on and off. It costs them though; they have to sleep for a day, day and a half, to recover.'

No one's in the mood for a Littledick lecture, least of all Roisin Dunbar. There's information she needs from the computer before this morning's meeting,

Ten o'clock sharp Willich comes in. Chairs are pulled round into a ragged semicircle. Littlejohn perches on the edge of a desk at the back. There are times when he wants to be one of the lads and times when he does not.

'First off, congratulations to DC Healey on the birth of a son, Wayne.' Applause, whistles, whoops. 'He'll be off this afternoon for two weeks on a much more difficult job than this.' The parents all exchange knowing looks. 'Seriously, well done, and good luck. OK, what have you got for me this morning? Technology smuggling; what's the word from the players?'

'The hard men will pay up to six grand for a maser.' Ian Cochrane's been running a string of grasses since the bad days of the Troubles. Dunbar's not sure that he isn't too close to his sources. 'They're arming all their enforcers with them; they use them to keep their people in line. Seems having your head blown up is scarier than a bullet through it.'

'They go for the head shot?'

'I'm guessing. There are rumours of an arms race; Inla's after some Sheenie device—'

'Hey. We don't use that name. We don't even think it.'

'Something called a Cloak of Shadows. Could be a code name. But if Inla want it, the Proddy boys want it first, except no one can tell me what a Cloak of Shadows is.'

'Dr Littlejohn?'

Heads turn. Littlejohn stands up, shrugs.

'I don't recognize the name. It suggests some hunting device, maybe with ritual connotations. If I had it in Narha, I could hazard a guess.'

'Jesus Christ,' Cochrane whispers to Roisin Dunbar. Then, aloud, 'I'll go back and see what my contacts can find. Ahm, they aren't exactly the Rotary Club . . .'

'Let me know what you need. Second round of door-to-door?'

Tracey Agnew's as bright and glowing as ever. All that jogging keeps the arches supple and the tits firm. Lucky you have time for it. 'We got seven who hadn't been in for the first round. One saw Ongserrang going in, another couple were at the Queen's Film Theatre on the night, but remember seeing an Outsider on a small motorbike pay a call that afternoon. It was a pizza delivery bike.'

'Our friend Ounserrat Soulereya. Does she check out? DC Thomas?'

'She's legit. The Not Afraid of the River Hold.' (Sniggers, 'What the hell kind of a name is that for anything?' Thomas smiles and continues) 'has confirmed that she is a qualified *genro* appointed by them to protect the interests of one Sounsurresh Soulereya, originally of that Hold.'

'The name sounds familiar.'

'It could. Sounsurresh Soulereya is actually a bit of a minor celebrity: one of those Outsider models who're the fashion at the moment. She came over here with her kids; it was in the papers.' Murmurs and nods. 'She came over to visit the family she was born into.'

'This isn't unusual,' Littlejohn says. He's been feeling ignored on his perch at the back. 'They're a much more mobile people than we are. It's likely that the father of her children is still resident in that Hold, and she wants them to meet him.'

'Anyway, she didn't go home. When she failed to turn up at a photographic shoot, her people got worried and sent this lawyer to find her. When I called, they thought it was because we had found a body. They were quite relieved to find out we hadn't.'

'So what's Gillespie doing with her?'

'The Hold she was visiting was South Side of the Stone, down at Islandhill. The one where Ongserrang went.'

'Connection? Agnew, check it out. Right, now you'll be fascinated to know that DS Dunbar has found another possible player in the game. This is while Mr Gillespie is getting his head kicked in by party unknown.'

Dunbar chokes back embarrassment.

'In fact, I think we'll have her up to the front to tell us all the good news.'

Fuck you, boss.

The team hoots and slow hand-claps as she pins up her printouts on the board next to the shots of blood-sprayed rooms and headless bodies on slabs annotated with computer-printed arrows. She got three prints from the machine. One is a grainy long-lens image from a RAM camera of a man standing in front of a Chinese grocer's window with a single lacquered duck hanging in it. It is night. One is an enhanced clipping from a newspaper of a heavy, beefy man in a terrible anorak and a dog collar, with another man partly hidden behind him. It is day, it is wet, they are standing on the steps of the City Hall. The photograph suggests they are part of a much larger crowd. The last is a prison full-face and profile, with a number under it. There are fingerprints, iris scans and the intimate bar-codes of a DNA profile along the bottom, and a name.

'Gavin Peterson. You may remember him; he got sent down for fifteen for his part in a series of sectarian murders committed by the Red Hand Commandos back in 1995.'

'I was part of the team put him away,' Willich says. 'I was in Antrim Road then, in the RUC days. We wanted the bastard in for life. He was running the North Belfast Commando; he carried out those killings personally, but his defence brief did a demolition job on our evidence. We were lucky even to get fifteen for illegal weapons and conspiracy.'

'He got out last year after some kind of prison conversion or something, and walked straight into a job as head of security for the fragrant Reverend McIvor Kyle.' She taps picture three. 'Gavin Peterson then.' Picture two. 'Gavin Peterson now.' Picture one. 'Gavin Peterson at two forty-seven this morning, leaving the premises of Mr Lee Pak Yu, who is running a frook club from the upstairs storeroom of his Oriental grocery on Little Howard Street, in our parish. If you look carefully, you can see he's carrying a package of some kind. Peterson had a meeting with Gillespie and the Outsider Ounserrat Soulereya at the club. They did time together in the Maze. They both have paramilitary backgrounds; everyone knows the Dee Pees and the UDF are in with the Free Men of Ulster.' She looks around the faces: anyone going to object? Anyone going to stand up and declare that McIvor Kyle is a good man and holy, and stands truly for God and Ulster? Any of you ones who leave anonymous tracts in my desk drawers about how Catholics too many earn salvation by turning from their church of error. I know you're there, the police draws you like flies: Dee Pees and Free Pees and Ee Pees.

Right-wing fellowship churches, wee gospel halls, suburban faith tabernacles with thousand-strong youth choirs; Lodge and Order and Temple. The Orange and the Black. Prior claims to your loyalties? Remember the first commandment, and keep it wholly: the Northern Ireland Police Service is a jealous god and shall have no other gods before it.

'Peterson's Gillespie's buyer,' Willich says adamantly. 'And the lawyer, the Outsider, she's the supplier.'

At the back of the room, on the corner of his desk, Littlejohn is rolling his eyes.

'If we're going with the arms smuggling theory.'

The room is suddenly silent. Not even the creak of chair leather, the squeak of stressed tube steel, the soft sift of cigarette ash to the floor.

'You think there's something wrong with this approach?'

'No. But . . .' But. Yes. But those buts. You have to. They force you. Deep breath. 'Gillespie and the Outsider went to another club before the frook joint. Club Ochre, on North Street. He caught me; I know, I got careless. He went to great pains to let me know exactly what he was doing and where he was going and who he was seeing. He was at Club Ochre because Sounsurresh Soulereya had been at the opening a couple of weeks back. From there he was going to the frook club on Little Howard Street to find a businessman called Gerry Conlon, the Gerry Conlon who owns GreenGene, who seems to have made some arrangement with Sounsurresh Soulereya. Now, why tell me this? Why lead me, not to Conlon, but to Peterson, if it's going to further implicate him? This does not make sense.'

'Then it could have been Peterson's boys gave Gillespie a digging,' Richard Crawford says.

'Why, if Gillespie's the contact?' Dunbar says. She doesn't like the shade Willich's face is going; apoplectic red.

'Maybe he's asking too much.'

'Or maybe word got back to Gerry Conlon,' Ian Cochrane says. 'Wants his mucky little secrets kept quiet.'

Bless you my son, Dunbar thinks at Ian Cochrane. Willich's holding up his hands.

'Hey hey hey. Let's not get ahead of ourselves. Too much

good solid bobbying gets flushed down the crapper by wanting everything at once. OK, we need a fast result, but we need one that's going to stick. So we do it methodically, we do it thoroughly, we do it slowly. OK? This is good work. This is a good lead. DI Cochrane, have another word with your grasses, see if they've heard anything about the Free Men. Dr Littlejohn, any chance you could pick a team to make some inquiries among the Outsiders about this Cloak of Shadows thing? I am going to have a little chat with Mr Gavin Peterson. Dunbar, you made the connection, you come with me. But first, a wee word in my office?' That headmasterial lowering of the head and lift of the eyebrows. Jesus. Six of the best.

Willich's office is a box room with a view of the back of the DSS. Come Christmas, you can watch the civil servants banging in the car park. He's got a big computer because everyone has to have a big computer but the screen saver has been sending its lissajous looping around his screen for five uninterrupted years. There's room for a desk, a chair, and one other person standing.

'Dunbar, do you know what the Eleventh Commandment is?' People are moving slowly beyond the ribbed glass door, trying to overhear.

'Never, ever, contradict the boss, boss.'

'You made me look like I didn't know what I was doing out there.'

'Sorry, sir.'

'You know what keeps this place going? There're thirty highly intelligent, highly ambitious, highly determined people out there; do you know what stops them tearing each other's throats out? Respect. Yes, it's like the Lion King. You question my competence, you challenge my authority, I lose respect and once that's gone it never comes back again. Never. And instead of a team we've got thirty individuals who don't like each other much, spending more time fighting each other than fighting the enemy. So, whatever you may think, you keep it to yourself. You got that?'

'Yes sir. It won't happen again, sir.'

'Damn right it won't. You see, I can forgive – just – you fucking up by getting spotted in that night club. I can even forgive you – though it will take time, and a hell of a lot of good behaviour from you – for taking your eyes off your client and letting him get the shit beaten out of him. But the unforgivable sin, the sin against the Holy Spirit, is to make me look stupid in front of the pack. So, you will never, ever, do that again.' He waits for a response.

'What more do you want me to say?' Dunbar says. 'I saved Gillespie's ass.'

'The Outsider saved his ass. Now, if we're done here, let's go spoil Gavin Peterson's Lord's Day.'

The sign's the size of a hoarding and it says 'Faith Tabernacle, Christ Centred, Full Bible Salvation, Minister: Rev McIvor Kyle, BD Hons, DD, All Welcome', with a painting of the Reverend McIvor Kyle at the top so there's no mistake, but Roisin Dunbar knows what anyone with even a vestigial spirituality knows, that you can't build a holy place out of red brick. God is a function of architecture: the Outsiders have got that right. Build in grand perpendicular, send Gothic piers and vaults shooting up and fill the spaces between them with glowing lights, and the God of Mystery will abide there. Build in the intimate, woody, inward-looking enclosures of contemporary Catholicism and you will meet the God of Harmony and Tranquillity. Build in housing-estate red brick, fit the thing out with PA and overhead projection screens, wrap it in a car park, and the God of Shopping Centres dwells therein.

The place looks like a gun battery. Those tall slit windows will retract and put out big black muzzles. That shallow domed roof will slide back for howitzers and siege mortars. The front line of the war against Romish error. The Verdun of the Reformation. A meaner deity than the God of Shopping Centre inspirits here. The God of Heavy Ordinance. The God of Protestant Armageddon. They want it. They really look forward to that final battle when they drive the forces of Popishness from their holy Israel. No nuns and no priests and no rosary beads, and each day is the twelfth of July. Jesus. But you don't get a look in here, do you? You're too soft and forgiving and loving and lefty; these are Old Testament believers.

The church seems to grow taller and wider and heavier as Roisin Dunbar drives across the thousand-space car park. It's an hour after the end of the morning service but there are still a lot of cars. Dissenting Presbyterianism runs long on Volvos, Rovers and Toyota people movers. All those good little Protestants they're encouraged to spawn.

'I bet you feel out of place here.'

'Any twenty-first-century person would feel out of place here.'

After-service hangers-on stare as Willich and Dunbar come through the brass double doors. The big, cold vestibule is glassed in with illuminated Lives of the Martyrs. Deaths of the Martyrs, more accurately. Above the Junior League of Church Loyalty table a naked, inverted, spreadeagled man is being sawn in half. The books in the wire book carousels are all by McIvor Kyle. They have names like *Thy Quickening Ray*, or *Thy Great Vouchsafefulness*, and photographs of sunsets on the cover. The cassettes in the wooden cassette rack also have pictures of sunsets on their covers, and names like *Ten Studies in Ephesians* or *The Vestments of Royal Priesthood*. Those that aren't by Reverend McIvor Kyle are by a group of fat men smiling up into a quickening ray from out of the sunset. These men are called the Revival Trumpets.

An usher who smiles far too much directs them to the offices, which are buried like a command bunker under levels of protecting masonry. Roisin Dunbar can't resist a look into the big church. You could fit an Outsider landing craft under the domed roof. It must be half a mile up to there. The seats are tiered, but she doesn't see a cinema or a theatre; it's an arena, a colosseum where dramas of death and blood are acted out every Lord's Day. Stark white walls, high bright windows. The decor runs to red plush, Bibles, crowns and swords. 'Ulster for Christ' says the fresco behind the pulpit. Other way round, surely, Pastor Kyle.

She can't get the smell of furniture polish out of her nose.

Another over-smiling usher in a too-neat suit tells them the Head of Security is in today. Knock, enter, out with the warrant cards.

'DCI Willich, and this is DS Dunbar, from Donegal Pass

Police Station. We're making inquiries concerning the murders of five Outsiders in University Street. We'd like to ask you a few questions.'

Hitler in the bunker. No SS defending the German people with their curved, triangular shields, but pictures of beloved Bible stories made horror stories by over-literal painting, super-intended by photoportraits of Pastor McIvor Kyle and King Charles III. He visited a Shian sacred space last month, the self-styled Defender of Faith, your semi-divine monarch. Said it was a truly transcendent spiritual experience.

'Sit, please. Chief Inspector Willich now. Things have changed a bit since last time we met. Can I get you tea, coffee?'

'Nothing, thank you.'

'So, how can I help you?'

Willich looks to Dunbar. It's a game of patience, of laying cards on the table and turning them up, one by one. Card one: a long-lens photograph of Andy Gillespie stolen in the moment it takes him to fumble for the keys to his flat.

'Do you know this man?' Dunbar asks.

'Looks like a man I was inside with.' He's up front about that. 'What was his name? Gillespie?'

'Did you know him well?'

He shakes his head. 'Just by name, really.'

'He's been in prison. Like you. Do you know what he was inside for?'

'I understand he was driver on an attempted murder of a drugs dealer on the Newtownards Road in 2001,' Peterson says. Wise, Dunbar thinks. While you don't know how much we know, you'll play along.

'It was set up by the Third Battalion of the UVF,' she says.

'You think that because he was in the paramilitaries, and because your commanding officer put me away for paramilitary activities, we were all best buddies in the Maze?' Peterson says. 'That hit was probably against another Loyalist group, UFF, someone like that. They all sold themselves out for drug money. Gangsters, the lot of them. I tell you this, we never, ever, dirtied our hands with drugs.'

'Have you seen him since your release?'

'Only on the television; that murder you're investigating. Do you think he did it?'

Roisin Dunbar takes a long, slow tactical look out of Peterson's window. The hard wind from off the hills is chasing empty crisp packets round and round in the lee of a buttress. Different climate this side of the city. Three degrees colder in any weather. There must be a pattern to the way the cars come off the motorway on to the Glengormley roundabout. Card two. Ounserrat Soulereya, leaving Pizza Di Action with a pizza box in one hand and her helmet in the other.

'Do you recognize this Outsider?'

He purses his lips.

'They all look the same to me. I don't know any Sheenies. I don't want to know any.'

'You've never had any contact with Shian?'

'There was one, in the Maze same time as me. Your friend Gillespie hung around with it a lot. Him and another guy, a Catholic.' He says the C-word like it's a bad taste in his mouth. This C-word policewoman's got you by the balls. You're smiling, you're liking it, you're enjoying the attention because now she's playing with them, stroking them, tickling them, but you'll be singing a new song in a higher key when she starts to twist them.

'Do you know what a frook is, Mr Peterson?'

'I don't recognize the word.'

'A frook is a human with a sexual fixation on the Shian. It takes many forms, but primarily it's a kind of fetishism.' Littlejohn mode. Effortless. Willich's concealing a smile, but she's watching Peterson's reaction. 'Sometimes it's just a desire to dress Shian fashion, wear body make-up, contact lenses, and be as close as possible to Outsiders. Most often, it's a desire to have sex with a Shian, male or female, regardless of season. In the more extreme states, they may undergo cosmetic surgery to make themselves look like Shian. It's a small, close subculture. They have their own clubs, newssheets, Internet bulletin boards, contact magazines.'

'As a member of a Bible-believing, born-again Church, I find this morally repugnant.'

Twist.

'But not so morally repugnant that you weren't at a frook club on Little Howard Street between one thirty and three o'clock this morning.' Card three. Ace of trumps. She had waited, finger on button, until he stepped from the shadowed door into the full light from the street lamp across the road. Harry Lime moment. No mistaking. No possibility of error. You, you sanctimonious bastard. You. In the window, the Chinese duck swings.

'Gavin, you were a lying turd then and you're a lying turd now,' Willich says. 'I think we're going to have to have you down at the station for a wee chat.'

Got his balls, and chained them to the fucking floor.

At five she takes a break for a Diet Coke and a sandwich and a call to Michael that it's going to be another late nighter. Wee Millie's got dexies. God knows where from. Dunbar pops a couple with her Diet Coke. She'll be questioning Peterson from the ceiling of the interview room, but at least the question will make sense. A long slow slash, while she finishes the Coke. Silence. Solitude. Something very settling and centring about bare bum on cold government plastic. This is the moment when, if she smoked, she would smoke. Ready for round two. The dexies must be kicking in already.

It's way past his quitting time but Littlejohn is lurking outside the ladies.

'Cracked him yet?' She really doesn't want to talk with Littlejohn, here, now. She keeps walking. He keeps step with her. He will talk with her.

'He admits he was in the club, he even admits he met Andy Gillespie but denies any knowledge of a gun-running ring.'

'Of course he does. He's nothing to do with gun-running. You know as well as I that's complete bullshit.'

'I got bollocked by Willich for agreeing with you.'

'At least you still have your soul. Willich isn't going to get the real story out of our born-again friend Peterson. He's asking the wrong questions.'

'Who's going to ask the right questions? You?'

'Before I made a career path switch to aliens, I used to be a middling-to-good human psychologist. You don't lose the old skills. Like riding a bike.'

'What will you ask him?'

'Why did he kill five members of the Harridi Nation at University Street on March the second 2004?'

She stops in the corridor ten steps short of Interview Room number three.

'Get serious.'

'He fits the profile. I read your files. This washed-in-the-blood praise-the-Lorder blew three Roman Catholics away and would have blown away a whole pother more if Willich hadn't caught him. Shian are just Taigs with funny haircuts.'

'And the fact that Gillespie was in the club with him?'

'Ireland's a small world; frooks are even smaller. He and the *genro* were following their own investigation. There aren't that many places for them to look. Peterson was there looking for prey.'

'You're grasping at straws. When I found Eamon Donnan, you told me categorically it was him.'

'Him, someone like him. No shortage of contenders, I'm afraid. This country is the mother of fuck-ups. The facts are Donnan fits the profile, Peterson fits the profile. Half of the male Loyalist population of Belfast fits the profile. But Peterson's the one you've got in your interview room and I know I can crack him, I can find out what he's really about. Willich can't.'

Dunbar hands Littlejohn the empty Diet Coke can and the bottom left corner of her tuna and mayo sandwich. There's onion in it. Great for interview intimidation: onion breath.

'One thing I know for certain, this has nothing to do with a weapons smuggling conspiracy,' Littlejohn says, hands full of snack. 'Rosh, get me ten minutes with him.'

Don't call me that. She hesitates just a moment before opening the interview room door and going in.

'DS Dunbar has re-entered the room at seventeen twelve,' Willich tells the tape. He sighs, lights up another cigarette. The atmosphere already carries a health warning.

'Would you mind not doing that?' Peterson says.

'Since when were you Mr Health and Efficiency?'

'The body is the temple of the spirit.'

Willich stubs the cigarette out and says, 'So, try and convince me of this again. If you weren't attempting to buy Outsider weapons off Andy Gillespie, if you don't have any connections with the Free Men of Ulster, if you haven't the least idea what I'm talking about when I mention Cloaks of Shadows, then what the hell were you doing in that frook club?'

'Maybe he likes them,' Roisin Dunbar says. 'Maybe he's got a wardrobe full of their clothes, maybe he's got his bedroom wall covered in pin-ups of supermodels. Maybe he's got a heap of mags and video under the bed. Maybe that's what he had in the envelope, a porny video.'

'Is that the best you can do?' Peterson wears a look of weary disgust. 'Wee girls pretending they're Elliot Ness? Well, go on with it. I'm enjoying the show. I'm not under arrest, I haven't done anything you can charge me with, I just sit here a couple more hours listening to you doing your double act, and then I'm home. Or you could save everyone's time and let me go and that wee girl home to make her husband his tea.'

'Boss.' He's made her mind up for her now. She was going to leave it, but he's earned it now. 'A wee word, outside?'

'I'm pausing this interview at seventeen seventeen to leave the room temporarily with DS Dunbar.' Willich hits the pause. A yellow light comes on.

'Oh aye, this is where the lads with the big sticks come in,' Peterson says.

Outside, Littlejohn is in the same position she left him. The Coke can and the chewed tuna and mayo have disappeared.

'Boss, let him do it.'

'What for? It's nothing to do with him.'

'Peterson's taking the piss out of us. We can't charge him for being at a frook club, he knows it. Littlejohn'll scare him.'

'He'll eat him with salt.'

'I know how these people work,' Littlejohn says.

'You know fuck.'

'Had a profitable and enjoyable five hours then?'

'A change of tack can't hurt,' Dunbar says, quick to mollify

145

the breed bulls. Jesus, you can almost smell the testosterone. 'Boss, with respect, he's getting back at you for the time you sent him down. He's playing with you, and you're just feeding him lines.'

No one moves. No one speaks. On the edge of hearing, the sprinkler drips. Count of twenty, fhlat fhlat fhlat.

'OK.' Dunbar close her eyes: a prayer of thanksgiving to the policeperson's god. 'But Rosh and me both sit in with you.'

'Agreed.'

He's started before Willich can complete the recording formalities.

'Tell me Gavin, did you ever have greenfly? Did you ever have a house plant and one day you'd see maybe a couple of greenfly at the base of a leaf and next time you looked the thing was crawling with them? No stopping them, was there? And no matter how much you sprayed them, you couldn't get rid of them completely, could you? They kept breeding, and breeding, and breeding. If you left a greenfly to breed, and nothing ate it or killed it, at the end of one year you'd have so many greenfly that if they stood in a line they'd stretch two and a half thousand light years. Light years, Gavin. Quite something, aren't they? Wee grubby pasty things you can hardly see, but they're the winners in the reproduction stakes. Humans can manage one new human every year, and it's thirteen years minimum before they can breed new humans. Greenfly've got us well beaten. No wonder you have to keep them under control. If they can reach halfway to the centre of the galaxy in one year, how long before they take over the world?'

'Who let this clown in here?' Peterson says. Senses stretched by dexedrine, Roisin Dunbar imagines she can hear an edge of tension in his flat voice.

'Maybe the greenfly are the heirs of the earth. Maybe God intended it for them, not for us. They're certainly better at subduing and possessing it. Maybe they should have it. What do you think, Gavin?'

'You what?'

'I'm interested in what you think about greenfly. Should we let them rule the world or not?'

'Do I have to answer this fool?'

'You do,' Willich says.

'OK. Greenfly. You get a big bug spray. You take the top off. You point it. You press the button. Greenfly problem sorted. They aren't ruling the world any more.'

Littlejohn pauses, fiddles with his beard. He is playing, Dunbar thinks. He has power here. He controls language, and who controls language controls thought. He loves this power. His children are gone, his wife is gone, his job is going nowhere; the only thing he can control are the words. Psychologist, shrink thyself.

'You're not married, are you, Gavin?'

'I'm not.'

'You never were, were you?'

'If you know this why are you asking me?'

'No girlfriends, no live-ins.'

'No.'

'It wasn't a question this time. Did you ever have any girlfriends, Gavin?'

'Yes. Plenty. I'm not a homosexual pervert.'

'I never said you were, Gavin. OK, plenty of girlfriends, but nothing longer than' – he shrugs, opens his hands – 'six months? Three months?'

'A couple of months, if you really want to know.'

'Your mates, Gavin. I suppose they're lost causes. Wives. Houses. Cars. DIY. Home furnishing. Trips to B & Q on a Sunday. Satellite TV. Big stereos. Holidays in Disneyworld. Big repayments. Big mortgages. Children. Children all over the place; you're tripping over their bikes and slipping on their roller skates and kicking their toys, and when you go to see your mates all they talk about is babies and schools and who's got what sickness and will have to go to the doctor and they've got their sprogs' scrawls stuck up on the fridge with magnets and you can't even take them out for a wee jar or two because the wee wifey's at her step aerobics on Tuesdays and they can't get a minder. Great lads, gone to pot. And you're the only real, free man among them.

'Are you, Gavin?'

'They've got their lives, I've got mine. I've got the church, that's my family.'

'But no kids, Gavin. When you die, you don't leave anything behind. You don't continue. You stop. Your geneline withers and dries up. All your mates are reproducing like greenfly, offspring everywhere, new generations, they're going to live for ever! And you're sterile, Gavin. You're going to die out from the earth.'

'I don't want kids. I don't like kids.'

Littlejohn says nothing, but he has that Littledick, too-smart, over-educated look in his eyes. Roisin Dunbar feels sorry for Gavin Peterson. Almost.

'Did you ever take a look at the last census, Gavin? The one back in 2000? Of course that was before the Outsiders arrived and bollixed the figures up. You should have a read of it some time. You'd find it fascinating. It makes some interesting predictions about the demographic make-up. It seems that one dividend of the Slow Peace no one foresaw was a baby boom. All of a sudden there's a future to bring children into. The good people of Ulster have been rutting like rabbits ever since. What's really interesting is how this baby boom is structured. It looks like the old clichés were true after all: the Catholics finally outbred the Protestants. All those priests, forbidding them sinful, evil contraceptives, urging them to have more and more children, winning this country for the true faith. They've got a paper majority already. By 2013 it'll be a political majority. They reckon by 2020 the position of a hundred years ago will be reversed. It'll be seventy-thirty Catholic to Protestant. A century to bust Protestant Ulster.

'And then there're the Outsiders. They're real greenfly. We took a full shipload, one hundred thousand. Do you know what the Shian do when they settle a new planet? They breed. Like greenfly. The universe is a big place and even with those light-speed ships of theirs they can't rely on back-up arriving. They're on their own, so they make babies. The pioneers are biologically engineered to have multiple births. In a year that hundred thousand is two hundred thousand, next year four hundred thousand, year after that a million. They come out of the womb walking and talking, by the time they're eight they're pregnant and the great thing about only having sex twice a year is if you want to get pregnant you are guaranteed to get pregnant. You think Catholics are outbreeding you? The Outsiders are going to bury all of us in bodies. The country's more than half gone now, between the Catholics and the Outsiders. Everything you've done for it, all the love and devotion you've spent on it, and you still couldn't keep it safe. How have they done it? With their bodies, and the bodies of their children, and their children's children. You're in a state of siege, like Derry's Walls again, but they keep piling up the bodies against the fortifications and they climb up them, and they keep piling them up and climbing up them, and one day they're going to pour over the wall like a tidal wave. Their descendants have won it for them. Their children, their immortality. You see, Gavin, in the end their children are going to give them everything they want, and you will have it all taken away because you have nothing to come after you. Abstract principles, political ideals, stirring words and deeds and military glory; they sound mighty fine, but they don't count. Bodies count. Bodies win. The greenfly take over the world.

'So tell me Gavin, how does that make you feel? Envious? Angry? Impotent? Don't you wish you had a big can of that bug spray you were talking about, and you could blow them all away, just wipe them out and have it clean and good and safe again?'

'Do I have to listen to this clown? What is he talking about? What is he going on about?'

You've got him, Littledick. Now all you have to do is reel the poor bastard in.

'Actually, Gavin, I've been bullshitting you. I'm a xenologist. I study Outsiders; what they are, what makes them tick. I'm interested in your church's attitude to them. Really, I am. They're just animals, isn't that what you believe?'

The silence is an indication to Peterson that this question is not rhetorical.

'You have to understand that there's a spiritual battle going on,' Peterson says. 'These are the end times, when the creatures of Satan will be loosed upon the earth and Satan will dazzle men's hearts and reign until Christ comes again to overthrow him and establish his kingdom. The devil is the counterfeiter of all God's work; for God there is the Anti-God, Satan; for Christ there is the Anti-Christ in Rome; for Adam, there is the anti-Adam, the mockery of man.'

Eschatology always gave Roisin Dunbar the creeps. In school the wee over-holy girls had timetabled the end of the world and looked for signs of its close approach and gone around warning everyone that they had better mend their ways should Jesus find them like foolish virgins. A unimpeachable excuse for a shag; the end of the world is nigh, unvirgin me, now.

'The Shian.'

'They say they come from another world, but the truth, the scriptural truth, is that there is only this world, created by God, and that man is his highest creation, and that these are made things, creatures sent to pervert our God-given manhood and womanhood.' Peterson's getting hot about this. His mouth has a head of steam behind it.

'So, if they are made by the devil, then they have no souls.'

'Only God can give spiritual life.'

'So they're no different from animals. It wouldn't be any more of a sin to kill one than it would be to kill a cat. In fact, you'd be doing the world a favour, getting rid of a minor demon.'

'What are you getting at?'

'I'm not getting at anything, Gavin. Just trying to put things together. So, they're a threat to your identity, you envy them their extraordinary fecundity, and your church basically gives you open season on them.'

'What are you saying? Are you saying that I killed those ones on University Street? Do you think I did? Gillespie accused me of that; he was like you, he thinks that anyone who hates them wants to kill them. I didn't do it. I wouldn't do it.'

'You did it to three North Belfast Catholics, and they're the same species as you. They have souls. These are only animals.'

'That was before. I've been washed in the blood. I'm a God-fearing, God-loving man.'

'But not as much as you fear the Shian, isn't that right? You

150

fear them, and you love them. You just told me you're the kind of man who loves what he fears, fears what he loves. They scare the shit out of you, but they attract you at the same time. They've got the things you want. Community, children, identity – every Shian knows what it is, where it comes from, it's got ten thousand years of recorded history behind it. What've you got? Four hundred years since the plantation – these people had planted five entire planets by then. And now they've got the thing you dedicated your life to: they've got your country. That's why you go to that club, to look at the thing you fear. You wouldn't touch them, you wouldn't do the things the others there do, that's bestiality. You go to look. Look good and long and hard. Love. Fear. Like that old film with Robert Mitchum where he had love and hate tattooed on his knuckles. He was a God-fearing, God-loving man too. He killed people.'

'I didn't kill anyone.'

'Then why were you in that club?'

'I was on business.'

'Exterminating Outsiders is business?'

'I didn't exterminate anyone or anything.'

'I don't believe you. I'll tell you why. We have a psychological profile of who we're looking for. It fits you like a glove. Everything you say, everything you do, everywhere you go, everything you've done, the profile was there first. How do you think I was able to tell you all those things about yourself? The profile. The profile tells me that you killed those Outsiders, Gavin.'

'You are talking bullshit now. This is bullshit. Complete bullshit.'

'The profile even predicted you'd react that way when directly accused. You did it, Gavin. Why not tell me? This is true, no word of bullshit: I've seen cases like this before. They protest and they protest that they didn't do it, but the funny thing is, deep down inside, they really want to tell me. They want someone to know. Some because they're proud of what they've done, others because it sickens them, they can't live with it inside, eating them away. Are you proud, or is it eating you away? And I'll tell you something else. The ones it's eating up, when they do tell someone, it stops. The looks of peace on their faces; it's amazing, Gavin. You can tell me, Gavin. Why not? We've already got you. This way you get to tell it how you like. You killed them, didn't you?'

'For fuck's sake, I keep telling you I didn't kill anyone.'

'Then why were you in the club? What was your business?'

'The tape. All right? The fucking tape. That was why I was in the club. You think I'd go to something like that? I was there to get the tape.'

The silence seems much longer than measured by the wall clock.

'The tape?'

Peterson sighs. The wind and the spirit go out of him, he crumples, withering. Littledick has him, but it's not the fish he was angling for. The Shian-killer is still out there, swimming in dark water.

'There's a DUP councillor. Sammy Dow. He's on the Planning Committee. Wife, kids, goes to the old Paisley church on the Ravenhill Road, and every Tuesday evening when his wife thinks he's at a committee meeting he's at that place. The Chink has other rooms, out the back, where you can go with them. We have a camera in one.'

'We?' Willich asks.

'The UDF.'

'You're blackmailing a Belfast City Councillor,' Dunbar says.

'It's bigger than that. It's who leads the Protestants in Belfast. The Democratic Unionists went downhill after they stuck Paisley in Purdysburn. They're finished. The UDF is the voice of the Protestant community. There're elections coming up in May. By then we should have enough on enough DUP men to swing the North and East Belfast wards.'

'You're going to smear them?'

'And show the pan-Nationalist front we're as dirty as them? No; so as not to split the Unionist vote, we'll arrange a series of electoral pacts where the DUP will stand aside in favour of a UDF candidate.'

'Jesus, it is Kincora all over again,' Willich says. Then: 'How high does this go?'

He's trapped. Learn this from the Taigs: confession is good for the soul.

'To the top.'

Roisin Dunbar closes her fist under the interview table. Yes! Got you, Pastor McIvor Kyle, you smug bastard. I'm coming to winkle you out of your big brick bunker and God is going to turn his face away. She looks at the clock on the wall. Eighteen thirty-five. An hour and ten minutes to crack.

The cars are going out. The barrier is up, and they are going out in convoy. Ten cars, four police in each, five teams of two. They have search warrants, and an attitude. Ten minutes before, Roisin Dunbar had come through the CID office and her search team had fallen in behind her while the others cheered and applauded and shouted encouragements like 'Go, Rosh!' and 'Fuck the bastard', and she had felt like gangbusters. Underneath that beige trench coat there're Batgirl's boots and black lycra.

The cars turn out on to Donegal Pass. A uniform stops the traffic for them. Down on to the Ormeau Road. Along Cromac Street into Victoria Street and on towards the M2, a big line of dark-coloured Fords. They lose the first two cars at the lights on York Street by the Art College. Two for the Crumlin Road Dissenting Presbyterian Church. Four more at the turn off on to the M2, accelerating smoothly up to high speed cruise, for the Glengormley Faith Tabernacle. Another two straight on into the York Road, for the Dee Pee Fortwilliam Mission. Detective Sergeant Roisin Dunbar leads the last two, left up the Limestone Road, right at the lights up by the Waterworks on to the Antrim Road. Two cars for Pastor McIvor Kyle's Victorian residence at Ben Madigan.

Batmobile! Yah!

Two cars turn between the sandstone gate pillars and crunch up the pink gravel drive between the rhododendrons.

'We're doing the wrong jobs,' Detective Chief Inspector Willich in the passenger seat comments, observing the Scrabo sandstone pile of nineteenth-century bourgeoiserie among the mature shrubs. 'If you really want to coin it, invent a religion.'

'Tell me that again when we've got him in an interview room,' Roisin Dunbar says.

The two dark Fords draw up at the foot of the worn steps leading to the glassed-in porch. Security lights flick on, AI-guided security microcameras lock on to the figures stepping from the open doors.

Her team orders up behind her. Roisin Dunbar faces the front door and assertively presses the bell push. A speaker gives her three bars of 'Nearer My God to Thee' and a chip-personality says. 'Welcome to the home of Pastor McIvor Kyle. Please state your name, your business, and whom you wish to see.'

'Detective Sergeant Roisin Dunbar. Police. We have a warrant to search Pastor McIvor Kyle's premises.' The team try not to laugh as the door-dog prissily answers, 'Pastor Kyle has been notified of your presence and will receive you shortly. In the meantime, I shall play you some music.' It's 'Burdens Are Lifted at Calvary'. The door-dog gives them all of it, followed by 'Safe in the Arms of Jesus, Safe in the Arms of Him'. After that, 'The Old Rugged Cross'.

Roisin Dunbar is not going to ask pretty-please of a chunk of silicon.

'Barry, give him a call on your mobile.'

The police admire Pastor McIvor Kyle's view of the lough and the lights of Holywood beyond. An aircraft lifts off from the City Airport across the river. Container ships are moving in the channel.

'He's not answering.'

'Right, lads. Barry, Doug, Kev and Joe, round the back.'

Dunbar tries the door-dog again. She gives it one bar before using the police over-ride to put it into receive-only mode. Still Pastor McIvor Kyle does not answer the call.

'Sarge! Boss!'

She's glad she's wearing heels she can run in. The big plastic cod-Victorian conservatory juts out from the back of the house like a penis extension. It glows with lamps. Dunbar wonders how they did that nice pink speckle effect on the glass. She wonders further; why are her officers standing on the lawn with strange, lost boy looks on their faces? There's a figure sitting in a cane chair in the conservatory, lolling back against the glass. She stops. There's something amiss with it. It has no head. That pretty pink dapple effect is blood.

'Jesus,' Willich breathes.

The seated figure is dressed casually, but its identity is immediately apparent. Below the ragged stump of neck is a clerical collar, once pure white, now washed-in-the-blood red. Its lap is a mess of raw flesh. Through the smeared glass Dunbar can make out another figure front down on the floor. Hands are outspread, gripping the tile-effect vinyl. A lake of blood has leaked from the cauterized arteries of the neck and congealed. This figure is wearing a long floral print dress with a cardigan.

'Sarge, one down in here!' Barry is at the kitchen door, peering through the glass.

'An ambulance. Get a fucking ambulance!' Dunbar screams as she runs to the kitchen door.

'Bit late for that,' someone says as Barry unsnaps his mobile.

The third body is on the kitchen floor, another woman, curled around her own dismemberment as if in shame.

'Get us in there,' Willich says thinly. 'There may be survivors.' But he isn't convincing anyone. Nothing has been left alive in that house.

'It's open,' Barry says, looking in amazement at the handle in his hand as if he has broken something not his.

'Boss!' Kev has made it to the double garage, where there is an Alsatian-sized dog kennel. There is a dark huddle half in, half out of it. 'They killed the dog! They killed the fucking dog!'

In their last couple of years on the Woodstock Road, Karen had had a cat, an evil black bastard tom with half its tail missing. Stumpy, she had called it. She hadn't so much had the cat as the cat had had her. It had come in out of the entry and she'd given it chicken bones and scraps and once you start that you never get rid of them. It fought and it sprayed and it stank of piss but Karen had to have it on the bed at night. It would sleep between them, languishing in body heat, purring asthmatically. If you tried to move it, it would draw blood. Gillespie would toss himself awake in the night, not knowing why he had woken, and though he could never see it, for no one can see a black cat in a dark bedroom, he knew that the thing was staring at him. He could feel the heat of its eyes on his skin. He could not drift back into cramped sleep while he felt its eyes on him. He knew that the reason he had woken was because the cat had opened its eyes. It could do this any time it wanted, open its eyes, and wake him.

He wakes, but it is not dark. It is not the front bedroom of the terrace house on Hatton Drive. In the waking moment he does not know where he is; it feels like some fragment of a dream, but eyes have woken him. He can feel the heat of cat eyes watching him. He tries to sit up. Enormous pain. Everything pain. Everywhere. He can't find the top of the bed. It seems to go on for ever. Jesus fuck, the pain. He rolls on to his side and meets the eyes. They are watching him from a distance of centimetres, cat eyes, slitted eyes.

'Piss away off, cat,' he mumbles at them.

The cat lifts its head off the bed. It turns it to one side, quizzically. It blinks its big eyes and then says something to him.

'Fuck!' Andy Gillespie is halfway across the bed that seems to go on for ever. It feels like he's getting smacked about all over again, but he wants away from that *thing*.

The cat that talks shrieks and leaps up. It lands on its back legs and skitters away with cockroach speed, across the bed, on to the floor, through the open door. Flailing stick arms, spindly legs; it's a cat-monkey thing from hell, wailing.

'Jesus!' Gillespie bawls.

A silhouette appears in the door. Outsider tall. Outsider thin. Ounserrat Soulereya, dressed in a pair of baggies and nothing else. The cat-monkey thing from hell is clinging to her side, like a cat-monkey thing from hell should. Its mouth is clamped to her single breast.

'You are awake at last, Mr Gillespie. I am glad. I am sorry that Graceland alarmed you.' She murmurs something in a language Gillespie does not understand. The thing on the tit looks up at her, blinks and twitters a response.

'What?'

'The doctor in the casualty department advised that you have rest to assist your recuperation. I was recovering from *kethba* so Ananturievo gave you some pills to make you sleep. I fear he may have given you too many.'

Lying on the back seat of the cop car, watching the street lights strobe through a pain so intense it was almost bliss. Feeling he'd brought the car seat with him, glued to his back, into the casualty department, into the cubicle, into the X-ray department, can't you see it?, I've got the back seat of a car rammed up my spine. Faces asking him his insurance details and when he couldn't provide them, trying to sell him a policy. Faces doing things at very great distances, with immensely long arms, like machines. Robot cleaning, robot bandaging, robot injecting. He remembers saying the word 'No' a lot to a policewoman in a beige coat who kept morphing into a vision of the Virgin Mary. No, no no, no charges. No pressing charges. Another car – a taxi – more lights, and something picking him up and leaving the back seat where it should remain and carrying him up endless stairs that smelled funny. Funny smelling stairs. Immensely long machine fingers, undressing him.

He's bollock naked, in a bed, in a room, in a flat, in a *planha*, in the Annadale Embankment Hold. He's freezing cold. There's what feel like fur under his ass. The bed is the room. It looks like it's grown from the walls. Several people could sleep in it together. Several people probably did. They like to sleep together, curled up in each other's body heat. Kiddy and Mummy and non-paternal Daddy and wur Andy. There were four in the bed and the little one said . . .

'Graceland?'

'I wanted it to have a human name as well as one in Narha. Is it not a fine designation?'

'Graceland.' The thing is looking at Gillespie now. Way too much knowing behind the slits of its eyes. It spits out the tit, scrambles down its mother and scurries across to the edge of the big bed. It props its chin on the fur mattress and stares at Andy Gillespie. 'What time of day is it?' he asks. He's not sure what way the light falls this side of the river, but it looks odd.

'It is sixteen o eight. You have been asleep for ten hours.

Fortunately, you avoided major injury or fracture of limbs, but you have sustained heavy bruising and contusion.'

He can't move. His muscles have locked. He looks at his hands gripping the edge of the silky white covering; they're swollen and black. He doesn't want them to be his. They don't look like the hands he knows. They look like vile black insects that have swallowed his good hands while he slept.

'I am not long awake and aware myself,' Ounserrat is saying as Andy Gillespie tries to lift the sheet and look at the damage down there without tearing himself into pieces of pain. Oh Jesus, it's a mess. 'It is a strain, going into *kethba*. And I was concerned about the blow I had taken to the belly. I had to monitor the state of the embryo.'

'You're pregnant?'

'Semi-pregnant. Graceland is one of a pair of twins, but I chose to bring only it to parturition. I am holding the other embryo in stasis until such time as I can afford to raise another infant.'

Semi-pregnancy. 'And is it, ah, all right?' Graceland's squealing something to its mother. Ounserrat speaks to it in the same familiar-yet-alien burble. Is there a Shian kid-speak? He thought they all learned Narha the way he learned Narha, through the chemicals. He can make out a word here, a word there, but they're either inappropriate or incongruous.

'All is well, Mr Gillespie. Lesbianism will be born whole and sound.'

'Lesbianism?' Some time he's going to be able to stop asking questions. But not quite yet. 'You have a name for a foetus?'

'It must be called something. It is at the stage where an identity is imprinted. The name spoke itself in a dream, while I was recovering energy after *kethba*.'

Gillespie tries to lie back in the huge bed that fills an entire room. Slow agonies. Is that a heartbeat he can feel underneath the soft, warm fur? The fucking thing's alive. Everything's flesh with these people. Then: 'Who hit us?'

'I suspect it was minions of Mr Gerry Conlon. While you were talking with your acquaintance, I noticed the club owner speaking on the telephone and looking in your direction.'

'Shit.' Then; for it's an afternoon of abrupt transitions, 'Shouldn't you be out delivering pizzas?'

'Not today. Not any day. I have been made unemployed by Pizza Di Action.'

'Ach, I'm sorry.' You and me, both touching bottom now. Heroes without a dime. It's never like this on the television. Perry Mason never has to worry about his bank balance.

'It is not so bad. I would have had to give it up soon anyway. The case is becoming demanding. The loss of income will affect us, but Not Afraid of the River will come to an agreement with this Hold to allow us to continue to reside here in the transients' hall.' Gillespie winces as he tries to sit upright. It takes a second for Ounserrat to read the expression. 'You are in pain, Mr Gillespie. Would you care for a painkiller? The doctor in the casualty department gave me a prescription. Ananturievo had it filled this morning at a dispensary before he went out to hunt. They are most powerful.'

'Actually, could you turn the heat up? I'm freezing my balls off in here.'

Ounserrat wrinkles her nose. Perplexed. Puzzled.

'Really? If anything we find this apartment too warm.'

'At least give me my clothes back, then.'

'They are being cleaned. But you are most welcome to borrow anything of ours that might fit.' And look like a nightmare drag queen. He pulls the pure white sheet around him. There're miles of it, like God's parachute. He tries to get up. Grit teeth. Close eyes. Shit.

'Mr Gillespie, this is not advisable.'

'I need to, you know. Go pee.'

'Do not trouble yourself, please. The bed will take care of it.'

'The bed?' Still no end in sight to the questions.

'Yes.'

They expect him to piss himself. A grown man, wetting the bed. Does it handle number twos as well? Probably, knowing these people.

'I think I will have that painkiller now.'

*

He sleeps without realizing he's slept and wakes in the dark. Same bed. Same room. Same smells. It was not a dream then. Ananturievo's home from the hunting. He's a couple of inches shorter than Ounserrat, otherwise the only distinction is his smell. It was the smell that woke Gillespie. Like fungus and whiskey. Gillespie remembers that smell quite well. The season is starting. He's brought two seagulls strung through the nostrils with a bootlace, and a Jack Russell terrier. He caught the seagulls down by the King's Bridge, and the terrier in the Ormeau Park. When the season comes no small animal is safe. Public parks become killing fields while the *kesh* chemicals are flowing. Dog walkers beware. Ounserrat examines the bag and feeds it to the protein converter in what had been a Housing Executive standard-issue fitted kitchen. In a couple of hours something like an edible turd will extrude from its sphincter.

Ananturievo's itchy, agitated. He can't stay still. He frets and rushes around the little flat while Gillespie eases himself out of the big fur bed and painfully gets dressed. Graceland clings to the Outsider's hip, protesting endlessly. Ananturievo's smell is everywhere, even on Andy Gillespie's freshly laundered clothes. It's the dancing, Ounserrat explains. It's harder for males. The hormones are harsh with them, and he is an early starter. Ounserrat follows him, smoothing his hair, stroking his skin. They throw streams of high-velocity syllables at each other. The words fly past Andy Gillespie, wrapped up in layers of shirts and socks and shawls and still warming his swollen fingers in his armpits. Words he thought he knew now seems to have a totally different meaning, while familiar names are replaced by unfamiliar. This is more than the mode Eamon Donnan used for the inadequacy of a word to fully express a concept. This is like a new language growing out of the one he understands. A forked tongue. But he doesn't ask them what they mean when they say a word. He holds himself at a distance, like a guest in a house where a married couple want desperately to have sex.

He takes himself out on to the balcony to lean painfully against the wall and see how the Annadale Embankment looks from a different side of the river to the one he's used to. How it looks from the inside. There's an ugliness to the wall of post-war red-brick public housing that the curves and sinuosities of Shian design cannot soften. They've hung their Hold and Nation banners from the balconies and stairwells, but the long swathes of fabric hang limp, barely stirring, hiding their emblems from the concrete. Down on the green in front of the flats, where they'd used to start building the Eleventh Night bonfire in April, and guarded it every night, rain or shine, things like tall, thin mushrooms grow. Twenty, thirty feet, their caps gleam in the street light along the embankment. Each one is a complete farm, capable of growing a Shian Hold's requirement of vegetables, meat and drink. Some of the old bonfires had reached thirty feet. The guards, he remembers, had always sat on leatherette sofas. The Electric Flats, they called them. He never knew why. The Electric Flats, and the Electric Houses. They demolished the Electric Houses and the Electric Flats are given over to aliens. He's known them under both occupancies and he's no doubt which tenants he prefers. Maybe the reason the Shian banners and the balcony gardens do not convince is because there is a deeper ugliness that decoration cannot erase. The ugliness of history. The ugliness of ugly men, who thought the things in their heads noble and beautiful. They'd beaten a woman to death in that flat over there, the one with the cat skins hanging out to cure, because they thought she was turning tricks out of it. He knew the boys did it. They felt no shame. They had done it for the community. Hard men, one woman. Result.

Then the Joint Authority move one Outsider Hold in, seven individuals and children, and overnight the hard men are gone. You can't push these people out like you could the Taigs. They've come sixty light years, they can't go home again, they are not going to be scared off by the lads. You intimidate them, you threaten their children, they intimidate you back. Harder. But it will still be a long time before the graffiti along the balcony walls fades. War by acronym. UFF. UYM. FTP. Rem 1690. B.1st FB. MUFC. No Surrender! Just letters to the Outsiders. Just letters to most of humanity. Good.

They are out in their streets and walkways tonight. There's something down at the south end of the flats that draws them; lights are shining, there're stray notes of music. There's something in the air he can't quite identify but it smells like electricity. You have thrown in your lot with these people, Andy Gillespie, these things that look like humans but aren't, but what do you know about them? What do they do of an evening, where do they go, how do they live? All you've ever seen of them is what they are like when there are humans around. You've never seen what they are like to themselves.

A cold wind is blowing around the river, meanders in off the sea. Chilled, Gillespie goes back into the room. Ananturievo is standing in the middle of the floor at the centre of a ring of bioluminescents. The chill is enough to make Gillespie's teeth chatter, but the Outsider's naked. He's shivering, but not with cold. Ounserrat is crouched at his feet. The child is clinging to her back. Ounserrat has a broad-tip black felt marker in her hand. Ananturievo is spastically licking his arm. He pauses and Ounserrat draws a scribble on his skin with the felt marker. He bends down to lick his thigh. No human could bend like that. Ounserrat draws a spiral. His body is already half-covered in black hieroglyphics. The smell is overpowering. Against his will, Gillespie can feel his lad stirring in his pants. His balls tighten. Disturbed by what he sees and his physical reaction to it, he retreats to the big warm bed. It is a living thing, he's discovered, grown for fit and comfort. He thinks of it as a dog, and so it's a companion for him, a pet. A live Jack Russell.

He examines his bruises. They're yellowing now. The pills keep the pain well down, so he can pretend he's really all right until he moves quickly. Then his body remembers. He dozes on the big dog-bed. He's woken a timeless time later by the warm poke and press of Graceland against his side. He's coming to terms with it. And it is an it. Ounserrat had politely corrected him: it won't be a he or a she until puberty. Just a kid, but it still spooks him. It's three months old, and it walks and talks and wants to know things. Proper kids aren't even kids at three months. They're babies. They blink and wave their fists and sleep and cry and shit. He's never heard this one cry, but it babbles constantly in its odd newborn-Narha.

Graceland feels for a nipple. Sorry, kid. Ounserrat comes into the bedroom and the thing slips off him and shinnies up her like a monkey.

'Good evening, Mr Gillespie. Ananturievo has just left for the dancing.'

'That's what the big do down the end of the flats is?'

'It is the opening of it, yes. A few males will meet there to practise and compete, but the females will not arrive for another few days yet. Maybe the rare early starter.'

As a way of getting girls it beats big cars, bottled beer and fights in the pub car park. Competition by display has to be easier than competition by combat. Clothes, that's the one point of similarity. And competition. Lead-foot Andy Gillespie wouldn't have got very far. Lead-foot Andy didn't anyway. Even the clothes looked wrong on him.

'I am thinking, maybe you are hungry,' Ounserrat says. 'Our food is not very palatable to you. If you like, I will go out and buy something.'

'Not pizza.'

'No, that would be ironic. There is a shop on the big road does very good chips. I could fetch you a fish with it.'

'Salt. No vinegar.'

'We shall eat it together. It will be many hours before Ananturievo returns, if at all.'

'He may get lucky.'

Ounserrat puts on her street clothes and leaves Graceland clinging to Andy Gillespie's thigh. She's back ten minutes later with a fish supper, an extra portion of chips, and a six pack of Harp. The furniture in the big room doesn't fit Andy Gillespie, so they sit on the floor. Ounserrat pulls off her too-hot streetwear, down to a green ribbed body. Gillespie wraps himself in the bed sheet and slooters ketchup over his fish. Graceland winkles chips out of the foam styrene tray and sucks them down. The child burbles to itself.

'What's it saying?' Gillespie gets the preposition right and pops a tinnie. 'It's like Narha, but the words don't make sense.'

Ounserrat stirs a soluble aspirin into a glass of water with a long forefinger.

'It is indeed Narha.'

'Not the Narha I learned.'

She's giving him that look again. Hey, who's the stranger on this world?

'How is it that you speak Narha like one born to it, Mr Gillespie?'

The scent of memory. It's all chemicals in the end, little bits of bits of things. Little bits of bits of Ananturievo haunt the corners of the big cold room and draw him back to that other spring, a year ago – one year, God, so much in so little time? He had been cold all the time in there. They'd heated the place like a furnace, but he couldn't get warmth into him. He still can't, he never could. Destined for the cold. The cold, the smell, the strange cries in the dark corridors. The spring, the season. Another time, another season, it would have been all right. Bits of bits of things – lives, season, chemicals – come together and make what they will make.

He's never told anyone about it. Those who knew, knew because they were part of it. Players, or victims. But they were part and so all they know is part. Only he and Eamon Donnan know it all, and Donnan's gone alien. No word in Narha for guilt, Eamon Donnan said. That gets him out of it. So it's all yours now. But if there is no guilt among the Shian, why don't you tell this Outsider sitting in front of you eating chips? She will not blame you. She will not punish you for what you failed to do. No one can punish as much as you've punished yourself, Andrew Gillespie. Just carrying it around, this huge sack of shit, like it's precious treasure, like it's a beautiful baby, isn't that punishment enough? Maybe if she tells you you did nothing wrong, you might start to believe it and maybe you could put this big bag of shit down and dare to look into it and see that perhaps it isn't old, dark, fermented shit at all, but just bits of bits of things that fell around you in a certain way.

Why not? What the hell have you got to lose? Why choose silence over speaking?

'How I come to speak Narha. Do you people like to tell tales?'

Graceland has eaten all the chips and is now trying to eat the styrene tray. Ounserrat takes it off it.

'We have old song and dance cycles, many thousands of years old. Tales of lust and hunting, and righting wrongs.'

'We're supposed to be a nation of story-tellers. We're supposed to gather around the fireside and listen to some old fart tell some long and stupid "Come here 'til I tell you" tale about the ould days. They're always about living in the counthery, in nineteen and twelve and all that shit. Never about living in the city. Never about living here and now. Never about you people. But they should be. This one is; my tale. I'm no story-teller, but at least it's true.'

Ounserrat picks up Graceland and presses a finger behind its left ear. The child immediately falls asleep. Ounserrat cradles it in her lap.

'One funny thing about humans, we like to think everything's connected. Everything means something, is part of something. Some folk call it God, to some it's fate, to some it's coincidence.' Jesus, I even look like Mother Macree, wrapped in shawls. 'Sometimes we get an idea of what this fate is going to be. Like I knew the moment I heard on the radio that you people had arrived that my life was going to be involved with you. Whatever I did, wherever I went, it would always come back to you.

'You see, when I heard on the radio that the American space mission had found your Fifteenth Fleet out at Jupiter, I was driving for a job on a drugs dealer. I was waiting in the car on Tower Street and there it was, on the news. I was waiting for three boys with shot guns in their sports bags and suddenly nothing could ever be the same again and I thought, what is this all about? What the hell are we doing that's so fucking important? Maybe I lost it deliberately, maybe that was in the back of my mind, that you had come and everything we thought was important was just stupid, maybe that was why I crashed the car.

'I can still see that kid, that wee girl. She went straight out through the back window. Like an angel, in this glittering cloud of glass. You have angels?'

'Some of the *hahndahvi* are like your angels.' Ounserrat has been drawing in the ring of biolights, closer, more intimate. 'Some of them are defiantly not.'

165

'I got five years. Her Majesty's Prison, Cellular, Maze. By the time I came out it was His Majesty's Prison, Cellular, Maze. My own reason to be thankful for Joint Authority: they had a general amnesty for paramilitary-related crimes. Some of the hard men, the Loyalist ones, refused to be released, because they wouldn't accept freedom if it came from Dublin. Jesus. They had to throw the bastards out. Not me. I'm Joint Authority's number one fan.

'What's it like? It's not losing having things, or privacy, or freedom; you grow up on the Woodstock Road, nobody has anything, everyone knows everything about you, everyone owns a bit of you, everyone's opinions about you matter more than your opinions about yourself. It's being scared. Yeah, that's what it is. Always scared. Big scared, little scared, always scared. You wake up scared, you go to bed scared, you sleep scared and dream scared. Scared of everything, all the time; scared something will happen to you, scared someone will do something to you; hurt you, try to stick it up you, take something from you, say something about you, make you do something you don't want to do. Scared that just when you think you've got it sorted – got your own little place, nice job, good mates, learning something, making something, got some money – it'll all change. There'll be new faces, and you'll have to learn what they want, and teach them what you want. What you want most is just to be left alone, but they won't do that. No one ever leaves you alone. Maybe you get to earn a bit of space, a bit of respect, but you won't be left alone.

'I think I had a headache all the time I was in that place. Tension. Scared, that's what it was. Neck muscles like iron bars. All the bad things you get on the outside you get on the inside ten times worse. The war-lords were organizing their wee gangs: orange and green, battalions and companies and officers and volunteers and saluting and all that fucking army shit. They weren't cons, you see. Oh no; they were Prisoners of War. They painted their wee coats of arms on the walls; wankers in black balaclavas with Armalites and shit about Sometimes Honour Is Like The Hawk, It Must Go Hooded; Let My Last Shot Be For God And Ulster. The green stuff was the same; just different *hahndahvi*. The bosses had heard I'd been on the edges of the paramilitaries, so they all had to have me. I didn't want anything to do with their toy soldiers; Jesus, there were *aliens*, folk from sixty light years away, wanting to come and live among us. In Holy Mother Ulster, for God's sake. Lucky for me, some of the boys from the job went in with me at the same time; Big Maun, and Soup Campbell. They told the bosses that I fucked up and got them busted and that they couldn't trust me to do it right. They lost interest in me then.

'I'd done a year when Mehishhan came.'

'That is a Shian name,' Ounserrat Soulereya says. She has moved closer, to the edge of fingertip range. Her private musk has a longer reach. But cold Andy Gillespie isn't afraid of it. He isn't afraid of her, or her child, or her people, now. He wants her to move closer still.

'He was a Harridi, a *genro*, like you. He got banged up for perverting the course of justice. He really couldn't see he'd done anything wrong. He hadn't a fucking idea why he was in there.'

'What had he done?'

'Followed the Shian law further than human law allows. Then when the cops brought it to court he had some big argument with the judge. His client got off. He got six months. So I know all about this price of the Shian law you keep warning me about. Fucking judge had to ask him what sex he was so he could decide which jail to send him to. He shouldn't have been in there. The screws didn't want him there; they hadn't a clue what to do with him. They gave him a room on his own, down the end of my block, well away from everyone else, but they were all scared of him. Everyone was scared of him. Even the hard-liners. Scared they would catch something, or he'd try some kind of weird perversion on them. They thought because he wasn't a man like them he was queer. He was always smiling at them, they thought he fancied them. They didn't know a thing. But they couldn't lay a finger on him. They got one of their big lads to try and teach him good manners, but he was too fast. He was like you, last night. And he did that thing you did.'

'*Kethba.*'

'That. Yeah. So they sent him to Coventry. He didn't mind. He didn't need them. He read a lot. He was never out of the library. Everyone else would be down the gym, he was reading. All hours. All the classics. I suppose he was trying to find out what it was about humans that they had to have a place like the Maze. He used to go to classes.'

'This is a place where humans have their rights removed by the law, and they can read books and receive education?' Ounserrat asks.

'And better food than outside, and exercise, and free medical care, and watch television and listen to the radio. Costs more to keep a man in the Maze for a week than to keep him at the Europa Hotel.'

Ounserrat blinks that blink. I'm blinking that blink too, Andy Gillespie thinks.

'Anyway, he went to these classes – the teachers asked him more questions than he asked them. That's where I met him. I'd been thinking for a long long time about myself – it's good for that I suppose, the Maze – and how letting things move me along, just going along with other people with no ideas of my own, had ended me up. You see, I'd never had a real idea of what I wanted to do, everything I did was just, well, OK. I was doing it because it was something to do and I couldn't think of anything better. Same with my mates; I didn't really like them, I wasn't really interested in what they were interested in, but they were better than nothing. Never really fitted. Same with the job; I got into cars because it was there and it was easy and the money was OK. I didn't really like it. Cars wasn't really what I wanted to do. I just drifted into things. Ended up drifted into five years. Right, Andrew Gillespie. No more drifting. Do what you want. What do you like? Well, at school all the other kids thought I was weird because I liked reading. Most of them lived in houses where the television went on first thing in the morning and off last thing at night, the most they ever read was the *Sun*. No kid wants to be weird, especially in Euston Street Primary School, so I gave up reading and went and kicked a ball against a wall, but it wasn't what I really wanted. It was boring as hell, kicking a ball against a wall. So, I'm banged up and I'm thinking, what do I really want to do? And I remember, well, I liked reading. And I'm sure as shit coming out of this place different from when I went in – and I don't just mean older – so I stick my name down for a university degree in English. English literature. And off I go to classes. There was me, another guy called Eamon Donnan, a wee skinny lad who was in for drugs, for fuck's sake, and Mehishhan Harridi.'

Ounserrat is closer to him now. They're sitting in the right-angle configuration that psychologists say is best for threat-free, intimate communication. She has taken his hand and is examining it, worrying out the dirt under his nails, smoothing down roughs of cuticle, tracing the grooves of his knuckles and the lie of the hairs on the backs of his knuckles. And it's all right. He doesn't flinch from it the way he would flinch when Karen tried to stroke him, because there it meant something and here it's just touching.

'After a couple of weeks Eamon and I both realized that what we were interested in wasn't Thomas Hardy and your woman who did all those books about marrying ministers for money. It was them, you, him. The Outsiders. The Shian. Why? Maybe because he was what I'd always felt. An outsider. Not part. Different. Weird. The ultimate weird kid ... For Eamon, I don't know. I've seen him, since. He's living over in the Harridi Hold on Queen's Quay. I think with him it's the opposite of how it was with me. With Eamon, he needs to be part. He wanted something to belong to. He didn't want to be an outsider.' But now he is. Both ways.

'There are humans like this at home in Docklands,' Ounserrat says. Her fingers are very delicate. Their tips are soft and warm. So long Andy Gillespie's been working with the Shian, and he's never noticed that their fingernails are narrow and pointed. Hunting claws. They're tracing the lines in the palm of his hand. Those are my past and future. Another part of the human need to connect everything with webs of meaning. Are your hands empty? Just hands?

'We were real cautious to begin with. Worse than asking a girl out, we didn't know what to say, or how he would react, or if he'd want to have anything to do with us. I'm still not sure what he thought of us, if we were friends, if he liked us, if he trusted us even. But he was willing to talk, and we were more than willing to listen. Eamon wanted to know about what it was like to be a Shian; their – sorry, your – history, your Hearthworld, the World Ten Migration, what kind of people you are, how you live, all that. For me, it was the law interested me. Everyone in jail's always interested in the law. I suppose they want to know how it got them in there. I was interested in a legal system that could put the lawyer in jail while his client walks. What I couldn't get was how he was so cool about the whole thing. Talk to twenty cons, fifteen'll tell you they shouldn't be in there, they're innocent, the police stitched them up, it's a fucking miscarriage of justice. Mehishhan, he didn't seem to mind. It was like he was almost happy to be there.'

'It is the *gehenshuthra*, the personal contract between *genro* and client.'

'I know that now. But then, Jesus. It didn't make sense. He made it make sense. He told me about how the Shian law is based on individual rights, and how one set of rights can violate another, and that the job of the law is to reconcile those sets of rights and I thought, what a fucking sensible system, not like our law, where you owe it everything and it owes you nothing and just when you think you get something the government changes the law and moves the goalposts and takes it away again. An unwritten constitution isn't worth the paper it's printed on. He explained about how the law was always between people, even the lawyers, and that they could get burned by it same as anyone else – maybe more. I'm telling you, my brief back when I was up in court would've put a hell of a lot more work into it if it'd been his ass in the Maze. Mehishhan told me about the stones, the white ones for guilt and the black ones for innocence; and the staff and that it was a thing from thousands of years back when the path finder would lead the Hold to new hunting grounds and mark the way with scent from the staff.'

'It has evolved in sophistication since then,' Ounserrat says. Her fingers are finding fascinations in his wrist, the swell of the blood tubes. When Karen had played there he had always snatched his hand away. The juice of him was too close to the surface. But this Outsider does it and it's OK. More: good.

'It saved my fucking life, my friend.'

'Mr Gillespie, do you have difficulty speaking my given name to my face?'

'Do you have difficulty speaking mine?'

'I have only known you four days, Mr Gillespie.'

But you've slept beside me in your skin, we're sitting side by side in sort-of candlelight and drinking our drinks and your fingers are doing tricks that, if we were people, would be an invitation to sex. Except that it isn't. It's a kind of loving, but not a kind of sexing. That's why I can bear you doing it.

'Mehishhan taught me the Shian law, and I thought, yeah, this makes sense, it's simple, it's good, it's responsible, this is what I want to do when I get out, this is the thing I've been looking for, because it's me, on my own, using my own abilities. When I was a kid I'd always wanted to be a knight. But how the hell does a human become a Shian lawyer? Well, you start with what you see around you every day. Donnan and I took on our own sort of *gehenshuthra* with Mehishhan. We would be his knight-advocates, though I think Donnan loved him. He didn't need minding, but we minded him anyway. Thanks for what he'd given us; maybe to show him men weren't complete animals. Weren't knights supposed to be noble and good; chivalry, all that shit?

'I don't know what it's like for you folk to travel through space in those big ships of yours, but I imagine that being in the Maze is sort of like it. All crammed together, shit-scared, nothing outside. Inside, everything you get from outside seems fake. We're all supposed to really value visitors and contact with the outside, but what it's really like is a television programme you switch on once a week and switch off and it disappears. No outside. No world, no change, no seasons. You look out your window one morning, there's snow on the ground, Jesus, it's winter. Another morning, you hear birds singing, it's spring. Doesn't matter. There's nothing you can do with it. But it mattered to Mehishhan. He knew about it. He smelled it coming.

'We didn't know, you see. We thought it was us. He'd be talking about something or other, and I'd find I wasn't concentrating, I couldn't follow what he was saying, and I was pissed off with him about this, like it was his fault I'd lost his attention.

Or you'd just want him to shut up for once, or someone in the library had taken out the book you wanted and that was the end of the fucking world, or the guy in the upstairs bunk would have his Walkman on but you could hear his music coming out of the headphones dish-di-di-dish-dish and you wanted to strangle him with the wire. The number of times I would look at Eamon Donnan and find I was thinking, you fucking fool, look at you sitting there thinking you're an alien. like you're really special and there's never been anything quite like you before on the face of the earth and in fact you're just a little wanker from Andystown. Jesus, I want to smash your face into that table. I know now he was thinking the same things about me.'

'Mr Gillespie,' Ounserrat Soulereya says, 'you have made your hands into fists.' She touches them. They open.

'Within a week we'd all caught it. Jesus, the place was like a landmine, waiting for one wrong step to set it off. Eat each other's faces off the least wee thing. Fights every night; folk making knives and things. The governor thought it was the warlords, stirring it up, trying for a takeover. He'd break a room up, move prisoners. Of course they stopped the moment they moved to another block and the new boys moved right into it. He didn't have a clue. Neither did we.'

'Humans are susceptible to Shian *kesh* pheromones.'

'Yeah. Both female and male. The male pheromones make us men aggressive. Some kind of competitive reaction, so the Littlejohns say. I know what it is now, but it's hard to fight the chemicals. I even get it a bit off Ananturievo. I'm kind of irritable when he's around.'

'And what do the female pheromones do?' Ounserrat asks. Her thin hands have moved to his neck, hunting out the memories of old anger in the muscles.

'Turn us on,' Andy Gillespie says. Third thing he remarked about Ounserrat Soulereya, after the pizza and the leather: that turn-head, sad-lost-woman smell. Left his flat full of her musk. And in the Welcome Centre it had been so strong he couldn't concentrate. But now he realizes he doesn't smell it any more. He doesn't smell it because it's inside him. He swallows something that's appeared in his throat that's not a clot of perfume.

'The air conditioning was blowing Mehishhan's pheromones all over the block,' he says. 'Everyone was running at about eight million degrees. One word, one look, and they'd fight. Every day someone ended up in hospital, but the fighting was because we couldn't get what it was really about. What it was really about was cunt. Fuck, or die trying.

'It was in the library, at half twelve. I remember, I won't ever forget it. We were in our corner by the window, at our table. Mehishhan was telling us about his birth Hold returning to the Hearth from World Four, and then the door burst open and in they came. Twelve of them, carrying bits of wood they'd knocked off from the joinery shop. That man I was talking to at the frook club, Gavin Peterson, he was there. Jesus, I can still see the bastard. The screw was up and out of there like shit off a shovel – he must have been thinking, Christ, the whole place's going to blow. They came right over to our table. Didn't say a word, not one word. I wanted to fight them. Twelve of them, big bits of wood, and I'd've taken them all on. They'd have fucking killed me, and I think maybe there was one wee bit of sense left in my head that the pheromones hadn't fucked up that made me stand back. I shouldn't have. I should have let them kill me. They came in, the twelve of them, and they lifted Mehishhan. He didn't make a move to stop them. They picked him right up and the weird thing is – I can remember this exactly – when they came in, there was total silence, not a word, not a sound, nothing, and when they got their hands on Mehishhan suddenly they all start cheering and singing and they're running off down the corridor with him and cheering and howling.

'They took him to the gym. They made a big pile of crashmats, and bent him over it, and then made another big pile on top of him and piled a couple of the lads on top of that, just in case he got some idea about doing that *kethba* trick, and then they all took turns to fuck him up the ass. They were clapping and cheering and shouting 'In, in, in, in,' and going 'Yo!' when someone came and I stood in the door and watched. I stood in the door and watched them stick it up him and I didn't do a fucking thing. Didn't lift a fucking finger. They were singing. They were singing Loyalist songs: "The Sash" and "Derry's

173

Walls" and "Give Me Bullets In My Gun, Keep Me Shooting" and "The Twelfth of July in the Morning" and the fucking National Anthem. God save our gracious King, Long live our noble King, God save the King. Send him victorious, happy and glorious, long to reign over us, God save our King. Everyone got to have a go before the screws came with the riot gear. There was come dribbling out his asshole; there was a pool of the stuff on the floor, they were slipping and sliding on it and they were laughing their heads off, and I just stood there and I watched.

'They had an inquiry, made a report. The bastards who did it lost remission, Mehishhan got a separate room over in the governor's block with its own closed airconditioning system, even though the season had ended and he wasn't giving off any funny fumes. Took me days to get the courage to go and see him. You see, I was his protector, his *genro*, me and Eamon Donnan, and we let them get him. We let them do that to him. We – I failed him. But you can't see that, can you? How can I explain it to you? It would be like – yes, it's exactly like this – it would be like you let someone hurt that kid there. How would you feel about that?'

Her fingers have been working their way like little creatures, coming, going, over his head. They freeze among the short stubble. Her low voice is shockingly intimate in his ear.

'Mr Gillespie, I would kill whoever hurt my child.'

Pour petrol on them, set them on fire. That's your way.

'But how would you feel? Would you feel you had failed? Would you feel you'd done something wrong?'

She sits back, looks into his eyes. Her cat's eyes are wide open in the dim light.

'Is this guilt, Mr Gillespie?'

'It's part of guilt.'

She cocks her head to one side. It's a strange, animal gesture. Andy Gillespie can't read it, doesn't like it.

'I went to see him. He looked like shit. He'd lost weight – you folk are skinny, but you could see the bones. His hair had gone yellow, like he'd bleached it with toilet cleaner or something. He smelled really weird. He wouldn't talk to me. Sat a whole hour, close as you and me, not one fucking word. The governor called me in. Me and Donnan were the nearest things the Maze had to Shian experts. He wasn't eating. He hadn't eaten a thing since. He wasn't drinking neither. Or sleeping, or anything. He hadn't moved or pissed or shat in a week, just sat in this nest of blankets on the floor. And he hadn't spoken a word to anyone. They were shit scared of another hunger-strike, only this time with an Outsider.'

'This was not a hunger-strike,' Ounserrat says. Her fingers are doing things with the backs of his ears.

'I know that now. And I know that he didn't blame us for anything, because he broke the rules for us. He spoke to us at the end. You're not supposed to do that. You're supposed to go silently. With great dignity. It's an ancient and honoured tradition. You even have a name for it: *deheensheth*. Jesus, you people. But I think he broke the rules about silence also because everything else was broken. We sat with him for hours, Donnan and me; we watched him go down, hour by hour. It was like he was eating himself, from the inside. Willing himself to death. We tried to talk him out of it, make him see sense, human things like that. It was Eamon got it first: he was just bringing his body into line with his soul. He couldn't understand what they'd done to him, those bastards. They'd killed what he was, his Shian-ness, his spirit. He was dead, the meat was just running down to join him.'

'Rape was a strange lesson for us,' Ounserrat says. Graceland is dreaming in her lap, twitching and muttering. 'The violence of one sex against another is most alien to us; at first, we thought *men* and *women* were different species. You do not even look alike, how can you be attracted to anything so different? And for one sex to be larger and stronger than the other, and be able to force intercourse on the smaller, less strong sex; this is quite horrifying.'

'It's all chemicals with you. Nothing goes up or comes down without the right chemical signal. So everything's always good and right and when you want it and how you want it. Vanilla sex.'

'Are you using ironic/satirical mode, Mr Gillespie?'

'I'm using fucking disgusted with my own sex mode, *genro*

Soulereya. There are women say all men are potential rapists. I used to laugh at them; fucking Malone Road tight-arse Queen's University bitches; half of you probably dream about it. Then I watched them rape something that isn't even human, something the same sex as themselves, another male, and I saw that it isn't sex at all, it's nothing to do with sex. It's power. It's being bigger and stronger and saying, I can do this to you and you can't do a fucking thing about it. It's nothing to do with your dick. It's the size of your fist. And if it made me feel this, what the hell must it have made Mehishhan Harridi feel?'

'Like death,' Ounserrat Soulereya whispers in Andy Gillespie's ear.

'You got no word for guilt, but you sure as hell got one for shame.' The fingers are at his neck again, pushing out the male rage. 'We watched him will himself to death. He didn't seem to be in any pain, most of the time he looked like he was somewhere else, inside his head. Talking with the *hahndahvi*, picking one to guide him to his next life. I don't know. Anyway, one night, way about two o'clock in the morning, I get banged up out of my bunk by a warder. Seems Mehishhan Harridi wants to talk to me. Two o'clock in the morning. I'm there and Eamon Donnan's there and in we go and he's sitting there in that pile of blankets like a skeleton wrapped in old leather stinking like God knows. Jesus, one look, we knew it wasn't long. He can hardly talk, but he tells us he has something he wants to give us, something important, something rare and valuable. He asks us to kneel in front of him, and then he bends forward and kisses us, on the mouth. I feel something slip into my mouth but before I can spit it out or boke it up, it's shot up the back of my nose and I'm trying to sneeze the thing out but it's like it's clinging up there, in my sinuses. I'm thinking, what the fuck?, but he sits back and closes his eyes and never moves again. He dies a couple of hours later. Next morning I wake up, and there're words in my head. More than words, sentences, grammar; a whole fucking language. Narha. He's given me and Donnan his language.'

And that's the tale of how Andy Gillespie learned Narha. It ends there, but it's not complete. There's much more to it, but the for ever after is made up of guilt and regret and things for which there are no words in Narha. And there is much more in it, but they're things you can't say to an Outsider even if she is running her fingers over your skin, so close you can taste her breath. A species born to just walk away won't understand the long ache of a man who either loses or gives away every valuable thing he ever had. Forgive me for this, forgive me for being a mad bad bastard, forgive me for getting into these things I have to get out of. But you can't. To you it's nothing wrong to lose partner, child, family, home, friends, jobs, ambitions. Just walk out on to the hunting path and turn your face to the north wind. But I can't live that free. I walk, but I'm guilty. Every footstep says, this man done wrong. The five people who were the nearest thing I have to a family are dead, and this time I'm not going to walk away. I'm going to stay, and this man'll do right, this time.

'Except that he didn't give you and Eamon Donnan the whole fucking language,' Ounserrat Soulereya says. Her voice is very quiet, but her words shatter Andy Gillespie's reflection.

'You what?'

'You only have half the language. This is why I asked you how you learned to speak Narha. You speak it as well as any human might, for you learned it the way we learn it, through the chemicals, but you only learned part of it.'

'What do you mean?'

'*Kesh* changes everything. Our bodies, our minds, our relationships, our society, the words on our tongues. We have two Narhas. One is the language of every day, of the cool seasons, the other is the language of *kesh*. The names for things change, sometimes the name remains the same but the thing changes. Grammars change, tenses change. We have genders for things in Hot Narha that we do not in Cool Narha. He, she, his, hers. Chair: she. Light: he. Floor: he. Walls: she. Food: she. Drink: he. The *kesh* hormones change the words in our heads; one set of chemicals is reinforced, the other suppressed. The *genro* Mehishhan was out of season when he secreted a *souljok*, therefore what he gave you was Cool Narha. A week before – even a few days – and he would have given you Hot Narha.'

Half a language. All the time walking around thinking he

knew it all, he could say anything to anyone, and he was speaking with forked tongue. But how could you know? How can you think about language, except in language?

'That's what Graceland is burbling on in. That's why I can't understand half of what you and Ananturievo say to each other,' Andy Gillespie says, but he is thinking about language again. He is thinking about the Insufficient Vocabulary mode Eamon Donnan used in the Queen's Island sacred space, when he said that Littlejohn was a fool. He would have learned to speak with a whole tongue. Hot and Cold. Maybe the thing he couldn't translate was something that can only be said in Hot Narha.

He knows what the next question has to be, and he knows in his gut and in his balls what the answer will be, but he must ask it.

'How do I learn Hot Narha?'

'From me.'

Suddenly he realizes he isn't cold any more. He can hear music, distant drums. Like a far-off Orange parade. No flutes massacring great tunes. The dancing's started. On the other side of the river a lone car alarm is yelling.

'How?'

'Like a child.'

How else? It won't mean anything. None of it has, or will. She can't help it, and you won't make something of it that it isn't.

'Teach me.'

Ounserrat sits back. She slips her arms out of the green body suit, pulls it down to her waist. Her breast is swollen, leaking milk and wisdom from the teat. She presses her body close against Gillespie's. Her meat is fever-hot. Gillespie lifts the long, thin breast and gently takes the nipple in his mouth.

Roisin Dunbar has a professional resolution never to be murdered. It's not the thought of dying violently she hates – she hates the thought of dying in any way. It's ending up on the pure Protestant porcelain of Belfast City Morgue. Indignity enough to have died violently and been taken away by the police in a black bag, like so much rubbish. Post mortem is the second indignity, the second death. Naked, vulnerable, helpless, you lie under the lights, open for examination. In the first death you might have tried to stop your killer, fight him off, put up a struggle. In the first death all he did was kill you. In the second death they come with their power saws and scalpels and forceps and they do whatever they want for as long as they want. And when they are satisfied, they bag you, tag you, slide you into a hole in the wall and sluice your juice away with the overhead shower sprays. Spiral pinkly down the plughole. Like the shower in the Bates Motel. This is no chocolate sauce.

Dear Police God, let me die a copper's death: fat and fermented and boozy, with a margarita slipping from my fingers to smash on the sun terrace of the sea-view retirement haciendas in the hills behind Fuengirola. Let twenty grandchildren fly in for the funeral, let them weep, let them curse me to hell when they find out I've spent their inheritance on drink and golf lessons. Grant me a gentleman's death, not a player's.

Funny; Michael doesn't feature in this memento mori.

'Absolutely no other possibility?'

Barbara Hendron unpeels her rubber gloves with sharp, sadomasochistic twackings. She gives Willich the same look of expert condescension Littlejohn uses. They must read the same crime books.

'Unless we've just discovered spontaneous detonation. Like

179

spontaneous combustion, only more dramatic. And whoever did this knows about the mutilations you wanted kept secret.'

The green-scrubbed assistants smirk as they do their things with trolleys and sacks.

'They'd been dead how long when we found them?'

'Couple of hours. They'd hardly even started to cool. It'll all be in the report.'

'Sunday evening, people everybloody where and no one sees a thing? Who is this, the invisible fucking man?'

'We've checked the door-dog's memory,' Roisin Dunbar says. 'Nothing on it, or the security cameras.'

'Except the bastard walked right into their conservatory and blew their heads off.'

'We think we have footprints. Forensic is running them through a neural net.'

'Littlejohn, are you absolutely sure that an Outsider couldn't have done this?' Willich asks.

Grasping at straws. Willich may not be Roisin Dunbar's contender for the police brain of the century, but she doesn't like seeing her boss have to eat Littlejohn's shit by admitting that the weapons-running theory is as fucked as Pastor McIvor Kyle.

'I keep telling you: their biology makes them incapable of this kind of sexually motivated violence. They're peaceable non-aggressive folk, unless you threaten their children.'

'Maybe Kyle knocked a kiddy off his tricycle or something,' Dunbar says. She needs to be flip in this Godawful place.

'A human did this. A human male. The most dangerous creature on the planet, or any other for that matter, is the young, unattached human male.'

'Like Mr Andrew Gillespie,' Roisin Dunbar says. Littlejohn looks at her. That smarter-than-thou look again.

'The Amazing Invisible Mr Andrew Gillespie?' he says. 'Who, despite getting the tripe knocked out of him, manages to haul himself up the Antrim Road, slip, unseen by half a dozen security devices, into the house, and blow the entire family away?'

'But it's not the entire family.' Barbara Hendron's voice is as shocking as a concrete slab falling from a roof. 'There's a son. He's at university.'

'McIvor Junior.' Roisin Dunbar remembers reading about it in a Pro-Union free sheet she can't stop dropping through her door five mornings a week. 'He's up at Coleraine.'

'Media studies. My daughter's on the course with him. He's got a room in the same unit as her.'

Dunbar's mobile is already open.

Chief Inspector Willich is driving back to the station like a maniac. He insisted. He's got a police licence, Roisin hasn't. His woo-woos are on and his lights are flashing, but Belfast traffic has no respect for police sirens. Too many times they put them on to get to the burger shop quicker. Belted in in the front, Roisin Dunbar's got cramp in her left foot from stamping on brakes that aren't there. Road kill is an alternative route to the big porcelain slab. Littlejohn in the back is wearing exactly the expression Woody Allen wears in *Annie Hall* when spooky Christopher Walken drives him to the airport.

Roisin Dunbar's mobile rings. Willich switches off the woo-woos. Roisin Dunbar says, 'Ah-hah' and 'Uh-huh' and 'OK' and 'You do that'. Then she folds up her mobile and puts it on the dash.

'Michael,' she says to the pale faces. 'Louise is running a bit of a temperature and he's calling the doctor.'

Shit shit shit shit shit.

Willich switches the sirens on again, but the traffic down the Ormeau Road still won't take him seriously.

The mobile rings again.

'Yah.' The sirens go off, again. 'Ah-hah.' Littlejohn is leaning forward, trying to overhear the twitter in Dunbar's ear. 'Uh-huh.' Long silence. Big twitter. 'OK. Thanks.' She sighs and seems to crumple in the front seat. She very slowly puts the mobile back in its place on the dash.

'They got him too,' she says. 'The Coleraine force went to his room. It was locked, they broke it down. Exactly the same.'

'Hell,' Willich says. 'And let me guess, a student hall of residence, and no one saw anything or heard anything.'

'The others on the corridor reckoned he was late back from the weekend or something. Scene of crime reckon he'd been there two days.'

'Two days?' Littlejohn says. 'When two days ago, morning, evening, night?'

'They won't know until they've done a pm,' Roisin Dunbar says. I know what you're driving at Littledick, because I'm there with you. While party unknown was blowing McIvor Jnr's skull up like a dropped melon, prime suspect Andy Gillespie's every movement was being observed and recorded and they did not include day excursions to Coleraine.

'Littlejohn,' Willich says, 'I need a suspect.'

'Eamon Donnan.'

'The one's gone Sheenie, over in Queen's Island?' They stop at the lights on the Ormeau Bridge. The pedestrian light is green, foot traffic is crossing. An Outsider passes in front of the car from the park gate side, with a back pack inside which things seem to be moving like fighting rats.

'He was in the Maze with Gillespie, and Gavin Peterson. I've been doing some research into what went on in there. You might remember – it made the news – that a Shian lawyer – a *genro* – fell foul of the majesty of law pursuing personal justice for his client a tad over-zealously and got sent down for six months. He was a Harridi, same sept as the University Street ones. Gillespie and Donnan befriended him, they got close. In Donnan's case, maybe too close. Maybe a little over-enamoured with the condition of being alien. Anyway, there was an incident – *kesh* chemicals in a confined environment, the place was like a pressure cooker full of testosterone – and the Shian died. There was an inquiry. It's different nowadays, but they'd only been here a couple of years and none of us really knew anything.'

The lights have changed and the car is on the bridge now. Dunbar glances out of her window at the flags and emblems flying from Annadale Hold. Whole family murder; the horrifying, implacable premeditation of the hunter. The thing that will not stop until it has completed its task.

'You think this Eamon Donnan is getting his own back?' Willich asks.

'Nothing so simple. Human male sexuality is a fragile and frightening thing. Bend it out of shape, everything else bends with it.'

Willich drives up the tail of a pony and trap laden with old forklift pallets and flashes his lights to intimidate the tinker holding the reins.

'All right. Eamon Donnan is now our prime suspect.'

They can see the crowd from the bottom of the Pass. Up at the station both sides of the street are lined with bodies. Light glints from lenses: journalists. Uniforms clear the hacks from the car park gates. Hands wave tape recorders at the windows. Voices are shouting about confirmation of rumours and Antrim Road.

'Well, someone's found something out from somewhere,' Willich says as the uniform swings the barrier down behind the car. The press mobs them across the road from the car park. First time Roisin Dunbar's had fifty men barking after her. And women too. They're waving machinery in her face and shouting the same question in different phrasings: can she confirm that police raids on premises and property of the Dissenting Presbyterian Church are connected with the University Street killings?

'Sergeant Dunbar, can you confirm that you're investigating Pastor McIvor Kyle in connection with the Outsider Welcome Centre murders? Is he in custody?'

No, he's lying in the mortuary up at Foster Green Hospital. His wife's on one side of him, his daughter's on the other. Just like all those photographs you took of him on the steps of Faith Cathedral. Family values unto the last. She puts her head down, Diana style, walks on. Willich stops at the security gate and turns to talk to the news.

'I can confirm that we are holding Gavin Peterson, Rev Kyle's Security agent, pending further inquiries,' he says. 'We will be making a full press statement later today clarifying the situation.' As he follows Dunbar and Littlejohn into the station he adds sotto voce, 'When we've got Eamon Donnan's backside in the next cell down.'

*

The cars are going out again from Donegal Pass. The usual agents of the law are in them – even Darren Healey. EU paternity leave bows to police expedience. There are vans this time, with uniforms in them. Queen's Island Hold is a big, alien country, with many places to hide between the detritus of failed heavy industry and the new habitations and agri-industrial plants. They go by a back gate; they are halfway down to the Ormeau Road by the time the journalists realize something is happening without them. The press breaks camp and gives chase in a flotilla of hatchbacks. Potential scandals involving ministers of God, born-again terrorists and aliens are unmissable copy.

The line of cars goes along Cromac Street into Victoria Street. But this time it does not shed cars at each junction. This time all the vehicles go over the bridge to the quay. They're driving fast. They like the speed that pushes everything from in front of them, that asserts the implacability of law. Human, Shian, just move it. They slam to a stop all around the sacred space. The Volkswagen kids throw up their hands in surrender, but the police storm past them and their camp-fire and their wet wool and their hash and their busting bass. It's Go Go Go time.

It's not like your ordinary church, Littlejohn told them at the briefing. Unlike any other kind of religious architecture you've ever seen, this works. It's like an acid trip. Be warned. They listened carefully, they made notes, and now they're ignoring him. There's a fucker to grab. One team for each entrance. If he's in there, they'll get him out. No bother. Some Sheenie in a frock comes out flapping its hands and jabbering. Someone grab hold of the bastard, keep it out of our way, right? If it make a fuss, charge it with obstruction. There's work to be done. Right. In.

'What the hell do they think they're playing at?' Littlejohn says, in the passenger seat of Roisin Dunbar's car. 'I told them go by the north entrance. Can you people not follow simple instructions?'

Littlejohn and Dunbar and the rest of the police watch and wait. They watch and wait much longer than they expect.

'Right,' Littlejohn says. Roisin Dunbar thinks of Basil Fawlty. He takes a small jar of Vick vapour rub out of his pocket, rubs a dab under each nostril, offers the jar to Dunbar. 'It's difficult enough keeping a clear head without *kesh* chemicals turning you into a slobbering pussy-fiend.' She puts a smear on her upper lip. Woof. Goodbye sinusitis. They get out of the car. 'I'll handle this,' Littlejohn shouts to Willich. The uniforms and detectives stand down.

Littlejohn goes to speak with the Shian – the keeper of the sacred space, he tells her; more a curator than a priest. Janitor of the mysteries. Dunbar realizes that this is the first time she has seen the consultant xenologist with an Outsider. A live one. A complete one. That's the thing about academics. Everything's abstracted, removed from source. The second-hand is better than direct experience. Like Michael and his virtual newsgroups and virtual communities and virtual friends. The empire of the fake. Like the dance club: appearance, seeming. God, is this all we have, a choice of surfacings?

'Dr Littlejohn, I protest at this unwarranted and unmannerly invasion of my wardenship. You would not do this if it were your own St Anne's Cathedral.'

'I can only apologize for their disrespect.'

'I have told the officers that Eamon Donnan is not in the sacred space. He has not been here for two days.'

'I'm afraid they don't believe you. They want to see for themselves.'

'I think that they are seeing more than they had bargained for, Dr Littlejohn.'

Littlejohn and Dunbar go round to the north entrance. At the door Littlejohn produces an unlabelled quarter bottle of transparent liquid. He uncaps it, swigs down half the bottle, grimaces.

'God, that's rough. I thought this might happen, so I nipped back home and brought a chemical ally.' He offers it to Vick-besmeared Roisin Dunbar. She sniffs it. Poteen.

'This is hardly the time.'

'This is the time, believe me. You want something that's going to hit your nervous system hard and fast. Like I told you, I'm a gin man myself, but this is the quickest.'

She forces it down. A few seconds, and then it hits the inside of her skull like a punishment beating.

'I'll bother you about where you got it from later,' she says, and they go in.

Woo, goes Roisin Dunbar, immersed in glory. She almost falls to her knees and it's proof that the poteen is working that she realizes that if she did she wouldn't get up again. Like those other dark huddles on the floor. What's the line from the old hymn? Lost in wonder, awe and praise, something like that. Exactly like that. Is that Darren Healey?

'Healey?' she asks and stops to listen as harmonies and cadences swoop around the curves of draped fabric like swallows. So many voices in my voice. She walks to him. He seems miles away. 'Come on.' He looks up into her face with awe. What does he see? Angel face? Long time since a man looked at her like that.

Something in the electromagnetic signature of the sacred space has blanked her watch, so Roisin Dunbar has no idea how long it takes to help the God-shocked police out into the mundane light. The light seems quite different every time she comes out towing her crocodile of officers. They sit around on the damp concrete outside the loading dock, arms on knees, blinking. The Volksfolk offer them coffee. Meanwhile Littlejohn has proved that the Shian Thetherrin was truthful and there is no Eamon Donnan hiding in the folds of God's mantle. Willich marshals his remaining officers. Three cars go to shut down the access routes into Queen's Island. The rest go out into the Shian town.

The day is rare and bright, high clear March. A scattered flock of small cumulus is driven on an east wind, shadows swoop over the rooftops, dip into the streets. The season has come and the shipyard unfolds like a blossom. Place and people shed colour: banners of Nations and Holds older than human history crack in the stiff wind; on ladders and scaffolding settlers touch up paintwork buffeted by the winter gales. Blues and greens are the favoured hues. The live polymer skins of the new architecture have grown patterns: complex scrolls and leaf forms, variants on the universal Shian symbol of the fourfold yin-yang. Tattooed buildings. Squeezed into the Queen's dry dock like a queen termite, the beached orbiter puts out spring colours; a reticulation of orange over dark red. In the adjacent Musgrave dock the miniature forest the Shian have engineered out of the rust-stained concrete is coming into bloom. Pursed crimson leaf buds open; the branches drop clusters of tiny white blossoms. Unseen things call and dart through the canopy. The wild wood grows in the heart of every Shian.

Kesh perfumes sweep through the wide, puddled streets. Unseen clouds of *hahndahvi* congregate about the crane gantries like the flocks of starlings, thousands strong, that dash and plunge around the city's bridges. The wind carries snatches of music; down on the dance floors it will not stop until the season ends. The *koonteesh* can drum for days on end, without eating, without sleeping. Theirs is a special grace, to sublimate the sexual energy of *kesh* into music. In the streets the males clutch at their fanciful headdresses, gather in folds and flounces of costumes that have been added to and decorated and modified for centuries, and now have been carried across interstellar space and sixty years of time. For many of the males, their costumes were the only possessions they brought. In the old cutting and plating sheds teams of males work on new costumes, designing, cutting, sewing, constructing head pieces. Everything may be appropriated for a dress: fabric, fashion, history, architecture, irony, industrial waste. Twice a year the city's haberdashers are besieged by high-spending costumiers. The council dumps run a profitable black market in recyclables. *Kesh* customs differ between Nations; among the Harridis the way is for teams to select and prepare a champion, like an entourage readying a knight for chivalrous combat. Bodies are decorated, hair is dyed and woven with ornaments. The retainers share the glory of their star, should his display and dance attract attention. They will get their fuck. Beneath tents of live skin rigged from crane gantries, old males dried to leather by pheromones and dance feed the forms and patterns in a drop of musk to just-pubescent eight-year-olds, shaking with the surge of unfamiliar chemicals and emotions through their bloodstreams.

Groups of females in traditional hunting costume call to the males. Ribaldry is exchanged, looks, scents are remembered for the night's contests. Many of the females' staffs bear strings of prey; rats, cats, gulls. No shortage of any of those in the shipyards, though carloads have been chased off the big landfill on the other side of the lough, and the RSPB has mounted a guard on the swans in Victoria Park. *Joy* is everywhere, in the looks, in the clothes, in the music, in the air. Children run through the joy; to them it is as palpable as weather. Some chase balls, some rush around on low-rider tricycles, all are completely ignored by the simmering adults. Everything is put away when the heat season comes. No work is done, no projects are begun, no business is conducted, no vendettas are executed, no law is practised. There is only heat, and lust, and *joy*.

The police scurry like cockroaches through the world party. They go along the wide human streets, and through the narrow Outsider alleys, and across the walkways and bridges that tie the disparate elements of Queen's Island into one sprawling unit, a great Hold house, almost as large as the enormous Holds of the Shian Hearth, thousands of years old, sprawling for miles across their demesnes. They go into its living areas and its sleeping areas and its manufacturing areas, they go into its dance floors and its workshops and they go through the coiled chambers of the big lander in the dock, spooked a little by the stacked stasis coffins in which the settlers slept through the forties and fifties and sixties and seventies and eighties and nineties on their journey to World Ten. They go down into the plantation in the Musgrave Dock, between the red trees, and they wonder what the hell is making that noise? But when they look they can never see. They knock on doors. They stop people. They ask questions. They show photographs. They try to be polite, but they get smiled at because it's the season, and blood is hot and emotions are smoking. They grow angry, but not because of the smiling. The pheromones have got inside them. Their blood is hot, their emotions are smoking. And they are the Northern Ireland Police Service. They get impatient. They get arrogant. There are disputes. There are arguments. There are threats of arrest. Females in hunting garb stare out officers in dark green uniforms. Names start to be used. Politically incorrect language. Then a police Ford driven too fast, too aggressively, with too much testosterone, clips a child's tricycle. The driver hits the brakes but the trike flips twenty feet across the road. The police are out and over in an instant – the kid's all right, it's landed on its feet – but in that same instant fifty shipyarders bubble out of the brickwork. Fifty more appear the next instant, and they are all smiling. The police call for back-up, and within two minutes there are twenty officers facing two hundred Shian. Concentrated chemicals. Shian crests rise. Human pituitary glands thump. Hands on guns, boys. Potential riot situation. Break out the baton rounds. Shian children go skittering around their ankles, oblivious. Littlejohn and Dunbar go in as Willich opens a channel to Mountpottinger and asks them to stand by a tactical support group.

Just like the old days.

The wind that carries the *kesh* chemicals through the shipyard streets is cold and keen, but Roisin Dunbar feels hot and constricted in her beige trench coat. It marks her as blatantly as it did in the dance club: she wants to tear the fucking thing off; tear all her heavy, heavy clutching clothes off. Her panties have her fanny in a grip of iron: she wants them off, she wants cool wind in her muff. Like being on holiday in a warm country, a hot and sensuous culture. It's some mighty mood, blowing in the wind. Carnival of flesh. Stronger even than Vick menthol rub. But she's a policewoman and policewomen don't get to do what they feel like doing, so she follows Littlejohn in her iron panties and her concrete suit and her beige trench coat flapping around her legs.

A Shian steps forward from the crowd. She is carrying a long staff: Dunbar recognizes the badge of a *genro*. Littlejohn greets her. They talk in Narha. The Outsider talks very fast. Littlejohn's replies sound ponderous and hectoring, like the thumping growl of Saturday afternoon street evangelists. Dunbar can guess what they are saying. The Outsider will be listing objections and violations of custom and Shian law. Dunbar's reminded of the wee hard Falls women, in the early days of the Troubles, who would pour out of their back-to-back houses at the warning clatter of dustbin lids on concrete to face off army search parties with a barrage of accusations and legal protests. Every one of them a civil rights lawyer. Nothing changes. Somebody's got to play the role of minority. Littlejohn's talking again. He'll be agreeing with everything the Outsider says, but regretting that the police do have warrants entitling them to search for their suspect, and yes, the officer was driving recklessly and the child's life was endangered and while he recognizes that Shian law sanctions any act in defence of children, human law takes precedence, even in a Shian town, and there are proper channels for complaint and if the *genro* would file a complaint with the proper authorities the matter will be dealt with objectively and effectively and justly. But this won't help anything. This will just make a bad situation worse. Really.

The *genro* rests on her staff. She says nothing. Clouds pass over the Shian town. To the north are the grey veils of a rain shower. The police look at each other. Dunbar looks at Willich. He has the car radio handset in his fingers. Waiting for the word.

The *genro* blinks at Littlejohn. She does something with her staff, it disappears into her hand. She lifts a fist, opens her fingers. The crowd see the sign and disperse, so fast it's like a soft explosion. It's just people on streets again, going their ways. The police stand down. Willich talks on the radio. Mountpottinger demobilizes.

The kid's already back on its trike sucking a violently orange ice lolly someone's found it. The trike isn't even scratched: smart plastic, bounces right back, every time.

The search teams report back. Nothing. They've been into every building, down every street, along every walkway, every place and Eamon Donnan's not there. Nothing.

'Fuck!' DCI Willich shouts. He bangs the wing of his car with his fist, dents the malleable metal. 'Bastard's done a runner!'

Words have been in his head all night, muttering, maithering, but it isn't words that wakes him. It's licking. Loud, slow, licking. Unh. Huh. Agh. And eyes open.

He's alone in the bed as big as a room. No slender red body curled beside him. No monkey-kid-thing clambering over him, sniffing for smart milk. Just Gillespie in his sagging underwear, and the bright light of day.

190

Oh Jesus, I sucked her tit. In the dark of the night, I drank her milk. It's different for them. It really is. It doesn't mean anything to them. Doesn't matter at all. Yes it does, the bright light of day says, shining straight into his soul.

Bright light of day, remorse, and licking.

In the big room, framed by the door, Ananturievo Soulereya is licking himself. It's such an incredible operation that for a long time Andy Gillespie can't do anything but stare. How can anything fold over like that, twist that to there? He is naked. His skin is still marked with black felt-tip hieroglyphs. He bends over and licks his crotch. I wish I could do that. His milk-swollen breast swings.

Tell me it doesn't matter if you'd suck hers, but not his.

Ananturievo notices Gillespie watching him. He blinks. Hello.

'Good morning Mr Gillespie. I trust you slept comfortably? How do you hurt today?'

It hurts like fucking hell. His body has turned to concrete in the night. Pain to move, pain to stay still. Ananturievo uncurls and Gillespie notices furrows of scrapes on his sides, chest, face, thighs. Three parallel lines. Those fine claw-nails he noticed last night. Tough love.

'Ah, good night?'

'Yes, thank you. Most successful.'

Most successful. Must remember that one, if I ever score again.

'Ah, where's Ounserrat?'

'She has gone out to hire a car. She told me to tell you that you must come with her to Dublin today.'

'Jesus, I can't go anywhere today.' It hurts to speak.

'Ounserrat knows this, and therefore will drive you. All you have to do is sit. Here, I have brought your clothes. Shall I help you put them on?'

No fucking chance. It takes ten minutes to put his trousers on. Like microsurgery; very, very little movements. T-shirt stinks like a used suppository. No one'll notice with the ming in here. He can't get his arms through the holes.

'Help,' he says.

Ananturievo gently assists. The door opens. It's Ounserrat,

with Graceland toddling at her side, skinny fingers linked with its mother's. The kid's dressed in too-short pink leggings and 'Princess in my Pocket' T-shirt.

'I am glad to see you are dressed, Mr Gillespie. I am most eager to get to Dublin today.'

'What's the rush anyhow?' he asks. Ananturievo, dressed in felt pen and saliva, is in the kitchen trying to put a human breakfast together.

'I am now very concerned for my client.'

'Why?'

'That is a matter of *gehenshuthra*.' Her eyes are flat and dull and alien. Gillespie knows he will get nothing more from her. Last night I sucked your milk from your teat, this morning I'm not even sure what you are. What do you know, that you won't say? If I find you've been lying to me, I'll . . .

You'll what? Hit her? Smack her around? Be a *man*? Do the *man*'s thing?

But they do the man's thing; they do it all the time, when someone threatens their kids.

'Okay. We'll go to Dublin. We'll see if Hot Sweat Video knows anything about your client.'

Andy Gillespie and Graceland shovel down Rice Krispies. The kid is entranced by the sound effects. And they're ready to go. Ananturievo and Sounsurresh talk in quick-draw Hot Narha, a blur of gentle touchings and syllables that strike echoes in Andy Gillespie's skull. *Gelemhai*: dancing. But not the waltz or the slush or 'Let's Do the Timewarp Again': dancing like your life depends on it. *Kesh* dancing. Real Saturday Night Fever. *Yesouldok*: a female sexual partner of more than one night. *Yekankin*: a male sex partner. As opposed a *lover* of the opposite sex.

Andy Gillespie wishes he didn't have the echo for that in his head.

Farewells made, the *planha* parts. Graceland clings happily to Ananturievo's leg, singing goodbyes to Mummy. Humans' kids would be having hysterics at this point. Separate words for Mummy and Daddy in Hot Narha, Gillespie notes, as opposed to Cool Narha generic *parent*.

The car's a new model Fiesta; a zero-point job. Electric blue. Double bad vibes. Fords, and metallic paint.

'This must have cost.'

'It did, Mr Gillespie.'

Gillespie painfully folds himself into the car. The bastard smart dash reminds him it won't start the car until he's fastened his seatbelt. A thought:

'Are youse pushed for cash?'

She starts the engine. Hydrogen and oxygen purr into water.

'We are a little concerned, Mr Gillespie. The loss of my pizza job has hit us hard. I do not want to have to go to Not Afraid of the River for a subsidy.'

First lawyer he's ever met didn't want money. If she can hire a car, she's got more money than him. He's been suffering cash point belly most of the week; the sick gnaw of not knowing but not wanting to know how much he has. He should stick his card in and get the awful truth, but not today. You always have less money than you think.

This never happens to Inspector Morse.

It's as she tries to turn out on to Sunnyside Street to go across the river to the motorway south that Gillespie realizes Ounserrat Soulereya is the worst driver he's ever sat beside. She pulls out in front of a C&C lemonade lorry. She misses major injury by a scrape of paint. The lorry driver follows them over the bridge and up the Stranmillis Road, flashing his lights. Road rage of the lemonade lads.

'Where did you learn to drive?'

'Another planet, Mr Gillespie.'

'Pull over here. Here. Just do it.'

Drivers hate being driven, but he only makes it to halfway down Stockman's Lane before he has to stop. It's not the pain in his hands and arms and shins. It's the words. Words, flying at him out of everything his eyes touch. Lorry: *psoulning*, a girl. House: *riehensh*: another girl. Bicycle: *niesvat*, a boy. Cyclist: *keniesvalskin*, a girl. Pedals: *sounjeng*, a boy. Wheel: *reenk*, a girl. Names like plagues of midges, flapping improbable genitalia. Hes, shes; the whole material world touching and pressing and fondling. Is this what it's like for French and Spanish, all their words with that little kiss inside, every sentence a tiny battle of the sexes? Or is it all a whiff of chemicals whirled through the demister?

'Are you all right, Mr Gillespie?'

'You take it from here.'

Maybe fear of being mashed underneath a forty-tonner will push the words back into their objects. It wasn't like this the other time, inside. He woke up, and it was laid out in his head like a city that had grown up in the space of a single night. But this is like being given a Berlitz rather than a map: it tells you what to see, what things are, but not how they're arranged, what street you have to walk, what bus you have to take to here, than change to the subway to get to there.

Jesus, she really is the worst driver he's ever seen.

By the time they get to the turn off to Dublin he's wound the window down. It's bitter, but better than breathing in Outsider *kesh* stink. He hopes she can't see his hard on; he's had it since junction three. Like being a wee lad again, on the bus suffering Coachman's Lob, trying to move your jacket to cover the thing up, sitting well past your stop because you're not going to get up and walk down the aisle with that thing pushing the front of your trousers out like a big top. Penis: *genshent*. Boy. Erection: *riesoulgenshentsin*. Boy. Cold, fresh March air. Ahh. She won't mind it. She likes the cold. They're a cool climate people.

'Whereabouts do you come from?' Talking helps.

'How do you mean that, Mr Gillespie?'

'On your home world. Whereabouts. We like to know where folk are from in this country. Where they belong to.'

'Belonging to a place. That is a most strange concept.' She takes a roundabout at fifty. Maybe talking is not such a good idea. 'One belongs to a Nation, and a Hold, but those are not places. They are people. The Soulereya Nation is everywhere. Perhaps it is that you mean the place I was born. That was Ruvstupehai. I was born and grew up there; my mother lived in three Holds in that region before I became a female. It is in the north-east of Great Continent, under the breath of the northern glaciers. That is where our hunting grounds are, I have seen them. I have hunted in them, with my mother, and when I went

194

out on my travelling. They are very beautiful and rich, they have been maintained by forest keepers for five thousand years. My mother was not a forest keeper. She was an intelligence designer. It is a traditional profession in my Nation; that is what our name means.'

'Like "Smith" means someone who makes things out of metal, or coopers make barrels.'

'Yes. Soulereya means people who program things.'

'You people have way too much civilization.'

'You would not say that if you knew us, Mr Gillespie.'

The cold air is doing the job. The big sore hard-on is going down. Traffic is light off the motorway. Ounserrat can drive and talk without putting lives at risk. Field: *mang*, boy, Andy Gillespie's brain whispers to him like an aside he can respond to or not. Tree: *frull*, girl. Ounserrat talks about her childhood in the cold northern Holds where winter was half a year long and the other five months coming and going. Whatever it was her mother did, she was good at it; Holds competed for her membership. The Soulereyas were not among the most powerful Nations – even the mighty Harridis were second division on the Hearth – but they held licences on basic assembler programs which had withstood centuries of legal challenge by the big manufacturing Nations, and had forged long-standing alliances with the Huskravidi and Tollamang Nations which had made them minority partners in the Shian-forming of their outer moon, Blascort. Soulereyas, she says with pride, were instrumental in the World Six colonization three hundred years ago, but Andy Gillespie's never been able to understand the complex Shian system of favour, duty and ability that passes for an economy. He likes the idea of it, but he can't see how anything can get done without money. Trader-ape thinking, he supposes. She describes her birth land, her travels across its mountains and valleys; the ancient, sprawling Holds, big as towns, in their pristine demesnes; the hunts and *kesh* encounters in those red-branched forests; the *love* and *bliss* in wooden rooms older than the pyramids. Gillespie hears her words, and the nostalgic pleasure with which she names the places she can never return to, but he can't see it. His imagination is a long way out of the

Woodstock Road, but light years short of envisioning another planet. He wants to apologize to her, it's just story, I can't believe in it, I can't believe in you in any other setting than this country, this climate, this landscape. You might as well have come out of faery hills as from another star. She's talking now about the World Ten migration. Her migration. It seems to have something to do with a colossal breach of etiquette. Gillespie can't see how that would make you want to come on a one-way trip to another world. Just another *wanderjahr* for these people. Jumping up and down in the genepool, lapping a little over the sides. If you carry the Nation inside you, one place is as much home as any other. But another world; it's not like Canada. You can't get Friends and Family Chieftain Travel packages, call cheap rate on Sundays. Phone home. Sixty years. You can't go back if you decide you don't like it. Gillespie can only think of the World Ten Migration wrapped around human history. Nineteen forty: Second World War. Phoney war well over, proper war begun. Bombs over Belfast. Herr Hitler hitting the shipyards with H.E. and incendiaries. Eighty-eight starships pull out of orbit around the Shian Hearth, flick on their Mach drives and start moving at near-as-damnit the speed of light. And there's Ounserrat Soulereya, folded into a stasis coffin tucked into the belly of one of a hundred landers clinging to the improbable spire-work of the big light-speed ships. He's thinking of when he was a kid, and there was an outing from Euston Street Primary to an open farm, and all the others had gone ooh and coo and ahh at the wee goats and lambykins and the piggie-wigs, but what he brought back with him was the beehives, the beekeeper in his creepy veil and gloves lifting out a slab of comb, oozing liquid sunlight, brushing off the squirming insects to show him, curled in each tiny wax cell, a bee, wings and legs and feelers folded, embedded in honey. That's how he sees her, curled up, breathing thick gold. My parents were kids when you left, kid. You slept through their courtings and their kissings and their hasty wedding. You dreamed your private dreams as they realized it wasn't ever going to be good but it was all they had, and the squeezing out of three children into the uncertainties of the sixties, which, Ulster being Ulster, didn't arrive until the

1990s, when I was twentysomething and intently fucking up my life, and still you slept, maybe moving a little in your honey sleep, sensing that the big ships had turned around ten years out, back in the days when we were still blowing each other up and blowing each other away and acting like five-year-olds with heavy ordinance. You are an old woman, you come from another generation, let alone another world, and here you are driving me in a hired Ford and there are road signs for Dromore and Banbridge and Newry and truckloads of Moypark frozen chickens and Tyrone brick and a fucking tractor hogging the slow lane, like there always is.

'How old are you?' he asks, made curious by his train of thought.

'It is difficult. I am measured by two different lengths of year.'

'Our years, rough guess.'

'About fourteen.'

Jesus. Under-aged driver. Under-aged mother. Under-aged lawyer. Under-aged to feed you her tit in the cold of the transients' hall. Under-aged everything.

'How did you get a driving licence?'

'Your government made exceptions for us.'

He shivers, chilled not by the wind but thoughts of brief, pure Shian childhoods. Karen had always dressed Stacey and Talya older than their years. Little women. Heels and satin and fabrics that clung where there was nothing to cling to. It had given him that same shiver; too much too young.

'And your family, Mr Gillespie?'

Can you read my thoughts, space-babe? 'My ex-wife, my kids?'

'The place you come from. The Nation you belong to.'

He laughs. 'I belong to the Andy Gillespie Nation. Very small, very selective, population one. No admission to latecomers. Trouble is no one recognizes this Nation but me. You're almost as bad as those Equal Opportunities forms you have to fill in that ask you, not if you're a member of the Protestant or Catholic community, but if you would be *perceived* as a member of the Protestant or Catholic community. Someone else telling you what you are.'

'This is strange to me. I could not imagine how it would feel not to be part of something.' Ounserrat muses on the strangeness by taking the roundabouts on the Newry ring road at forty-five.

'Light, but lonely,' Andy Gillespie says. 'Right here.'

As the car takes the long climb out of Newry towards the old border, he tells Ounserrat about the slow decline of the fifteen streets where he grew up from working-class pride to the redeveloper's cracking ball. He tells her about kick the can and building guiders out of planks and string and pram wheels and giving them names like William of Orange and True Blue without any self-consciousness. He tells her about the scary years, when he was very small, when the Troubles were bad and people were blown up without warning, and he tells about the angry years when policemen and prison officers were burned out of their houses by men who claimed to be loyal to crown and country and there were marches every weekend protesting about some deal or other Her Majesty's treacherous Westminster Government had done with Ulster's enemies, and about the dark years when it was all hard men with guns, evening the scores, going one for you, two for us, three for you, four for us. He tells her about the Slow Peace, and how good it was to just be ordinary, forgettable people again, and how he had sung along down at the City Hall when Van Morrison sang about no religion, and booed the Lord Mayor when he had tried to altar-call fifty thousand people, and cried when the President of the United States stood up behind his Great Seal and spoken about hope and work and the future, and how he had gone home feeling, yes, maybe it will be like this all the time. He tells her about the good years, and the love he found for cars and their oily orderliness, and for Karen when he saw her in the Glens Supporters' Club that night she became something more than just the wee girl from down the street, and for the two shocking parcels of red, boiled flesh she forced out of her into the world. By the time he is done telling it they are well over the painted line which the troops could go up to but not cross, well past Dundalk, well past Drogheda and the megalithic tombs of the Boyne Valley that were being aligned with the sun when the Shian were discovering the principles of chemistry. It takes so long a distance to tell because when he starts talking about Stacey and Talya he realizes there is so much that he wants to say about them. And he can say it, because Ounserrat won't condemn him. In her eyes he is no failure as a husband and father.

They come to Dublin. Word storm, bone-deep pain or not, Andy Gillespie insists on driving. They decided back around Balbriggan to find a cheap hotel. Hot Sweat Video might take more than an afternoon to investigate. Tourist Information gives them a cheap hotel in the south of the city, by the canal. The girl behind the desk keeps slightly too-firm control over her features. Andy Gillespie risks his card in a cash machine. *Check Balance?* Bite the bullet. The bullet hits him in the heart. Fifty quid in the entire planet. He closes his eyes.

'How much cash have you got?' he asks Ounserrat.

'Are you in difficulty?'

'Not if you pay for the hotel.'

'Then we will have to share a room, Mr Gillespie.'

'You in difficulty too?'

'Soon.'

They go south, to the canal. The girl behind the desk in the cheap hotel amends the booking for one room and does not look at either Gillespie or Ounserrat. Gillespie hobbles upstairs to survey the room while Ounserrat checks the vending machine in the lobby for something nutty that she can eat. The en suite is a curtained-off corner of the room. Emphasis on cheap here. No mini-bar – he wasn't expecting one at these prices – but there is a television/keyboard unit with full Net access. One big bed. Slept in bigger. No scandal in it, wee receptionist girlie. They get directions to Hot Sweat Video's address from the receptionist and drive over there in the rented Ford.

'You got your *genro* stick?' Gillespie asks.

She pulls it out of the breast pocket of her denim jacket, holds it in front of his nose.

'For fuck's sake don't set it off in here!' Gillespie says.

'Mr Gillespie, I may be young in years and professional experience, but I am fully adult,' Ounserrat says. But she seems agitated, in the kind of mood that might just set off a *genro* stick in a small car, because.

Hot Sweat Video is based in an ugly Edwardian workshop unit skulking at the back of a Regency terrace close by Pearse Station.

'I would like to handle this inquiry,' Ounserrat says as Gillespie sidles the car into the parking space marked 'management'. She is visibly quivering. Nervous, knight-advocate? 'This is my case and client. I do not think it is either necessary or desirable to mention Mr Gerry Conlon, do you, Mr Gillespie?'

Mr Gillespie agrees.

The girl on the front desk looks at Gillespie and looks at Ounserrat Soulereya. She's the only Dublin receptionist so far not to be surprised by a man with an Outsider female. She does look at the bruises on Gillespie's hands.

'Friends of your boss,' he says.

'We're not auditioning today, but I can give you an appointment for tomorrow afternoon,' the receptionist says, scowling.

'I am not here to audition,' Ounserrat says. 'I would like to have a few polite words with the manager. Might that be possible?'

'He's got a very full diary today. I know, I do it for him.'

Andy Gillespie's studying a shrink-wrapped step climber machine in the corner by the coffee maker.

'Is there then someone else in a position of moderate authority to whom I might speak? Please be assured that you have nothing to fear from me, I am trying to find Sounsurresh Soulereya, who I believe did some work for you some time ago. She is a well-known model. I fear she may have come to some harm. I am her *genro*. Knight-advocate.'

'And him?'

Gillespie looks up from the typescript catalogue he's been scanning.

'A friend.'

The receptionist purses her Carmine Lake lips: really doubtful now. She gets out of her chair – the length of her legs and the glossiness of her panty hose draw Andy Gillespie's eyes up, up – knocks on a door marked 'Studio' and goes in without waiting for an answer. She's away long enough for who they are and what they want and will you see them?

'You can talk to the director,' she says coming back into the reception area.

The Studio is a big glass-roofed factory. Cast iron pillars, concrete floor painted green, roof lights grey with Dublin dirt and pigeon shit. There are still drive belts for machinery up in the roof trees. Sweat shop then, sweat shop again; but the machinery is human-powered now. Treadmills, exercise bikes, step climbers, weight machines: working like a dog and going nowhere, earning nothing. The air has the sour tang of sweat and rubber matting Gillespie remembers from gym at school. He shudders. Always was a very fine line between work-out and S and M. Big A1 full-colour posters on the brick walls of alien babes getting sweaty. Red brick, red babes.

The director is a skinny wee lad of about nineteen with a beanie hat and an attempted beard. Andy Gillespie knows a thousand of him. If they still put occupations in passports, he would read 'glipe'. He's sitting on a Reebok step poking with a screwdriver at parts of a video camera that probably shouldn't be poked at. He nods at Ounserrat.

'You're looking for an Outsider.'

'Sounsurresh Soulereya.'

'Can't get round those words of yours.'

'She did a video for you.'

The glipe's eyes take in besieging posters.

'We do a lot of videos. We get a lot through here. 'Course, most of them aren't real, but we don't pay them as much. We reckon they get enough just dressing up and pretending.'

'You would remember this one. She is a quite well-known model. From London.' The big gym lends an authoritative echo to Ounserrat's contralto voice, but Gillespie can hear a tremor. What's she so tensed up about?

'Oh, her. Yeah, I remember her. *Space Baybee Step 'n' Sweat*. Expensive, but I think it was probably my finest work to date. Even better than *Big Red Stomp*. So, she's disappeared?'

'When did she make this video for you, Mr . . . ?'

'I'd have to look it up.'

'Please.'

He flips out a Psion, doodles with the tracker pad.

'Shooting schedule was the nineteenth and twentieth of February. We overran a morning into the schedule for *Lean Burn II*.'

Ounserrat blinks very slowly.

'Do you know if she had any appointments after this? Did she give any indication of her movements or future plans?'

Glipe snickers at her precise language. Shakes head.

'Didn't tell me anything. Went back home couple of grand the heavier.'

'You sure work-out videos're all you shoot here?' Andy Gillespie says.

'Your meaning eludes me, my Northern friend.'

'Just that, well, some frooks might get off completely on step aerobics, but maybe there's a more, ah, specialized audience wants something more, ah, intense?'

'You asking do I shoot porn here?'

'Do you?'

'Hey, I'm a fucking artist, right? I've got some fucking artistic integrity. How they reprocess the images when I've edited them down, that's nothing to do with me.'

'You mean, videos get manipulated?' Gillespie asks.

'Software they've got in there, they can make anyone do anything. Mostly it's movie stars; personally, I'm more than happy to see Julia Roberts suck a pig's dick. Fuck Hollywood.'

'Your images of my client may have been sold on?' Ounserrat asks. 'With or without her knowledge?'

'What do you think, red babe? Not sold on; kind of in-house. It's a separate division; nothing to do with me. Shouldn't really even know it exists. Well, that's my line for the peelers. So, sorry, but that's all I know about your client. She came, she did the business, she went, she's doing more business that's not in the contract. Anything else I can help you with?'

'No, that will be all, thank you Mr—'

Mr Nothing. 'Hey,' he calls out as Gillespie opens the door for Ounserrat Soulereya. 'You want to make some quick money? You got great bone structure.'

'*Gehenshuthra*, sir,' Ounserrat Soulereya says. But back in the car she's disconsolate. Gillespie has learned to read that one, it's a widening of the nostrils and pupils.

'All my client's movements are accounted for within the time period,' she says.

'Maybe it's nothing more terrible than she really has run off to join another Hold,' Gillespie says. 'If nothing else, we've got a good guess why Gerry Conlon's boot boys jumped us. Amazing what they can do with computers these days.'

'I am very hungry, Mr Gillespie,' Ounserrat says. She's still trembling. 'Please drive me to somewhere I can eat chips.'

There's a kebab van underneath the railway bridge at Pearse Station.

'Have these been cooked in animal fat?' Ounserrat asks the Turkish proprietor. Gillespie asks if he can borrow the van-owner's mobile to call the hotel and cancel the room. He'll pay for the call.

'They would only accept payment in advance, Mr Gillespie,' Ounserrat says, inspecting chips and flinging the imperfect into the gutter. 'They will not give me my money back. And I think you will have a reason to use it. I will be engaged tonight.'

'Engaged? At what?'

Ounserrat exhales loudly through her nostrils. Impatience? 'Mr Gillespie, I shall be away from you all night. Should you wish, you may drive back to Belfast. I will take a bus in the morning.'

'Where are you going, what are you doing, all night, in Dublin?'

'Mr Gillespie . . .'

'Oh, Jesus.' It's the cash-point bullet through the heart, but someone's carved a cross on the end of this one so it opens up inside you and tears you apart. It isn't stress that's making her shiver.

'It is the season, Mr Gillespie. We are not as free as you about sex. There are disciplines *genro* are taught to delay the onset, but we all must succumb to it in the end. There is a Shian community out by the sea at a place called Ringsend, some of the lovers of Not Afraid of the River have passed through it. I will go there. I must do this.' The van owner is utterly fascinated. Onions are turning to charcoal on the hot plate. Ounserrat says to him, 'I will give you two pounds if you will call me a taxi to Ringsend.'

Sex, betrayal and a Turkish kebab van.

'You're going off for a fuck?' Gillespie says, suddenly needing to be bestial and wounding. 'You're going to go down there, pick out some boy because you like his make-up or he's got a cute dress on or great thighs or moves real neat, and just fuck him?'

'It is our way, Mr Gillespie. Please, you have nothing to be jealous of. It will only be sex.'

The onions have caught light. Distracted, the kebab man is smacking them out with a fish slice.

'OK. OK, you want to go, I'll fucking take you myself.'

'That would not be a good thing, Mr Gillespie.' The taxi's arrived, hovering at the kerb. Ounserrat folds her height into the back seat. 'I will be back in the morning for breakfast at the hotel. This does not mean anything, Mr Gillespie.'

The taxi pulls out into the traffic.

'My name's Andy!' Gillespie shouts after it. 'Why can't you use it?'

He paces up and down outside the kebab van, buys a doner, bins it, sits in the car, drums his fingers on the wheel and then good thing or not, drives to Ringsend. He's only five minutes behind the taxi, but that's enough to hit the traffic. A huge evening is unfolding over Dublin in golds and purples. It could be lead and shit for all Gillespie sees of it. He hurts. Not the outer beating of Conlon's boys trying to scare him off. This is inner GBH, like a fist in the throat, and another two under each eye, driving them up into his skull. This hurt's no stranger to him. It's called on him many times. It lived with him when the divorce was going through, it still calls when he sees Karen with another man. When she comes over to the flat those nights she wants him to mind the girls, it comes through the door with her.

The night Conlon's boys jumped them she'd talked about sex without love. It's what men are supposed to want. But you make it different, Ounserrat Soulereya. You turn everything round, you Outsiders; you reflect us back on ourselves, men, women. Sex without love, love without sex. I think I wanted to fuck you, Knight-Advocate Ounserrat Soulereya. Not because I'm a frook, not because your body presses buttons in my head. Because I feel something for you. Love you. But if you had let me, it would have made me a stranger. Someone you didn't love. And off you go in your taxi to pick up the first bit of skin takes your eye and fuck him senseless and it's like you say, it won't mean anything, you won't feel anything for him. You won't love him. You love me, and I feel everything. Any way you turn it, Andy Gillespie gets fists in the heart. The Shian way kills him every time. No word for *guilt* in Narha, Hot or Cool. Any word for *jealous*, or hasn't she fed that one to him yet?

He doesn't want to have to listen to these bull-horn thoughts, or to the words he sucked out of her breast, so he'll listen to the radio. It's an easy-listening station. Heavy on the Gershwin. They're having a theme day. They'd better not play 'Someone to Watch Over Me'. So he drives angry and pushy and bangs his horn oblivious to the hurt it does his fingers and cuts up whatever he can cut up and takes it out on the people of Dublin driving home after their day's work who look at his plate and say *bloody ignorant Northerner*. The light is a low edge of crimson behind black Howth Head when he arrives in the Shian Town. The Ringsend Shian live under the red and white striped chimneys of the big derelict power station by the sea. Those chimneys can be seen all over the city, like Belfast's cranes. The Shian seem to be a people who steer by landmarks and obsolete technology. Their lander is beached in the shallows beside the south mole. Environmentalists, dog-walkers and racists have stuck protest posters on its hull, now resplendent in spring tiger stripes. He parks the car by the sea wall, sits a time on the birdshit-spattered concrete in the huge evening. He can hear the music. He can see the colours. He can smell the perfumes. But he's suddenly reluctant to follow through the picket wall of processor plants. He's here without knowing why he's here. Do you want to see her down at the dance floor, finding, stalking, catching? Do you want to follow her and whatever she's chosen through the alleys and walkways to his room, up the stairs, to stand outside the door and listen to the shove and pump of their bodies?

What the fuck are you doing here, Andrew Gillespie?

Chemicals. That's all love is. A small surplus of *this* in some bit of your head. At least they're honest about it. They don't go on about love being the key to the universe and supreme and holy and mystical and make a million songs and poems and religions out of it. Just stuff in your head. Chemicals. That's all you feel. She gives them off, you take them in, and you die inside for love.

Ships are moving out in the dark water, he can feel the grumble of their big engines through stone and sand and sea. The aircraft warning beacons on the chimneys are flashing, red red white, red red white. He can hear incoming Boeings up there.

Fuck it.

He gets into the car, drives back to the cheap hotel by the canal. Across the street, as he remembered, are a cash point, a pub and a takeaway. He takes his last fifty out of the first, drinks most of it in the second, buys curry, chips and sausage in the third with what's left, loses the lot to the gutter outside the hotel and still can't get the chemicals out of his head. In his room he lies on the bed watching MTV with numb incomprehension. After an hour, when he realizes that this is really all there is going to be to it, he flicks the set to com mode, picks up the keyboard and calls up the frook pages.

I'm pissed, my inhibitions are switched off, I can do what the hell I like in the privacy of my cheap hotel room, I'm not ashamed.

Right, Andy.

He looks, and it hurts, and he sighs but it won't go out of him in breath. Chemicals. That's all it is. Right again, Andy.

He steers through the pin-up pages. He doesn't want hot porn, the reprocessed images, the stolen souls. He just wants to see her, things like her. They all look the same, any one will do. Look, there's even one with the same name. Soulereya.

Jesus.

He knows the name. He knows the face. He knows the place.

More long-lens stuff; telephoto sniffs of Sounsurresh Souler-eya, Space Baybee, Hot Sweat Video Star. The usual day-to-day stuff: getting into the car, strapping the kiddies into the back seats, driving through a farm gate, overtaking the lensman in the fast lane, getting a ticket for a car park. I know that piece of road. I've seen that farmyard, and those processors standing behind the barn in that arrangement; I've been through that gate, it's got those four-spiral symbols painted on it. This is South Side of the Stone. But the dates on the bottom of the videoprints are two days after Ounserrat says they told her her client and kids disappeared.

Write this down, you pissed bastard. This is important. This is detective work. Two days after she disappeared. They are lying. He finds a pen in the hotel stationery set but someone's stolen all the paper so he scribbles site address, dates, places down on the back of the Do Not Disturb/Please Service This Room sign. Check it. Double check it.

You've got it right. Now you can fall into unhappy jealous rat-arsed sleep.

It's a life-long malevolence of Andy Gillespie's metabolism that his brain wakes him when it sobers up and won't let him go back to sleep off the hangover. Unkh. Wide awake. Hours of lying like this ahead, unable to move because you feel so shit. Fully dressed on his back on the bed throw. Freezing cold. Body rigid with ache. Early light, grey rain on the window. Dark shadow against the glass, something huge, perched on the crappy wee dressing table. Watching him.

He finds he can move.

'Good morning Mr Gillespie. It is sixty twenty-three a.m. and you smell of an over-indulgence in alcohol.'

Ounserrat gets down from the dressing table. Her shadow fills the room.

'How long have you been there?'

'A time.'

'Did you have – ah, you know, um?'

'Intercourse?'

Gillespie winces. Ounserrat tilts her head to one side in an expression he can't read.

'No.'

'Ah.' He can't say he's sorry.

'A female would have to be desperate to the point of mania to have intercourse with a male from Ringsend Hold.'

'No luck then.'

'They dance for themselves. They dress and make themselves beautiful for their own admiration. They are vain and preening and have no appreciation of a good female.'

'We have a word for men like that.'

'What is it?'

'Wankers.'

'Ah. Masturbation reference. How fortunate you people are that you can enjoy sex with yourselves. It would be preferable to the males I met last night.'

His body's shit, his mind's pissed-on concrete, but inside, his heart's warm and happy and smiling. He lies back on the bed.

'Mr Gillespie, there is something of the gravest importance that I must tell you.'

'There's something of the gravest importance I have to tell you. South Side of the Stone lied to you. I saw it, at the web site. I saw her. Sounsurresh.'

'Mr Gillespie, please be quiet. Listen to me. I am extremely concerned for my client since I heard the early morning news on the radio in the taxi. Mr Gillespie, Pastor McIvor Kyle, his wife and his children are dead. They have been murdered. The fashion of their killing is the same as that at the Welcome Centre. It is humans now, and I am most afraid.'

In an instant Andy Gillespie is awake and aware and alert and sober as a tomb stone.

Fear and loathing on the border that isn't a border any more. Fear that while his attention was turned south – for a moment, just a moment – the killer struck again. Fear, because Andy Gillespie knows that the killer isn't going to stop. He's working to a pattern now. A pattern that only he knows, that he loves more than anything. He has to work it through. He has to weave it whole. Humans now. I am most afraid. What does Ounserrat mean by that?

Loathing: memories of last night; *Oh, Christ did I really say mean do intend that to you?* Afraid she'll say, *yes, you bastard*. Ounserrat hasn't spoken a word since he made her stop the car at Malahide because he thought he was going to boke. He hopes it's because she's angry at having been lied to by her own species, because she's concerned that the killer has started on humans now. High profile humans. Ironic: all those people who wished McIvor Kyle and his bastard theology dead, and now their wish is granted.

Is this the pattern? Ulster fuck-ups?

But there was Seyoura and Senkajou and Muskravhat; Seyamang and Vrenanka. What was their crime against the great killing pattern? Being alien?

Ounserrat drives up through St Patrick country and the drumlins of Down where the early lambs are blinking in unaccustomed sunlight and the air is rich with pigshit and slurry, through the loughside towns and the oyster and mussel farms and they turn on to the causeway to the island past Sketrick Castle and follow the sign for the right fork along the shoreline and through the gates of South Side of the Stone.

For people with a racial mistrust of water, they like putting their families next to it, Gillespie thinks.

In the days since Gillespie was last here, months have passed. It's another season in South Side of the Stone; a brighter, warmer, noisier, more colourful, more fertile one. Pheromones respect no boundaries; the human settlement on the bay is responding to the changes blown in from its new neighbour on the island. Houses are being repainted, boats spruced up for a season that is over a month off; the water is busy with little yachts and slightly early water skiers and windsurfers. Sails and Hold blanners crack in the wind.

Ounserrat Soulereya blows in like a squall. South Siders move out of her way; her *genro* staff is extended in her hand. She smells capable of using it. She goes to the middle of the dance floor which is the heart of the Hold, plants the heel of her staff on the painted concrete and scatters her one hundred and twenty-eight jury stones on to the ground. The Hot Narha is too hard and fast for Gillespie's infant vocabulary, but he knows a calling out when he hears one. This is a matter of *gehenshuthra*.

Gun-fight at the South Side corral. Beats the hell out of wigs and gowns and *m'learned friend*.

South Side rises to the challenge. Five *genro*, staves ready. Two are in dancing costume, one other in seasonal female hunting gear. Gillespie doesn't recognize the bastard lawyer who gave him the run around when he came to talk to Ongserrang. The *genro* lay their staves on the ground, five pointing to Ounserrat's one. They kneel. The males carefully tuck up their elaborate costumes. Could be a clever wee legal ploy, call them out in the middle of *kesh*, hope that the chemicals will make one of them slip. Nah. Ounserrat's too green and too angry and too honest for law games. They're talking now, everyone at once, so quickly it's almost a song. Andy Gillespie stands back and lets them talk. The people of South Side of the Stone carry on their business around the arguing lawyers. They know it can take days for a compromise to be struck between clashing rights. Children kick footballs over them. A car arrives full of young males and shopping bags from Next and Top Shop and Miss Selfridge. They grimace at Andy Gillespie, uncertain about this *man* in their place. He blinks slowly. Reassured, they blink back. The lawyers talk on. A cloud darkens the sun, a sudden, hard spring shower. South Siders take shelter as the first fat drops spot the dance floor. Then it comes down hard. Gillespie takes cover in the car. Through the rain-smeared windscreen he can see the kneeling *genro*, water streaming down their bodies, clothes and costumes clinging to them, arguing law. The rain passes, the sun comes out, the ground steams. The lawyers fight. Gillespie turns on the radio and thinks about a doze. Not to be. A tap on the window. Another. It's a kiddy on a too-small BMX. Gillespie blinks at it but it won't go away. Tippety-tip-tap. He winds down the window.

– *This for you*, he makes out of its Hot Narha. This being a slip of paper. Gillespie unfolds it. *Message from Saipanang Harridi. Mr Gillespie, it is now in the interest of my client that we speak. Please meet me at the Nendrum ruins on Mahee Island at your earliest convenience.* He looks for the sender, not even sure he'd recognize the Harridi lawyer. No one. The kid's pedalled off too.

He takes the note to Ounserrat kneeling, saturated, negotiating.

'Um, I think you should have a look at this.'

What he finds he's looking at are the sharp ends of six *genro* staves, forming a neat arc five centimetres from his eyes.

'OK. It's not that important.'

He backs off. The lawyers put down their weapons.

All right, then. I'll do it myself. Haven't played Andy fucking Hero in a while. And if it's Saipanang Harridi, then it's nothing to do with you and everything to do with me. Whose name is it on the note anyway?

From South Side of the Stone to the stump of the old round tower and the ruined monastery walls is a hundred yards across the short neck of water. He can see figures moving on the neatly shaved lawns. A boat would take you over in two minutes; by road it's a twenty-minute drive along the deeply indented shoreline of Strangford Lough, over bridges, along causeways, past private islands and peninsulas. In the monument car park dog-walkers are unloading springer spaniels from the rears of hatchbacks. The women all look vigorous and corduroyish. Gillespie hobbles up through the concentric ditches and walls that failed to protect the Culdee monks from Viking raiders. The *genro* and his client are waiting at the top of the hill, in front of the weathered High Cross. Saipanang is holding his staff.

'Mr Gillespie.' Saipanang shakes hands the human way. Ongserrang offers a palm. Gillespie licks it.

'Got your note.'

'*Genro* Ounserrat is not with you.'

'She's fighting a case with some of your South Side lawyers.'

'She will be there some time. The Harridis are masters of obfuscation.'

'You're not there with them.'

'No. My legal priorities have changed since our last meeting.'

'So Ongserrang will answer my questions.'

'Commensurate with his rights and interests.'

'What do you need to tell me here that you can't tell me back at South Side?'

Ongserrang looks his lawyer a look that says *I am trusting you on this.* The doggy women throw sticks and whistle mutts and walk around the concentric rings of monastery wall while their spaniels squat and shit on the neat grass. None of them will come near the two Shian and the human. Ongserrang takes a disk out of the breast pocket of his floral print canvas jacket. Gillespie turns it over in his fingers. There's nothing to identify it but his and Ounserrat's names written on the label.

'What's this?'

'The input log of number six matter processor for the twenty-eighth of February of this year,' Ongserrang says. 'I have transferred it to human disk technology. It records what was input as feedstock material on that day.'

'It includes a 1998 Ford Transit van, registration UBZ 1875,' Saipanang says. He's holding his *genro* staff in a death grip, Gillespie notices. His fingers are shaking. 'Also, the bodies of one Shian female adult and two children.'

The hill of Nendrum is suddenly huge and high and cold and terrifying and Andy Gillespie naked and vertiginous, clinging to its grass roots with his fingertips.

'I . . .'

'The bodies were those of Sounsurresh Soulereya of the Not Afraid of the River Hold in Docklands, London, and her children Neneenhoun and Arroumsajang,' Saipanang says. 'They were found in the Ford Transit van on the morning of the twenty-eighth, having failed to return to the Hold after walking in to Whiterock village the previous evening to show the children the boats. We mounted a search and found the van parked in a gateway on a farm lane a mile from South Side of the Stone. The bodies were in the back of the van.'

'How did they die?' Gillespie asks. He knows what the answer will be, but he must hear it spoken.

'Each had been killed with a single maser shot to the head. Sounsurresh's body had been mutilated.'

'Her, um, genitals?'

'That's correct. We brought the van back to South Side of the Stone . . .'

Wait.

'The twenty-eighth? Before the University Street killing.'

'That's correct.'

'Then this was the first, and it was covered up.'

'That is why I was taken in by this Hold, Mr Gillespie,' Ongserrang says. 'To control the information.'

'And the matter processor would take everything apart; there wouldn't be any evidence.'

'To the last atom, Mr Gillespie.'

Beats bodies in the foundations. Complete annihilation. And reincarnation, in a hundred different forms. The fat guy in the Pringle sweater, does he know that his custom-golf clubs are made out of the body and soul of Sounsurresh Soulereya, London hyper-space-bay-bee, Step 'n' Sweat? Hope you never get a good round with them, fat Pringle man. They're haunted. He shivers. He's cold. He's always cold.

There are 'why' questions coming. Why didn't they call the police? Because they knew what they were seeing. Because they wanted to keep it secret. And so they could control what any of us should know?

Because they know who's doing it. The Shian don't die for love, but they will kill without thinking to protect their children, Eamon Donnan had said. You're a threat, he had said. Humans. Can you think of anywhere more human than this place? What were you telling me, Eamon? A Shian did this? To protect the children? That would fit with McIvor Kyle and his Nazi mouthings, but how is a model and her kids, how is a drop-in centre setting newcomers up with Holds a threat to a child?

He's always feared the 'why' word. Never an easy answer to it.

The Outsiders are looking at him.

'You have worked it out, Mr Gillespie?'

'I don't know. Some of it fits, some of it, I don't know.' He looks at the disk in his hand. 'Why are you telling me this now? Last time, you wouldn't give me a fucking thing. Why this, now?'

'Sometimes the price of secrecy is too high,' Saipanang says. 'And before any loyalty to Hold or Nation, I am a *genro*.'

'They've threatened your client?'

"It is a possibility."

'And you too, then. But why bother? The police are involved, you can't hope to keep it secret from them.' And it's another self-answering question. Unless . . . 'Unless the Harridis reckon they can get to it first. Then they can keep it quiet. And then it'll just be a few wee loose ends to tie up.' His head is spinning, the circles of thousand-year-old masonry are orbiting around him. Too much too fast.

'Precisely, Mr Gillespie.'

'But why tell me? What am I supposed to do with this?' The Judas disk is in his fingers again. He holds it up like an accusation. Exhibit A.

'Insurance, Mr Gillespie. Give it to the police. It may help them solve the crimes. Then my client will be safe. It is the most I can do.'

'Why don't you just tell me who we're up against? Who am I facing?'

'*Genro* Ounserrat must have told you that the Shian law is practised at a price. Her price is that investigating too deeply into her client's disappearance may put her in the same danger as myself and my client.'

'She could be a target?'

'She, and those associated with her, Mr Gillespie. I warn you, because my price is moral quandary. I am a Harridi, and I believe that it is in the best interests of my Nation and children that humans do not find out information about us that might jeopardize their future safety on this world. We are guests after all, and guests do not murder their hosts. However, *gehenshuthra* binds me to my client's best interests, which would not be best served by the Harridis' plan succeeding. My children, my client. Please understand my crisis of conscience, Mr Gillespie.'

'Fuck your crisis of conscience!' Gillespie shouts. The doggy women look around, scandalized by this interruption of nasty loud foul-mouthed *maleness* into their afternoons. 'How many more is your fucking moral quandary going to kill?'

Saipanang flares his nostrils and bares his teeth, just a glint. Just a gleam.

'How much Hot Narha do you know, Mr Gillespie?'

'I got some words from Ounserrat. Not much more.'

'This can only be said in Hot Narha. Cool Narha does not have the words.'

Saipanang closes his eyes. He does not speak for many seconds. When he does, it's a low whisper: – *Sacrifice of Fools*.

'What?' Gillespie asks. The word strikes echoes from the surfaces of his mind. Distant voices, like neighbours behind thin walls. He can hear them but he can't make out what they're saying.

'I have said all I may. We must go now. This meeting is terminated. I trust I have made the right decision for my client, and for my children.'

Ongserrang is already heading down the hill. Saipanang turns to follow.

'Where will you go?' Gillespie shouts. 'You can't stay in South Side. Not now.'

'I cannot leave, not now. When the season is ended there is always great unrest and movement between Holds. We are a moving people. Then I and my client shall disappear. The world is a big place, Mr Gillespie, even for Shian. We shall not meet again.'

They drop below the brow of the hill. Andy Gillespie sits down on a flat piece of chapel wall and tries to make out what the voices want to tell him about *Sacrifice of Fools*, but there's so much else stuffed into his head that he can only hear his own thoughts trying to fit his experience around the facts that Saipanang and his client gave him. Too much. Way too much. He's not a *genro*. He's not a cop, nor a private eye. He's not even Andy fucking Hero. He's a grease-monkey from the Woodstock Road. He's a cheap hood with bad friends; he's a con who got given a present he wasn't expecting. He's an out-of-work translator with all the money he has in the world jingling in his back pocket.

Dog-walking hour ends. Nendrum is left to the birds and the cows beyond the perimeter fence. Andy Gillespie sits on his stone and listens to the cows farting. A tractor chugs up a drumlin side across the bright water, drawing a line of wounded brown earth behind it. Birds bicker and flock in its soil wake.

Yes, I'm all these things and I'm not all those things and I shouldn't be here and I shouldn't have anything more to do with this, but when did 'should' ever have anything to do with my life? I'm here, I'm in it, I can't leave it. The only way out is through. You go where the ride takes you, so you might as well put your arms over your head and scream tough.

After a time a front comes in from the west, covering the sun. Cold and still not able to make sense of either of the worlds he occupies, Andy Gillespie gets up and goes down to the hire car. By the time he reaches the causeway off Mahee Island it's raining.

She's standing by the gate in the rain, leaning against the post inscribed with the Shian fourfold yin-yang. The rain's soaked through more than her clothes. She's drowned inside. Her *genro* staff is all that's holding her up.

The car stops in a crunch of wet gravel. Gillespie opens the door. She drips on the floor, the seat, the upholstery.

'Nothing?'

'They fought me every step.'

'And?'

'I could not get past them. They insist that the photographs are in error and that my client has not been at South Side of the Stone since February the twenty-second.'

'Your client is dead,' Andy Gillespie says, reversing the car and swinging it round on to the bridge. 'She and her family were killed by the same person who killed the Harridis and McIvor Kyle. They used one of the processors to get rid of the bodies, and they hushed the thing up. This disk lists the inputs to the processor the day they were killed.'

He sets it on the dash. Ounserrat isn't looking at it. Her eyes are closed. Her teeth are bared.

'You are in danger,' Gillespie says. 'You're in danger, I'm in danger, everyone who has anything to do with this is danger, and I want to know what the hell is going on.'

Her answer is not in words. The noise that comes out of her is so sudden and so unlike anything he's ever heard before Gillespie almost drives the Ford off the causeway into the lough. If a liver or a lung had cancer and could voice how it felt to be consumed from within, it would sound like the long, piercing keening coming from Ounserrat Soulereya. He stops the car in the middle of the single-track road.

'Jesus God, what are you at?'

She doesn't answer until she's finished, and the noise takes a long time to finish.

'You cannot understand what it is like for a *genro* to discover she has failed her client.'

'Your client was dead before they sent you over from Docklands.'

'*Gehenshuthra* exists outside time and death.'

'Well that's just fucking stupid,' Gillespie says and regrets it the moment it's off his lips. She's only a kid, for God's sake. Three years older than his own wee Stacey. This isn't just law. She can't take the money and walk away like human lawyers. It's like that saying about football: it's not a question of life or death, it's more important than that. This is her first case and she has singularly failed to protect her client's rights. Being made into a fucking golf club is a hell of a desecration of the dead. But he's pissed off at her because of the sex thing, and for shutting him out of that legal farce at South Side, and he's pissed off at her people for shutting him out of everything.

Her nostrils are wide. She's nakedly smiling.

'Mr Gillespie . . .'

'Hell, I'm sorry. It's just – I am angry, right? I've been pissed about and fucked off and lied to and made to look like a fool and nobody will tell me what the hell is going on and I don't know who to trust any more, and to tell you the truth, I'm not even sure I trust you. You've all got your wee hidden agendas, you've all got your games and teams, but nobody's told Andy Gillespie the rules. Even you. You've got your Shian law game in your head, your personal soul-contract with your client, even though your client is dead, even though you never even properly had a client, you still owe her; you'd fuck me right up the ass if your fucking *gehenshuthra* told you it was in your client's best interests. You'd shaft me and wouldn't even feel bad about it.'

'Mr Gillespie, this is not a good time to discuss this with me.'

'I don't care. I just want to know what is going on.'

'You seem to know more than I.'

'I don't think so. That's the evidence that I've been lied to.' He nods at the disk, nestled against the demister vents.

'I also have been lied to, Mr Gillespie.'

'But you're Shian.' And he regrets that too, though he had to say it.

'Have I ever lied to you?'

'I don't know.'

'How can I prove to you that I am worthy of your trust?'

'Tell me what *Sacrifice of Fools* means.'

She hesitates. Just an instant, but it's enough for Gillespie to know that her answer will not be the truth.

'It is a story. A thing made up to frighten and entertain, like your vampires and beast-men. It is nothing real, nothing that can harm us.'

'You're lying.' Andy Gillespie says very simply. 'You are lying to me.'

'Mr Gillespie . . .'

'Mr Gillespie nothing. You are fucking lying to me; all of you; all you've ever done is lie to me. Fuck you! Fuck you to hell!'

Ounserrat lays her hands flat on her thighs.

'Then this partnership is dissolved,' she says. She opens the door and gets out. 'I shall make my own way home. Please have the car back at the depot by seventeen thirty.'

'Oh, for fuck's sake, it's twenty miles and it's pissing down. Have a bit of sense!' But she's already halfway to the main road. 'I'm the one's lied to and you get to storm off in anger!' he shouts at her. 'Jesus, you people!' He starts the car and drives beside her. 'Come on, will you?' She does not acknowledge his presence. She breaks into a jog. Gillespie matches pace with her. Her clothes are clinging to her bones but she will not look at him. She can keep this hunter's lope up for hours and miles.

'OK then, we're finished,' Gillespie shouts and then shrieks the engine and spins the wheels like he's a twentysomething in a Ford, and not a late thirty something, and drives off.

Fuck her. Fuck them all. Fuck them and their secrets and their lies and their law that says it's better to deceive a friend than betray a client. Even a dead client. Fuck them and their sneaky creepy chemicals that get into your head and turn it all inside out so that a man doesn't know what he is any more, let alone what he thinks he knows. Fuck them for having to come to this world, out of all the worlds around all the stars, as if it wasn't complicated enough with just people on it. Fuck them for making everything we do look mean and crude and smelly and brutal and stupid. Fuck you, Ounserrat Soulereya.

But he didn't. And he wanted to. And he still wants to, and he almost turns the car around to go back for her, but only almost and that isn't enough to put out his anger. So he turns on the radio instead and it's that same bloody station that has to play a Tina Turner track every hour, and this is that track, and after it, the Mystery Record.

'Bryan Adams,' he says after just the intro. '"Summer of Sixty Nine".'

Answer after four. By then he's into the Belfast traffic. He sort of wonders where Ounserrat's got to. Wet. They're supposed to hate getting wet, like cats. Well, I'm really really surprised no one got the Mystery Record, the DJ says in his dumb Ulster-American accent, I'd've thought it was obvious: 'Summer of Sixty Nine', Bryan Adams. Gillespie could have won the Top Twenty CDs. He didn't know they still had a Top Twenty. Of anything.

He uses one of his last fifty pees on a meter and then does a thing that he's never done before. He voluntarily goes into a police station.

As the desk sergeant is in the back calling up DS Dunbar, Gillespie sees a figure he knows coming towards him along the corridor. His Sunday suit is crumpled, his jaw is shadowed, his hair is tousled, he looks like shit. Gavin Peterson sidesteps the sprinkler drip and in that moment sees and recognizes Gillespie.

'Gavin.'

'Gillespie.'

'Looks like they've had you in the prime suspect suite.'

'They think they can make a conspiracy charge stick. Do you know how many top-ranking policemen are members of the Dissenting Presbyterian Church?'

'Conspiracy?'

'Come on, Gillespie. The NIPS set you up with that Outsider bitch to break our leverage operation. I must be getting old; back then, I'd've seen through you like that.'

He holds Gillespie's gaze, snaps his fingers.

'You won't believe me, but I don't have a fucking idea what you're talking about, Gavin.' Gillespie is not intimidated by Peterson's smile.

'You keep saying that, Gillespie. Keep saying that, and keep looking in mirrors, over your shoulder. You keep your eyes open. Someone will get to you with a little message from God.' He forces a laugh. 'I see someone already has. Just keep looking back, Gillespie. God is not mocked.'

He brushes past towards the security door and the street.

'Haven't you heard, Gavin?' Gillespie calls, 'God is dead!'

'His civil service is still working,' Peterson says.

He's been threatened in a police station, but Gillespie feels pity for Gavin Peterson. Now God's hard man understands what it's like to lose the thing that gives your life goal and spirit. Gillespie's still staring at the street door when Roisin Dunbar arrives. She looks greasy and tired and very very pissed off.

'You look rough,' Gillespie says.

'Rich coming from you. You still not want to press charges?'

'I've other ways of getting back at Mr Gerry Conlon and his porno video operation.'

'OK, I can give you two minutes,' Roisin Dunbar says, opening the door to interview room three. Gillespie slides the disk across the formica-topped table to her and starts to talk. It takes more than two minutes but Roisin Dunbar isn't watching the clock any more.

'Jesus,' she says when Gillespie has finished. She makes a call upstairs on the intercom. 'Boss, I've got Andy Gillespie down in interview room three. I think you should hear what he has to say. Oh, and bring Littlejohn too, if he's still around.'

'I'm on a pay and display,' Gillespie says.

'I'll pay your ticket,' Dunbar says.

Willich comes into the room, Littlejohn following. Gillespie notices Dunbar's expression. It says she's going to enjoy making Littlejohn eat shit. He doesn't like it. Littlejohn is a smug beardy bastard who wanted Gillespie for a devo serial killer, but Gillespie doesn't want anyone to have to eat police shit. He takes a deep breath and tells it all again and then sits back and listens to the police lay into Littlejohn about how he was so sure that the killer couldn't be a Sheenie, couldn't possibly be, biologically impossible, wasn't that it? And here's the man you profiled for us as prime suspect telling us he knows who the killer is. It's not nice. It's not good to hear. Police are supposed to be noble and upright and heroic, and not vicious bitches when they get it stuck up them. Not *people*. Not *men and women*.

Willich bangs out of the room with the disk. Two seconds later, Dunbar goes after him. Littlejohn and Gillespie are left in interview room three, sitting on adjacent sides of the God-ugly table.

'Sorry about that,' Gillespie says after a time.

Littlejohn looks at him.

'Xenology is not an exact science,' he says.

Gillespie smiles.

'I need your help,' he says after another time.

'Are you sure you can trust it, Mr Gillespie?'

'What do the police know?'

'What, indeed?'

'Do you speak Hot Narha, Mr Littlejohn?' Gillespie asks.

'I know its grammar and syntax and vocabulary and I could name you fifteen classical song cycles composed in it, but speak it? I take it you do.'

'I've learned some of the words, but I can't speak it.'

'You know,' Littlejohn says, 'there's something decidedly not kosher in the world when I spend years setting up the first xenology department in Ireland, learning a language with seventeen tenses, seven genders including two potential forms used exclusively for pubescent children, five modes and which completely up-arses itself twice a year into an entirely different language, and you swallow something and wake up with it in your head the next morning, word fucking perfect.'

'You mean, a wee glipe like me,' Andy Gillespie says. 'Like you say, it's not a fair world.'

Littlejohn smiles and Gillespie realizes that he is trying to be friendly. This is as nice as he gets.

'I heard something in Hot Narha today, but I don't know what it means.'

'Tell me.'

'*Sacrifice of Fools*,' Andy Gillespie says. Littlejohn frowns.

'Give me that again.' Gillespie repeats the phrase. 'Your accent is flawless. Who taught you Hot?'

Gillespie cups a hand against the breast pocket of his jacket.

'It's just the way they do it,' Littlejohn says. 'Care to introduce me to him or her for a few advanced language lessons? This expression, where did you hear it?'

'From Saipanang Harridi.'

'You didn't tell the officers.'

'It wouldn't mean anything to them. Does it mean anything to you?'

Littlejohn shrugs, sighs.

'It's a very formal mode. Hot Narha is a nightmare of modes: they've got modes for addressing sexual partners and non-sexual partners, and each has a different gender form. This is in Hot Dream Mode, the spiritual language the *hahndahvi* speak in the *kesh* cycle.'

'It chimes with other words in my head, but I can't make any sense out of them.'

'I'd need to check back at home. It does sound vaguely familiar though, I might have come across it in one of the eddas, or maybe a research student brought it up in a meeting. You think it's important?'

'It cost him a lot to say it.'

'You know better than me, their motivations are nothing like ours. We understand each other more by luck than affinity.'

Gillespie thinks of Ounserrat Soulereya, soaked to the bones but doggedly pushing on through the rain. Twenty miles to home, and she won't even slow down. Pride isn't it, nor anger. Humiliation, despair, arrogance. Human names, human feelings.

'Tell you what,' Littlejohn continues, 'I'm neither use nor ornament here. You can see what the Northern Ireland Police Service think of me.'

'Sorry about that,' Gillespie says.

'Life's a learning curve or it's a flat line, my friend. Come back to my place and I'll see what I can find about your Sacrifice of Fools. At least it'll show these smug police bastards I'm still good for something.'

'Could we go by way of McAusland's car hire?' Gillespie asks. 'I've ten minutes before I go into an extra day.'

Gillespie could see himself living in Littlejohn's house. Big early Victorian terrace backing on to the Botanic Gardens, but the wall tall enough to prevent the cider drinkers from throwing their bottles over. High ceilings. Big rooms. He likes the plaster mouldings, and the little glass cupola on the return. So what if it leaks? This is a house that suits the rain. Looks good in it. Upstairs living room. Dining room at the front. Class. He could go some of this. Not like those executive estates out at Upper Malone, with two feet between the red-brick mansions so they can feel detached and islands unto themselves. Arranged in closes and cul-de-sacs. Pseudo California. They don't suit the rain. They look like surfers caught in a downpour. You'd think we'd been colonized by the Americans, not the Shian.

But he can see himself in this place, yes, if things had turned out differently from how they did.

'Drink?' Littlejohn's study is at the back of the house, looking out on to a closed yard cluttered with rusting gardening tools and terracotta planters filled with the rotted straw of last summer's annuals. A red plastic bird feeder half full of peanuts swings from the washing line. 'Not much else than gin, but there might be some beer at the back of the fridge.'

'Beer would be good.'

Gillespie studies the study while Littlejohn rummages in the fridge. He's always wanted a room furnished with books. One wall, nothing but books. The books on Littlejohn's wall are all about the Shian and look new. New subject, new books. He leans over the shelf and sniffs. He's always loved the smell of fresh book. Lamps are lit against the gloom; that's the way to light a room, Gillespie thinks. Photographs on the wall facing the books. His graduation, her graduation. Their wedding. Kids, growing through baby shots and school photographs and high days and holidays. Did girls really dress like that in the nineties? Were boys' hair-cuts that grim? Memory is kind, photography brutal. Their graduations. Their weddings. Their baby shots. On the desk beside the computer, a silver-framed photograph of a handsome woman.

'When they went we discovered they were all we had in common,' Littlejohn says, handing Gillespie a tin of Caffrey's and a glass. 'Classic empty nest syndrome. Just because you can describe it to five decimal places doesn't prevent you from becoming a victim.'

'Sorry,' Gillespie says.

'Don't be.' He sets his gin on his desk and himself behind the computer. 'This could take a while. I may have to uplink to the Fifteenth Fleet Colonial Library and it's difficult getting satellite time booked.'

'Isn't that expensive?' Gillespie pops and pours his beer and watches the head surge out of the creaming liquid.

'Appallingly. However, best efforts of my children and my wife's lawyers notwithstanding, I am fucking rolling in it. More than I know what to do with.'

Gillespie sits back in the cat-clawed chair and sips his beer and watches the rain outside the window and Littlejohn moving across the plane of streaked grey, fetching a book here, a file there, a magazine somewhere else. The click of the mouse is loud and metallic. The screen lights Littlejohn's face. Fifteen minutes pass. Half an hour.

'Nothing in the main dictionaries, but I wasn't really expecting anything,' Littlejohn says. 'We learn enough new words and phrases and modes to bring out a new dictionary every other week. The formal mode might make it worth having a juke at religio-social studies. The trouble with these people is that they cut right across our established academic disciplines.'

Back to the mouse-clicking. Gillespie picks a book off the shelf. It's not everywhere he feels comfortable enough to read. This house, this room, this man, are the life he once imagined. Alternative Andy Gillespie. The book's a survey of the better known Shian *hahndahvi*. It's a popular work, with plenty of pictures. Gillespie flicks over the glossy pages. They smell good. He pauses over some of the more bizarre avatar masks. Imagine these things walking in your dreams. An open-mouthed face, painted with white spirals.

Ongtith, guardian of paths and fords. This avatar occupies a central place in the Shian Dreaming, and existed in proto-forms thirty thousand years ago, when, at the end of the Shith Glaciation, she led the Old Hunters into the newly habitable north. In the historical period, this *hahndahvi* guided the nomadic nations across Sounyok, the continental forest, and is associated with both astronomy and the reading of forests signs. Frequently appears to new adults as they embark on their *wanderjahrs*, and thus has a secondary aspect as the guide of the young. Huge renditions of the Ongtith mask are painted on the ablation shields of Shian interstellar vehicles.

Her environment in the Dreamplace is always the forest clearing, her associated symbols are the fire, the staff, the *petoun*, the scent-laying stick, and the bare footprint. Her manifestations are as a female dressed in white. She is always barefoot and bareheaded and never speaks. If addressed directly, the *hahndahvi* will disappear. Though a guide, she is an ambiguous figure, she can lead both to and away from a situation, and her destinations may not always be those the dreamer might consider most beneficial.

Please rub the scratch-and-sniff panel at the bottom of the page for a sample of her identifying perfume.

Gillespie holds the book up to his face. It's hard to make anything out over the glossy paper and printer's ink, but then he catches it and for a moment the book unfolds around him and he's standing in that clearing among the dark red trees and the light of a different sun is falling through the leaves and a creature in white is beckoning him down a path that curves away into darkness. Then he's back in the big scruffy chair and it's raining and the table lamps are lit and all he can smell is himself.

He shivers.

Another mask: a Shian face with wooden skewers sticking out of its nose and its head hair. *Plouterhai: the Questioner. Spirit of Penetrating Inquiry.* Penetrating inquiry all right, up its nose. This your one, Ounserrat Soulereya? The patron saint of lawyers? What would the *hahndahvi*, ex-con, ex-grease-monkey, Narha-speaking amateur knight-advocates be? I'm sure there's something suitable, way down in the really obscure dream creatures, the bottom nine thousand that have about three followers each. What kind of mask would it wear? Dazed and confused, and under-shaved. Pouchy around the eyes, too much chin. Half an inch of stubble all over. Tired. That most of all. I know exactly its characteristic scent.

'No luck then?' Gillespie asks. Littlejohn grunts and waves a hand. Deep into it. Warmed within by beer and without by zero-point electric central heating, Andy Gillespie dozes in the big tatty chair. It's been a long time and much happening since rashers and sausage and two eggs in the cheap hotel on the canal.

And Eamon Donnan, he thinks. What came to you out of the flapping things that live in the folds of the sacred space? What stepped out of your life into your dreams? Was it something you made up out of your memories and hopes and fantasies, or was it made-to-measure, an off-the-peg deity? How did you learn to dream? Whose tit did you suck it from? And when the *hahndahvi* came to you, did it know what it saw? Or did it say, get away from me weird half-thing, I don't recognize you?

He settles into the chair and almost dreams of open-mouthed, staring-eyed, spiral-painted masks of Ongtith hurtling through space. He's woken by the consciousness that there is a face looming over him. Littlejohn.

'I think we have something.'

The mask of the Littlejohn *hahndahvi* is worried.

The desk is covered in printouts. A starship icon in the top corner of the computer screen shows he's uplinked to the Fifteenth Fleet Library at ten pounds a minute. Open windows all over the screen. He fetches fresh drinks from the kitchen. 'This is going to take a bit of telling.

'I had to go right back to the *Geduldehanna*, the epic poems of the founding of the Nations. They aren't exactly religious texts because the Shian don't have a religion, as such, but they're the most ancient documents their race possesses; they've been preserved unchanged for ten thousand years, and before that they were passed down for God knows how many thousands more years as oral literature. They're a sort of snapshot of the Shian in transition from a nomadic hunter-gatherer society to a technological culture. There are hundreds of the damn things, each Nation has at least one, and each is a thousand pages long; they make the *Mahabharata* look like a shopping list. And they're bloody difficult to read, *hahndahvi* step in and out of them, you can never be sure whether we're in the physical world or the Dreamplace, and the literary styles fluctuate between modes and Hot and Cool Narha, according to the season in which they're set. Which is just to say it's a bitch of a job, so you'll properly appreciate the magnitude of my discovery.'

'Which is?'

'Let a man tell his tale, will you? I went to the *Corrosoun Geduldehan*, which is one of the oldest stories in the cycle. The Corrosoun Nation's fallen a bit from glory over the millennia, but they were one of the most powerful of the early Nations in Central Great Continent, which is the birthplace of Shian civilization as we know and love it today. Basically, it's this incredibly long and complex and quite unnecessarily detailed account of the establishment and defence of the Corrosoun hunting demesnes against the neighbouring Huskravidis, whom history has treated more favourably than their ancient rivals. I went to this cycle because it's the only one that makes any mention of something we would call *war*.'

'I thought the Shian didn't fight wars.'

'They don't. Not as we fight wars. Nations don't mobilize against Nations, they don't even have nations as we recognize them.'

'I know this.'

'Sorry. Lecture mode is a tough infection to beat.'

'War is displaced rape, and their sexual make-up makes rape impossible for them.'

'You sound like me.'

'I should. I got it from an *Irish Times* article you wrote about a year back.'

'I used to say something similar about serial killing too.'

Gillespie smiles wryly, apologetically.

'I'm a scientist,' Littlejohn continues. 'If the facts don't fit the theory, you're supposed to throw out the theory.'

'Supposed.'

'We're human. We like a familiar universe around us, that we know how it works, even the nasty stuff, like killing each other. And then these folk come and we don't know how things work any more. They've rewritten the rules on everything else, why not murder?' Littlejohn downs half his gin in one swallow. 'When you were a teenager, you know, full of idealism and putting the world to rights and wouldn't it all be very much better if only we did *this* instead of *that*, did you ever think wouldn't it be great if, instead of fighting wars, like, say, the Gulf War, or even the Second World War, someone had just quietly blown away Saddam Hussein or Hitler before they started fucking things up, and then there wouldn't even be a war? One death to prevent millions?'

'Most of my teenage years were talking about girls or football or cars.'

'Lucky you.'

'I mean, sure, everyone's thought of it, like if they'd killed off Gerry Adams, or Paisley. Or McIvor Kyle. Jesus God.'

'For some people it's more than just a good idea,' Littlejohn says. 'Now listen to this. Two passages from the *Corrosoun Geduldehan*. The first is in Cool Narha; I'm translating roughly: "Then the Hold of, ah, Good Killing by the Waterhole made war with the Hold of Fifteen Trees" – the text specifies a species of tree but it won't translate. "They met at the open place and they fought until the close of the day with sundry weapons." This is a shit translation.'

'I think that should be "the green before the skinning hut" instead of "open place", and "edged blades" for "sundry weapons",' Gillespie says, coming round the desk to peer over Littlejohn's shoulder. Littlejohn bristles a moment.

'I bow to your superior knowledge of the vernacular. It goes on . . .'

'"Many eyes were taken by the Good Killing Hold",' Gillespie translates. '"The people of Fifteen Trees were shamed and did not leave their Hold for hunt or *kesh* or journeying for a year and a lesser moon. The earth was drunk with blood. Birds gathered in that place to gorge for many days, and the *hahndahvi* came to live there so that all who passed through that spot were visited for many nights by ominous dreams." So they do have war.'

'Where were you when I was doing my doctoral thesis?' Littlejohn asks. 'They have war in the same way as South American Indians or tribal people in Borneo do: small group to small group. Hunting parties clashing, conflict of demesnes, stuff like that. Small scale, like Scottish inter-clan warfare. Or our own home-grown ethnic head-hunting. More a vendetta than a war. You haven't heard the second one. This is from a Hot Narha passage, written either during, or about, incidents that took place during, a *kesh* cycle.'

Windows close and open. It's dark outside, the wind has risen and is driving the rain against the glass. Something is flapping in the yard.

'From the *Corrosoun Geduldehan*, canto thirty-seven, part nine, stanzas twenty-five to twenty-seven. "Sestrahunna" – she's a kind of Cuchulain figure, a Shian superheroine, cantos thirty to forty-five are dedicated to her exploits – "Sestrahunna's people had been much troubled by the Hold of Great Safety, who were stirring up the other Holds to challenge the Corrosoun demesne. Therefore she went to the residence of the spirits" – what we'd now call a sacred space; the Shian dreaming has evolved a lot in sophistication since these things were written. "There she met a man dressed in crimson with a head-piece set with a thousand mirrors. He carried in his right hand a gutting knife. He greeted her and told her he was the Drinker of the Red Earth, the Divider of the Waters, the Cutter. He said that the people of Great Safety Hold were committing great folly. They were trying to hunt a river." Note the "she" here.'

'It's the *kesh* form.'

'Exactly. Couple of important points. The Shian didn't go through a semi-aquatic phase in their evolution like humans did. They're a very terrestrial species, they don't like water, they don't trust water. It can't be contained, it's liquid, mercurial, and it's dangerous. You can drown in just a puddle of it. They have a great fear of drowning; it's the most terrible death to them, because it's always done alone, separate from the community. It's a kind of annihilation. Water, the sea, lakes, rivers have sinister connotations in the *Geduldehanna*. It's full of stories of lone Shian who were entranced by their reflection in water, fell in and were drowned. Trying to hunt a river is the ultimate folly, wasting the energy of the Hold on catching something that cannot be caught. The gutting knife is important as well. It has semi-ritual connotations. After the hunt the intestines and sex organs of the prey are removed – the sex organs are thought unlucky, except during *kesh*, when they are eaten as a delicacy. The text goes on: "Drinker of Red Earth, Divider of the Waters, the Cutter gave her the gutting knife, and told her to commit upon them the sacrifice of fools".'

'It what?'

'There's more. "She called upon herself shadows and wearing them like a cloak, she went to the Great Safety Hold and passed through its fences and hedges. She came unseen to the people of Great Safety, and their children with them, and with the gutting knife committed on their bodies the sacrifice of fools, unto the smallest child, sparing none so that their folly might not be perpetuated. Then she took the organs that she had cut from the adults and cooked them on the fire, and ate them, and the folly was ended and there was peace between the Corrosoun and their neighbours."'

Gillespie looks at the sinuous Shian script on the screen. He shivers. The cold has got into the warm room, inside him.

'You're telling me that Sounsurresh's family, the Harridis, McIvor Kyle's family, have been killed by a legend?'

'There's often truth behind our monster stories. Let's take vampires. Solitary hunters of human beings. Damned souls. Deeply disturbed individuals, we'd call them these days. Ritual aspects to their killings, mutilation of the victims. Displaced sexual desire.'

'Serial killers,' Gillespie says. 'And this sacrificer of fools, he's stepped off the legends into our world. Into Belfast, Northern Ireland. No shortage of fools here. Christ, when I asked Ounserrat what "Sacrifice of Fools" meant, she told me it was a story, a legend, something made up to scare children.'

'She didn't lie to you.'

'No wonder they want to keep it secret.'

'Perfectly rational behaviour to them. Eliminate the threat before it even starts to threaten. Makes a lot of sense to me.'

'But the family, the children.'

'Eradicating the taint from the genepool. These people are deeply unsentimental when it comes to eugenics. What's a few bodies in the foundations, when you look at our head count in two world wars? There're enough nuclear warheads to kill every human on earth fifty times over, and a male sexuality that positively seeks conflict. Who's scaring the shit out of whom?'

Gillespie sits down in the comfortable, tattered chair again. Empty beer cans and glasses are at his feet.

'I'm finding this a bit hard to believe. OK, we've worked out what, but we haven't a fucking clue who.'

Littlejohn's silence is political.

'You do have a fucking clue who.'

Littlejohn rolls his eyes.

'Someone you got before all this broke. When you thought it was a human. Except it isn't, but you still have a suspicion. Oh, come on. For fuck's sake. You can't be serious.'

231

'He fits the profile.'

'Eamon Donnan is no more a fool killer than I am.'

'You fitted the profile, for a while.'

'You were wrong about me, you were wrong that it couldn't be a Shian, you're wrong about Eamon. He's a mate.'

'This working-class ex-con male bonding is very touching, but Charlie Manson was once somebody's mate. You say he's a mate. All right. So what kind of a mate fucks off the moment he gets out to join the Shian? What kind of a mate is it thinks so little of humans that he wants to be an Outsider? Humans, including you, mate. Counts for a lot, doesn't it? Did he ever give a moment's consideration to what his good mate Andy Gillespie might feel about him turning himself into a Shian? What do you know about him? What did you ever know about him? Really know?'

'Do not, ever, try to stick your fucking psychology up his ass, right?'

'I'm not doing anything. I'm just telling what's happening. You know what a sacred space can do to your head, let alone the *kesh* chemicals. He's on his own, not one of them, but definitely not one of us, taking this stuff into him with every breath, and every breath is taking him further from what he hates into what he loves. But he can't love them. He's not Shian enough for that. He's got a dick and he knows what to do with it, but what he wants to do with it the Shian don't. He can't love them how they want to be loved.'

'He kills them because he can't fuck them?'

'Killing is never that simple. It's like a very fine liqueur; there can be dozens – hundreds – of ingredients in the recipe, all reacting and co-acting with each other, infusing, imparting their particular combination of flavours over a long time. Years. Decades.'

Murder like Drambuie, or Galliano in a tall yellow bottle. Jesus.

'You're talking bollocks. Why start by killing the people you want to be part of?'

'To show how much he loves them. He's sitting in that sacred space, trying to find a way of loving them so they won't hate him, and then this *hahndahvi* comes out of the light dressed in a crimson robe with this big tall headdress and a gutting knife in one hand and says, *I know how you can show how much you love us.* Those bodies are a love-offering to the Harridi Nation, like a cat leaving a dead sparrow in your slipper. Look what I've done, I killed for you. I've sacrificed fools to you, dangerous fools, threats to your children and the Nations' genelines. Look how much I love you. Murder is sex misspelled.'

Gillespie's standing up now, agitated, about to pace up and down the study carpet. Littlejohn's behind the desk, sitting down, lower than Gillespie, but he's the one in command here.

'I'll go to Queen's Island, I'll find him, I'll prove to you that Eamon Donnan is not a killer.'

'You'll have a job.' Gillespie remembers that smart-smart tone of voice quite well. You can't stop it, can you? For a wee time we had it, we were two guys, working together, getting along, respecting each other's abilities, but you had to make it so there's a high and a low and a clever and a stupid and a university lecturer and a mechanic from the Woodstock Road. The world has to tell you how clever you are.

'What do you mean?'

'The police went in yesterday morning. They turned the place upside down; nearly started a riot. Donnan's flown the coop.'

Gillespie balls a fist but there's nothing to strike it against.

'Stupid stupid stupid.' Suddenly decided, he grabs his coat and pulls it on.

'Where are you going?' Littlejohn asks.

'I'm going to make Ounserrat Soulereya tell me the truth, the whole truth, nothing but the truth, so help her God. *Genro* to *genro*. She knows. She'll tell me. I'll prove it's not Eamon Donnan, and you can stick your psychology.'

'I'll give you a lift.' Gillespie senses that Littlejohn's genuinely conciliatory, that he knows he's pushed too hard and too far, but he's not going to sell forgiveness for a ride in a car. That was working-class male bonding. This is working-class male pride.

'I'll walk.'

'It's pissing down. You're in no condition to go anywhere.'

'I don't want your fucking lift, right?'

It's a cunt of a night. Within twenty footsteps Gillespie's wet through. He turns up his collar, puts his head down, limps on through the dark and the wet. Sour Belfast rain runs down the back of his neck, into his eyes. It's been doing that to him all his life. There's not even a single masochistic jogger on the embankments tonight. The people in the cars that pass stare at him like he was out on Care in the Community.

At first he doesn't make anything out of the fact that he can't hear any music. Males go crazy on hormone heat, but they couldn't dance in this weather. Then he sees the crowd on the ground beneath Ounserrat's flat. There are males in dance gear, females in and out of formal costume, kids, standing in the rain, thin and wet as refugees. There are more of them on the steps, and along the landing and at the open door. One at the top of the steps spots the human first. All the heads turn simultaneously.

'What the fuck is going on here?'

Two big females at the top of the stairs try to stop him going on to the landing.

'You would be advised not to proceed any further,' one says.

'I'm Andy Gillespie, I work with her.'

'We know,' the other says.

'What's happened? Something's happened, what's going on?'

'We would emphatically advise you to leave,' the first one says. They move closer together to better block him.

'Get the fuck out of my way.' With a grit of pain, Andy Gillespie picks up one of the females and throws her over the low stair wall. He doesn't look to see how she falls, he doesn't hear her odd high-pitched wail, or notice the Shian rushing to help her. All there is is the open apartment door, and Outsiders that, if they are sensible, will keep out of his way. They're sensible. He bulls into the tiny hall.

'Ounserrat,' he bellows.

Into the big living room.

'Oh Jesus fuck.'

The first body is face down on the carpet, feet towards the door. Arms outspread, fingers splayed. Face down. It hasn't even got a head, let alone a face. Just that big fan of red on the carpet, like a river delta.

All he can hear are his careful, measured breaths. He goes up to the body, stands over it. It's dressed in a pair of blue baggies. Its bare torso is covered in faded patterns in black felt marker. Gillespie closes his eyes, to enjoy the come of guilty pleasure that it's not her.

The second body is by the window. It's sprawled back on the sofa. It's dressed in black leather jeans and a denim jacket. He knows those clothes. The blue denim is purple with blood. Gillespie advances towards Ounserrat. Her left arm is missing from just below the shoulder. Blood everywhere. So much blood. Blood oozing from the seared stump of the arm. Her face is a mask of blood. She has a face. An erect *genro* staff lies at her feet. The window is pink with meat drizzle. Gillespie kneels, sobbing, trying to stop the blood, stop her life running away through his fingers.

The body twitches.

Gillespie is too terrified to move.

An arm comes out from behind the body. A head, shoulders, a body wriggles free. A spindly homunculus, covered in blood. It staggers to its feet on the sofa.

– *Gillespie, Gillespie*, it sings in Hot Narha. – *Fool Slayer, Fool Slayer, Fool Slayer.*

'An ambulance!' Andy Gillespie roars to the Shian that have ventured into the hall. 'Get a fucking ambulance!'

'Hi, honey, I'm home. Early.'

What makes John Willich boss of bosses is that he knows when you're shattered and bruised and just about thinking but still have a gallon or so in the tank, and when you're shattered and bruised and just about thinking and if you have to run any further you'll fall out of the sky.

'Hons? Michael?'

Saying enough, done, quitting for the day grates Roisin Dunbar's soul. She could never trust others not to fuck it up. And if they do, it'll come back to her. But Willich said go home, eat, drink, have a bath, play with your kid, take your husband

235

out to dinner, see a film, just do something that isn't this investigation, in his tone of it isn't an order now but it will be if I have to repeat it.

'Mikey?' If he's got the VR rig on he mightn't be able to hear her. She checks the downstairs anyway. Mugs balanced on the arms on sofas and chairs. Can't he grasp the simple principle of sticking used coffee mugs in the dishwasher? Except he can never be bothered to empty the dishwasher. You buy a dishwasher because you're too lazy to wash dishes, and then you're too lazy to unstack the thing. She sticks the Chilean Chardonnay she picked up on the way home in the fridge. OK, if she has to take time off, she's going to make it work for her.

'Mikey? Hons?'

Upstairs now, but she can't feel the house breathing. She can always sense another human presence in a building. Prickle of body fields rubbing past each other. He's probably nipped out to the wee shop. If he's left Louise home alone, he'll be getting his balls on a plate for dinner. With Chilean Chardonnay. Come home early and catch all your little domestic sins. She can hear the infrasonic whine of an active television screen in his study. Monitor's on.

'Mikey? Louise?' She sticks her head in to make sure her instincts aren't fooling her. They aren't. Screensaver superheroes swoop across the monitor, fists out-thrust.

On the chair, what's that?

There's webbing to it, and buckles and snaps fasteners, and padded bits and bits that stick out and stick in and cable. Lots of computer cable. She holds it up and it falls into shape and it's obvious how it's worn and where everything fits and what they do. She can smell the wheaty, bready musk of come.

The first thing she wants to do is drop it. The second is be sick. The third is somehow convince herself she has never seen it. The big thought in her head is my life is over. Everything I thought I had is nothing, everything I believed is a lie. Ashed and blown away in a single second.

She doesn't drop the suit. She isn't sick. Nothing will convince her to unsee what she has found here. She sits down in Michael's chair. Her elbow nudges the mouse. The Captain Screensavers disappear. Underneath is a net connection document. CyberSex On-line Interactive.

I don't want to look at this.

Look at this.

Meatmaster@genesis.com to Miss Sylvie@demon.co.uk.

Meatmaster. She's going to boke again. She fights it down. Com. commenced 17.15. Com. session ended 18.18. Total elapsed time, 63.45 mins. Full interactivity: 48.1 minutes.

There's a message in a little window surrounded by red hearts at the bottom of the screen. *To Meatmaster: oooh! you hit my G-spot, and my HIJKL and M spots too. Same time next week! Can't wait, big boy.* Above it is a picture of a big-tittied slapper pursing Marilyn Monroe lips at a camera.

And what picture did Meatmaster Michael Dunbar show you?

The net holds a lot of lies.

She sits back, hand on chest, breathing heavily. She sees the computer link. She sees the suit. She sees the desk lamp.

Do it, Rosh.

Miss Sylvie answers her Meatmaster after three rings.

Back so soon, darlin'? Dunbar imagines a Deep Saath drawl behind the e-mail. *Well, I'm hot and ready for you.*

Good, darlin'. Dunbar jerks the flex out of the desk lamp and shoves the live wires into the plastic penis holster. The socket circuit fuses with a bang. The computer dies. Did that perm your little pussy, Miss Sylvie@demon.co.uk?

She hears the front door open.

'Rosh?' He'll have seen her car. He won't know if she's found his toy, so he'll play it innocent and cool. 'You're home early.' For a third time, she wants to throw. That sickening fake innocence.

'Could you come up here a minute?'

There's a pause before he climbs the stairs. In that pause he knows she knows. He appears in the doorway. He's got Louise in her baby carrier.

'Um.'

'Give me Louise.' She puts her on the floor. She doesn't want her near that thing. 'Well, say something.' But he doesn't. He never does. He just stands and says nothing because he knows that anything he says she will wrest from him and use to run him through. She has always hated this passive silence. She hates it especially now, now that he's not Michael any more but an alien in her house that she wants to hurt and wound and slash and drive out into the rain. 'Explain it to me. Tell me what it's about, what it does for you, how good it is, what it can do that I can't. Tell me why you need to buy this stuff and hook it into the net and hide it from me. Tell me, do you have a set time for doing it, is it a wee ritual, do you watch the lunchtime news and *Neighbours* and then get hot thinking about getting the suit out and putting it on and hooking it up to the computer? Tell me, what do you feel like when you put it on? Tell me what they do, all these wee vibrators and sensors and motors and pressure pads? What do they make you feel? Is it better than me? Is it more exciting, or is it more gentle, or is it that it can be whatever you want it to be? What do you see in those goggles? Can you make her look like whatever you like? It's computers, isn't it? Everything can be anything, but nothing real. Do you stand here, stark naked, in this room, with this thing on your dick and that up your ass and those over your nipples? Do you stand there with that helmet on, bumping and grinding, fucking air? Do you smile? Is there that stupid goofy grin under your goggles? Can you stroke her tits with those datagloves, can you twang her clit? Can you do oral? Is it good at oral? Is it better than me? Or do you fiddle it so that what you see in the goggles is me, and not fucking Miss Sylvie@wherever the fuck she is?'

'It's not real,' he blurts out. 'It's just a game we play between ourselves. It's not serious, it's not real. It's virtual.'

Roisin Dunbar dips her finger into the penis holster, scoops out white slime.

'This is virtual semen? Meatmaster?'

He winces at the name.

'I never touched any of them,' he says.

'This is supposed to make me feel better? It's only virtual adultery, so it's not really adultery at all? Because it's just computers, we still have a good, healthy, loving marriage? Jesus. Every day I go out to work and you rub your hands and say yippee! she's gone, now the fun really starts! And where's Louise when you're doing this? Sleeping in the next room, or do you stick her downstairs watching television while you have your own wee private party up here? Or do you have her in here with you? Sure it's only virtual. I don't want to know. I don't want to hear anything from you. Oh; just go. If I have to look at that fucking mashed-potato cocker-spaniel look one more second I really will throw up. Get out of this house. Get out of my sight, get out of anything to do with me.'

The trill of her mobile is so sudden and incongruous it's rung several times before Roisin Dunbar realizes what it is.

'Yes. Fuck. All right. Jesus.'

'Work?'

Don't try that Mr Sympathetic understanding voice. Do not try it. She picks up Louise, waving her little fists in her plastic baby-trug. What are you going to do with her at a murder scene?

'Take her. You have one night. Say all you have to say to her, play all the wee games you want to play with her, read her all your favourite stories, play her your favourite CDs because tomorrow morning you are going. And I shouldn't need to tell you you're in the spare room.'

Dunbar shoves daughter and trug at Michael. She sees Grateful/Triumphant/It'll All Blow Over With a Little Sweet Talk on Michael's face and wishes for a five pound sledgehammer to plant in the middle of it.

Jesus, nine-to-five-and-beyond you pick up the bodies and the wreckage and wonder at other people's lives, and you come home and without anyone asking your permission it's your life that's trapped in the wreckage.

She's halfway down the close when it hits her: how come he gets thrown out, but she's the one ends up leaving?

There is no more terminal sound to Roisin Dunbar than the rip and zip of a body bag being sealed.

The men in the white plastic boiler suits and the rubber boots struggle the load down the slippery concrete steps to the black van. The Outsiders press close, trying to touch the black bag. They are making a curious humming sound.

'Get these people back,' Willich shouts. 'You, Dunbar, get the fucking lead out.'

Dunbar shakes black webbing body harnesses with fully interactive dildonics out of her head. In blow the rain and the white glare of the emergency floods. Don't smile, she reminds herself, advancing arms outstretched towards the Outsiders. Not even that pacifying half-smile they taught you in training for crowd control situations.

'OK, could you give us some room, please?'

The back door of the van is open; the bag slides in on the smooth chrome runners.

'What the hell is up with you tonight, Dunbar?' Willich has stopped on his way to the control car for a wee word with his sergeant. 'I don't know where you are but it isn't here.'

'Boss, I'm going to need some time off.'

'You are joking.'

Doors slam. The black van moves off, slowly. Always slow, Dunbar thinks. Always dignified. Why? The back seat passenger isn't going to mind. They could do wheel spins, hand-brake turns. Off up the road to the porcelain table.

Littlejohn comes down the steps from the flat. By being busy and moving around a lot he's trying to create the impression that he's got a vital role here. He's as much use as hog nipples. He turns up his collar, grimaces at the rain. Dunbar's so wet she doesn't care any more.

'How is it in there?' she asks.

Littlejohn shakes his head.

'If they hadn't had that Shian medic up at the Royal, she'd be dead. Even so . . .'

There's a small commotion at the door of the flat. Heads turn on the landing and down on the street. The ambulance sends its blue rays sweeping over the wet faces.

The crash team is coming out. People in green coveralls are shouting at each other, trying to get the chrome stretcher down the stairs without further damaging its passenger. Some green-suits are holding up bottles of drip. Some are bending down. Andy Gillespie is helping to carry the stretcher. Half carry, half embrace. He looks in pieces. He looks like his world has ended.

I should look like that, Roisin Dunbar thinks. I should feel like that. But all I feel is numb and wet, and very very cold. One of the greensuits is a Shian, standing close to the head of the stretcher, calling 'Careful, careful' as they negotiate the wet concrete steps. A skinny elf-thing in a *Hunchback of Notre Dame* T-shirt is clinging to the stretcher. The crash team try to push it away but it comes right back as if magnetized.

Willich goes up to the crash team. Dunbar hears him ask. 'When do you think she'll be ready to give a statement?' The human doctors have looks of naked amazement on their faces. The Shian doctor says, 'If she lives, it will be quite some time.' They slide the stretcher into the open back of the ambulance. Medics pile in beside it, Dunbar can see them hooking in monitors. The Shian doctor is arguing with one of the humans.

'With the greatest respect, you do not have the facilities for trauma of this degree.' Polite, even with minutes between life and bleeding to death. She can't make out what the human doctor says, but the Shian replies, 'The stasis coffin will keep her stable; there is a full regeneration unit on Ship Sixty-Four.'

The kid keeps trying to clamber in and getting unhooked from the back of the ambulance. It's making a weird whining noise. One of the greensuits sees Dunbar and shoves the kid at her.

'You're police, aren't you? Look after this, will you? Keep it out from under our wheels.'

Assuming that because she's a woman, she'll know what to do with children. Of any species. She holds its hand. It blinks at her. A Shian steps forward from the crowd and extends a hand to the skinny thing. It sniffs the hand, then jumps on to the Outsider's hip, wrapping its long arms around the adult's waist. Monkey-kid. Andy Gillespie's arguing with the greensuits now. He wants to go with her. The humans are dubious. The Shian doctor beckons to him. He jumps in. The doors slam. The ambulance moves off. Sirens open up. The kid struggles and jerks but its foster parent has it held tight. The Shian opens its saturated blouse and offers teat. The kid hauls it to its mouth and sucks greedily.

'Bloody fucking mess, boss?' Roisin Dunbar asks.

'Bloody fucking arsehole of a mess,' Willich says. 'Of course, no one saw anything. No one heard anything, no one knows anything. No one's going to tell us anything.'

Scene of crime are going up the stairs with their big metal cases. The Shian are dispersing to their homes. Much to talk about but nothing more to see. Willich goes to sit in his car and tries to wipe his head and face down with tissues.

'Look at this suit. It was new last week. Pure new wool.'

Roisin Dunbar sits in the back and watches the rain. Thank you, whoever you are who blew that family apart. Thank you because it stops me thinking about my blown-apart family. Thank you that it gets me out of that house where every wall and door and window shuts you into this new world that is so very different from the world it was this morning, and every picture and magazine and book on the bookshelves and CD in the CD rack is stupid and false and as insubstantial as this rain.

'Boss, I need to talk to you about this time off. It'll only take a moment.'

Someone's banging on the window. Darren Healey, head bent, trying to keep the rain off him.

'Boss, got something. In the van, come and look.'

'What?'

'I don't know.'

It smells of wet coats, wet shoes, fart and Darren Healey's aftershave in the electronics van. With Willich, Dunbar and Littlejohn crammed in behind Healey and the tech, the humidity reaches one hundred per cent.

'We got this off the security cameras at Wellington College,' Healey says. 'Now, you have to watch carefully. We didn't catch it the first time.' The tech runs the tape. It shows street, rain, yellow light, passing car headlights on the main road. 'Coming up,' Healey says. 'There.' He points at the screen. 'Freeze it here.'

Dunbar sees it. They all see it. It looks like a thickening of the air, like a floater in the eye caught against the light. The video clicks on a frame. Another. Another. It's moved. It has no shape, no form, it is defined purely by absence.

'What the hell is that?' Willich whispers.

'We're running it through enhancement,' Healey says. 'It should be ready.'

'Ready now,' the tech says. 'It's on screen.'

The software has sharpened the edges of the thing. It's a shadow of dryness inside the rain, twisting, twining. Dunbar imagines she can get the sense of it, that it's a thing she knows, knows very well. Then the frame jumps and it's something alien. It's moving very, very fast; this eye of not-rain in the heart of the storm.

A needle of pure frozen superstitious dread slides up Roisin Dunbar's spine.

It's a ghost. The shape of the rain falling around a person who isn't there. The other night upon the stair, I met a man who wasn't there . . . No. It can't be. No such thing. Then you tell me what it is, logic. There has to be a physical object there. The rain's running off something. You just can't see it.

'Oh, my God.'

She understands what they're up against. They can't beat this. No one can beat this.

'Now I know why the paramilitaries are so desperate to get their hands on a Cloak of Shadows,' Littlejohn says.

One day Miss McClure in P3 in Euston Street Primary School asked her class what they really, *really* wanted to do most in all the world. The wee licky girls had said they wanted to be good or have a cat or pony or get some doll or other. Some of the wee boys had wanted to walk in a band with their Das, or play football for Manchester United. Andy Gillespie age seven had said, 'Miss, I'd like to ride in a nambulance with the woo-woos going and all the lights flashing and going through traffic lights and everything getting out of your way. Miss.'

It's turned out to be a real disappointment.

It sways. It bounces. You can't see where the hell you're going. It's the closest Andy Gillespie's ever been to car sick. He presses himself against the door, keeping out of the way of paramedic elbows and needles. They're talking fast and low among themselves in a language stranger than Narha.

A medic clambers around the stretcher to sit opposite him.

'Need some information from you. Do you know if the customer has any next of kin?'

Customer. Jesus.

'Only her partner, the one who got killed, and her kid. Someone's looking after it. Her home Hold is called Not Afraid of the River. It's in London, Docklands, somewhere. I don't know who you'd talk to there. She's pregnant, you know.'

The Shian medic looks up, looks at Andy Gillespie, shakes his head in the human *no*.

'Any insurance details?'

'Get to fuck.'

She writes something down on a clipboard. Not what Gillespie said.

'And what is your relationship with the customer?'

'Her *genro*,' Andy Gillespie says. The paramed frowns. 'Her lawyer.'

She notes that down on her clipboard too.

When the medic is looking at Ounserrat again, his hand steals into his jacket to feel the cylindrical bulge of a *genro* staff in his inside pocket. Probably withholding evidence, taking her staff from the flat. Different law claims jurisdiction here.

The woo-woos are on again. They've hit traffic. Gillespie braces himself against the sway. He could touch Ounserrat's body, he should touch her. She's only inches from his fingertips but it feels miles. He can't connect this hurtling box of plastic and blood and steel implements with his last sight of her, stalking away from him across the causeway from South Side of the Stone with the rain falling on her. He tries to colour in the unseen between: her coming home, Ananturievo and Graceland greeting her, listening to what she has to tell them; then the door opening on the uninvited, and two clean shots. He can't see it. Something won't fit. Something not right, but he's missing it.

The ambulance lurches to a halt. Gillespie jumps out into driving rain and blinding light. They've stopped right on the edge of the dock; the hull of the lander curves over him. Up, up, up. He's never seen it close to before. It's bloody big. It looms over him, so huge and high it seems it must topple over and crush Andy Gillespie to a smear of juice. White light pours down from the crane-mounted spots, turning the rain to needles of acid. It strikes the skin of the lander and seems to disappear. Everything and everyone else the rain pierces to the bone. Gillespie touches the orange/red mottled skin. It's warm, soft, granular, like sand. Not what he expected. What did you expect a spaceship to feel like? He doesn't know, but not this.

The crash team have the gurney out, the wheels kicked down and their drips and tanks and tubes clear. A hole has opened in the side of the lander, a ramp extends from hull to dock. A crew of Shian comes down it to take the gurney. There's a brief altercation in the rain between species, but the Shian crew make it quite clear that the humans will not be permitted into their ship. The human medics withdraw to their ambulance. Andy Gillespie is forcefully turned back when he tries to follow the gurney up the ramp.

'She's my client,' he protests. 'I am her *genro*.' He pulls the staff out, shakes it to its full height. 'You're violating her rights.'

– *Do not be a fool,* the Outsider says in Hot Narha.

He waves his stick but the Shian go up into the lander and shut their door behind them and the orange-red skin heals like a wound. Gillespie steps off the ramp before it withdraws and dumps him twenty feet into the rain-filled dock.

When the first one died, he vowed that he would protect them, but more died and he vowed again to make sure it would never happen again, but it has, and third time he's made the vow even though he now knows that he'll never be able to protect them, because you can't protect anyone from themselves. He will find this one, this Executioner of Fools, and stop it, and it will happen again, and keep on happening.

Nothing to save. No world to right. No justice to pursue. It's personal. It always was. He understands the thing about the Shian law now.

'You couldn't give me a lift back over to the University end of town?' he asks the paramedics.

'We're not a fucking taxi service,' one of the greensuits answers. They're pissed at being made to look stupid by weird Outsiders.

'At least lend us a fiver for a cab. I'm skint.'

'On your cycle, Michael.'

He ends up walking. Thumb's out, but the cars wush past over the flyovers. No one is going to stop for a man carrying a stick taller than he is. After a while he stops trying. There is so much in his head he would love to be able not to have to think. For brief moments, he attains that state of mindlessness, Zenned out by wind and rain and cold and borderline hypothermia. He gets back, fumbles out his key, staggers into upstairs' mountain bike which is all over the fucking hall again. The racket and the swearing bring Upstairs Mountain Bike out on to the landing.

'Where the hell have you been?' he asks.

'What's it to you?' Gillespie lowers the staff to point the head up the stairs at the skinny figure in the Coors T-shirt and sag-crotch jogging bottoms.

'It's to me when your kids have been asleep on my sofa since eight o'clock, mate.'

And they're there, behind him, blinking in the bright light and the dislocation of waking up in unfamiliar terrain.

'Stacey? Talya?'

Wednesday

What do you do the morning after a killing?

If you are Andy Gillespie you set the alarm for quarter past seven, up-for-school-hour, and when it goes off you feel for a moment like the world has ended and you discover you're the one waking up disoriented in the unfamiliar terrain of your sofa and your neck's got a lump in the back of it like a second head sprouting and the room smells like someone has died.

'OK, kids, come on, we got school. Yeah, I know, horrible old school, but you have to go.'

Then he realizes that it's five miles across town and he hasn't the bus fares, let alone a taxi, but by then they're in the bathroom with their Disney toothbrushes and Punch and Judy banana toothpaste and the day has begun. Fucking Karen.

'Sorry it's only toast for breakfast,' he says. 'But I make the best toast in the world. I've won medals and international prizes.'

Talya's staring at him, still disconcerted to see daddy-hero covered in bruises and moving like an old, old man. Stacey pulls a Kellogg's variety pack out of her backpack and sets it on the table like a royal flush.

They fight over the Cocopops. Gillespie compromises by mixing Cocopops with Banana Puffs and dividing them between the two bowls. A true Joint Sovereignty solution. The milk goes chocolatey and banana-ey. Both traditions honoured. While the girls eat and drink him out of milk, he calls Karen. No answer. He tries again, three times. Four times. Then he tries her mother. She's as surprised as Gillespie, and as angry.

'That wee girl, she'd turn your head, she would. Probably away off for the night with some waster with a company car.'

As opposed to wasters without company cars. Or any kind of car. Mean thought, Gillespie; Karen's ma always had a soft spot

247

for you. You got on well with her. Just the daughter you couldn't stick. However, no man from the Woodstock Road can admit to his mother-in-law that he's busted.

'OK kids, here's the plan.' He's coming on like a UTV linkman. Moderate. Modulate. 'I have decided that because it's a special occasion, there is going to be no school today.' Genuine, heart-melting glee. Big chocolate-banana smiles. 'In fact, we're going to have a wee treat. A wee day out.' It's no sooner said than regretted. What kind of day out can you have on three pounds fifty? 'We'll go to the museum. They've got dinosaurs.' It's cheap. It's free. Problem: they'll want Coke. They'll want crisps and stickies. They'll want dinosaur erasers and pencil sharpeners from the shop. 'In fact, we'll make a real expedition out of it. We'll pack a lunch, and we'll go to the Tropical Ravine and eat it there and it'll be like we were back in the age of the dinosaurs, right?' He feels like a pound and a half of eel shit at their excitement for his cheapskate day out. Might as well spend your last three pounds fifty on dinosaur erasers and stickers as anything else.

Improvising sandwiches from the odds and sods living in Andy Gillespie's fridge proves to be a great game. While they try and match up slices of bread from different bags, he fetches the free sheet from the hall. All over the front page. HORROR SLAYING AT OUTSIDER GHETTO. *Sexual tension at the Outsider commune at the former Annadale Flats last night erupted into violence which left one Outsider dead and another critically injured . . .* Jesus wept. Fucking *Newsletter*. It's not even accurate, but when did that ever matter? Any chance to have a dig at the Shian, all the dirty-dealing-by-Dublin-to-minoritize-Unionists bullshit. Anyone who isn't for us is against us. Worse than the Taigs, you know. *Detective Chief Inspector Robert Willich refused to speculate on possible connections with the recent horrific multiple murder of Pastor McIvor Kyle and his family, but firmly denied rumours of a crazed alien sex killer.*

Gillespie bins the shit.

'OK, girls, what have you made me?'

'Peanut butter and raisin, ham and apple, and banana and jam,' Stacey says.

'Daddy, what's this?' Talya comes out of the coat alcove with the *genro* staff.

'It's a very special magic stick that was given to me by a very, very good friend. She can't use it any more, so she gave it to me.'

'An Outsider?' Stacey asks.

'Yeah, an Outsider. It's for people who have a very special thing to do.'

'Do you have a very special thing to do?' Talya asks.

'Yes, I do,' Gillespie says. 'A very special thing, but the trouble is that I don't know what I can do to do it right.'

He shows them how the *genro* staff collapses and extends, and it delights them so much he does it a dozen times. As they put on their coats to go out, he slips the collapsed staff into his pocket. A reminder of special things to do.

They're first into the museum. The attendants unbolt the doors, and in they go. Straight to the shop. Then the displays. As well as the dinosaurs and the stuffed animals in the natural history gallery and the geological map of Ireland with press-button coloured lights for the different rock types that, with three pairs of hands, you can make all light up at the same time, there's a good new exhibition about genetics and inheritance. Even Gillespie can understand it, though the kids wander ahead to the mummy in her glass case. *Let me show you why you look like your parents*, says Mr DNA, who's sort of springy and spirally. Gillespie stands in front of the family tree with the photographs of the generations all the way back to Victorians who look disgusted to have been hijacked into something as vulgar as a display on reproduction, and the lines of inheritance and dominants and recessives and the nose which passes all the way down from the start, and the joining-up eyebrows that come in the nineteen thirties with Uncle John, from Swansea. All in the blood. All passed down and passed sideways.

And looking at Uncle John from Swansea's joining-up eyebrows, Andy Gillespie realizes what it is about the HORROR SLAYING AT OUTSIDER GHETTO that doesn't feel right.

He scoops Stacey and Talya away from the three-thousand-year-dead Egyptian princess with her cracked black skin and eye-sockets filled with mortician's wax.

'I've had this great idea,' he lies. 'Wouldn't you like to see what it's like inside a police station?'

What do you do the day after a killing?

If you are Roisin Dunbar you find you are lying in your bed far far past your getting-up, even past your work time, because *he*'s downstairs and you don't want to have to meet him, even see him.

Willich is going to kill her.

Let him. It can't be any worse.

She lies in bed, listens for Michael down there. Usually it's his noise that drives her to distraction. Today it's his silence. It's as political as his noise; creeping around, being good, being quiet, not disturbing poor wee Rosh, giving her peace, understanding that, yes, he's done a bad thing, a bad bad thing, but he's not going to compound it by selfishly making a racket.

It's got to be better in the office than this.

'I'm getting up,' she yells. 'I'm going to the bathroom.' In the shower she examines her body: these tits, slight sag? This belly, slight bulge? This face, slight wrinkles? This fanny, slight withering? They're all right. They're pretty damn good for a working, child-bearing, woman of her age. She'd fancy her. But not enough for him. She dries, dusts, dresses, then shouts, 'I'm coming downstairs now. I'm going to have something in the kitchen.'

She hears doors creak and close, but doesn't catch even a glimpse of him. But halfway through her muesli with dried apples and apricots she finds the fury stoking up inside her until she throws the bowl against the dishwasher and it shatters and spills its load like vomit.

'Fuck you wherever you are, just get out of here, just go away, I want this house empty, right? I want it just me and Louise; I don't want you hovering around like some invisible presence. Just leave us alone.'

The doorbell rings.

'What?' Roisin Dunbar says.

It rings again.

While she thinks about not answering it, it rings a third time.

'Yes? What is it?'

It's Andy Gillespie with two little girls, peeping out from behind his legs.

'Sorry about this,' he says. 'I need you to help me. You see, I just worked out something.'

'How the hell did you get my address?' Not so much an ex-con calling on you first thing in the morning – albeit with kids in tow – as God's way of telling you to change the locks.

'Littlejohn.'

'Bastard.'

'Hey. Kids here. You weren't at the station.'

'We saw inside the pleece station,' says the older girl, finding boldness. 'It wasn't very nice. There was water falling out of the roof.'

Maybe if she goes back inside and comes out again, it'll be the Jehovah's Witnesses this time. They'd be easier to get rid of.

'What are you doing here?'

'I need you to come with me to Queen's Island. I've got questions need answering, and I want the police with me to make sure they get answered. By the way, um, you couldn't lend us a tenner to pay the taxi?'

Another thing about the great detectives, Andy Gillespie realizes, is that as well as never running out of money they never have to worry about child care. It takes the best part of an hour for Roisin Dunbar to persuade her sister to take not only Louise but a perfect stranger's two daughters.

'Mikey busy today?' the sister asks.

'He's seeing a client,' Dunbar says hastily. Don't even think of phoning my house.

Gillespie stands in the middle of the sculpted tuft among the Early Learning Centre non-endangered wood toys and feels like a refugee from an African civil war. The cook on the *Good Morning!* show is making Moroccan lamb tajine with apricots and cinnamon.

'When will you be back?' the sister asks, a little apprehensively, as the detectives say their goodbyes. Dunbar looks at Gillespie. He shrugs.

'If anything happens, call this.' He writes Karen's number on the message pad. 'Ask for Karen. My home address is this.' He puts it below the girls' mother's. 'OK, I have to go now, girls. I'm sorry about this, but we'll have that picnic some time, I promise. Be good.'

'This had better be worth it, Gillespie,' Roisin Dunbar says as she steers the car around the loops and curves of the development. 'That was perhaps the most diabolical liberty I have seen in my entire life.'

'I think so,' Gillespie says. 'You see, I think whoever did the killings at South Side of the Stone and University Street and Kyle, and whoever killed Ananturievo at Annadale last night, are two different people.'

'You have evidence?'

'Can't prove a thing. But it's Graceland gives it away.'

'Graceland?'

'Ounserrat Soulereya's kid. She calls it Graceland because she likes the sound of the word. You saw it last night, the wee thing clinging on to the stretcher for dear life.'

'And?'

'It should have been dead. What's the factor in all the other killings? The family is wiped out down to the last child. You know about the Sacrifice of Fools thing?'

'Littlejohn explained something about legends and ancient epic poems and why the Outsiders haven't had a war, ever. Can't say it made an awful lot of sense to me.'

'It's how they fight wars. Wars to avoid fighting wars. Stamp out the fools before they get dangerous. Weed them out. Eradicate them. And make sure they don't breed their foolishness to any other generations. That's the reason they cut the sex organs out. Symbolize that it's been sterilized. And the children, so they won't pass it on. Tell me: Ananturievo, Ounserrat's partner: were there any cuts or mutilations?'

'No.'

'And Ounserrat. The killer missed the first shot; why didn't he finish the job? And the kid was a sitting duck, why didn't he blow it away? It's a different person. Someone who'd never done it before, and bottled when it came to making a clean job of it.'

'Copycat?'

'Clean up. The Harridis want to keep the thing secret, take out the killer, and anyone else who knows too much.'

'Gillespie,' Roisin Dunbar says, effortlessly merging into the inbound motorway traffic, 'this puts you in the firing line.'

'And Stacey and Talya. And Karen – my ex – too. And that's why we're going to Queen's Island, to let them know that it's out, that they can't hope to keep it secret any more.'

'Gillespie,' Dunbar says, 'my kid is with your kids.'

'I know,' Andy Gillespie says.

'Gillespie,' Dunbar says again after a time, 'just to make your day absolutely perfect: we know why no one ever saw the killer. Killers. We know what a Cloak of Shadows is.'

'Tell me.'

'It sounds like something out of a sci-fi film, but it's a kind of, ah, invisibility device. As far as we can tell, it bends light around the target.'

'No wonder none of them ever put up a fight.'

'They probably let him into their homes. He switched this thing on and sat there until someone opened the door, then just walked in. No one saw him come, no one saw him go. Perfect camouflage.'

'Jesus. So you can't even warn me to watch my back. How are you going to catch a killer you can't see?'

'I have absolutely no idea.'

Neither has Andy Gillespie.

'One wee favour,' he asks, after a time. 'It's probably well out of your way, but could we make a detour via an off-licence?'

Queen's Island feels morning-aftery. Hung-over. Not the residents – there are no residents, the big wide streets are deserted – but the district. The buildings are tired of holding themselves up against gravity; the big wide deserted streets are lying down on the nice cold solid earth; the vehicles are hunched over gutters, just in case. The flags can't be bothered flying; the colours are too bright for themselves and the lamp posts are

253

leaning on each other. The day is clear and headache blue and whatever way you turn you can't get away from the light.

There's music somewhere deep in the Shian town, a little feeble, a touch fragile. Roisin Dunbar's car rolls through a moraine of wind-blown trash: paper cups, styrene chip boxes, kebab bags, wooden chip forks. The fast-food vans make big money out of on-heat Shian needing to eat every twenty minutes. Among the disposables are articles of clothing: lost, discarded, ripped off; body ornaments and pieces of jewellery; streamers, aspirin packets, empty mineral water bottles, musical instruments, flags, banners, emblems.

'It must have been some party,' Roisin Dunbar comments.

'It is.'

The Volks folks have taken themselves off their stand outside the sacred space. Too close to the *kesh* winds. Dunbar stops the car. Gillespie uncaps the quarter bottle of vodka he bought at the offie, offers it to Dunbar. She downs a slug, winces, downs another.

'I'll be OK as long as traffic branch don't stop me,' she says. 'They are complete bastards.'

Gillespie finishes the rest of the bottle. He waits until he can feel it tickle the base of his brain. He goes to the north entrance. Dunbar is at his back. Gillespie can feel the powers contained in the sacred space moving over his skin like shadows.

– *Thetherrin Harridi*, he shouts in Hot Narha. Birds explode upwards from their roosts on the rusting cranes. – *Andy Gillespie calls. Must speak.* A calling out. High noon in Shian town. For the time it takes a ship to move up the channel to the sea, nothing happens. Then the north door opens. Gillespie shakes out the *genro* staff.

'What is that?' Dunbar asks. The rising wind flaps her coat tails like wings.

'Tool of the trade,' Gillespie says.

'Mr Gillespie,' the warden of the sacred space says. She is dressed in long greys but her face bears the dusty white marks of *kesh* decorations. 'And Detective Sergeant Dunbar.'

'I'm representing my client, Ounserrat Soulereya,' Gillespie says. 'I've got some questions I need answered, and under your

254

law a *genro* may be refused no reasonable request. Can we come in?'

'You want to talk with me in the sacred space?'

Yeah. Because even though you keep the thing and run it, even you aren't immune to its effects and you're going to find it harder to lie to me in there than out here. Me, I've nothing to hide, and nothing to lie about. The *hahndahvi* can blow right through me.

It's nothing like it was like last time. It probably never is; always something different to everyone at every occasion. The presiding spirit today is a slightly edgy expectancy. Tense, bass line of something-awful-is-going-to-happen, high notes of thrill. Knot in the stomach. Hitchcock *hahndahvi*. He looks at Dunbar; by the expression on her face he can see it's something altogether other for her. All things to all people. Like a good god should be. Or maybe it's really done with mirrors. Reflects back on you your own dominant mood. Like most gods are. Tricks of the lighting.

'I know about the Fool Slayer,' Gillespie says. The acoustics lend his voice a sonorous ring. Authoritative. 'We worked it out. Me and Littlejohn. It was the *genro* Saipanang gave it away. We know about Sounsurresh Soulereya and her family, what you did with the bodies at South Side of the Stone, how you thought you could hush it up. And we know who did the job at Annadale Flats. We know you've someone out there, hunting for the real killer, taking out anyone who knows too much.'

'You know a lot,' Thetherrin Harridi says. The perspectives shift behind her, making her at once far away and immensely tall. She seems to lean over Andy Gillespie with his stolen staff like a redwood tree. 'You are to be congratulated. I advised the Council of the Nation that they could not possibly hope to keep this an internal Shian affair, especially after the killing of the religious. But some of us are less trusting of humans; they have good reason.'

Gillespie fights down the dread rising like bile in his belly. It's all inside your skull. It's just stuff. Head-games.

'You were for us?'

'Mr Gillespie, none of us are "for" you. We are for ourselves.

Some of us think that our interests are best served by rapprochement with humanity. Some of us disagree. Some of us resent having to share this world with other sentients. The Shian are a hunting species. We are a proud species. We have great achievements behind us. We do not like to be second-class citizens, refugees who have sold their inheritance for land that we could have taken. And we could, Mr Gillespie. When the fleet picked up your radio broadcasts in flight and it was discovered that World Ten had given rise to a technological civilization, there was a motion to reduce human civilization to a level at which we could achieve technological dominance. It could have been simply achieved: moving the fleet into earth orbit and focusing the Mach drive fields on the tectonic plate boundaries would have generated seismic activity sufficient to destroy ninety-five-per cent of your industrial capacity. Likewise, cometary heads could have been manoeuvred out of the Oort cloud into impact orbits; after fifty years the ecosphere would have stablilized sufficiently for colonization. The colonial council of Nations was brought out of stasis to debate and vote upon these motions. They were rejected. The margins were exceedingly narrow.'

'Yeah,' Andy Gillespie says. 'But you didn't and we're here and you're here and we're stuck with each other.' He's shifted weight on his feet, but that's enough to move into a new emotional focus. Concentrated ballsiness. He's not taking this from anyone. 'Who is it, Thetherrin Harridi?'

'I do not know.'

Gillespie takes another step forward, moving through moods, pushing Thetherrin into the deep mysteries around the south door.

'But you must have some idea. Your hunter has to have some trail to follow.'

'A profile, Ms Harridi,' Roisin Dunbar says. 'Give us the same trail. We have a law here, you know. It's different from yours, we can't just blow each other away because some angel-thing in our heads tells us it's a good idea, or to save the honour of your Nation.'

'You kill each other by the millions for the honour of your nations,' Thetherrin Harridi says. 'And your law gives you full permission. Our way, I think, is the saner. There is a little blood, and it is always personal. There is no collateral; there are no innocent victims.'

'The children,' Gillespie says. 'What about the children?'

'Where do you get this idea from that children are innocent?' Thetherrin says. 'Children are terrible creatures. They treat each other with cruelty and injustice and blatant tyranny. They inflict pain without thought, both physical and mental. It is the same with your children, I have seen how they are with each other. Any difference, any imperfection or deformity, is mercilessly exploited. They make victims of each other. They have no kindness or compassion. They are not innocent, neither yours nor ours. They are terrible, yet we will go to any length to protect them.'

'And the killer?' Roisin Dunbar asks. In her beige policeperson's coat, she's cold, a shiver in the soul. She doesn't know if it's the architecture of the sacred that's put it there, or the truth behind Thetherrin Harridi's words. Our young are aliens to both of us. We imagine that because we necessarily passed through childhood ourselves we can communicate with our children, but they are as alien to us as the Shian are.

'Little more than a child itself,' Thetherrin says. 'Are you authorized to negotiate?'

'The law doesn't negotiate.'

'Ours does. It is what our law is, negotiation. If I give you the information you need to find the Fool Killer, the Queen's Island Hold will recall its hunter and you will blame the Soulereya death on the Fool Killer.'

'You have got to be kidding. I can't make a deal like that. There is no way we could agree to that. Your hunter killed one Outsider and seriously wounded another. We have a law, it's called Withholding Evidence. You can go to jail for a long time for it. Ask Gillespie what it's like for an Outsider in jail.'

'I do not need to ask Gillespie,' Thetherrin Harridi says. 'The *genro* Mehishhan was once a lover of mine, on another world.'

'I'm sorry,' Andy Gillespie says.

'His communications with his children counted you and Eamon Donnan as his lovers,' the Outsider says.

257

Andy Gillespie knows that Thetherrin is using the Shian sense of the word. 'It's over,' he says, sadly. 'They've got you. Tell her.'

Thetherrin is silent for a long time. The dimensions of the sacred space stretch its few seconds into a long pause. Things flock in the edges of the humans' vision. Then the Outsider says, 'Sergeant Dunbar, were any of the bodies you examined in this position?' She clenches her fists, places them on the middle of her belly a few centimetres apart.

'The adults at the Welcome Centre. Why? What does it mean?'

'At the end of the hunt, when the quarry is run down, there is a moment when it knows that it cannot run any further, that escape is impossible, that all its skills and evasions have been bettered and that death is inevitable. It cannot run, and it will not fight, for the prey does not hunt the hunter. So it turns to its hunter and goes gladly to the blade. That is a moment of most pure and intense love between hunted and hunter. Death is a joyful culmination. The mystery of the hunt is celebrated. My fellow Harridis in the Welcome Centre understood that they could not escape the hunter, and so gave themselves gladly to it. This is the gesture of it, a baring of the heart for the knife. I am making it to you, Detective Sergeant Dunbar.' Thetherrin shifts a step. In those few centimetres she seems to grow in stature. Miles high. Towering.

'I met a *hahndahvi* the other day,' she says. 'It was not one I had ever met before. I met it at the place where two rivers join. One river ran down to the sea, the other river straight. It did not follow the curve of the world, it was not a prisoner of gravity. It flowed into the mountains, it flowed around the shoulders of the mountains, it rose up through the mountains and beyond the mountains; it flowed over the edge of the world. The *hahndahvi* that I met had sailed down this river in a boat clasped in the skin of human women and human children. The skins were of all the colours of the human races; the faces had been cut away but the scalps left whole so that the hair floated in the river like weed. The *hahndahvi* stood in the join of the two rivers, its feet were in the water. It was not at all tall; it was dressed in denim, with brass buttons on the pocket flaps. Its hair

258

was black, its nose pointed, it had round white eyes. Human eyes. It had muscles on its muscles; ropes and knots of muscle, like cables, like the roots of trees. It could rip out the roots of trees by its own sheer strength. In one hand it carried a long club, in the other a football. It called me to it and told me it might harm me or it might not harm me; it was all a question of feeling. From across the water I told it that I had not seen its like before in my travels across the Dream Place. It answered that I should not be surprised, for it had come from another dreaming in its skin boat. In that other dreaming it had owned no form, no smell, no name. It had been shapeless fear, it had lived in the dark at the base of human brains for all history. But in this place where the rivers joined, it had a body, it had a face and a spirit and it could walk and talk and kill things, for that was its chief delight: to fight, to overcome. Then I asked it its name. Its name, it told me, was Sex and Violence.'

Gillespie waits for the kicker. It doesn't come.

'Nice story. So, what does it mean? That you've discovered men are dangerous?'

'It is not a story, Mr Gillespie. Your archetypes are infecting our dreaming. There is leakage between our racial unconscious-nesses. You are taking from us, we are taking from you.'

'Sex and violence.'

'Perhaps we are more alike than we thought, Mr Gillespie.'

'What does that mean?'

The warden of the Sacred Space does not answer.

'Why won't you tell me? Why does everything have to be a riddle with you?' And he feels himself losing it, like he almost did that time in this place with Eamon Donnan. The subtle dislocations of sacred space kick out the blocks, the big ship slides. He lunges for Thetherrin Harridi. She's fast; he's faster. Two fistfuls of shirt pull her down to his height. Face to face. 'I've had enough of your pissing around, never being straight, never knowing where you're coming from. I've had enough, you hear me? I want to know how to find this Fool Killer. Tell me how to find this fucking Fool Killer or I will break you in two.'

Thetherrin Harridi blinks slowly. Her throat convulses, she spits into her hand. Then, too fast for Andy Gillespie's anger, she clamps the hand over his mouth. Something squirms over his lips, up the back of his nose. He retches, chokes, reels backwards.

Roisin Dunbar has her gun out, aimed two-fisted at Thetherrin Harridi.

'I'm all right. I'm all right.'

And then suddenly he isn't.

Suddenly he is somewhere else entirely.

He is in woods, by running water. Broken light falls through the branches of conifers, reflects from the surface of the slow-moving brown water. There are shapes moving in the surface. Ducks. Mallards. A path runs by the water's edge, following the bend of the river. Gillespie smiles. He knows this Dream Place. He used to come here as a kid. He's in Belvoir Forest. Walk down that path and you'll come to Annadale Flats, the city, the docks and shipyard, the sea. His *sounyok*, his private world-forest. Joggers round the bend in the riverside path, a dog-walker emerges from the trees on the far bank. The dog leaps into the river, chasing a thrown stick, dog-paddling happily in the water. Of course your dreaming is a place you know.

He can smell the water, the resinous scent of the trees.

Beats the shit out of that so-called virtual reality bollocks. Computers fake it. Lookee no touchee. The chemicals embody.

He hears movement in the branches behind him. He turns; a figure stands at the edge of the trees. It is a tall Shian, dressed in a long crimson coat. On its head it wears a tall, out-flaring crown woven from tree twigs, hung with mirrors and tiny bells like you put in budgie and parrot cages to stop them pulling out their feathers in boredom. The figure carries a short, thick-bladed hooked knife in its left hand.

'Red Earth,' Gillespie says, remembering the names of the *hahndahvi*.

'Divider of Waters,' it says.

'The Cutter.' Gillespie completes the trinity.

'As your *hahndahvi* have entered our dreaming, so we enter yours,' the Slayer of Fools says.

'Who are you?' Gillespie asks. The joggers bounce past. They show no surprise at the Shian avatar standing by the path. That's how Gillespie can be sure he is in the dreaming.

'Sex and Violence,' the figure in red says. 'It is for us as for you. Sex and violence.'

'What do you mean?' Gillespie says. 'You can't even be straight with me in dreams.'

The Slayer of Fools smiles. It flips the knife end for end, catches the point, offers the hilt to Gillespie. He finds he has a *genro* staff in his hand. He does the Shian 'no' and shakes out the staff.

The Fool Slayer looks at the staff, looks at the blade, looks at the joggers vanishing around the bend and the dog paddling up and down in the water with a stick in its mouth, and lunges forward, too quick for Andy Gillespie, seizes him as only a dream can seize. It leans over him, bares sharpened teeth. Jesus, I'm dead, Andy Gillespie thinks; throat bitten out in my own childhood dream. And the Fool Slayer whispers the word of grace in his ear.

In the Shian dreaming, when you are given the word of grace, you know that you can trust it absolutely. God has spoken. Alleluia.

And he's back, kneeling on the floor, trying to cough the clinging, niggling thing that isn't there any more out of the back of his throat. The concrete is very hard and cold and solid. The arcane geometries of the sacred space whirl above him. But he knows. The word of grace is sharp and clean and true. Sex and violence.

'Are you all right?' Dunbar actually sounds concerned.

Gillespie shakes the scraps of dreaming out of his head.

'Woo.'

'It would not have worked had your brain not been imprinted with receptors for Narha,' Thetherrin Harridi says. 'It worked for Eamon Donnan, it should then work for you.'

'What did he see?' Gillespie asks.

'What you saw.'

'You were telling the truth,' Gillespie says. 'All along.'

'Of course,' Thetherrin Harridi says. 'You had to see it for yourself.'

'The children,' Andy Gillespie says.

'Yes, the children,' the Outsider agrees.

'The children?' Roisin Dunbar asks as Gillespie buckles his seat belt. And again at the lights at the end of Queen's Quay Road.

'The children?'

'The children,' Andy Gillespie says carefully.

'What did that Outsider do to you in there?'

'Showed me how to work it out for myself. Showed me the Slayer of Fools.'

The traffic is slow over the bridge. Not even woo-woos can get you through solid crush-hour.

'And what did this Slayer of Fools looks like?'

'A child,' Andy Gillespie says. 'It's all sex and violence. Like Littlejohn says, murder is sex misspelled. It's the same for them as it is for us. The mechanics are different because the biology is different, but it's still sex and death.'

'The mechanics.' She treats Cromac Street to a two-second excerpt of woo-woos. The traffic scatters like seed. Ah, the abuse of power.

At least something will move for her. Something will recognize her.

'It's all chemicals with these people. They make them love, they make them fuck, they make them travel between stars, they make them kill. We've no idea, no idea at all, what *kesh* does to them. We think it's like a good party, or doing a dozen poppers, or a Marbella night club on an eighteen-to-thirty holiday. We think it's a couple of degrees hotter than the hottest we can go. We aren't even close to it. It tears their fucking souls out. It burns away everything they are. It destroys their minds. It's insanity. Racial insanity. The whole species goes mad. If it turns adults into animals, can you imagine what it's like for a kid when the chemicals hit that first time? Nine, ten years old, you've just got used to having a sex, when one morning you wake up and you're someone else full of desires that scare you stupid, that you have to obey or you'll explode. And you're far away from home, on your own, a stranger in a very very strange land, no one to help you, no one to guide you, except the dreams

262

in your head. You turn to them, those old friends you've grown up with through your childhood, who've guided you and helped you and seen you right and all that; and you can't find them. They're gone, the chemicals have changed them into something else. Something with a knife in its hand that's telling you what you already know, that it's a big, wide, scary world full of shit and humans. You're alone, you're afraid, you don't know what to do, except stop the things that scare you, any way you can.'

'Kids.'

'*Gensoon*. Shian singletons on their first *wanderjahr*. Transients caught out by the season. The ones who've found Holds have the support to make it through the season and back to sanity.'

Dunbar turns into University Street, slows down to cruise for a parking space.

'And you have records of all transient movements into the province at the centre?'

Gillespie nods. He's still rocky, but Dunbar can't judge if it's the lingering effect of vodka, sacred space and whatever that Outsider put into his head, or the vertigo of the Shian species falling from grace.

'You admire them, don't you?' she ventures, finding a space, swinging the car into it.

'I did admire them. I thought I knew them. I thought I could trust them. Now I don't know anything any more. I don't know what anything means. I've got these words of theirs in my head, but they're just jabber. Just sounds.' He pauses. You look in hell, Roisin Dunbar thinks. 'I'm going to need your help with this.'

'Certainly.'

They both stop in the hall outside the open office door. Each knows the other is seeing it as it was, and that they will never be able to see it any other way. Gillespie takes a deep breath.

'Hardcopy or computer?'

'I don't know your database architecture. I'll shuffle papers. What am I looking for?'

'*Gensoon* referrals since the autumn season. If they don't find a Hold within six months, they either move on or form one with whoever's around. You can probably chuck out any that have been sent direct to Holds, unless the Hold's called back here to ask us to refer him or her to another Hold. They move about a lot, these people.'

Us. These people. Which are you, Gillespie? Which Nation do you belong to?

Roisin Dunbar opens the filing cabinet and groans.

'Oh, God. Any chance of some coffee?'

'There's a jar in my office. They were allergic to it. Came out in lumps. Break in fifteen minutes?'

All those clambering clockwork names. Jangs. Ongs. Anks, Ouns. What kind of place is Shelter from the Sky to come from? Or Cool in Summer, or We Built it Good? As much as Dungannon or Dunmurry or Ballymena or Belfast would, literally translated. Sasammaven Seyonk, from Fifth Small Hill Hold in Ontario. Eleven years old. You read eleven years old and you see a human eleven-year-old sitting strapped into a seat on a 747, wandering lost around airport transit lounges, being scammed by taxi drivers, driven off into white slavery. At eleven they are adult. Fully grown, complete sexual beings. We think our children grow up too quickly. But our children want to grow up. They've no patience with childhood.

How would you feel if it were Louise fully grown, flying out on her eleventh birthday into the rest of her life? How would you feel if Mikey could breast feed her too, be as much a mother to her as you are?

Redundant. Old. A walking womb.

If you were Shian, you would just walk away from Mikey. No recriminations, no unravelled ends to tie off, no mess, no fuss. A little hurt, a few tears – except they don't cry, they go dark around the eyes – and onwards to new lives and loves. Maybe there is a big sanity in the way they keep sex and love separate. Love is sanity, sex is insanity. But could you live that way, never having sex with those you loved, never loving those you have sex with?

And how do you feel about Mikey right now?

'Got one.' She never noticed that coffee has arrived, and gone cold.

'There'll be more.'

She finds the next one within the minute. Gillespie's got three.

'We'll need to cross-check these. It's possible some of them may have formed their own Holds,' he says. Pages flick at epilepsy speed across the screen.

'I can see the connection in this, but I still can't get the logic,' Dunbar says.

'What logic was there to Jeffrey Dahmer, Fred West, Denis Nilson? There's a logic to this, but it's Shian logic. Dreaming logic. They've rewritten the rules of murder, like they've rewritten the rules of everything else we know. The killer is protecting his unborn children from the threat of the fools. That's the logic. And he won't stop until the threat is exterminated.'

'Where do you stop in this country?'

'Exactly.'

'I think I get the logic now. The children are protected by the adults, but who protects the adults from the children?'

'You've got it. That's the irony of the *hahndahvi*. Bitch, isn't it?'

They work without speaking for another hour. More coffee goes cold. It all comes down to going through the files, Dunbar thinks. Willich should have told her that as the third secret key of detective work. It's only in the movies that you get the car chases and final cliff-hanger shoot-outs.

'I'm done,' she says, stretching locked joints and stiff muscles.

'What've you got?'

'Four.'

'I've got three.'

Dunbar has her mobile out.

'Hold on,' Gillespie says. The cross-check takes fifteen seconds and reduces the list to three. Meshinkan Unshevret, from South Wales, in the transients' house at Annadale Hold. Genstevra Tolamang, from The Hague, in the transients' house in Mount Charles. Sinkayang Huskravidi in the transients' house on Palestine Street. Two hes, a she.

Gillespie spreads hardcopies on the desk.

'One of these is our Fool Killer,' he says as if he doesn't believe it can be that simple.

The unseen hunter. The shadow in the rain, with the maser

and the gutting knife of the Fool Slayer. Kids. Eleven-year-olds. Do you know what your children are?

'Any favourites?'

'Could be any of them. Sex doesn't matter. It's not like human serial killing, where it's almost always men. Could be a male, could be the female. They're all well-positioned.'

He'd visited the Palestine Street house. Stood on the doorstep and asked questions of a young Shian with a patient expression who might have blown half a dozen people apart.

They look at the three sheets of paper.

'I'm feeling a little anti-climactic,' Gillespie says.

Dunbar has her mobile up.

'DCI Willich, Roisin Dunbar. Boss, get yourself and the team over to the Welcome Centre. We're also going to need search warrants, squads and I think three weapons teams.' A lengthy pause. 'Andy Gillespie has found us our murderer.'

The NIPS excel themselves in University Street this time. Four Mobile Support Unit vans, five armoured Land Rovers de-mothballed, five squad cars and a dozen assorted Fords, Nissans, VWs, and Ian Cochrane's white Toyota. The heads are out in the Holiday Inn again.

Willich has the warrants. He divides the teams up. He and Cochrane will take one squad to Annadale; Darren Healey and Tracey Agnew will go up the road to Mount Charles; Dunbar and Littlejohn will call round on Palestine Street.

'Littlejohn says that it's highly likely there will be other, innocent, people in the houses. So knock first, smile second, say please; then sledge-hammer. But if something goes wrong, for fuck's sake get out of the MSU's way. Do not take any risks. Remember, we may be dealing with a stealth assassin. I do not want anyone coming back to me with no head or any other body parts missing, thank you. Got your paperwork? Good. We want to hit the targets simultaneously; we'll go in at half past exactly. I've got twenty past five.'

'Seventeen twenty, boss,' Darren Healey jokes. Whistling past the graveyard. Times are synchronized. Willich leads his team off first. They've the furthest to go. Then Healey's squad. Andy Gillespie demands that Roisin Dunbar take him on her team.

'I found the bastard. You owe me this.'

Dunbar tells him he's done enough, get away home, rest, recover from the shock of the *hahndahvi* contact in the sacred space.

'Littlejohn's going with you.'

'We want to minimize civilian risk.'

'The fuck you do.'

She resolves the issue by calling up her sister and asking her to drop Stacey and Talya at their father's flat, 28 Eglantine Avenue.

'You don't want them sitting on the doorstep.'

'Bitch. Let me know what happens.'

'Don't worry about that.'

She sends a uniform to make sure he goes straight home. And then she rounds up her squad and they move out and University Street is free and open again.

It's a small, red-brick Victorian terrace house, two storeys, flush to the street, no bay. Its only characteristic is the yellow brick around the door and windows.

It looks like a classic serial killer's house, Roisin Dunbar thinks as she glasses it from her car. Ordinary houses, ordinary people, no one ever notices them, everyone's surprised when they find out that the next door neighbour has thirteen bodies under the patio, or heads, hands and spleens down the drain. They were so quiet, kept themselves to themselves. We thought it was just a transient house for Outsiders, well you know how they come and go. We never suspected.

'Scared?' Littlejohn asks. He's noticed the binoculars are shaking.

'Shitless. What time is it?'

'Go go go time.'

The MSU Transit comes down the street. The squad cars come up the street. There will be two more cars moving into position at each end of the entry at the back of the terrace.

All the vehicles stop.

'Go,' Roisin Dunbar says quietly into the radio. And then, as she finds herself in the middle of Palestine Street with an MSU in full combat gear, four uniforms, two detectives and a consultant xenologist behind her, 'Jesus.'

People are gaping out of their windows. They're quitting their afternoon tea, getting up from the television – what's going on out there? It's so embarrassing.

The MSU move to cover her as she rings the door bell of Number 25. A figure moves behind the glass. The door opens. She fights an insane urge to say 'Hello, Avon calling.'

She shoves her warrant at the Shian face in the open door. Is that bewilderment, or some other Outsider emotion?

'Detective Sergeant Roisin Dunbar, Donegal Pass police. We believe that Sinkayang Huskravidi is resident here. We have a warrant to search these premises. Please step aside.'

Pushed aside is more accurate. The MSU goes in like gangbusters. They are gangbusters. Roisin Dunbar pushes the Shian into the front room. It looks strangely cramped in the low-ceilinged, jerry-built Victorian parlour. Littlejohn's on her right, Kev Barret on her left and there's a uniform with a submachine gun, just in case the alien suddenly fades into the Laura Ashley wallpaper and starts blowing heads apart, but her hand strays to her piece inside her coat.

God, this is scary.

'Are you Sinkayang Huskravidi?'

'I am Ounsunjot Beshedden. Sinkayang Huskravidi is not back from work yet.'

'She's what?'

'Today is her late shift at Europa Hotel Bar. She will not be home until seven.'

They are going to have to come back and do it all over again.

'Fuck.'

Her mobile rings.

'Dunbar.'

Willich. Scratch Meshinkan Unshevret at Annadale. He and five others have got together in a nice cosy little Hold and headed off down to Kerry in an old container truck to set up an oyster farm. Anything from Darren Healey? Nothing yet. Her? She bites the bullet. They've fucked up in Palestine Street.

'Sergeant Dunbar!' One of the MSU black shirts is calling from the landing. 'Up here. Back room.' She takes the stairs two at a time. The team are on her heels. She makes it three steps into the little box room overlooking the yard and stops dead.

'Boss, I think you can recall Darren Healey.'

The MSU torches swing across the room. Walls, ceiling, floor are covered in photographs cut out from newspapers and magazines. The windows are pasted over with clippings. The radiator, the back of the door, papier-mâché of pictures. Snippings have been stapled to the curtains. There is no bed, no chairs, no wardrobe or chest, no lamp, no light bulb in the ceiling rose. In the centre of the floor is a pile of sheets and throws, torn and knotted together into long strips and woven into a nest.

'Someone like to poke that?' Roisin Dunbar ventures.

The torches lock on to the heap of fabric. Assault rifles move to cover as a policewoman prods the nest gingerly with her gun muzzle. She flips over the wound cloth. A gust of stench sends the police a step back; musks, aldehydes, sweats and secretions and body odours.

'Clean.'

The police move into the room.

'Can we get some light in here?' Dunbar asks. Someone unscrews the landing bulb and passes it in.

'Jesus,' Roisin Dunbar whispers as the ceiling light goes on. The cut-out photographs are all of prominent people. Politicans, churchmen, sports personalities, entertainers, business people, lawyers, judges, police. Willich is up there, an *Irish News* photograph of him crossing the car park to the station. Roisin is just out of shot. 'There must be thousands of the things.'

'No shortage of newspapers in a hotel,' Kev Barret says.

Peter Robinson; Kenneth Branagh; James Galway.

'George Best,' Dunbar says.

Robert McCartney, Barry Douglas, Gerry Conlon, Gerry Kelly.

'No shortage of fools either,' Littlejohn says. He's found his own picture, a shot from a press conference. 'If I remember

269

rightly, I was telling the world that it was biologically and socially impossible for the Shian to be serial killers.'

Gerry Adams. Gerry Anderson. Mary Robinson. Tony Blair. King Charles III.

'Littlejohn, can you make anything out of this?'

A thread of black scrawl is wound around some of the photographs. It looks like writing, lines of it lead off to lasso outlying images.

'*Shinshan* script,' Littlejohn says. 'It's a formal mode of the standard Narha syllabic form. Looks like it was written by a five-year-old.'

'Eleven-year-old,' Dunbar corrects.

'Noticed anything about it, Rosh?' Kev Barret says. He traces some of the tributaries back from main stream to source. 'Look at what they're connecting.'

'Fashion mag pictures of Sounsurresh Soulereya. This one's from *Mizz*. What does it say, Littlejohn?'

'"The beauty space; unpleasantness in the heart of the beauty space; the wrong clothes, they're wearing the wrong clothes, the hat is too tall, the shoes too wide; wrong clothing demeans us all,"' Littlejohn reads. 'Gillespie could give you this better. Reads like a diary of the Fool Slayer's dream communications with her *hahndahvi*. Stream of unconsciousness word salad.'

Dunbar follows the stream of jibbering forwards, explores down the narrow backwaters.

'"Muskrahvat and Seyoura Harridi accepting a cheque for twenty-five thousand pounds from the National Lottery Heritage Division to help develop their Shian Welcome Centre in Belfast." There's a bit torn off the edge of the photograph. And here, "Members of the Shian Welcome Centre meet with Unionist leadership." There're dozens of the things.'

'Hundreds,' Littlejohn says. He's studying a patch of wall seven feet up, close to the corner. 'Looks like there's an order to this. McIvor Kyle and his clan are up here. Smiling their heads off.'

Kev Barret laughs.

'Ah,' Littlejohn says unexpectedly. 'Rosh, I think you should have a look at this.'

The change of tone in his voice is so marked that Dunbar forgives Littlejohn's use of her diminutive.

'I think I know who's next,' Littlejohn says.

Once you know how to see the lines of frenzied scribbling, the patterns become obvious. Entangled in black ink are fifty clippings of Doctor Robert Littlejohn of the Department of Xenology, Queen's University, Belfast. Littlejohn speaking. Littlejohn sitting. Littlejohn giving police press conferences. Littlejohn crossing the road to Donegal Pass police station. Littlejohn in the Xenology Department prospectus. Littlejohn in the background of the summer graduations in the *Ulster Tatler*.

'It seems that humans who get too close to Shian are as dangerous fools as Shian who get too close to humans,' he says in that same strange tone of voice. 'The human who thinks he can get inside an Outsider's head. Kind of a perverse compliment: that this Fool Slayer thinks I'm such a danger to her people I have to be eliminated.'

'Where is your family, right now?' Dunbar demands.

'Um, my kids are both in England,' he mutters. His smug has failed him. His arrogance has come apart. He's afraid and vulnerable and his powers are useless. Dunbar is sorry for him.

'I need to know addresses, places of work. This bitch tracked down McIvor Kyle Junior and killed him in his own room two days before she did the rest of the family. Your ex-wife?'

'She's got a new boyfriend, she's nothing to do with me. I haven't seen her in six months.'

'They take out the whole geneline. That's what you told me. They stop the fool gene being passed down. Littlejohn, you call your family, tell them to lock the doors, stay exactly where they are until the police arrive. Kev, call Willich, get him to put protection on to Littlejohn's ex-wife, and alert the local forces in England. Tell them this is deadly serious. Tell them – tell them they'll need infra-red.'

'Sniffer dogs,' Littlejohn says very quietly. 'Something with a nose as good as a Shian hunter.'

Barret takes Littlejohn out on to the landing to get addresses and make the call. Roisin Dunbar surveys the room. It's cold, but that's not the reason for her shiver inside her big raincoat.

'Right team, I want you to take this fucking place apart. We're looking for a maser, and a Cloak of Shadows, whatever the hell that looks like. I'm going to have a word with Wee Lad downstairs; I cannot believe he doesn't know what's been going on up here.'

'Rosh.' Ellen Moran, fresh out of uniform into plain-clothes, is on tiptoes staring up at the junction of wall and ceiling. 'Found something. Here, here, and here, and down here; there's writing, but there are no pictures.'

A line of policepersons forms, facing the wall, tracing lines of script. A reverse identity parade. There are fifty holes in the fabric of faces. The sticky fixers are still clean of dust and airborne dirt.

'They were up, they came down,' Ellen Moran says.

'Who was up and came down?' Roisin Dunbar asks. Then she sees it, caught in the crack between the floorboards and the skirting, a tiny flag of newspaper. She pulls it out. It's tiny, a thumbnail image clipped from a larger picture.

Obsessive dedication to minutiae gives her the creeps.

She holds it under the light. A face, little more than a blur of half-tone dots. But she knows it.

Andy Gillespie.

She's already moving.

'Call the Europa Bar, check Sinkayang Huskravidi actually turned in for work today,' she shouts to Ellen Moran from the top of the stairs.

'Where are you going?' Barret shouts over the bannisters.

'Twenty-eight, Eglantine Avenue. It may be nothing. I hope it's nothing, but get an MSU together anyway.'

Who is the greater fool, the one who imagines he can get a human mind inside a Shian, or the human who can get the Shian mind inside a human?

Stacey and Talya are pissed off with him. You have good reason, Andy Gillespie thinks. I am guilty, I am very very guilty, but it'll be a few more years before the sight of parental guilt will be its own reward. At eleven and eight, it has to be edible or entertaining. Preferably both. He can't afford either.

Dunbar's sister is pissed off with him too, but that is probably because she's had to drive a complete stranger's kids five miles through rush-hour traffic when she should be attending to the needs of her own family.

'Can I give you something for petrol?' Gillespie offers, hoping she'll say away with you, no.

'No, it's all right.'

She almost smokes the tyres in her haste to get off.

'I'm sorry about today,' Gillespie says, opening the front door. 'We'll have that jungle picnic in the Palm House tomorrow, I promise. I really really promise. It'll be good.'

'We had it in Aunty Emer's,' Stacey says. *Aunty*, is it? 'We built a big house out of chairs and sheets and pretended we were explorers in the jungle and had our picnic in the tent.'

Virtual reality jungle. He never had much imagination.

It's starting to rain. Gillespie herds his small tribe into the hall. 'Mind the bike.' They step carefully over it. Some day, some day soon, he'll dump that fucking thing outside upstairs' back door and see how he likes it.

'I'm sure you're tired,' he says, opening the flat, hoping they are and that they'll go to bed with no fuss because he's fucked, absolutely fucked senseless, and his plans for the evening are to drink much Guinness, watch brain-drip TV and fall asleep in his chair. 'Now, what do you want for tea?'

He closes the door on the world, thank Christ, and is halfway to the kitchen, girls skipping ahead of him, when something makes him pause a moment.

There's an odd smell in his flat. He knows his own smell. This is not single-man, small-apartment standard ming. He pauses, sniffs. It's most unusual. Most distinctive. Like musk, and leaf mould, and whiskey when the glass is dry, and strange, electric things. He knows this smell.

Shian.

'Come on girls, out, out now, quickly.'

The air beside the door boils. It curdles, thickens into an Outsider in black leather. She has something in her hand. It's black, it shines, it flows like liquid in the three-fingered grasp.

'Oh, Jesus,' Andy Gillespie says. 'Oh, Jesus God, oh no, not us, not us.'

The girls have their mouths open to speak. Gillespie scoops up Stacey and Talya and runs for the back door.

'Mr Gillespie.'

There is something pressed into the back of his neck. It's warm and soft but it's not flesh. Nothing like flesh.

'Please set the children down and turn around to face me, Mr Gillespie. You must face me. You must see me, and I you. That is the rule.'

He drops the girls, turns, swinging. The Outsider dances away to the far side of the kitchen in a twitch. He pulls out the *genro* staff, shakes it out to size.

'This is against the rule, Mr Gillespie. The hunted does not turn on the hunter.'

The children are screaming. Someone will hear. Mountain Bike upstairs will hear. He'll help. He'll call the police.

'Help me!' he bellows. 'They've got my children! Help me!'

The Fool Slayer swings the black nose of the maser a millimetre. A cardboard carton of milk left to rot on the work-top explodes. Sour milk sprays the kitchen. The girls scream again.

'You're going to kill us all anyway!' Gillespie shouts, deafened by the detonation.

'Yes, that is the rule.'

He's never heard anything as flat and reasonable as the Fool Slayer's soft contralto.

'Now, we really must get on. Do you wish to die before your children, or do you wish them to be eliminated first?'

Anything. Do anything, try anything, say anything. He can't think of anything. Not a deed, not a word, not a thought. Except one name, and the thought of that makes his balls freeze.

'Karen!'

The Outsider tilts her head to one side.

'Ah. This is the mother of the children.'

Shit. Fuck. Shit.

'We're divorced, we don't live together. She has a separate life.'

'Has she reproduced with another since you?'

'Why should I fucking tell you a thing? You're going to kill us, aren't you?'

'I most assuredly am.' She slides a hooked knife out of the lining of her leather jacket. 'However, the length and painfulness of your children's death is entirely dependent on you.'

'Fuck you, you fucking Sheenie bitch. Fuck you to hell. Fuck you in hell.'

'Please, what is her address, this ex-wife of yours?'

– *You owe me an explanation*, Gillespie says in Cool Narha. *Our rules are that the hunter owes the hunted the reason why.*

– *You have given the explanation in your question*, the Fool Slayer says. *You have something that is ours inside your head. You are not entitled to this, it is not for humans, it is ours, we demand its surrender.*

– *This was given me by Mehishhan Harridi, genro of the Shian law. His decision, his gift.*

– *It was not his to give. Mehishhan Harridi. Another Harridi. Their foolishness grieves me.*

– *Mehishhan Harridi is dead.*

– *Good. I can only hope that his dangerous foolishness died with him.*

– *Foolishness?* Gillespie says. Suddenly he doesn't care that he is going to die. It doesn't matter that his head is going to explode; it'll be quick, he'll never know. What matters is that he is angry, blazing angry, more angry than he has ever been in his life, and he is fucking well going to let this Fool Slayer know how angry he is before he dies. I am going to die at the hands of an eleven-year-old, the same age as Stacey here, and I am bloody angry about that.

– *Who are you talking to about dangerous foolishness? I am not the threat to the Shian Nations. I am not the one stirring up fear and resentment among humans, I am not the one sowing mistrust between the species, I am not setting Shian against Shian, dividing the Nations, dividing the Holds. Who is the fool here? You think that you can make the Shian Nations safe from humans? Eighty thousand Shian to a million and a half humans? That is a foolish idea. You are going to kill every human you feel threatens the*

275

Shian? Only a fool would think that. There are a million and a half humans in this country, all of them a potential threat to the Shian species. Are you going to kill them all? What kind of a foolish idea is that? Who is the fool? Where are you going to stop? How many will be enough? If anyone is the dangerous fool, it's you. We don't know the rules of your Fool Hunt. We don't play by them. We are hunting you, we will find you and stop you. Because do you know what your biggest foolishness is? That you imagine you can get away with it. That you imagine we won't find out what is happening, what you are, what you represent, and when that happens the Shian are going to be in real danger. Because of you.

'Ironic that the Fool Slayer is the biggest fool of all,' Gillespie says in English. 'Doubly ironic that Narha can't express the concept of irony.'

The Fool Slayer blinks slowly. A smile for the dying.

'Thank you for your diatribe, Mr Gillespie. You have made some intriguing philosophical points. I shall ponder them in future. Now, I have spent altogether too much time on this hunt. Have you decided the death order?'

'No,' Gillespie says. 'You decide.'

The Fool Slayer tilts her head back, flares her nostrils, levels the maser. She smiles.

It's useless, but Gillespie raises the *genro* staff.

And her head explodes.

Every glass and dish and cup on Andy Gillespie's drainer shatters. The back window blows out. The door panes fly to shards. Stacey and Talya won't stop screaming. Gillespie pants, helpless with shock, claws blood off his face with his fingers. There's something moving in the living room he has to see.

'Gillespie?'

His ears are still ringing. Did something call his name?

'Andy Gillespie?'

'Shut up!' he yells.

The kids go quiet.

A second Shian enters the kitchen. It moves careful as a cat, nostrils flared, maser held ready against chest. It steps in its black cowboy boots to the thing on the floor in front of the fridge-freezer. It studies the body, head tilted first to the left, then to the right. Then it turns to Gillespie and his children. A flick of the fingers folds the maser into a flat rectangle. The Shian folds the rectangle in two, then in two again and slips the weapon in the hip pocket of its PVC jeans.

'Andy?'

The Shian has a Belfast accent.

I have gone insane, Andy Gillespie thinks. I have died and these are the final hallucinations of my brain as its circuitry flies apart at the speed of light.

But there is something familiar about the Shian assassin in his kitchen.

'Oh, my good God.'

The Shian smiles the human smile. The tooth smile.

'Bout ye, Andy. Sorry if I scared the kids. They swore those nanoprocessors would eat out any lock in fifteen seconds. More like thirty.'

'What the fuck have you done to yourself, Eamon?'

Eamon Donnan spreads his hands. They each have three fingers. He touches his body.

'It's amazing what they can do, Andy. The bone grafts still hurt a bit if I walk too fast or try to run, and they warned me not to expose the melanin to strong sunlight for a few weeks. It's a real shame that the best stuff is all internal: they fitted me with these nanotech hormone processors tied to a solar rhythm. Near as shit *kesh*. Jesus, you have no idea what it's like, Andy. Like being on speed all the time, speed and poppers and ecstasy too. The surge of energy; you can't sit still, you want to dance all night, you want to fuck anything and everything that moves.' He sounds like a fan boy orgasmic over a new techno toy. 'You're living at about a million miles per hour, Andy. Vanilla sex, human sex, that's nothing. Nothing. Dead. Cold. Human.'

Gillespie hears the words, but he sees the *planha* at Annadale, and the bodies arranged in the inelegant geometries of high violence. Ananturievo Soulereya. Cold. Dead. Nothing. Ounserrat Soulereya, shielding her child behind her life. Cold. Human. Human sex. Human affection. Human love.

The Shian don't trade, but they have a price for everything.

With an inarticulate cry, Gillespie swings the *genro* staff.

Donnan steps back. The staff sweeps cereals, toaster, kettle, dish rack to the kitchen floor.

'You fucking fuck! You took their filthy wee deal. We'll make you one of us, but first there's a couple of wee jobs we'd like you to do, a couple of loose ends to snip off.'

Genro staff gripped in both hands, Gillespie waves the weapon in Donnan's face. He's shaking with fury.

'You don't understand the Shian way,' Donnan says.

'I understand you killed Ananturievo Soulereya, and near killed Ounserrat.'

Gillespie lunges with the staff, driving Donnan into the living room.

'And killed the Fool Slayer,' Donnan says. 'My mission is accomplished. The hunt is over. Now Eamon Donnan will disappear, and all there will be is Serrasoun Harridi.'

'Listen to yourself,' Gillespie shouts. 'They've got you talking like them. You aren't a Shian, Eamon, you never can be a Shian. You're a fake. You're a wee Belfast glipe done up in fancy dress. Serrasoun Harridi. Fuck! You're a man. You're human. If you were Shian, I'd be dead. You would have let the Fool Slayer kill me, kill Stacey and Talya, and then blown her away, but you didn't. You couldn't, because you're human, and you couldn't do that to a mate. And you can't do it to children. You couldn't let that happen to Stacey and Talya, you couldn't do it to Ounserrat's kid, Graceland.'

He shakes the *genro* staff at Donnan. Eamon Donnan smacks it away with his hand, Gillespie swings it back to bear, point aimed between Donnan's eyes. Donnan hits it away again, again it returns.

'Don't push it, Andy.'

'Pissing you off, am I? Getting you angry? Getting on your tits – have they done those too, will it swell up and you can feed some wee Shian sprog pure cream of fucking ambrosia? Want to try to stop me? What about it then? Come on, I know it's in there, I can see it in your eyes. You want to ram this fucking thing down my throat. You're thinking, I can take this bastard, he's older, smaller, fatter, slower. I can fucking take him no bother. Male violence, Eamon. Male aggression. Road rage. One-on-one competition. So, did they do it down there too? Wee tucks and folds, a wee stitch here, a wee flap pulled down there, cock and balls all nicely hidden away? So where's all this testosterone coming from? I can smell it off you like fucking Chanel, Eamon. You're not Shian.'

Eamon Donnan roars. The Shian surgeons have boosted his reactions: a blur of movement and the maser is out of his hip pocket, unfolded, aimed at the middle of Andy Gillespie's forehead.

'And that proves it, Eamon,' Andy Gillespie says calmly, evenly. 'The prosecution rests its case.'

Eamon Donnan grimaces. It's the deep soul pain of a creature stripped bare of faith and self. He is neither human nor Shian, and those are all the identities the universe allows. He tries, though.

'No. No. I know why you're doing this, Andy. I know what this is about. It's not me; it's all of us. You fucked up your own family, you fucked up your own life, so you turned to the Shian for a new family and a new life. Something to belong to that won't let you down. And we gave it to you, and you took it just as it came, without asking yourself, am I seeing just what I want to see, am I like those wise blind men and the elephant? You thought we were like angels, like gods, that we were a better people, without violence, without the basic biological inequalities of humans. Saner. Better. No sin. No demons haunting us. No dark side of the soul. And now that's all been fucked to hell. We let you down. You put your trust in us, and we weren't what you thought we were. We have our demons. We have our darknesses. We aren't fucking Shirley Temples. We didn't ask for you to make us gods, we didn't ask for your faith and your hope. What right have you to make these expectations of us, and then be angry when we don't live up to them? Are you God, that everyone has to live up to your moral standards? Who has fallen from grace with who, here?'

Andy Gillespie smiles. The staff is mighty heavy in his hands now, but he holds it firm and straight and erect and steady.

'Yeah, well, happens there's a grain in truth in what you say, Eamon, but the real reason I'm angry, so angry I want to tear your eyes out and jump up and down on them, is because I have been lied to, betrayed, cheated on, suspected, called any number of perverts by the police. My children have been threatened, my life put in danger, people I care about maimed, my best friend is a transspecies assassin and I. Have. Had. Enough. You get that? I have had a fucking bellyful.'

A noise in the hall. Gillespie stops, turns. The flat door flies open.

Driving thoughts of DS Roisin Dunbar. This car, this rain, this intent expression of my face is something absolutely awful about to happen; I must look like Janet Leigh in *Psycho*.

Once thought, she can't get those all-string *qheee, qheee, qheees* out of her head.

The mobile rings.

'Yes.'

Kev. The Europa Hotel reports that Sinkayang Huskravidi didn't arrive for work today. No phone call, no explanation, no show. No job, now. Also, they're taking the room apart – the floorboards are up, the plasterboards down: not a dead cockroach, let alone a maser and a Cloak of Shadows. Fool Slayer's out a-hunting.

'Kev, get any weapons units you can spare over to Gillespie's place. Tell them to prepare for a siege.'

She's at the street door when it occurs to her. What the hell are you doing here, on your own, one policeperson against an invisible enemy with a silent, sure-kill weapon?

Being gutsy and heroic and dramatic. Being good and useful and a martyr. Proving Roisin Dunbar is worth something in Mikey's and my parents' currencies.

Martyr.

Don't think about that word.

Hero. Being a Clarice Starling. Did she ever feel that she was about to wet her pants with fear?

Something has turned the street door lock to the goo that leaks out of dead batteries. The door swings open at her touch.

Gun out. Two-fisted grip. Deep breath. Keep to the wall. Stealthy advance. Her handbag keeps swinging around to obstruct her shooting arm. The mountain bike. Watch the mountain bike. You do not want to fall face forward through the door.

There's a hell of a din coming from the flat. She recognizes Andy Gillespie's rough-edged syllables.

The door is open a crack. This could be a good or a bad thing. She won't have to kick it in. She's not sure she could kick a four-panel Edwardian door in.

She presses herself against the door-frame. Where are you, Willich? Hurry up, just bloody hurry up.

There is a second voice in the room that Dunbar doesn't recognize. Jesus, they sound like they're about to tear each other apart in there. If you're going, you have to go now.

One more deep breath. She shudders with tension as she inhales.

Go go go.

The door flies open.

There is Andy Gillespie with a big stick. Facing him across the hearth rug is a Shian aiming a black object at Gillespie's head.

'Police! Drop your weapon!'

The Shian turns. Its mouth is open in astonishment. The maser wavers, hunting from Gillespie to Dunbar to Gillespie. To Dunbar.

'No!' Gillespie shouts.

She shoots. She keeps shooting. She can't stop. She empties all six chambers. The Shian jerks, spasms, flaps its hands as the bullets tear through it. The look of surprise, then sadness on its face is almost human. It hits the wall. It falls. It is still. The black maser spins across the floor. Slowly, deliberately, it goes flat and folds itself in half, and half again.

Roisin Dunbar realizes that she is screaming, short, shrill, furious screams. She was screaming those screams as she was shooting. She pants, breathing the screaming out of her, like birth breathing.

'You stupid fucking bitch!' Andy Gillespie shouts. 'My kids are here. My kids. My kids.'

He drops the staff, strides to Roisin Dunbar panting, shuddering, and hits her. He hits her with his fist. He hits her hard, with all his fear and pain and *man* rage in the blow.

'My kids!' he shouts again. 'It was over, it was all over. It's in the kitchen. The one you wanted. The Fool Slayer. The fucking Fool Slayer.'

Roisin Dunbar sprawls back, legs apart, stunned. She can't move. She can't do a thing but hold on to this hideous gun like it has grown out of her bones.

A face peers round the kitchen door. A little girl's face.

'Daddy?' she asks. 'Can we come in now?'

There are sirens in the near distance, fast approaching.

Two pounds fifty for forty-five minutes seems steep for an adventure playground to Andy Gillespie, even if it is a complete forest fort with five levels and underground tunnels and death-slides. At least parents get in free. When no one's looking he might have a wee go on it himself. Why does no one have the courage to come out and build one of these for grown-ups?

'Daddy! Look at me!' Talya's hanging upside down from the trapeze bars on the middle level of the wooden castle. Don't think about a four-foot drop on to the crown of her skull, Gillespie tells himself. The therapist says that the children must be allowed to take risks. They've had a severe trauma, but if the parents over-protect them they'll never properly heal.

Trust them, the therapist says. Trust Talya's innate agility. Trust the impact-absorbent play surface. Trust you're a good father.

That one will take time.

That's another thing the therapist says. It will take time. She says a lot, this therapist. At least she insists that Gillespie and Karen both participate in the therapy process, and that Stacey and Talya must have free access to their father, to break the association with the bad thing. The trauma. The killings. You should say it, the therapist says. You need to be able to say it.

Eamon's death.

It will take him time to be healed of that. His body is putting itself back together; the bruises are fading, the doctors say the limp will go but he may have trouble with rheumatism in that knee and his fingers in the coming years.

The coming years. He glances at the paper on the bench beside him that he brought to read but is so much less interesting than watching his children play. News heals with time, too. The Fool Killer scare has been relegated to the inside pages by the

UDF/Dee Pee blackmail scandal. The party is disintegrating. Inspectors and accountants are peeling open Faith Tabernacle and exposing the maggots within to the sun. Peterson will go down. This world really isn't your kind of place, Gavin. Get back to the Maze, to a world you can control and live in.

Stacey's clambering purposefully to the very pinnacle of the fort. She balances herself on the battlements, carefully raises her arms in triumph.

'I'm the King of the Castle! I can see for miles and miles from up here! I can see all the docks, and the other side of the lough, and Holywood, and there's boats coming in.'

It is a damn fine adventure playground, Gillespie thinks. The view alone is probably worth two fifty. The designers have built it into the castle park on the side of Cave Hill; even from his safe parent's seat, Gillespie can appreciate the sweep of his city laid out before him. It is a soft April day; shower clouds move fast and threatening, they cast their rain shadows over other parts of the city but they miss Cave Hill. She is some queen bitch, this city, he thinks. She's ugly, she's small, she's mean, she treats you like shit, but you can't leave her, you keep coming back to her. She fucks you like nothing else. She's not even faithful, she fucks everyone who comes to her.

The adventure playground warden, who is a Youth Employment draftee dressed as Robin Hood – Nikes over the green tights – is calling out all the red badges. The kids are yellow badges, they've got about another fifteen minutes. This is how they get you. Forty-five minutes, you've just discovered where the fun is. Why the hell not? He can afford it. Littlejohn told him he should be able to make three times as a consultant what he would as an employee. For once he was speaking the straight truth. Not even therapy three hours a week seriously dents his reserves. Andy Gillespie, xenological consultant. Try telling them that down the Linfield Supporters' Club.

Xenological consultant. You can't get away from them, can you? They won't let you go. They suit this city well, Nation of bitches. They need you, Andy. Both species. They need someone to stand between them and say, hey, wait a minute, stop and look and think. It's a lonely place, the gap between. It had killed

Eamon Donnan when he realized that he wasn't human but he couldn't be Shian either. But he needed to belong. You have something you belong to: hanging upside down from that trapeze, scaring the shite out of you; standing up there on the battlements ruling the world. And when he takes the rituals and becomes a *genro*, it won't be so that he can feel he belongs to the Shian as well as the humans. It'll be for his own reasons, his own rights, his own justice. Andy Hero. His place is between, the neither-place. You always said you didn't consider yourself part of any Nation or culture. Your own Nation. The Gillespies, ourselves alone.

He finds he thinks a lot about Ounserrat. Her thoughts are frozen in time in the belly of the lander, his flow to her like water. The Harridis have been helpful to him. They're all being helpful, and open, as the species study their positions. She hung a time over the edge of death, but she's stable now. The regen facility out at the L5 point can rebuild her. It'll take time. Months, a year, maybe more. They'll take her up next time the lander is scheduled for a resupply trip to the fleet. Even for the Shian, space travel is expensive.

He's glad her healing will be slow. Time for her to fade to grey in his memory. Time for him to change, so that if they should ever meet again, *genro* to *genro*, they will understand each other completely.

He leans back on the log bench and enjoys the touch of sun on his scalp. A sudden tremor runs through the wood. The bench is shaking. The ground is shaking. He can see the wooden fort quivering.

Stacey.

She's on the flat platform behind the battlements.

'Stacey! Talya! Come down now, come to me.'

Children are evacuating the wood fort like a burning skyscraper. Kids drop to the ground, run to be scooped up by their parents. The shaking grows. Earthquake. Can't be. Ireland is the world's most seismically stable country. It's a Shian spacecraft switching on its Mach drive.

'Stacey! Talya! Look!'

He turns them to look at the shipyards across the river. Follow the line of his pointing finger, there, between the cranes, do you see it?

They see it.

It lifts straight up, a big dark red arrowhead. Its *kesh* stripes have faded, all the colours of the Shian towns have faded, decayed back into the mundane sexlessness of season's end. The ship goes up and up and up. Even to Gillespie, it's impressive. The girls are thunderstruck. Up and up and up until it's level with the tops of the Holywood Hills. It turns on its axis towards the south, tilts its nose upwards. It's big. It's wonderfully big.

Talya's waving to it.

It seems a great idea to Gillespie. He waves, without shame or self-consciousness.

The trembling of the ground changes pitch as the Shian ship manipulates gravity fields.

'Ooh,' Stacey says, feet tickled by Mach's principle.

And then it's gone. Gillespie imagines he saw a dark streak stab the sky to the south. A sonic boom rolls across the lough. A long tube of white vapour tunnels up through the sky.

'Wasn't that something?' Andy Gillespie says. 'Wasn't that quite something?'

Stacey and Talya nod their heads. The line of white vapour slowly blows away on the wind from the west. The girls slip their father's hand, and run, shouting, back to play.

Other Vista SF titles include

VISTA books are available from all good bookshops or from:
Cassell C.S.
Book Service By Post
PO Box 29, Douglas I-O-M
IM99 1BQ
telephone: 01624 675137, fax: 01624 670923

VISTA